The Warrior's Game

The Warrior's Game

Denise Hampton

AVON BOOKS
An Imprint of HarperCollins*Publishers*

AVON BOOKS
An Imprint of HarperCollins*Publishers*
10 East 53rd Street
New York, New York 10022-5299

Printed in the U.S.A.

Chapter 1

Lady Amicia de la Beres stepped into Winchester Castle's royal apartment and froze. John Plantagenet, king of all England and once master of the better part of France, was standing at its center. The king's bedchamber should have been awash in men, men who possessed the king's favor, men who wished to own their king's favor, and those men who'd lost all favor and were brave or foolish enough to try and win it back. Instead, only a single common servant, dressed in the red and blue of the royal house, stood near the bed at the room's back wall. The only sound was the patter of rain on the window's shutter and the hiss and pop of the coals in the brazier's brass pan beneath it.

Ami's internal alarm bells clanged. Pulling her miniver-lined mantle closer, as if the garment could offer her any protection at all, she drew a shuddering breath. May God take John and his restless cock. After her husband's death four years ago, she came into royal custody, as did all gently born widows. For each of the subsequent years Ami had striven to avoid her king's roving eye. She had at last failed, and now she would become John's whore.

She scanned the room again, as if doing so might somehow produce the witnesses she craved. Expensive beeswax tapers stood about the room in wall sconces and bronze branches to drive back a drear November day. Golden light splashed against the wood ceiling beams and softened the plain braided matting that covered much of the floor. The brazier, a flat copper pan lifted on a tripod, gleamed as ruddy as the coals within it. Set beside the brazier was a small table, two traveling stools at its sides. Easily folded for transport, the stools were a testimony to this king's peripatetic lifestyle. From the back of the chamber, expensive metallic threads, woven into the king's bed curtains, winked at Ami in lewd invitation. Furniture was no witness. Neither was a commoner.

"Why, here you are at last, my Lady de la Beres," John said, as though he'd called for her weeks ago rather than this morning.

"I come at your command, sire," Ami replied, barely bending her knees to him. She wasn't going to pretend respect if John was going to unfairly use her.

Her king watched her, savoring his power over her. Although not the warrior his late brother, the Coeur de Lion, had been, John's build was no less powerful. Dark hair framed his handsome Plantagenet face, while his carefully sculpted beard outlined a sensitive mouth.

"I've so looked forward to this meeting of ours," he said.

"Meeting me, sire? Why? I am nothing to no one," Ami murmured, crossing her arms as she eyed the odd garment John wore, a rich green tunic trimmed in golden embroidery at the neckline and sleeves, split down the front from neckline to floor-length hem. Despite the wide belt that held it closed, the garment gaped enough at the top for Ami to glimpse the king's bare chest beneath it. There were but two instances in which men and women shed their shirts. The first was when they sought their nightly rest. Since it was presently only a few hours after midday and they'd be feasting tonight in honor of Saint Martin, the possibility that John meant to retire, at least to sleep, was unlikely. That left only that second possibility.

John smiled, the curl of his lips slow. "So, my lady, shall we play a game?"

"A board game, sire? Surely, there are wellborn men more appropriate to be your opponent?" Ami said, pretending innocence. How dare he turn her ruination into a game!

Well, she wasn't going meekly into her own destruction, nor was she as helpless as John might believe. Being a member of this court with its many schemes, ploys, and plots had honed Ami's game-playing skills well, indeed. There was a way to extricate herself from this awful bedchamber and his clutches, and she would find it.

The king's teeth flashed. "Oh, but you are supremely qualified to be my opponent. Indeed, I feel I must make amends. To my shame I find I know next to nothing about you even though you've been a member of my court for years."

If the familiar way England's monarch spoke to Ami promised intimacy, the phrasing of his comment suggested he knew more about her than she cared to imagine. John was a spider, forever building webs in which to trap his subjects, especially the gently born. It was something that had the country's better bred folk whispering of rebellion.

Taking a step toward him, as if willing but shy, Ami said, "Well, if all you want is to know me better, I can tell you everything in a simple sentence or two. I'm a dull creature, really. My only asset is my fine hand at embroidery, or so some folk say. I keep a decent house, or I did before I left my home to come into your custody."

Longing surged through her with her words. More than anything she wanted to go home, a pleasant manor house in Sussex complete with a fine bed and a sunny solar. Ah, but she wouldn't see her house again until she was married, and it would be no homecoming if she returned wed to a husband who had every right to abuse her for having been the king's paramour.

"As for board games," Ami continued, her voice soft and feminine, "truly, I am unworthy being only a knight's daughter."

John laughed. "Fie on you, my lady, to make so little of yourself," he chided. "And, here I thought that beauty and wit couldn't coexist in one woman. I don't doubt you'll prove an able opponent no matter how we spend our time together."

Ami caught back a grimace. Rather than deflect the king's interest, she'd just inadvertently dared John to peel her like an onion as he sought to discover what she might be hiding.

"What say you to a round of backgammon?" The lift of John's hand indicated the small table. Only then did Ami notice that the king's prized game board sat atop it, ready and waiting for a match to begin. The king crossed the room to stand before her, catching Ami's hand in his. His fingers were gentle around her own. "I pray you, my lady, come and share time with me," he invited anew, his voice deeper and, oh, so suggestive.

Game, indeed. Her king was toying with her, the way a cat pawed a mouse before finally snapping its neck.

With no choice in the matter, Ami let John lead her to the hearth and game board. When he released her hand, he claimed the seat facing the doorway. Ami dropped uneasily upon the opposite stool. The silent, watching servant appeared at his master's elbow to place a golden cup set with rubies on the table. The man moved a tall candlestick closer to better illuminate the game board, then retreated.

"Now, my lady, don't you dare let me win," the king warned. "In fact, to guarantee that you don't pander to me in any way, let me offer you this incentive: win this game and you may choose our next contest. Lose and—" John's smile broadened into what was almost a leer—"*I* decide what we do next."

Ami sourly eyed him. Only a fool set out to defeat her monarch in any sort of game. But defeat left Ami facing ruination. Heated words crowded into her throat. Over the course of her almost five and twenty years more than a few men had called her a bold bitch for her outspoken ways. Now was no time to hold her tongue, not when she had nothing left to lose.

"Highness, dare I point out that win or lose you retain the power to decide what we do next?" Even framed as a question there was no mistaking her chide for what it was.

John's brows shot high upon his forehead. His dark eyes widened. Ami braced herself for the arrogant blast that would surely follow.

Instead, honest appreciation took fire in his gaze. "So I do, my lady," he agreed pleasantly, "so I do. Wine?" He offered her the cup the way a lover might.

Damn him, and her as well. Her forthright manner had only encouraged his interest in her. Ami did her best to smile. "What, sire, drink when you've exhorted me to play as best I can? Nay, it's a clear head I need if I'm to triumph in this game of yours." This time her challenge was intentional, acknowledging that the game they played wasn't laid out on the board before them.

John laughed as he tossed the dice and made the first move. "How clever of you to discern that I seek to intoxicate you so I might have my way with you. Now that you're warned against me, I'm doomed to failure," he said as he shifted his markers.

Ami's heart twisted in defeat. Until this moment no

man had succeeded in luring her from a widow's enforced chastity, no matter how he wooed or schemed and despite how much Ami desired the pleasure of a man in her bed and body. Instead, she'd turned her pursuers' masculine game of seduction on its head, forcing them to dance to her tune while she whetted their appetites for what she would never give them. Once they were beside themselves in want of her, she refused them, watching in triumph as they retreated, tails between their legs and their desires gloriously unfulfilled. There wasn't the slightest chance that the king's game would end so neatly, or in her favor.

Move after move, their backgammon match flowed into the rhythm of the game Ami knew so well. She played with all the skill she owned. Why not, when she had nothing left to lose? For that moment, the only sound was the rattle of the dice, the pop of embers, and the gentle tap of the weather on the shutter.

A distant sound of footsteps echoed into the room from the antechamber that fronted it, followed by the muted rumble of masculine voices as the chamberlain greeted the newcomers. John's head lifted. He looked toward the door. Anticipation took fire in the his eyes.

Shock tore through Ami. John was expecting someone.

The noblewomen among the royal wards spoke freely of the king's sexual perversity, how he liked more than one woman in his bed and even invited those men among his favorites to join him in using a woman. Ami's stomach knotted. God help her, she wouldn't let John abuse her that way, she just couldn't.

The door opened. Ami's muscles tensed. If the chance to escape came, she meant to take it, even if running from the king was only a temporary solution to her dilemma.

More than a single pair of boot heels thudded against the floor's wooden planking, punctuated by the gentle jangle of knitted metal garments, then the door closed. Armed men, at least two of them. One of the men crossed the room, the tap of his footsteps stopping when he was a few feet behind Ami's back. Metal rasped gently as he shifted. The smell of the outdoors wafted from him, the mingled scents of rain, horse sweat, and wet woolen garments. His breathing, steady and calm, sounded like the roll of the ocean against a beach.

The skin at Ami's nape tingled. Was he the one with whom John meant to share her? A picture rose in her mind of herself left bloodied and humiliated by the king's base needs—for she would fight them.

John smiled up at his visitor, the curve of his mouth pleased. "Ah, Sir Michel, punctual as always."

Horror tore through Ami. Jesus God, the king was going to share her with one of the de Martignys! Nay, not just one of them. Of all the de Martignys—for John had hired a number of soldiers from that accursed family—Michel de Martigny was said to be the most vicious, and the most ambitious.

She shot to her feet. Her knee caught the backgammon board. It slid toward the table's edge, markers swimming across its face. Satisfaction flickered through her. So much for the king and his one-sided game.

"My lady!" John cried out, grabbing for his precious set.

Snatching up her hems, Ami whirled. She managed two long steps toward the door before Michel de Martigny caught her by the arm. His grip was so tight she felt the pressure of his fingers through the thickness of her mantle.

The mercenary yanked her back toward him. Pivoting, Ami flattened her hands against his chest to thrust back from him. As she did her fingers splayed past the edge of his surcoat—the sleeveless woolen garment he wore atop his armor—to touch the chill metal of his chain mail. The cold rings glistened like ebony when they should have been silvered. Rumor said he'd killed so many that he needed to paint his armor black to cover the blood stains. Her stomach twisted at the thought and she shoved with all her might. To no avail. He simply caught her free arm and held her in place in front of him.

The crown of Ami's head barely reached to his cheekbone. Utterly trapped and helpless, she looked up into his face. The mercenary had discarded his helmet and pushed back his mail coif to bare his head. Teased by November's damp, his hair curled lightly about his shoulders, its color so dark a brown that it was nearly black.

Michel de Martigny was a handsome man, some women said the most handsome at court, what with the line of his dark beard sculpted to accentuate the hollows beneath his high cheekbones, straight dark brows, hawk's beak of a nose, and well-made mouth. Aye, but no heart beat within his chest anymore than emotion showed in his cold, gray eyes. A man who needed to paint his mail could own no mercy, or be capable of either pity or compassion.

Fear circled around Ami, its maw opened to catch her in its grip. She tensed in refusal. It didn't matter that he was a vicious brute. She'd never in her life been afraid of a man. She wasn't going to start now, especially not when he was only a baseborn mercenary.

"Release me," she demanded. That she didn't use his title, but spoke to him as if he were a servant, was more to prove to herself that she wasn't daunted than in any hope that her rudeness would work where force had failed her.

Something flickered deep within his icy gray gaze. Although it was a subtle reaction, Ami read its meaning with ease. Those who claimed this knight impervious to the slurs sent his way were wrong; he was simply adept at concealing his reaction to the insults. Satisfaction lifted the corners of her mouth. Here was a weakness she could exploit if need be.

He blinked. The movement of his eyelids and the slight tightening of his grip on her arms was all it took to tell Ami that the knight had read and understood her expression just as easily as she had his. Everything in her rejected the possibility that he might own such depth of reasoning. Shrewdness of wit wasn't generally a trait given to churls whose purpose was thoughtless violence. The king's hired brutes were only that: hired and unreasoning brutes.

Ami's gaze once more swept across the forceful lines of his face, this time seeking proof of intelligence. Although she'd seen Sir Michel from a distance at many a meal and during the court's frequent travels, she'd never once been this close to him. Brute or not, he was a very handsome man.

The part of her most female stirred. Horrified at herself, Ami stomped on her reaction, then shifted as far back as possible from her captor. What in God's name was wrong with her? This lout wasn't just a knight who betrayed all honor to sell his sword to the highest bidder, he was common born.

"Release me," she demanded again, only to be appalled at the shrill note in her voice. It sounded like fear, even though Ami knew it wasn't, at least not fear of the mercenary. How could she have allowed her senses to be stirred by this man?

Sir Michel's hands shifted on her arms. The knight's brows drew down, just a little. The blankness dimmed from his gray eyes. In that instant, Ami confronted far more intelligence than she cared to imagine. Horror tumbled over her. Dear God. What if he noticed her untoward reaction to him?

"I am not yours to command, my lady," he said, with no sign of triumph in his face or voice.

Ami almost sighed in relief. Men always gloated when they thought a woman desired them.

Sir Michel shifted until he could see their monarch. "Sire? What is your will?"

Wood scraped quietly against wood as John's stool moved against the floorboards. England's master came to his feet with a mere glance at his ward. "You may release her, Sir Michel. After all, there's no place she can go that we cannot reach her."

That the mercenary merely nodded in response to his king's command proved just how high Sir Michel perched in John's favor. The knight's hand opened, freeing her arm. Ami wasted no time in putting a few steps between herself and the warrior.

John motioned toward the doorway behind her. "Do come join us, Sir Enguerran."

That sent Ami whirling again toward the door, seeing this time what she'd missed in her panic. Enguerran d'Oilly, the man who was both her neighbor and the administrator of her lands stood at the room's back. Sir Enguerran started toward his king.

Ami's neighbor had once been a good-looking man; he might still have been, even with his thinning dark hair and the heft of his two score years about his portly waistline. It was a lifetime of toadying that had disfigured him, bending his back and twisting his lips into a permanent and unctuous smile. All to no avail. As dearly as Sir Enguerran hoped to advance himself by clutching the tunic backs of abler men, he hadn't the discernment or wit to know which man to use as his vehicle. Thus, he stayed what he'd always been, a rustic, thick-witted country knight.

Without a glance of greeting to the woman whose estate paid him a nice stipend, Sir Enguerran stopped abreast of Sir Michel. As he did so, he turned a shoulder

toward the Frenchman. So it was with all the English
court, each man affording what subtle scorn they could
to John's favored hired knights, but especially to the
baseborn one.

"Sire, I come at your command." Enguerran
sounded only marginally less comfortable in the king's
presence than was Ami. "Dare I hope you call me here
to offer a response to my request?"

"In part we did, Sir Enguerran," John replied, reclaiming the royal pronoun. "We'd have you repeat
your request in Lady de la Beres's presence. We're told
that a woman likes to hear it from the man himself
when he seeks her as his bride." John looked at Ami, the
full heat of a man's desire burning in his eyes.

Ami felt the royal spider silk tighten around her.
Here was John's game. He would marry her to Enguerran, not so she could find happiness in what should
have been an holy estate, but so he could misuse her
without fear of censure. Toady that he was, Enguerran
would happily turn a blind eye as the king made a
whore and adulteress out of his wife. All that mattered
to Enguerran was how he could use each one of John's
thrusts into his wife's body to his political advantage.

"I won't do it!" Ami's refusal rang against the beams
crossing the ceiling.

John lifted his brows. "Do you dare to say your king
nay, my lady?" he asked mildly as the previous moment's desire heightened into bold lust.

Ami caught back her groan. She'd just whetted the
king's masculine need to dominate and conquer. Unless
she could save herself, she was doomed to ruin, and it

would happen within the confines of marriage, a state she'd once dreamed would be her comfort and salvation. Her spine lance-straight, she boldly met her monarch's gaze. She'd kill Enguerran before she let John use her this way.

The corner of the king's mouth twitched as he read the defiance in her gaze. A fine web of creases appeared at the corners of his eyes. Ami blinked as she understood. Each time she reacted, dancing to John's whistle, it fed something in him. Against that she strove to clear all emotion from her face. Disappointment flashed in John's eyes, then he looked at Enguerran.

"Well, sir knight, you've heard the lady's response to your proposal. We must take her reluctance into account. You cannot have her," said the man who had the right to marry his ward wherever he chose.

Sir Enguerran's jaw dropped. All the breath left Ami's lungs, so great was her surprise. The certainty grew that she sank ever deeper into some unseen trap. So did Ami's need to protect herself. The best she could do right now was bend her neck, donning the submissive pose that all women put on along with their gowns.

"Sire, you must pay her no heed," Sir Enguerran protested. "Women cannot choose their own husbands. They haven't the strength of mind or character to make a proper selection." As Enguerran pleaded his case, he stepped closer to their king, then knelt. The skirt of his mail shirt jangled softly as it piled onto the floorboards around him. "Perhaps you've forgotten, sire," he continued from this humble pose. "You promised her to me when I first became administrator of her estates. As we agreed, I've paid two pounds a year for the past four years so she wouldn't be given to any other man."

"So you have," John agreed, sounding like a reasonable man, something Ami very much doubted he was. "What a quandary. Give us a moment to ponder some way that might do justice to both of you."

Arm's reach from Ami, Michel de Martigny shifted, his movement impatient. Tilting her head just a little, Ami watched as the mercenary eyed Sir Enguerran the way a hawk studied its prey, his gaze nearly boring a hole through the metal that covered Sir Enguerran's back. The subtle curl to the corner of Sir Michel's mouth said that the warrior liked Enguerran d'Oilly no better than the rest of John's court.

Again, the possibility that Sir Michel wasn't the thoughtless brute she believed him piqued Ami's curiosity. Eyes narrowed, she studied him. What exactly did he hide beneath that chill exterior?

As if he felt her attention on him, Sir Michel looked at her. Their gazes met and held. Ami loosed a startled breath as appreciation again stirred within her. Before she knew what was happening, her long-starved needs seeped past the bars of their carefully crafted prison. Her mind flirted with the image of Sir Michel in her bed, his hands and mouth providing the pleasure she had so long denied herself.

To Ami's horror, an answering warmth flickered deep in the depths of Sir Michel's gaze. Cursing herself, she snapped her gaze to her toes. What was she doing? The mercenary was not only common born, but a man who deserved only her loathing. She wouldn't harbor inappropriate physical longing for him.

"Ah, we have just the solution," John announced a moment later, sounding far too pleased with himself for Ami's peace of mind. "Sir Enguerran, you must prove to the lady just how much you want her. What do you think, Lady de la Beres? Would two hundred and fifty pounds be bride price enough to make you reconsider Sir Enguerran?"

The sum made Sir Enguerran collapse from his knees to sit flat upon the floor with a clash of knitted metal. Ami gaped at John. *Two hundred and fifty pounds?* That was an amount appropriate for a baron's first daughter or an earl's second lass. Why, all Ami's properties together never generated more than twenty pounds a year. Once alms were given, her folk provided for, and John collected his ever-increasing amount of blanche and taille, the king's tradition taxes, there wasn't anywhere near enough left to make a payment on such a sum. Enguerran would have to be mad to agree; it would take his lifetime, and his son's after that, to repay the amount.

Enguerran staggered to his feet. "But, sire, she's not worth that much!" he blurted out.

"Tut, what a thing to say in the lady's presence," John rebuked his knight. "Pardon, my lady. We cannot think what's come over our man. He's usually far more amenable. Malleable, some would even say." The king made no attempt to disguise his contempt for Enguerran.

That sense of an unseen trap closed around Ami again. Bowing her head, she crafted a safe reply. "For love of you, sire, I can but forgive him."

Enguerran bent a burning look in her direction. "I have no need of your forgiveness," he snarled.

Ami took note. Here was the pattern of their marriage should she and Sir Enguerran wed. Her dull-witted tufthunting husband would crawl on his belly before his betters, then redeem his continuing failure to advance himself and degraded pride by abusing his wife with his tongue, and likely his fists as well.

As Enguerran once more faced his king he stood like the mercenary, his head held high, his shoulders in a defiant line. "She's worth the forty-five pounds I agreed to pay for her four years past and nothing more. Deducting what I've already given you, I can produce notes guaranteeing the remaining thirty-seven pounds by week's end."

"What's that you say?" the king replied, a gentle silkiness to his tone. "You don't even intend to pay us the original forty-five pounds we requested?"

"But I am giving you all," Sir Enguerran cried, his brow creasing. "What I paid to hold her aside was part of her bride price, sire."

"Hardly so," John countered. "That amount only held her for you. Ah, but that's neither here nor there now that she has a new price. Perhaps we do ask too much for her, but how much is too much? Sir Michel, you have no stake in this. Have a look at the lady and tell us if you think our price is too high for her."

Enguerran's back instantly bent into its former

curve. For John to request Sir Michel's opinion on an issue that should be solely between him and his subject was an insult of the most dastardly sort. John's words struck at Ami with no less impact.

"Sire, I am your ward," she protested, straining to keep indignation from her voice. "No man save yourself can determine my bride price. Moreover, your mercenary is a foreigner, an outsider . . ." She let her voice linger on the word to remind the king that there were many at court who deeply resented how he preferred men from other lands over his own folk. "You cannot expect him to give a good opinion of my properties when he knows nothing of me or my estate."

No man, not even the king, was going to disparage her or her estate by asking a commoner to determine her value, not if she could do anything about it.

Chapter 2

Michel de Martigny eyed Amicia de la Beres, in whose hands lay his future. Damn, but she had just proved herself as clever as some claimed, and courageous beyond most of her sex. There weren't many men, much less women, with gall or heart enough to scold a king, not even when using a shield of logical protest to hide rightful outraged.

John only lifted his shoulders in a shrug. "But, madam, only a few moments ago you reminded us that we can do with you as we please." There was enough amusement in his tone to suggest the lady would pay no greater price for her audacity than this mild rebuke.

Still, Michel had seen John's quietest reprimands force England's noblemen to their knees, while a single cross word could bring men like Enguerran d'Oilly to their bellies, crawling like the worms they were.

Not this woman. She met her king's gaze without

flinching. "Sire, I bow to your wisdom," she said, "praying only that I don't unwittingly become the cause of ought that might tarnish your repute."

However subtle, it was another chide. Grudging admiration stirred in Michel, even though the lady's fearlessness didn't bode well for him or for their future.

She wasn't only bold, but lovely as well. Beneath her blue, fur-lined mantle, her under- and overgowns were of rich scarlet satin, the hems and sleeves trimmed with thick golden embroidery. They were laced just tightly enough to reveal the lush curve of her breasts. A finely tooled leather belt encircled the turn of her waist, catching the skirts of her gowns into pleats. The folds weren't bulky enough to disguise her flat belly, a belly that Michel knew had never once stretched to accommodate a babe, although she's been married for almost six years to her first husband. Her potential barrenness had concerned him until he learned her previous husband had been thirty years her senior, old enough to be seedless or incompetent.

Framed by the folds of a fine white linen headdress held in place with a golden circlet, her face was a smooth oval. Wings of rich chestnut hair swooped down against the lift of her cheekbones, then back toward her nape. Her mouth was generous, her nose strong and straight. Dark brows as strong as she slashed above green eyes. Only a few moments ago those eyes had had been filled with subtle appreciation when she looked upon him.

Michel might have returned her interest save that Amicia de la Beres was an Englishwoman, born and bred. On the whole he found the wellborn bitches of this backward isle more bigoted and devious than those of his own country, and that was a feat unto itself.

John looked at Michel, the corners of his mouth lifted just a little. That expression meant a trap lurked. Then again, with John there was always a trap.

"What say you, Sir Michel? Can you prove our ward wrong about yourself, and render a fair value for her hand in marriage? Nay, do better than that. Tell us what price you'd pay for her if you were the one seeking to have her to wife."

Wondering if his patron would go so far in this game of his that John might breach his earlier vow of secrecy regarding Michel's interest in the lady, Michel turned to face Amicia de la Beres. He knew exactly what the court said of him and his black mail. Christus, but he'd started that rumor himself to prevent another raft of nuisance duels as had plagued him at his last position. They'd ended up consuming all his free time until he was heartily sick of wounding beardless noble lads armed with swords they didn't know how to wield.

Against his vile repute, every woman from maid to queen should have been too terrified to met his gaze. Not this woman. She glared at him without a hint of fear in her green eyes. Her chin lifted into an imperious angle.

Michel's regard for her dimmed as he recognized the gesture for what it was, a reflection of an inflated sense of her own worth. She looked at him and didn't see a knight, her equal in rank, but an upstart commoner. Such arrogance above her station required a worthy retort and he knew exactly how to repay her. Lady de la Beres was said to be a consummate player of the game of chaste love. Game! It was no game, but a way for women of supposed high morals to taunt men, stoking masculine desires with cooed promises of what they would never give to those men fool enough to admire them. Game or not, a show of masculine lust was a fitting retort.

Michel drew his gaze down, then up the length of the lady's body. Although his intent was to humble her, the image woke of her upon a bed as she yielded all to him in the ultimate female submission. It was a tantalizing picture. When he raised his gaze to meet hers, he lifted his brows and let the corners of his mouth rise, so she might know just how greatly he approved of her appearance.

Her eyes widened. She drew a sharp breath, then her jaw tightened and her eyes narrowed to spit green fire at him. She snatched her mantle close around her to shield herself from his view. Bitter amusement tugged at Michel. She could hide from him for the now, but matters would soon be different.

"Well, Sir Michel?" John prodded.

"Sire, no matter how long I look upon the lady I cannot offer the opinion you require," Michel said with a small shake of his head, knowing better than to swiftly give John what he wanted. "I'm a bachelor knight, hardly the sort of man qualified to determine a wife's worth."

Sir Enguerran grinned and shifted into a more comfortable stance, as if he thought Michel's comment in some way benefited him. Lady de la Beres lifted her head a little to shoot him a wary glance from the corner of her eye. Appreciation for Michel's subtle dodge flashed in John's dark gaze, but the set of the king's jaw said his mercenary wouldn't slither so easily from the royal grasp.

"How humble of you," John said. "Of course you would be reluctant to give your opinion, being as you are only a merchant's son," he added, using the reminder of Michel's base birth to jab again at Lady de la Beres's already bruised pride. If John meant the blow to strike Michel as well, the king missed his target. A lifetime of being despised for his tainted blood left Michel beyond reaction. Even his own cousins loathed him, having never forgiven Lord Amier, their grandsire, for advancing the common offspring of their disparaged aunt. They included him in their ranks because his skills and his growing repute were better than any of theirs. "Still, even commoners must know something of a woman's value," England's king persisted. "What of whores? You must surely assess a tart's worth before you pay out good coin for her services."

Although Lady de la Beres's head was yet bowed, she gasped and swayed as if struck. And, so she might. In comparing her to a daughter of joy, John lowered the lady to a whore's level, tarnishing Lady de la Beres's stainless repute.

Sir Enguerran threw back his head. Michel waited for him to protest. Instead, the man glanced at the woman he expected to wed as if he worried that she were, indeed, now dirtied.

Anger stirred in Michel on the lady's behalf. "Sire," he started, only to catch back his protest.

The pleasure was gone from John's face, which meant the king's insult had been a final and wild blow made by a man who knew he was defeated and now tantrummed against the loss. Thank God. It was time to end this game between him and his employer, once and for all.

"I frequent the stews as often as any man," Michel began again, taking care with his words. "However, the value a man places on a whore's tricks isn't the worth he awards his wife. You asked for my assessment of the lady's wifely value. As regards that, all I can say is that no knight's daughter can be worth the sum you named, sire. In all truth I doubt I'd pay even the forty-five pounds you originally asked for the lady, for I hardly believe her value can be as high as that." Michel glanced at Sir Enguerran as he spoke. It couldn't hurt to plant the idea that Lady de la Beres was worth less than her original value in the toady's mind; nor would it hurt for the lady to believe Michel had no interest in her.

Michel savored his triumph. It wasn't often that John so completely lost control of one of his schemes. For this brief moment Michel was the master of England's master, and a brief moment was all he needed to reap the reward he'd been promised.

It was at the siege of Nantes, after Michel presented the king of Paris's cousin to John as a hostage, that John had offered Michel any compensation he desired. Michel had bided his time until John's return to England last month before he made his request. What

Michel wanted was a wife, a woman who brought with her lands, wealth enough to free him of his common roots, and a good bloodline capable of lifting his future sons into a genteel future.

John, being John, had offered his mercenary an heiress too rich and too noble for Michel. But then, it wasn't his mercenary's happiness that concerned John. What the king wanted was to craft Michel into his weapon, using the mercenary to punish the lazy, cowardly Englishers who had refused to come to their king's aid in John's French war. Because of the betrayal of his subjects, John had lost control of his Continental patrimony from the Aquitaine to the fractious barons of Poitou to Normandy, that province turning its back on England for the first time in almost two hundred years as it paid homage to the king of Paris.

Michel was no man's pawn or fool. If he had wed John's high-born heiress, he wouldn't have survived long enough to enjoy his newly acquired status or to seed sons in his wife's womb. It had taken a month of sifting through John's available wards before Michel found the woman he needed, one of middling importance, decent income, and no family to protest against their kinswoman's degraded marriage. He cared nothing for the fact that some other man had opened the lady's maidenhead before him.

The only wife Michel would have was Lady de la Beres.

"Do you hear, Majesty?" d'Oilly cried. "Even your own man says she isn't worth what you ask for her."

Michel's muscles tensed as his hand clenched

around his sword's hilt. He pivoted to stare at the idiotic worm of a knight. Jesus God, but if it weren't already too late, he'd cleave that foul bootlicker in twain for opening his fool mouth! Everyone, even Michel whose acquaintance with John had been only these last few years, knew better than to rub the king's nose into a defeat.

Just as Michel expected, John's mouth quirked downward into a stubborn line. Damn the Plantagenet blood. Once challenged, John simply couldn't admit to defeat of any kind, even if persevering in this effort meant destroying Michel's future.

"Nay, we cannot agree with either of you," John said. "Any man can see that Lady de la Beres is a woman of spirit and intelligence. That, in our mind, is worth a great deal. If you want her, Sir Enguerran, you'll pay me every pence of that two hundred and fifty pounds."

John's voice was cold, but Michel knew him well enough to recognize the childish sulk in that icy tone.

Sir Enguerran's face flushed. "But sire, you yourself named your mercenary as objective. You must heed him when he renders his opinion," he cried, proving himself an even greater idiot as he drove his insult deeper beneath John's skin.

A small sound escaped Lady de la Beres. Her head was still bowed, but her shoulders were set in a harsh line and her profile could have been chiseled from granite. Then again, Michel didn't know anyone who cared to hear themselves called worthless again and again.

John's expression flattened. His eyes narrowed. "Sir

Enguerran, do you dare to imagine yourself our councillor?"

D'Oilly's head hung so far forward that Michel wondered that the man's beard didn't catch in his mail. "Begging your pardon, sire," the toady muttered, belated panic filling those quiet words.

"As you should," John announced to the room as if he stood among a crowd instead of only four other souls, if one counted John's body servant hovering in the corner. "Now, leave us, not to return until you have notes guaranteeing us the full amount. Aye, and until that day you are also relieved of your position as administrator of Lady de la Beres's estate."

That brought Sir Enguerran's head snapping back up, his eyes wide. Rather than outrage at being unjustly stripped of his position, the knight looked more like a guilty lad who'd just been rightly charged with some as yet undiscovered wrongdoing.

"Majesty," Sir Enguerran protested, "what reason have you to do me so? Is there someone who says I've misused the lady's properties in some way? If so, let me know that man's name so I can call him out and restore my honor."

Nothing of subdued amusement remained in the king's face. "No man speaks against you, nor do we accuse. We simply choose not to tempt you into using the lady's properties to raise the amount we require for her. What you give us must come from your own resources. Now, leave us." A brusque flick of the royal hand dismissed Sir Enguerran.

Reclaiming his slump, Sir Enguerran backed his

way to the chamber's door, bowing with each step. Once the door closed behind Sir Enguerran, John turned the force of his personality upon Lady de la Beres.

"You may leave us as well," he said, dismissing the gentlewoman as bluntly as he had his knight.

The widow raised her head to look upon her king. Although her shoulders were yet tensed, there was no sign on her face of the humiliation she'd just experienced, whether through Michel's appraisal, John's unfair insult, or Sir Enguerran's protests. Instead, the lady's pretty eyes filled with consideration.

"A question if I may, sire?" she asked, her voice reflecting only the gentle meekness men expected of all females.

The king gave his ward an impatient nod. "Speak."

"Sire, if Sir Enguerran is no longer the administrator of my properties, who is?"

John looked at Michel and smiled. Gone was the royal petulance awakened by Michel's small victory. Michel barely stopped himself from gnashing his teeth in frustration. Damn the widow. Still grinning, John looked upon his ward.

"Why, my lady, we have given the management of your estate to Sir Michel de Martigny."

The assault had all the impact John hoped and Michel feared. Shock drove the lady back upon her heels, then her spine snapped straight. Whirling, her hands once more clenched, she glared at Michel. She believed, just as John intended, that once Michel had control of her estates he would do as his fellow Frenchman and mercenary Gerard d'Athlee had done with the estates given to him: loot them of their wealth.

Or did she already understand more than that? Gentlewomen considered marriage to a commoner a fate worse than death.

No matter what she understood, Michel had no choice but to accept the appointment. He gave John a single nod.

Lady de la Beres freed another of those seething breaths. Without so much as a nod toward her royal master, she turned and stormed toward the door, her mantle snapping at her heels. If she meant the manner of her departure to insult John, she failed.

Laughing, John called after his ward, dropping royal formality for a manner and tone that was too intimate by far for Michel's tastes. "My lady, I cannot tell you how disappointed I am that our game was interrupted. You can be certain that I look forward to another match between us in the not so distant future."

Chapter 3

Ami ignored her king's parting threat and yanked
open the bedchamber door. Its leather hinges
squealed in protest. By God, but this was beyond all
toleration! If John thought she was going to stand idly
by as his mercenary impoverished her, he was sadly
mistaken.

Lost in blind rage, she slammed the door behind her
and strode into the antechamber, only to collide with
something. Gasping, she careened back toward the
door. The sound of subdued masculine laughter followed.

She'd collided with a large wooden tub set on its
edge. The royal bathtub. Behind it stretched a line of
menservants, snaking out the doorway, each bearing
a yoke hung with a pair of water buckets. Irritation
spiked anew in Ami as she understood John's suggestive dress. Of course the king hadn't seen fit to tell

his visitor that he waited on his bath. Why, when his attire aided in his purpose of tormenting his innocent ward?

Ignoring the startled chamberlain, Ami stalked around the tub. Another round of muted amusement escaped the beyoked servants as they shuffled to the side to let her pass. By God, but she couldn't wait to put distance between herself, these horrid men, her horrid monarch and his even more horrid mercenary.

Rage took fire in her. As if it weren't bad enough that, as one of the lowest ranking woman among the wards, Ami had to tolerate the snubs and arrogance of the women above her, the king and his mercenary had taken great pleasure in trampling her esteem to dust. Even worse than that, that commoner, that mercenary, that soldier derelict in all honor, had dared to name her worthless!

Ami's eyes narrowed. This after he'd looked at her as if she were a slab of meat or a length of cloth that he meant to purchase. Nay, that wasn't how he'd looked at her. He'd eyed her as if he sought a whore to serve his needs!

She strode for the exit from the antechamber as behind her wood rattled on wood as the tub was rolled into the inner chamber. The chamberlain's quiet call followed as he urged the water-bearing servants to make haste. Ami thrust out of the doorway and onto the balcony that overhung the king's hall, only to collide with yet another manservant and his yoke. The servant stumbled back from her. Water sloshed from his buckets onto the balcony's floor. The moisture spattered Ami.

With a cry, she yanked up her hems and danced to the side. While her mantle could tolerate some wet, it truly wasn't meant for wear outside the confines of court appearances. As for her best gowns, the water would stain them when she owned nothing else appropriate for the king's presence. Nor would there be new gowns for her, not in any foreseeable future. Last year's income had been far lower and so, consequently, was her allowance.

Ami peered down the length of the narrow balcony ahead of her. As in many of the keeps where there were second-story living quarters above a hall, this balcony served as access from the hall below to these upper chambers. In some castles, the balcony was open, with nothing but a railing to keep folk from falling down into the hall to their deaths. Here, wooden walls turned it into a darkened corridor, thus shielding the king from the noise of the household. Right now that corridor was filled with servant after sweating servant, each one with seeping buckets.

As dearly as Ami wanted to storm down the stairs, if only to vent her own rage, she wasn't willing to risk her precious garments. That left only one choice. She backed up a few steps.

Where the balcony ended just past the antechamber's doorway, the meeting of the walls created a tiny alcove complete with benches, so folk might sit while they waited to see their king. Ami sat upon a bench. It wouldn't be long before the servants were done and she could leave.

As the dimness in the alcove enclosed her, her rage

over her mistreatment sagged. That left her staring at the despair that lurked beneath it. Why had Richard de la Beres had to die? A lump formed in Ami's throat at the thought of her husband, gone these past four years. Although there had been many years difference in their ages, she had loved him. He would have hated the sort of quandry his death created for her.

Her good repute was the most valuable thing she owned. She'd managed to keep it even whilst under attack by hostile women and men determined to seduce her. Yet, today and in a single sentence the king had lowered her to a whore's level, doing it before witnesses. So fragile was the female repute that a woman who but spoke to one accused of indecent behavior could be tainted by that same sin. If one of the other ladies in John's custody heard that Ami had been compared to a tart, all of them would have to shun her.

From the moment Ami had come into John's custody she'd known she was exactly the sort of woman her king preferred. Not only was she a woman of middling importance, being a sheriff's widow with one insignificant keep, two manor houses, and a few mills to her name, but she was an orphan. That meant no inconvenient father or brother to complain over how John might misuse her.

That also meant there was no one to protect her good name if the king dared force her into his bed, something judging by John's final comment that was still a possibility. No one would care what happened to her, not even after John grew bored with her and married her to one of those land-hungry, low-born clerics he so enjoyed promoting, or if he wed her to one of those slavering French mercenaries whose company John so preferred over his own nobles. A flicker of rage pressed against Ami's despair as the image of Sir Michel formed in her mind.

That bitch's son, Michel de Martigny, had let his lusts run wild while he studied her. Flickers of anger turned into tendrils. Ami caught them close to her, stoking the emotion until it consumed her. Her eyes opened and she sat straighter on the bench, her hands clenched into her mantle.

It didn't matter how long it took or what she had to do. God help her, but she would find a way to shove John's *game* down his royal throat. But, before she repaid her king his insult, she'd find a way to gut that arrogant mercenary who now had control of her home, cutting out his heart and doing it right through his foul black mail if need be.

As Lady de la Beres had slammed the door behind herself, John whirled to face Michel, his eyes alive and his smile wide.

"By God, but she's magnificent! How could I have overlooked her? Dear God, I hope she never again so abuses my majesty. It would be a terrible thing to have to break that spirit. Ah, but the greater waste would be to squander her passion on a man who has no more appetite than a eunuch. You cannot have her, Michel."

Michel shrugged off the king's insult. John suspected the masculinity of any man who didn't nightly take a woman into his bed. Michel chose to be more cautious when it came to relieving his lusts. He no longer used city stews and brothels, having contracted one too many curable but annoying illnesses after a visit to the baths. That left him to choose from the scattering of healthy maids he encountered as John traveled from property to property. Marriage offered him the better choice. Since he had no expectation of visiting his wife's bed any more often than it took to create an heir or two. Once he was wed, he could find himself a willing woman, one from his own class. She'd be grateful for the promotion and security Michel's bed offered her, and willingly serve him.

"Sire, need I remind you that you vowed I could have my choice of wives?" Michel prodded quietly, in case John's memory of his battleground promise needed jogging. "The woman I choose is Lady de la Beres. However, if it pleases you, you may use her before I wed her."

Michel made the offer knowing John would refuse. As long as the king believed his mercenary didn't care what happened to the lady, then John had no incentive to use his ward, especially when bedding her against her will could lead to an outcry at court. That was something John couldn't afford, not when the present wrangling between the king and some of his barons might yet come to war.

"All I ask is that you support any bastard she bears you," Michel added, "and that you'll agree to meddle with her no more once our vows are said." Aye, it was sons of his own blood Michel wanted to raise, not one of John's by-blows.

"I'll consider it," John replied, but, just as Michel expected, the pleasure dimmed from the king's face when his jab failed to provoke the reaction he craved. "What befuddles me is that you still want the lady now that you've met her. She's disgusted by you, I fear."

A muscle along Michel's jaw tightened in exasperation. John had done his best to see that the lady was disgusted with his mercenary. "I care nothing for what she thinks of me."

"You should care. She'll fight you, making your marriage hell."

"She'll try," Michel replied with a shrug. "She can but fail." It was God who made men the masters of women, just as they were the masters of dogs and horses. Aye, and the only way that holy order could be defied was when a man made himself vulnerable to the women he was charged to dominate.

"I'm warning you, Michel," the king said, smiling still, "Lady de la Beres isn't the sort of woman most men would have as a mate. Living with her will be like riding an unbroken horse." Lust sparked in the king's gaze, rising until it darkened his face. "By God, but your offer is sorely tempting. I may have to accept."

Anger streaked through Michel. No man, not even a king, touched his wife. All that saved him from growling at his monarch was a tap at the door.

The chamberlain opened the door far enough to step halfway into the room. The golden chain that crossed his breast, the symbol of his position, was a yellow streak against the bright blue of his tunic. His brown cap was pushed far back onto his bald head. "Your bath, sire?"

"I am ready," John replied.

With a nod, the chamberlain threw open the door and stood aside as a pair of men rolled a large tub into the room. They snapped a greased cloth into place at the chamber's center, then set the tub upon it. Another greased sheet lined the tub, so it might better hold water, then men bearing water buckets appeared, emptying their burdens into it, one by one.

Michel gave thanks for the distraction for it allowed him to leash his strange reaction. The lady wasn't his, yet. If John caught even a whiff of his possessiveness, the king would bed Lady de la Beres every night until Michel's wedding. It was time for Michel to retreat and stay away until he was again fully in control of himself.

"Sire, I'd like to view the lady's estates before the wedding is arranged," Michel said. "By your leave, I'll depart today for Sussex. I should be gone no longer than a week."

"Wait a little before you go," the king said, his voice suddenly flat. It was a reminder that John wasn't willing to give Michel the bride he wanted, not if it meant admitting that Michel had won this contest of theirs.

Or, was it something else? The memory of Sir Enguerran's behavior as he was stripped of Lady de la Beres's properties returned to haunt Michel. His jaw tightened. As long as Michel insisted on flouting his king's will and insisted on Lady de la Beres for a wife,

Michel wouldn't put it past John to let him wed the lady, all the while knowing her estates weren't what they should be.

"How can I wait, sire, when you've named me as her administrator?" Michel countered, striving to sound sensible rather than impatient. "It's my duty to make myself familiar with her lands. Now that you've stripped them from Sir Enguerran I'll not have him enrich himself from her properties as he retreats from them."

Contempt darkened John's face. "That worm? He barely has balls enough to wipe himself much less to steal from me. Nay, it won't be long before d'Oilly accepts that he cannot afford the fee I named for her."

With a jerk of the royal head, John invited Michel to step farther from the door and tub, then continued. "I tell you what. In the next days I'll depart for Windsor, but leave you here as temporary guardian of my wards. That will give you access to the queen's hall, and my wards. Attend those interminable midday meals of theirs." John almost winked at his mercenary. "Better you dine with them than me. But while you consume those meals, you can use the time to come to know the lady a little better."

It took all Michel's will to keep exasperation off his face and out of his voice. "Sire, you know that I dare not spend any public time near the widow, else the whole of the court may take note of my interest in her. I shouldn't need to remind you that some folk presently collect tales of your supposed misdeeds to justify insurrection. A rumor that you plan another marriage between one of your wards and a mercenary will only aid their cause."

Aye, and with such a rumor, this militant faction's protest could make Michel's marriage to Lady de la Beres impossible. But then, that might be exactly what John wanted.

"Piss," John snapped, waving away the possibility of rebellion. Or was it Michel's connection to Lady de la Beres that he dismissed? "Let de Vesci plot as he likes," the king said, speaking of the lord of the powerful northern keep of Alnwick. "That cur is nothing but a hotheaded oath-breaker, a miser who refuses to pay the scutage he rightfully owes his liege. No man trusts him enough to follow him into a garderobe, much less rebellion."

Michel eyed his king, wondering if John purposefully blinded himself to what happened in his own country. No longer was it just the northern barons who whispered of rising. The lord of Dunmow had joined the malcontents, a baron whose extended family included the earls of Essex, Oxford, Hereford. It was said that Dunmow felt driven to it by Bishop Peter des Roches, another of John's Frenchmen, whom John had left as royal justiciar while out of the country this past year. The bishop had his own heavy-handed version of justice.

"This is a kingdom of cowards." John's voice rose as he again indulged himself in another round of outrage over his barons' refusals to join his Continental war. "Let them bare their swords to me and I'll squash them like the insects they are."

Although a lift of Michel's shoulders acknowledged his monarch's words, in Michel's opinion John had always trusted too deeply in the loyalty of men like the earl of Pembroke and John's half brother, the bastard earl of Salisbury. There wasn't a man in the world who wouldn't break his word, given the right motivation.

But then, Michel put little stock in ideals and oaths. That's why he'd chosen the mercenary life. A man who warred for pay knew exactly why he battled and what he stood to lose if he was defeated. So too was a mercenary free to turn on his employer, should that man refuse to render a promised payment. An oath-bound man had no such freedom, not unless he wanted to lose his good name as he broke his oath.

This was Michel's only reservation about marriage. To have Lady de la Beres and her properties, he had to give John his oath, promising unpaid service to England's throne for the remainder of his life. In his younger years, the thought of giving any nobleman his oath of fealty had been abhorrent. No longer. Michel supposed that had to do with having reached the age of more than a score and ten. That was old enough to fear death might come for him before he'd had the chance to seed either a legacy or sons to carry on after him.

"I'll spend a week at Windsor, then move on to Kensington and the queen," John was saying. "Is that long enough for you to convince the lady to choose you as her husband?"

For the lady to choose him? Instantly, Michel banished all expression from his face, a skill he'd cultivated during his violent squiring in Lord Amier's home. May God take England's king!

It took little imagination to conjure up the king's next ploy as he strove to dissuade Michel from the woman he wanted. D'Oilly was sure to complain to any who'd listen of Lady de la Beres's new bride price and how he'd been stripped of her properties. John, being John, would start a rumor of a second offer for the lady's hand. Michel, as the new administrator, would be the obvious candidate. Courtly outrage would follow. Pretending to bow to public pressure, John would give the lady the right to choose her own husband, and it wouldn't be Michel.

That would leave Michel with no English woman left to choose for a wife but the heiress John wanted for him. Michel knew very well what that meant. Outraged noblemen waiting in every city street and country lane, their swords bared to attack, until he was finally dead. As Michel felt the future he wanted for himself slipping from his grasp, suspicion ran wild.

What if this was John's purpose? That heiress of John's was also an orphan. If Michel died after their wedding, she, and her income of several hundred pounds a year, would return to John's custody.

He wanted to draw his sword and swing it until there was nothing left whole in this room. Michel clenched his fists. It was time to beat his retreat.

"As you will, sire," Michel said. "I'll serve as guardian to your wards until your return." With a bow, he turned and started toward the door.

"Do I catch a hint of concern in your voice, Sir Michel?" John called after him, sounding well satisfied, indeed. "Don't fret. You'll have what you want. Remember, I have promised."

Michel made no response as he departed around the steady stream of water-bearers. He crossed the antechamber, his attention focused only on the bitterness churning in his gullet. Only as he stood aside to let yet another man guide his yoke through the antechamber's narrow doorway did he realize that he'd agreed only to be temporary guardian of John's wards. John had never specifically forbidden him from traveling to the lady's properties.

The possibility of snatching victory out of defeat lifted in Michel. Once the king moved to Kensington, too far to be able to control matters here, Michel could make his journey to the de la Beres properties. If the lady's estates were in order, John could rush back to Winchester and rage all he willed. Michel would insist that he fulfill his royal promise.

And, if the lady's estates were impoverished? Well, there were other wars, other kings and other women to make into wives. Michel would sell what remained of his loot from the king's Continental war, and be done with England and its betraying monarch.

Chapter 4

Michel thrust out of the antechamber's door only to collide with yet another servant's yoke just beyond the doorway. Cursing beneath his breath, he stepped back into the alcove behind the antechamber's door.

"I've endured enough of you for one day. I won't have you ruining my mantle by standing on it with your filthy boots."

Michel pivoted. His shoulder caught the antechamber's door, sending it swinging back toward the servants on the balcony. It collided on the end of a man's yoke and stopped. That left it standing like a wall between this alcove and the rest of the balcony.

Amicia de la Beres sat on the alcove's bench, trapped just as he was by the line of servants. Coming to her feet, she lifted the corner of her mantle, then made a show of wiping his supposed boot print off its corner. When she let the garment's hem drop, she crossed her arms before her and looked down her nose at him. It was quite the feat, given that he was almost a full head taller than she.

"You, sir, are a man lacking in all courtesy," she snarled, her voice held low. "Had you any sort of manners you would have refused to participate in that little charade the king had us playing a moment ago." Rage flashed green in her eyes. "Ah, but why should you refuse when you so enjoyed playing along? You took advantage of the king's ploy to leer at me. How dare you!"

How dare he? How dare *she* throw her commands at him as if he were some lackey, not the king's knight? "You're hardly one to speak of manners, my lady," he offered in harsh retort. "It was you who leered at me first. Noblewomen or gentlewomen, you're all the same, gawking at me while trumpeting to the world that you'd destroy me if I dare return an iota of your interest or, God forbid, offer up a touch." He lifted a scornful brow. "What makes you think I might want any of your ilk?"

As often happened when Michel confronted these Englishers with their hypocrisy, the lady's eyes widened in a mingling of shock at his bold speech and denial of her actions. Color blossomed in her cheeks. "Cad!" She turned her body to the side to present her shoulder to him. "Leave me."

The gesture and her dismissal, something he had endured too often in his life, drove through Michel like a sword's blow. This woman above all others wasn't going to treat him like some servant. "How careless you are about the folk you antagonize, my lady," he told her, letting his voice lower to its most dangerous tone.

He took a step toward her. A step was all he needed. There wasn't much distance between them in this narrow space. His chest was so close to her shoulder that Michel could feel the heat of her body through his mail and underarmor.

She made a dismissing sound and tried to shift away from him. Her opposite shoulder collided with the alcove's wall. With nowhere left to go, she turned her back to the wall and faced him, the only barrier between them her crossed arms.

Michel waited for her to quake in fear for her virtue. Wellborn women all seemed to believe commoners incapable of controlling their bodies and their lusts, expecting rape from their masculine inferiors, even though every commoner knew that attacking a gentlewoman guaranteed his own death.

Lady de la Beres didn't shrink from him or turn her head to the side. Instead, with her sultry mouth once more held in a narrow line, she lifted her chin and tried to look through him as if he didn't exist.

It was the toss of a gauntlet. Michel knew just how to force her to acknowledge his presence. He set his hands on the wall behind her, positioning them low enough that she couldn't duck beneath his arms to escape him. Caught on his shoulders, his cloak came forward with his arms to curtain them in its thickness, lending an odd intimacy to what he did. Then, he shifted his body toward her until there was but a bare inch between them.

The blankness of her gaze dissolved, but not in fear.

"Retreat this moment! I am the king's ward. Touch me and I'll see that you regret it."

It was a viable threat; only a man begging for death made free with one of the king's wards. But then, it wasn't one of the king's wards Michel taunted just now, but the woman who would soon be his wife. At least, if he had his way.

"Then, I shall have to take care not to touch you, shan't I?" he told her.

Leaning forward, Michel lowered his head until his mouth was no more than a finger's width from her lips. They were so close he could sense the jut of her breasts a heartbeat from his mailed chest. Her breath was an angry hiss against his cheek. The faint scent of roses clung to her skin. He let the smell reawaken the desire he'd felt for her in the king's chamber.

"Now, madam, turn your shoulder to me," he whispered, his words the only thing touching her flesh. "Try and deny my existence."

Michel craved her fearful shiver, for it meant he'd mastered her. Instead, the lady who stood nigh on against him drew a quiet, shuddering breath. The heat of her body reached out to envelop him, her rosy scent now owning a new muskiness. In the next instant she softened in the most primal of invitations.

The urge to smile filled Michel. It wasn't his words this woman wanted to feel against her skin. Lust stirred within him. John was right. Riding her would be like riding an untamed horse, magnificently thrilling and, with mastery, ultimately satisfying.

"What are you doing?" she breathed in question.

Michel gave her no response, only shifted his head just a little, his breath again caressing her skin. She freed another shaken sigh. It would take nothing more than a kiss and her resistance would melt. But if he touched this woman, flesh to flesh, before their vows were said, all he hoped to achieve would slip like sand through his fingers.

It was the lady who offered him the solution to this dilemma. She turned her head to the side, as if to deny him her lips. Now, Michel's mouth hovered over her ear, or rather its outline. Her head was covered in a linen headdress almost matronly in its cut. Then again, linen was the perfect barrier between his mouth and her skin.

He lowered his lips to her concealed ear. She drew another shuddering breath. There was nothing of revulsion in the sound, only deep longing.

It was a siren's sound. His mouth moved on her ear, tracing its outline beneath the fabric. She sighed, then lifted her head a little to aid him in his caress.

His eyes closed. Painted on the insides of his lids was the image of this bold woman. This time, she lay upon his tangled bedclothes whilst he lay atop her. She writhed and clutched at him, her skin golden in the fire-light as she drove him into ecstasy.

Wild need followed, every inch of him alive and achingly aware of the woman almost pressed to him. Michel's shaft filled, straining against the confinement of his garments. By God, but he wanted her beneath him, now, even if that meant he took her on the balcony floor.

His hands shifted on the wall, moving toward her arms as he prepared to claim her. All it took was his fingers against the rich fabric of her mantle. Michel snatched his hands back as if burned.

What in God's hell was he doing! He shoved himself back from her, his hands dropping to his sides. Bad enough that John had already done what he could to set this woman against him. Now, here he was, aiding the king in that endeavor. Nay, he was doing worse than that. Rather than conceal his interest in her, he might as well have gotten down on his knees and begged for her hand in marriage.

Watching her, Michel took a backward step. Her shoulders still owned their proud angle. Her head was yet turned to the side, her eyes closed. Her lashes lay like dark fringe against the smooth landscape of her cheek. His gaze shifted to where her headdress gaped, revealing the length of her throat. There was something vulnerable and compelling about the arch of her neck.

That image of his shifted. All of a sudden it was no longer one of lust, but one of those extraordinary moments of satiation that followed lovemaking. She now rested alongside him in the bed, her arms around him, her dark hair streaming across the bare flesh of his chest. This woman would be his wife, his to care for and protect.

Michel caught back his imagination with a whispered curse. Fool! In one short moment he'd gone from making himself her master to rendering himself vulnerable to her by expecting what would never be between them. Wedded to him or not, no woman of her class would ever accept his touch, much less cherish it.

More likely he'd have to do as his own merchant father had done, and imprison his wellborn wife to ensure the births of his sons. The memory of Michel's dam brought with it the recall of her hatred for her children, whom she saw as living proof of her disparagement. Michel slammed an inner door on his past. It was dead and best left buried, save to use as a warning. Lady de la Beres must never be more to him than a vessel, a means to an end. He would use her body to make his heirs, then use his children to restore the prestige his mother's blood had once owned. If achieving that meant enduring his wife's loathing, then he would endure it.

Turning, he pushed the antechamber's open door to one side, startling yet another man in the endless string of yoked fellows bearing buckets. All it took was a glance at his black mail. Whether coming or going from the king's chamber, the men upon the stairs all shifted out of his path. Michel strode unimpeded down the steps, putting needed distance between himself and the woman who would be his wife.

Ami's eyes were clamped shut so she needn't look upon the reality of what she'd just done. She heard Sir Michel's whispered curse. That the mercenary called on God to take him offered her only the barest of consolation. It meant she wasn't the only one stirred by their nearness and his taunting. The humiliation would have been unbearable if he'd proved impervious to the sensations that had her knees quivering and her heart pounding.

The scrape of his boot heels against the balcony's wooden floor marked his departure, but she didn't need the tap of his footsteps to know he was gone. Nay, the cool emptiness in the air around her announced his absence. Keeping her eyes tightly shut, Ami sank down upon the bench.

The memory of his lips hovering almost atop hers returned. His breath had been fresh, his skin smelled of this day's rain. Sensations again streaked through her as out of her control as they had been the previous moment. God help her, but how could that have happened? Ami gave a cry and buried her head in her hands.

Never in all her life had she wanted to feel a man's mouth on hers as she wanted Michel de Martigny. In the space of a breath her determination to punish him for the insults he'd done her had melted into a fiery longing to bed him. A single touch of his mouth to hers, or even a whispered plea for her kiss, and she would have given him all he wanted and more, right here, where anyone might witness.

How could this be happening to her and with this particular man? Aye, there had been other knights at court who'd piqued her interest, but never one who'd pierced her barriers and stirred her lusts beyond the control of common sense. Perhaps the king was right to name her a whore.

Choking on that thought, Ami let her hands fall and peered down the length of the balcony. She breathed in relief that Sir Michel was nowhere to be seen. Good.

She could make her escape without having to confront him again.

Coward! Never mind that this particular man was capable of making her completely forget herself. For four years she'd turned men into poppets. She wasn't going to cry *yield* to an arrogant mercenary, especially not upon their first skirmish.

Ami regathered her shattered pride. A skirmish was all this little event had been, not a proper battle. She'd be ready, fully armed and defended against him when next they met.

Even as the steel returned to her spine, she reminded herself that this was nothing more than her just reward for putting the needs of vengeance ahead of practicality. What did it matter if one of the king's mercenaries thought her worthless? What was important was that this mercenary now controlled her property. If what had happened to others was any guide, then John wouldn't raise a finger as his favorite stole every moveable item from her estates.

Ami's eyes narrowed. She'd do worse than simply gut the mercenary if he stole her bed—

No more of this. What she needed was a way to stop Michel de Martigny from impoverishing her and that meant finding a way to control him. The only way Ami knew to leash a man was to use his affections to bind him.

On the balcony before her, two grunting men made their way into the king's apartment, carrying a heavy cauldron on poles between them: boiling water to warm the cold already in the tub. A few short minutes later they reappeared, moving easily now that their cauldron was empty. They were the last to leave.

Ami came to her feet, smoothing her skirts as she stood. The sooner she started leashing Michel de Martigny, the better for her. She almost smiled. Tonight was the perfect opportunity to begin that leashing.

It was the feast of Saint Martin. In the countryside this day was heralded as nothing more than the right moment in which to plant leeks, but John and his court took every excuse they could to celebrate—feasting, drinking, dancing and otherwise carousing. These amusements shattered all rules of rank, especially when the full court wasn't in residence as now. In this more casual atmosphere an earl might find himself holding a serving lass's hand.

Or a poor sheriff's widow might put her fingers into the palm of a handsome mercenary.

Chapter 5

At the end of the balcony, Ami descended the stairs toward the the body of the king's hall, one of the two royal dwellings at Winchester's castle. So large had old King Henry's family grown that a second, temporary hall had been constructed within these walls to accommodate his expanded household. Although it was but mid-November the weather had been colder and windier than usual. Against the chill a fire roared on the hall's central hearth stone. Yet that wasn't enough noise to drown out the clamor of a hall being prepared for a feast.

Servants shouted one to another as they arranged the dinner tables; dogs yipped and chased the ends of white tablecloths as maids snapped them into place. Their raucous activity stirred the piney scent of rosemary that had been strewn into the reeds covering the floor. The king's table, dressed in cloth of gold, already stood upon its dais. All along the hall's length, garlands hung, the fruit of Ami's and the other wards' labors. For the past week they'd spent their days turning stalks of wheat, late autumn flowers, and rosemary into long ropes.

At the base of the stairs, Ami looked toward the door's screen—the tall wooden panel that guarded the hall from drafts—seeking her escort. A woman of good name never strode outside of her own house without a chaperone of some kind, not even if that woman was only going from hall to hall in this castle. The two soldiers who had come with her from the queen's hall started forward when they saw her.

Only when they were by her side did Ami start for the doorway. Once around the screen, they left the hall, making their way down the exterior stairs. For defensive reasons, the hall was built of stone and had a slate roof and narrow arrow loop windows. Its door was placed a full storey above the courtyard floor.

Once at courtyard level, Ami pulled her mantle more tightly around her as chill rain spattered her. Despite the weather, the yard bustled with servants and soldiers, all of them intent on doing their masters' business, whether their master was the king or only one of the king's lowly clerks. There were laundresses with their baskets on their backs, clerks with ink-stained fingers and sheaves of parchment tucked beneath their arms, men bearing parcels from their yokes along with liveried, bejeweled messengers bearing missives on horseback.

Beaten into permanence by two centuries of use, a pathway led Ami and her escorts through the clutter of outbuildings that every defended residence needed to serve it. Stables and barns were placed farthest from the living quarters, to spare delicate noses as much as possible. Closer to the halls were the buildings that housed the king's body soldiers. And, nearer still, was the jumble of thatch-roofed constructs that was the kitchen complex. What with feasting tonight, smoke streamed from its many roof vents, the wind filled with the scents of stews, roasting meats, and baking bread.

Ami's gaze caught on the small bathhouse, its back to one of the ovens to borrow heat. Unlike the king, who took his bath in his own chamber, the rest of the court had to share a tub in yon house. If not for the fact that the water would be well used by this time of day or that Ami had taken a swift plunge before coming into her king's presence, she might have considered a long soak. After her interview with the king and that . . . experience . . . with Sir Michel, she felt the need to rinse the day from her skin.

The second of the two halls within Winchester Castle's defensive walls was nearly the same size as the one the king used, however it was built of wood and lacked the stone foundation of the main hall. Instead of slate for roof, it had wooden shingles. Because the hall had no defensive purpose, wide windows had been cut into its sides and where its ell harbored private apartments. These were covered with shutters.

To others, the queen's hall might exude an aura of homely comfort. But to Ami it represented nothing less than her prison. Once she climbed the few steps that led to its door, she would be again trapped within its walls, held in barren confinement while John had the use of her properties.

As Ami reached the steps to the door, her escorts fell back, retreating to their barracks. This hall was being used by the king's female wards, thus no man save those vouchsafed by John entered. The porter waited by the door, shielded from the weather by the porch roof. The door he guarded stood slightly open behind him, so that air might be drawn within to feed the hall's fire. What went one way could go another. The opening was big enough to let the sounds of female life escape it. Women chattered. Dice clacked and clattered. Someone played a mournful tune on a zither.

The porter, Walter by name, bent a friendly smile on Ami as she stopped before him. Walter could afford to be amiable. Those wealthy women imprisoned behind his door often bribed him to look the other way as they escaped confinement to tend to private business, whatever that business might be.

"Well now, that was a right swift audience, my lady," Walter said, sending a meaningful glance at Ami's clothing and her yet perfectly arranged headdress.

That he overstepped himself in addressing her was because Ami encouraged it. In her past visits to Winchester, Ami had found Walter useful as she led those men trying to seduce her through the maze that was the game of love. The porter was a veritable fountain of information about courtly folk. Still, Walter's crass comment was a reminder that those folk who'd heard the messenger calling her into a private audience with their king expected her to return sullied.

"It doesn't take a woman long to tell a man no, Walter, even if that man is a king," Ami retorted, doing what she could to hold on to her already suspect repute.

Walter laughed, then dared to wink at her. "Don't I know that all too well, my lady? For myself, I couldn't be more pleased to learn of your strength of will, but then I expected nothing less of you. There'll be a few others painfully surprised when they must forfeit their coins to me."

Ami's stomach knotted at the thought of anyone wagering over her ruination. "Fie on you, Walter, risking your hard earned coins that way. Doesn't your confessor tell you that gambling is a sin? And, if you won, then I'd better hear that you lifted your cup in thanks to me this night."

"That I will, my lady," Walter assured her, stepping aside so Ami could pass him.

She swept into the portal, then around the wooden screen to reenter her prison. In no more time than it took to blow out a candle, all the noise in the hall ceased. The silence was so complete that Ami could hear the patter of the rain upon the hall's shuttered windows. Someone cleared her throat. A dog whined. The bells on a hawk's hood jingled merrily as it blindly turned its head, disturbed by the change in the room.

Ami's footsteps rang on the hall's wooden floor as she started toward the wee space at the far side that was allotted to her. With no sun to drive back the day's gloom, and the fire upon the central hearth providing even less light than it did heat, expensive candles stood about the chamber. That gentle illumination made the occupants of the room gleam, their gowns and mantles almost rainbow brilliant. Jewels flashed in rings and necklets, while metal threads sparked at nearly every hemline and sleeve. A man might judge his merit by how well he wielded his weapon, be that pen or sword, but in this hall it was the weight of gold and silver worn upon a body that was the measure of worth.

The candlelight was bright enough to reveal avid interest on the face of every woman, be she gently born or servant. Again, Ami's stomach knotted. Pretty vultures, all of them. They couldn't wait to feast upon one of their own.

Calling them to witness that she returned untouched and too swiftly for wrong to have been done wouldn't stop them. Confinement and boredom made these women eager for any sort of distraction. Ami's life would be their plaything until some new scandal arose to replace it.

What she needed was to offer them a new scandal.

Ami almost smiled. All she need do was shift their thoughts onto Enguerran d'Oilly's replacement by Michel de Martigny. There wasn't a woman in the room who wouldn't tremble over the disparagement of a mercenary as her property's administrator. Rather than tear Ami's repute to shreds they'd rage on her behalf, their emotions driven by the fear that someday the same would happen to them.

Let this be her first blow in her new battle to leash Sir Michel. Stones or not, the walls around Ami could be transparent when it came to rumors. Once news of Enguerran d'Oilly's replacement reached the rebel-mongers, whispers would fly as they fomented hatred for John and directed even more contempt toward de Martigny. Anything that might weaken him was to her advantage.

Ami stopped to curtsy before the woman in the massive chair near to the hearth. Slim, fair, and several years Ami's senior, Eleanor of Brittany was the highest-ranking woman in this hall, what with John's queen presently residing at Kensington. Eleanor was John's niece by his next eldest brother Geoffrey, now deceased. She was also sister to the deceased Arthur, the lad who might have been England's king if he hadn't all too conveniently died while John was visiting his home.

"How quickly you return to us, Lady de la Beres," Eleanor said, her raised hand holding Ami where she stood for a moment. "Did you find my lord uncle well?"

Interest beyond the scope of her question glittered in Lady Eleanor's eyes, suggesting the countess intended to skewer her inferior. Instead, Eleanor had unwittingly offered Ami the perfect opportunity to save herself.

"His majesty seemed well enough, my lady," Ami replied, her strong, clear voice filling the quiet room. "As did Sir Enguerran d'Oilly, my trusted neighbor and administrator of my properties, who was included in my audience." Ami congratulated herself on her phrasing. Now, no one would think she'd ever been alone with the king.

"However," Ami continued, "I fear the news our liege had for me was to my detriment, and to Sir En-

guerran's. May God take those filthy churls who misuse our sweet king's generous nature," she cried, her
voice rising, reaching every corner of the chamber.
"Most of all, I pray God might destroy that baseborn
brute, Michel de Martigny. That lout has misused royal
favor to strip my estates of a trusted administrator and
claim that position for himself. Mary preserve me, but I
can only think that the foreigner means to take what is
mine for himself."

Her words were like the opening of a mill gate. Outrage flooded the room as women shot to their feet,
spilling embroidery and half made garments onto the
floor. While within the safety of these walls, only a few
women, among them Ami's maidservant, the frail
Maud, cowered at the thought of Sir Michel and his
black mail.

"That monster," protested the homely Lady Sybilla
in tune with the others, when the truth was that Sybilla
would have rendered up her virginity to Sir Michel, or
any man, if he but crooked a finger in her direction. At
two and twenty, and ten years spent in royal custody,
Sybilla had begun to believe she'd live out her life as a
nun without a convent, just as Eleanor surely would.
John's treasury needed the profit Sybilla's estate generated. If she wed, that profit would belong to her husband.

"May God take that arrogant upstart," shouted the
northern born Lady Adelberta, her words as tortured by
her thick accent as her opinions were by her rank and
youth. "I tell you all, it's not right that our king should
favor foreigners over our own folk. I say the whole

country should rise and drive these meddlers from our shores."

That comment brought Lady Eleanor sharply forward in her chair. Despite that her royal uncle had likely murdered her brother and that John would never risk his niece's marriage, Eleanor remained his willing spy. Every word spoken here might as well be spoken to the king. Ami considered warning Lady Adelberta. Then again, it wouldn't be the first time the king had heard the lady's opinion of him.

"Do lower your voice, my lady," called Mistress Milicent in tart reproof.

Like Ami, Milicent was a widow of middling means, but Milicent was well past the age for bearing children. With no illusions that she might ever remarry and no desire for convent life, Milicent was content to let the king feed and clothe her while her sons paid a fee to administer her dower properties. In return for royal generosity, Milicent took it as her duty to guard the morals of all John's younger wards. It wasn't a role appreciated by any of the women who'd experienced one of her tongue lashings.

Now, Milicent aimed a reproving finger at her better. "My lady, it seems your rough upbringing has been derelict. Someone forgot to teach you that no well-bred woman raises her voice to a shout. Nor does she express interest in what is masculine province."

Both Lady Sybilla and Lady Adelberta turned on Milicent. Other ladies came flying to join the fray. Spindles scattered across the floor. Baskets fell. Dogs barked and yipped in the excitement, while tethered hawks flapped and screeched in complaint. Some of the women crassly raised their voices to remind Mistress Milicent of her station, while the old woman's usual cadre of supporters rushed to her side, claiming that it was every woman's duty to see that none of their sex misbehaved.

Ami could have crowed. Let them argue about anything they wished as long as she wasn't in any way connected to the topic. Blessedly unnoticed, she slipped through the crowd to the wee corner of the room allotted to her, the size of the space based upon her rank. In that area were all the possessions she kept at court, the whole of them, clothing and other personal effects, contained in a little brass-bound chest. Two pallets, one for Ami and one for her maid, were rolled up behind the chest, waiting for nightfall when they would be spread upon the floor to serve as beds. Ami had never seen the inside of the private bedchambers in this hall, contained in its second-storey ell, much less slept in one. Such apartments were reserved for women of rank like Lady Eleanor. That left the remaining gentlewomen and servants to find their rest on the floor of this big room.

In front of her chest stood Ami's stool. That folding seat with its carved legs defined her world. For most of the day it was upon this wee chair that Ami could be found. Crouched like a lost kitten at the stool's foot was frail Maud. Tears glittered in the maid's eyes as she looked up at her mistress. Although Ami's sole maid servant was only two years younger in age than Ami, she was far younger in experience. Four years at court, and Maud still hated being left alone with her betters.

"What of the holiday?" Maud breathed in question, her tone brokenhearted, as if she already knew what answer she'd hear.

"I never got the opportunity to ask," Ami said with a sigh as she once more settled into the confines of her world. Guilt shot through her. In truth, with all that had happened, she'd forgotten about asking to go home.

Maud's head bowed in disappointment. More than anything, the maid wanted to return to her family for Christmas. Ami sighed, feeling the same longing for their shared home, the larger of her two Sussex manors.

Unlike some of these women who had family to watch over them, as an orphan Ami couldn't come and go from John's custody. Why, last summer, when she asked to attend the wedding of her distant cousin, Gerard of Essex, a man raised at court as John's own foster son, the king wouldn't release her until Gerard promised to pay a fine if Ami were kidnaped and forced into illegal marriage. However little Ami's estates could mean to John, the king still wouldn't risk losing control over her and her womb.

Ami's lip curled. As if any man would be fool enough to incur royal wrath by taking her. After all, wasn't she the woman that even a godforsaken mercenary had declared worth less than the forty-five pounds she knew was her true value?

It wasn't anger that answered this challenge. Instead, the sensation of the mercenary's mouth pressed against her ear rose. Primal longing, sharp and completely unwanted, shot through her. Ami destroyed it. It was the memory of how he had humiliated her she needed to be remembering.

"Wine," Ami said, and touched her maid's bowed head. "I think we could both do with a little wine."

The girl gave a shuddering sigh and raised her head. "Will that help, my lady?"

"Better than you can imagine," Ami replied with a little laugh. Aye, right now she'd like nothing more than to drink until she could drive this entire day from her mind. Since such excess wasn't something Ami allowed for herself, and there would be wine at the feast tonight, she wanted something even more special just now.

Releasing her purse from her belt, Ami tested its heft. From inside soft leather came the weighty clink of coins. There was still plenty left from her Michaelmas allowance. Aye, but common sense warned that it had to last until next Easter, when the time came to again collect rents from her lands. Ami tossed aside caution. Who cared what it cost? Tomorrow, the king might call her back to him and it wouldn't be an innocent game of backgammon they played.

She smiled at Maud. "I say we share a posset flavored with cinnamon."

Maud's lips quivered into an almost smile. She adored the taste of cinnamon, but the spice was so expensive that Ami, herself, rarely had the chance to enjoy it. But when she did, she never failed to let Maud sip with her.

"Thank you, my lady," the lass said. Taking Ami's purse, Maud found her mistress's cup in the chest, then set off across the hall on her way to the kitchen.

Once Maud was gone, Ami turned her attention on the hall. Some of the women were still arguing. Most had returned to their respective spots to soothe ruffled feathers. Only one woman watched Ami in return. Lady Roheise de Say smiled and started toward Ami's corner.

All Ami's pleasure ebbed. Not all of the king's wards were like herself, Milicent, or Sybilla, helpless and or-phaned, widow or heiress. Some of these women were so rich or so highly placed that the king held them like he would a male hostage, using them and his power over them to check their families' behavior. The newly come Lady de Say was one of these, cousin by mar-riage to the powerful Lord Geoffrey de Say.

Sharp of feature with eyes the color of slate and dark hair streaked with that same hue, the middle-aged widow stopped before Ami. Lady Roheise was an earl's daughter; her rank demanded that Ami stand and bow before her. This Ami did, reminding herself as she bent that while the lady could wrench this display of respect from her, Lady Roheise didn't have the right to bend Ami to her will. Not that this stopped powerful women like Roheise from trying.

One of the first things Ami had learned upon coming into John's custody was that there were only two ways to survive at court. One was to choose a faction—these days there were but two, either for or against a rebellion—and stay attached to it through thick and thin. Of course, that meant doing all sorts of onerous tasks, such as spreading rumors or spying or carrying secret mes-sages, the sort of thing Sir Enguerran wouldn't mind. Ami had opted for the other path, which was to avoid

all the factions and make herself as invisible and in-
nocuous as possible.

"My Lady de la Beres," Roheise de Say said with
what she no doubt supposed was a friendly smile. "I
wanted to offer you what comfort I can. How dare our
king put that lout in charge of your properties! Tell me,
since you've been here years now and I am only newly
arrived, does one actually learn to tolerate these indig-
nities? You seem so calm when I think I'd be thrashing
upon the floor, so great would my rage be."

Wondering if this was some sort of backhanded insult, Ami slipped behind the shield she'd devised four
years ago. "Many thanks for your concern, Lady Roheise. No matter my manner, believe that I am outraged. You cannot imagine the arrogance of a man like
that baseborn de Martigny," she added, taking an opportunity to throw yet another blow at Sir Michel.
"But"—here Ami adopted an exaggerated pretense of
female helplessness, bowing her head and wringing her
hands—"I am only a woman with no control over my
own fate. Against that, all thrashing upon the floor will
accomplish is the ruin of my gowns."

Roheise loosed a startled laugh, the sound filled with
genuine amusement. "I like your wit, my lady."

The snap of the noblewoman's fingers brought one
of the de Say maids running, the woman dressed in the
blue and green of Roheise's dead husband's house. The
servant carried a traveling stool, which she assembled
near Ami's seat. Lady Roheise sat, motioning that Ami
should do the same. The maid took a stance at her mis-

tress's side, her head bowed as she awaited the next command.

"Was that your servant I saw leaving with your purse and your cup?" Roheise asked Ami, her brows cocked. "Tell me the king doesn't also require that you buy your own drink."

Ami shook her head. "Nay, not the wine, but the cinnamon and sweetening. I fear my audience with the king sapped me. A posset seemed just the thing to restore my strength."

"Why, doesn't that sound lovely on a cold wet day," Roheise exclaimed. "I think I'll have one as well. I have a recipe, one of my own devising. It's wondrous. Why not let my maid"—the lift of Roheise's hand indicated the waiting servant—"make one for you as she makes mine? Oh, let me do this for you. Not only will it spare you the expense of purchasing what you need for your own drink, but I promise you'll enjoy it."

Had Ami been newly come to court she might have believed the lady sincere. But spices were too dear to be a casual gift, especially to an inferior. Nay, what Roheise was buying was privacy. The lady didn't want Maud returning too swiftly and interrupting them, when Ami didn't care to be private with this noblewoman.

She opened her mouth to demur and send the lady away. Before she could speak Roheise gave a lift of her hand. Her maidservant trotted away toward the door, chasing after Maud.

Anger surged through Ami. Just who in Satan's hell did this woman think she was?

Then, Ami wondered why Roheise's presumption surprised her. The noblewoman was no different from their king and that horrid mercenary. Well, she'd had enough of games for one day. She put her hands on her thighs, leaned forward, and prepared to vent the vastness of her anger onto the unsuspecting scheming bitch, even if paring away the lady's subterfuge earned her the noblewoman's enmity.

Chapter 6

"**H**ow grateful I am that I have something to offer you after such harrowing news." Roheise patted Ami's hand. "I think we shall come to be great friends, you and I."

Ami's eyes narrowed. It took all her will not to jerk her hand out of the lady's reach. "I doubt that, my lady. Why don't I spare you the charade? Tell me how you believe I can aid you and your cause."

Astonishment flashed across Lady Roheise's expression, only to fade into caution. "I see those who told me you were unusual didn't mislead me, my lady. You're right to think I want something of you, but make no mistake. Aid me and you'll be aiding yourself as well."

"Is that so?" Ami ladled disbelief into her tone.

Lady Roheise smiled again, showing a little too much tooth in the process. Leaning close, she wrapped her fingers around Ami's wrist as if she feared Ami might escape her. "Do as I ask and you'll save your own properties while becoming the cause of de Martigny's destruction."

Ami blinked as the possibility of freeing her properties from Sir Michel's grasp dropped into her lap. Nor was Roheise's offer of the mercenary's destruction an empty promise. Lady de Say's relatives were powerful, the sort of men who could force a king to do things he didn't wish to do without worrying too greatly over royal repercussions. Caution sounded. Women like Roheise never gave, they only used, taking care to see that blame for their plots never fell upon them. Still, it wouldn't hurt to hear the lady out.

"Tell me more," Ami said, her voice flat.

Satisfaction flared in Roheise's slate eyes. "It's justice I want, for you, my lady, for me and for all England. These last years our king has wreaked his worst upon the great men of this country, treating lesser men with more kindness than their worth and encouraging some of these men to act above their stations. Someone must check him. Our king has strayed too far from the good laws of our land, those crafted by our sainted Edward. I say no prince should be allowed to steal estates from good English families, then use them to reward men with no connection to this land. When I heard you name Michel de Martigny, the lowest of John's foreign churls, as administrator of your properties I could hardly believe my luck." Roheise smiled, this time the turn of her lips vicious. "You are but a knight's daughter and a sheriff's widow. In you, lesser men will see their own wives and daughters. Your disparagement, my lady, will become the flint upon which the spark of rebellion is struck. Here's what you must do. Using the pretense of estate business, you'll seek out de Martigny as is your right now that he controls your properties. On the pretext of privacy, you'll send away your chaperone. That baseborn lout hasn't the refinement of birth to restrain himself and the privacy will be more temptation than he can bear. He'll take advantage, doing rape against you."

Ami reared back on her stool to better see the madwoman's face. Roheise spoke of a woman's ultimate destruction as if asking someone to render up her virtue was a commonplace thing. It wasn't lunacy Ami saw in the noblewoman's eyes, but sincerity. Dear God!

"Aye and when the mercenary is finished with you," the lady was saying, no hint in her voice or manner of any prank, "you'll come to me. With my arms around you, I'll cry to all the land that a commoner under John's protection has done this terrible deed. When the lesser barons and knights hear, they'll demand again that John rid himself of his mercenaries, which of course our king will refuse to do," the lady added with a sneer. "His refusal is the justification every man needs to wield arms against their liege lord. John will have no choice but to address our complaints and restore our stolen rights."

A bubble of hysterical laughter escaped Ami's lips, sounding all too much like a whimper. She yanked her arm free of the lady's hold, cradling it close to her. What was it about this day and her virtue? Whatever it was, Roheise would never get what she wanted. Brute Sir Michel might be, but he was an intelligent brute, far too clever to indulge in rape when it would bring him nothing but trouble. Besides, if he meant to do rape, he'd have attempted it in that alcove.

"So, all you need of me is that I allow myself to be raped?" Ami asked, as if she was urged every day to spread her legs for men.

Lady Roheise frowned. "Do you mock me? I know well that this is no small thing—"

"Begging your pardon, my lady," Ami dared to interrupt, "but I'm very aware of what you plan. You not only want me ruined, you want every knight in England to know of it. What you haven't told me is how this will rid me of Sir Michel as administrator of my properties."

"Why, the commoner can't possibly control your estates if he's dead, my lady," Roheise said, pouncing on this like a cat upon a mouse. "Such is the fate for the commoner who rapes his better. Drawn and quartered, he'll be, and you'll have the satisfaction of watching him die."

After four years living among the nobility, Roheise's response shouldn't have astonished Ami, but it did. The noblewoman truly believed that a virtual stranger's death might compensate for the ruination of all Ami's hopes and dreams.

"And, what happens to me after the mercenary is dead and your precious rebellion has succeeded?" Ami asked. "Nay, better yet, tell me what's to happen to me if your uprising fails. How will you protect me once I've been stripped of any hope of marriage, and my ruination is used to enrage our king?"

The noblewoman's gaze shuttered, all emotion

draining from her expression. "I am patroness to a nunnery." It was a flat statement.

"Ah, so you'll buy me a position?" Ami suggested, knowing this wasn't at all what the noblewoman intended.

The lady's expression again tightened as she was forced to reveal what she'd hoped to avoid. "I'll pay them a stipend to keep you."

"How good of you." Ami held her voice to an almost whisper to hide what boiled in her. "You'll pay the nuns to keep me in barren and comfortless confinement. Meanwhile, your cousin or some other powerful man will purchase control of my properties from the king and make free of its profits."

The noblewoman had grace enough to look chagrinned. "What difference does it make who controls your properties?" Roheise snapped. "A convent is no less barren and empty than this place." The jerk of the lady's chin indicated the room around them.

"But at least here I have my virtue and my name. However petty you may think me for it, my good name is my pride," Ami retorted, daring to scold. "Find someone else to play the martyr for you." Her words died into silence as something glimmered at the back of her brain, something important. And in the next instant it took shape. Then the tool Ami needed to leash the mercenary dropped into the palm of her hand.

"But I don't need to martyr myself," she whispered, speaking to herself.

"What?" Lady Roheise demanded, a hopeful edge to her voice. "How?"

The how of it rose to the surface like a bubble in almost boiling water. For the first time, Ami would play the aggressor in her game of love, turning the game on its head. De Martigny already desired her. If a man could be turned in the right direction, it was a short step from desire to affection. When his heart awakened, she'd use his affections to control him. If she were careful enough at it, she wouldn't need to replace him as her administrator. Then again, rejecting him, both as administrator and as lover, would give her the satisfaction of a little vengeance, her status as king's ward protecting her from any retribution de Martigny might think to offer.

Achieving this without compromising her good name could be tricky. What Ami needed was someone to shield her repute as she pursued the mercenary. Aye, and before her sat just the woman capable of that protection.

Warning bells clamored. Pawns didn't often survive striking out at lusty kings, bloodthirsty knights who painted their mail black, or noblewomen who owned the arrogance of queens. Ami shook away the concern. This was too perfect, giving her all she craved: John humbled, Sir Michel leashed and broken, and Lady Roheise duped for so foully trying to use someone beneath her.

Ami slanted a sly look at her soon-to-be victim, preparing the trap. "What if I'm able to drive the mercenary to the point of attempting an assault? Would an incomplete attack serve your purpose?"

Lady Roheise's eyes took fire as she willingly stepped into Ami's snare. "But, of course."

"Then, my lady, I will aid you, only if you vow to me that should you hear any slur against my name you'll leap to my defense. Only if my repute remains unsullied, will the effect of his attack on me be potent. Know that if at any time I doubt you or your motivation, or fear your betrayal, I'll cease my efforts on your behalf that instant."

Roheise's answering grin was filled with mastery. "I so vow." She came to her feet, deigning to fold and lift her own stool. "I go, leaving you to enjoy your posset in privacy. Know that I expect swift results, so begin your endeavor this very night. By the by, don't try to approach me. We won't speak again until you've accomplished your goal."

Chapter 7

A mi sat in her usual position at a feast table, a good ways distant from the fire. Outside, the world lay trapped deep in night's hold, but the hall was as bright as day. Ensconced torches clung to the walls, each one sending up black tendrils of stinking oily smoke to stain the painted ceiling. Golden threads sparked from the weave of the embroidered fabric into panels covering the walls. Where the panels gapped, the plastered walls showed, their surfaces painted in gaudy reds, forest greens, and brilliant yellows.

On the raised central hearth, a great fire now sent crackling swords of flames high into the air. King John and his hostess for the night, Lady Eleanor, were barely visible through its roaring curtain. Dressed in vivid blue, John wore a small crown, hardly more than a golden circlet decorated with jewels and pearls to mark his royalty. It flashed as the king tossed back his head to laugh at something his niece said. The sound of his amusement didn't rise out of the din of so many people all talking at once.

Ami gave an impatient huff. John should pay better attention to the rest of the room. The meal was long over and it was time to move on to the dancing.

Excitement strained within her at the thought. To use dancing, an amusement, to achieve her goal of leashing Sir Michel was only sauce for the gander. Chaste love was a woman's game, just as dancing was.

Following her thoughts, Ami's gaze shifted to Sir Michel. He sat with the rest of John's favorites, near the head of the opposing line of tables, where nobles like Roheise should have been seated, which was surely part of the reason that John's noblemen despised them so.

On this night, all of the de Martignys wore the deep red color that identified their house and family save Sir Michel. His tunic was so dark a gray that it was almost the hue of his armor. Silver embroidery glistened from its neckline and sleeve, the trim modest considering what festooned the garments of his relatives. The chamber's flickering light found dark glints in his hair, then cast shadows on the arrogant line of his nose and the sharp lift of his cheekbones.

He sat so still among his more animated kinsmen, his elbows braced upon the table and his untouched cup caught between his hands, that if not for the occasional gleam from his shadowed eyes, Ami might have thought him asleep. Pondering this, she studied him, only to acknowledge an unwelcome recognition.

He looked as out of place among his own family as Ami felt among the bejeweled wards in the King's custody.

Ami touched her hand to her ear, tracing the spot Sir Michel had touched with his mouth. Gone was her thick linen headcloth of this afternoon, donned in the hopes of deflecting John's interest. In its place Ami wore her best silken wimple, one so thin that it was nearly transparent.

Disgusted with herself, she lowered her hand from her ear to wrap her betraying fingers about the cup she and Milicent had shared this night. Milicent was Ami's seatmate for the least, and unlike Sir Michel, Ami had no fine cup to bring to the feast table.

"That's a beautiful fire we have tonight, isn't it?" said Milicent, leaning closer to Ami.

Startled by the old woman's comment, Ami tore her gaze from Sir Michel to look at the dowager, her brows raised in question.

Milicent's lips took a sly twist. "But I think there couldn't be anything more beautiful than yon man," she added at a whisper with a jerk of her head in Sir Michel's direction.

Ami's heart dropped. There could be no worse calamity than for Mistress Milicent to discover Ami's interest in the mercenary. The old woman would only cry to everyone else that she was pursuing the commoner.

"I suppose I'd be less than honest to say he's anything but handsome," Ami said, bringing the cup to her lips for a sip, only to discover it was dry. Since

Milicent wasn't much of a drinker, claiming that wine left her stomach unsettled, that meant Ami had drained that second cup all by herself. Setting the vessel back in place, Ami leaned back on the bench and smiled at Milicent. "However, it's hard to think of Sir Michel de Martigny in that way. Perhaps you don't know him. He's the mercenary who now controls my property. Between the fire and the man, I think I prefer the fire."

Milicent's dry laugh sounded like a hen's cackle. "A wise choice. I can't speak for you, my lady, but in my life I've learned that a man might burn hot enough to warm me, but his sort of warmth only lasts a little. As for a fire, I can feed the flames until the heat penetrates the very stones of my home, keeping me warm throughout the night. That is something no man has ever done for me, at least not without great effort on my part." Gaps marked Milicent's crooked smile, each missing tooth a mark of what she'd sacrificed to bring forth five living babes and six stillborn children from her womb.

"No truer statement was ever made, mistress." Ami laughed in honest amusement, then gave the old woman's hand a pat. "Who would have expected such a comment from one as proper as you? Could it be there's more to you than some of our fellow wards suspect?"

Milicent offered her seatmate a bawdy wink. "There may be, but I'll never admit it. Why, I'll even deny we had this conversation."

At that moment a servant appeared across the table from them, an alms basket in hand, collecting the used bread trenchers for distribution to Winchester's poor. Ami almost smiled in her relief. At last, the meal was done and they were to be released from the table.

All around them diners begin to rise and make their way toward the darkened screen at the hall's door. Milicent groaned a little and started to her feet, signaling to her maid as she rose. "Pardon, my lady, but I think I'll take a bit of air before the dancing begins," the dowager said.

The corner of Ami's mouth lifted a little as she nodded to the old woman. Ah, the pretense of manners. Take the air, Milicent said, when the reality was that she and all the others would be holding their breaths. It was the latrines that called to them.

It took another quarter hour before all the trays, trenchers, spoons, and cups were cleared from the tables, then every man and woman came to their feet. Before they could dance the tables needed to be moved. That was one chore that knew no rank. Everyone would lend a hand. Only the high table would stay in place throughout the evening.

More than ready to do whatever she could to speed the process, Ami rose with everyone else and threw a glance toward the de Martigny table. Sir Michel was gone.

Ami found him slowly working his way toward the door, sidling through folk lifting tabletops and shifting benches. Sir Michel bore his golden cup in his hand. That could only mean the mercenary was leaving for the evening.

Ami's plans collapsed into the rubble of worry.

How was she supposed to lodge herself in his consciousness if he didn't remain within her reach? Dear God, but if he left now, who knew when her next opportunity to meet with him might arise? It was only at public events like feasts and fairs that men and women could interact without winning criticism for their behavior.

Damn her arrogance! Sir Michel wasn't a fool. He wasn't going to let her repay him for what he'd done in the alcove any more than he'd stand idly by as she worked her wiles on him. If she wanted him leashed, she needed to take the initiative this very moment.

Giving herself no chance to reconsider, Ami trotted down the hall's length, meaning to meet him at the door. For once her low rank served her; she was closer to the exit than Sir Michel. The night served her as well. Darkness had reached its chary hand through the open door and curled its inky fingers around the tall wooden screen. Praying the gloom would be enough to hide her bold approach from watching eyes, Ami melted into the shadows to await her nearing prey.

Discordant sounds, the musicians tuning their instruments, pierced the roar of conversation as Michel made his way down the room's length. Those folk who weren't assisting in moving the tables already stood at the center of the room, waiting for the first dance to begin. Across the hall, Michel caught a flash of bright blue moving through the crowd. It was Lady de la Beres making her way toward the hall's exit so swiftly that her mantle fairly flew out at her heels.

Desire seethed up from behind the barrier raised by Michel's common sense. His mouth tightened in disgust at himself as he battled the betraying lust back where it belonged. He cursed himself, then, in bitter amusement, cursed the lady for her honest physical reaction to him. Because of her, he'd been plagued all afternoon by thoughts of her in his bed. So great had desire grown that he'd even caught himself wishing she might forget who he was, and who she was so she could lose herself in her honest passion for him.

It hadn't helped that she'd tossed glances in his direction throughout the meal, although she did use enough circumspection to make them seem random. If she'd glanced, there could be only one reason for her interest. Lady de la Beres had devised some punishment to repay his affront in the alcove and she couldn't wait to wreak her vengeance on him.

As Michel watched, his future wife disappeared into the pool of darkness at one end of the door's screen. Little fool. That was no way to lay a trap. All he need do to avoid her was to leave around the other side of the screen.

That was what a wise man would do, picking the time for his battles, rather than be drawn into conflict, unarmed and unaware. Then, he was no wise man. Michel's feet turned toward her end of the screen. Perverse it might be, but he wanted to see how she would try to hurt him.

Lady de la Beres had chosen her spot with care, standing directly across from the screen's end, her back resting against the wall where the shadows were the deepest. Sucked into the hall by the greedy fire at the room's center, autumn's frustrated breath exploded around the wooden panel, holding in its depths the smell of rain and woodsmoke from the town below the castle walls. It moved past the lady with enough strength to tug at that farce of a wimple she wore.

Masculine voices echoed through the door behind the screen. Across from him, Lady de la Beres turned her face to the side, trying to disappear into the darkness. Michel backed away from the passage, moving until he stood at the center of the screen.

Two of John's body soldiers strode through the passage, walking past the lady without a glance at her. The musicians in the hall's center broke into a melody. The waiting dancers circled it into a romp. With a shout, the two soldiers lifted their heels, nigh on sprinting to join the dancers.

Here it was, Michel's second chance to withdraw. After all, his purpose was to disguise his interest in her, not engage her. Lust demanded a final glance. Lady de la Beres had lifted her head.

Michel froze in admiration. By God, but she was a beautiful woman. What little firelight pierced the dimness gilded her skin and found auburn lights in her dark hair. Her expression was soft, her eyes luminous. There was nothing of passion in her face save the natural, sultry curve of her lips.

Calling himself a fool, he stepped nearer to her once again. The corners of her mouth didn't lift in triumph as she looked up into his face. Michel said nothing, only waited.

"Pardon, Sir Michel. I hope I'm not intruding on your privacy," she said, her voice held low.

Michel, torn between desire for her and curiosity over how she'd wreak her vengeance, offered her a nod, nothing more.

Taking his nod as leave to continue, she said, "I wanted only to tender an apology. I was overwrought this afternoon. My behavior toward you in the alcove was untoward and rude."

That startled Michel. No woman of her rank had ever before begged his pardon. What sort of vengeance was this? Where was the trap in an apology? That he couldn't find either of these was worrisome.

"Madam, I am not your confessor," he told her. "If you want absolution for your behavior I suggest you consult with your priest. Good evening."

Stepping between her and the screen, Michel strode to the door, then exited from the hall. As he started down the steps leading to the courtyard a storey beneath him, it occurred to him that she hadn't been seeking immediate retribution. Nay, she must have a longer term plan. Why else would she be trying to lure him closer to her?

The corner of his mouth lifted. An apology. Now, that was a first. All in all, this little game of hers might prove far more interesting than he could ever have anticipated.

If she wanted him closer, then his next move had to be a retreat. The longer he kept her at arm's length, the more likely she was to do something that might reveal what it was she intended for him.

* * *

Ami watched Sir Michel disappear, waited yet another full moment, then grinned. The idea of apologizing had been inspired. She'd read her success in the confusion that flashed across his face. For the rest of the night she would be the only thing in his thoughts. And that was what she wanted: him to think of her each and every night until she was the only thing on his mind. The way to do that was to meet him as if by accident, day after day, in places where she need linger near him for no longer than it took to offer a sentence or two.

From the hall behind her, the musicians launched into another romp. The joyous, bouncing rhythm called to Ami like a siren's song. Her feet found the beat as she danced out of the shadows, only to have joy sour.

Coming from the body of the hall was Lady Roheise, two of her household soldiers at her side. Ami nodded in greeting and received a sharp glance in reply. With that single look Lady Roheise exhorted Ami to her best efforts, or else.

It was the *or else* that had Ami cursing herself. Noblewomen could be even more vicious than their mates when it came to extracting their revenge. Perhaps it had been a mistake to try and use Roheise to protect herself while intending to repay the noblewoman's arrogance.

Well, the best way to free herself of Roheise and such worries was to achieve her goal and leash Sir Michel. Ami's hand fell to her purse. Thanks to Roheise's purchase of the posset this afternoon, it yet had a friendly heft. Just as well, for Walter and his network needed to speak volumes, and that might cost her more than she really could afford.

Chapter 8

"**M**y lady," Maud whispered.

At Maud's touch upon her shoulder, Ami started from her dreams, her eyes flying open. Nothing but blackness surrounded her, the only sound that of a hall at its rest, the occasional snore punctuating the rhythmic roll of breathing. So many bodies all packed cheek to jowl in this chamber made the air close, even though the temperature outside Ami's blankets left her nose cold.

For a moment she strove to remember where she was. It was one of the stranger things about being John's ward; England's king craved travel the way some men craved wine. He moved so frequently from house to castle to manor that Ami often longed to never again find herself sagging in a saddle on a dreary, wet winter's day with nothing to look forward to save another journey on the morrow. All that shifting made mornings disorienting to one accustomed to a more set-tled existence.

Slowly, the darkness gave way to walls and Ami rec-ognized Winchester's queen's hall. Rolling onto her side, she found Maud leaning over her clad only in a blanket, her eyes glimmering circles in the darkness.

Concern shot through Ami. "What is it?" she cried, or would have if her voice hadn't yet been hoarse from sleep.

"I came to fetch my clothing," Maud said. Each night they removed their precious garments, shaking them clean and folding them for storage in Ami's chest. "I found this." The lass held out a fold of parchment. The wax that sealed it made a dark blotch on its lighter surface. "It was tucked beneath the edge of your pallet. I thought it might be important."

The appearance of an unexpected note, the first Ami had ever received, drove the cobwebs from her thoughts. She sat up, her unbound hair tumbling around her. Every night Ami retired with a cap upon her head, just as did everyone else in the world, the cap meant to hold in her body's heat and protect her health. How-ever, the bit of white linen that should have been pro-tecting Ami's head now lay on the floor beside her pallet. She wasn't certain quite how it happened, but the garment never made it through the night with her.

Taking the wee packet from Maud, she turned the thing over in her hands with a sinking heart. Ami could conjure up only one person who might have sent her a note: Lady Roheise.

This morning was the third dawn since the feast. In

the intervening time, Ami had done all she could to put herself in Sir Michel's pathway. Although they'd passed each other in the yard and hall time and again, the knight hadn't responded to a single of her inviting smiles, only eyed her in stony silence. Roheise wouldn't tolerate what she perceived as lack of success on her pawn's part. Breaking the seal, Ami unfolded the note.

"Is it important?" Maud asked in breathless excitement, her voice held at a whisper so as not to disturb any of her still sleeping betters. The arts of writing and reading were conundrums enough to Maud. To find a note, a secret message, this way was almost as great a mystery as the transformation of mundane wine into Christ's blood at communion.

"I don't know. It's too dark to see what it says," Ami replied at the same low volume. Unlike Maud, she didn't want to see what lay upon this skin.

Maud looked toward the hearth. "There'll be a fire in a moment. Gilly's on her way to the hearth right now. It's her chore to feed the embers this morn. Here"—the maid grabbed up Ami's chemise— "let me help you dress so you can go see what it is."

A moment later, with her chemise on and her blankets wrapped around her for warmth, Ami started toward the hearth. A few of the rising serving maids glanced her way, but there was no one of consequence to notice her as she stepped over a snoring Mistress Milicent, then around Lady Adelberta. Standing at the raised hearthstone was the lass Gilly. The child looked up from placing twigs upon what remained of last night's coals, smiled, then went back to her chore of teasing flames back to life.

It took a moment for those fiery tongues to appear. The homely scent of burning wood filled Ami's nose. She breathed it in, taking courage from the friendly smell. When the fire was bright enough for Ami to make out the words on the parchment, she held up the note.

Our king departs this day, behind him leaving his female wards. To that end Sir Michel de Martigny their guardian has been named, his term of service this very day beginning and throughout his majesty's absence from Winchester continuing. Make good use of your opportunity.

Ami's stomach knotted in unwelcome surprise as she read the words a second time. The odd phrasing and the stilted formation of the letters all smacked of a clerk's writing, or at least someone more accustomed to scribing in Latin than the French tongue used by England's ruling class.

What was the noblewoman thinking employing a clerk to pen a note like this? The more folk who knew that they plotted together, the greater the chance of betrayal. Then again, any clerk Roheise employed was likely well entrenched in the lady's cause. Such a man wouldn't be sharing what he knew with anyone.

Cursing herself for involving Roheise and shivering over the thought that anything might exist to connect her to the lady's scheme, Ami dropped the bit of parchment into the newborn flames. The note writhed as it hit the coals, browning and curling, stinking as it was consumed.

Gilly used a slender branch to shove the vellum deeper into the fire's heart, then lay the switch atop the other sticks. "It looks like there'll be no more rain for us today, my lady," she said, her tone pleasant and disinterested as she sent a glance toward one of the windows.

Ami followed the maid's gaze to find sunlight scratching at the shutters like a polite dog. Gilly wiped her hands on her gown as she finished her task, gave Ami a bob, and left the hearth. Ami looked into the flames to the area where the message had found its end.

That the king should depart Winchester after a visit of only a week wasn't at all unusual. Neither was the fact that he left behind his female wards; it was only the lads squired to him that John kept always at his side. However, that the king named Sir Michel as guardian of the wards was more than passing strange. That temporary position usually went to a man of higher rank.

Unless Roheise's kinsmen had somehow arranged this. With that, new excitement rose from the ashes of Ami's frustration. It was a wondrous opportunity, indeed. With John went most of his knights, squires, soldiers, and clerks, leaving so few here that the keep's meals would become casual family affairs. Ami smiled. As guardian of the wards, Sir Michel would be at her mercy and within her reach at breakfast and at the big midday meal.

She shot another quick glance at the window shutters. Lord, but it was already dawn and she had much to do before the midday meal. Her most important task was to discover what Walter had learned about the mercenary, although it hadn't truly been long enough to expect much in the way of results. Her blankets tight around her, Ami hurried as swiftly as she could back to her pallet and the waiting and now dressed Maud.

"My lady?" the maid asked, earnest interest filling her gaze. "What was in your note?"

Her question tamed Ami's excitement. It wouldn't do to let the lass catch a hint of what her mistress was doing. Nothing terrified Maud more than the plots she saw played out in this court, and the punishments exacted for participation in them, save perhaps the mercenary who painted his mail black.

"One of the ladies wrote a few words, giving me information about that mercenary who is now in control of my estate," Ami said, tiptoeing around a lie.

Disappointment quenched Maud's eagerness. "But of course it was. Silly me. Who else save a lady from this chamber might leave a note beneath your pallet?"

"Who else, indeed," Ami retorted with a quiet laugh. "Why, who did you think wrote to me?"

Maud made a face and shrugged. "I thought mayhap you'd found someone new to amuse you now that the man you so liked to gaze at this past summer has wed."

It was Ami's turn to make a face. Last summer she'd amused herself by playing the game of love with one of the king's young knights. Indeed, for a time she'd even let herself grow infatuated with him, only to realize he didn't return her interest with the same ardor. However, a new admirer was the perfect disguise for what might otherwise look as odd behavior to her maid.

"You've found me out," Ami replied with a laugh. "There is someone, although I don't think he knows I exist. It's a shame I can't wear my scarlet gowns every day. That's a color sure to catch and keep a man's eye. Since I can't wear them, will you take my second best to the laundress this morn for a good brushing? I'll also wear my best veil today, using the gold band to hold it in place."

To expose the fragile fabric of her better headdress to everyday wear was an extravagant risk. A single tear would ruin it. Aye, but the more Sir Michel saw of her ear, the more he'd remember what they'd already done between them.

Maud smiled in excitement and pride; she lived vicariously through Ami, having not yet dared to play her mistress's game of love with the lads who caught her eye, despite all Ami's encouragement. "These other ladies may have more jewels and better gowns, but you never fail to outshine them, my lady."

"Good of you to say," Ami replied with real gratitude as Maud leaned over their chest to dig through its contents for her gowns.

"Maud, wait. I think I'll bathe this morning." If a woman wanted to catch a man's attention she needed scent, and the only scent Ami owned was what came in her soap.

The maid straightened with a jerk to stare at her mistress in stark surprise. "Again? You bathed only two days ago, before your audience."

"A person can take a bath more than once a week," Ami countered.

"I suppose." Maud made her agreement sound as if she doubted frequent wettings were a good idea. "If you wish, you can go to the bathhouse right now. That will give you first chance at the water, using it before anyone else. You'll miss your morning meal, but I can hold something aside to break your fast once you're finished."

Having first use of the water sounded appealing. "Then, I'll bathe now," Ami said around a yawn, stretching as far as she dared under the cloak of her blanket.

Maud nodded, all efficiency now. "I'll help you don your third-best, then run to the bathhouse and see that they prepare a tub for you. While you soak, I'll take your second-best to the laundress. That way, they should be clean before the midday meal."

What was now Ami's third-best had ten years ago been her wedding attire, worn at her marriage to Richard de la Beres. Made of fine wool, the weave of the fabric retained its tautness even after all these years. The undergown was a pale blue, while the overgown was a shade darker. A woven trim of pink and green decorated the overgown's neckline and sleeves. Ami still liked the garments. The colors suited her, probably better than the scarlet gowns. However, here at court it wasn't how attractive the garment was, but how much flash it could generate. Aye, and when it came to her third best, there were servants in John's employ who owned richer garments.

Once Maud laced Ami into her clothing, the maid

grabbed up Ami's personal grooming items, contained in their tiny carrying case. She handed the kit to Ami, then returned to the chest for her mistress's second-best wear—a green overgown with wee beads embroidered at its neckline and sleeve hems, and an undergown of gold-colored sarsenet. Then, darting around those still sleeping in the hall, Maud made her way toward the door to arrange her mistress's bath.

Ami waited a moment, braiding her own hair, then tied on a simple headcloth. As she fastened the purse to her belt, she picked her way to the door. A yawning Walter was already at his post. Then again, he didn't have far to go to begin his day. Walter slept between the screen and the door.

Running his fingers through his disordered hair, the porter offered Ami a quick smile. "It's a lovely morning, my lady."

"So it is," Ami agreed, her breath clouding in the chill air.

As she spoke, she looked out across the castle's yard. The newborn sun pierced the veil of hazy clouds to cast rosy light upon the yellowish stones of Winchester Castle's enclosing walls. Dew glistened on the roof and wall, the moisture darkening the yard's hard packed pathways and clinging to the tufts of yet green grass that filled the spaces between the paths. With the fires in the kitchens banked, none of the usual smoke pall hung over the compound. For the moment the only scent was rain-washed air. From the barns that lay to the west end of the compound came the low of cattle and anxious bleat of sheep, waiting to be milked.

The sound tore through Ami, a poignant reminder of the slow and simple life she had once cherished and no longer owned. What she wouldn't give to again greet the morning from the porch on her own house. Then again, if Sir Michel remained unchecked she might well have no home left from which to greet anything.

Turning to Walter, Ami closed her hand around her purse and shook it just a little, so the coins within it would jingle. Walter's expression sharpened with the sound. His gaze dropped to Ami's hand and purse.

"So, Walter, what have you learned of Sir Michel de Martigny? What sort of man is the mercenary?"

"I fear I don't have anything new to tell you, my lady," he replied with a shake of his head. "I know what I think you already know, that he's a merchant's son and a soldier of great skill. He might be a knighted commoner, but I think he's not a common knight. Of all the king's mercenaries he endures the most challenges, no doubt because of his common blood. To date, those who have invited him to battle have lived to regret it, but live they do, although with wounds that heal into fearsome scars. So frequent are these challenges that the knight does not travel alone, instead he always keeps a troop of men at his back. Some say he pays for these men out of his own profits from wars and tournaments. Others insist that his merchant sire is so wealthy that he buys his son this protection. Myself, I think it's more likely our king gives these men to one of his favorites, not wanting a man he cherishes to suffer undue injury."

"If Sir Michel keeps his own troop, where does he

sleep within these walls?" Ami asked. As a rule those men in command of others kept their troop at their sides even when at rest. That meant Sir Michel couldn't be sleeping with the other bachelor knights in the barracks and outbuildings.

"He has never slept within these walls, not on any visit here," Walter replied. "Instead, he pays one of the merchants in town to house him and his men." The jerk of Walter's thumb indicated the town that lay to the south of the castle.

Ami shifted a little, instinctively following his gesture. From this vantage point she could see nothing of the thatched roofs that was Winchester town. However, at the town's opposite end, the cathedral's gray stone tower soared high enough to pierce the sky. Winchester had been the home of English kings from time immemorial. Where royalty went so did the treasury, and a court full of noblemen with coins in their pockets. Thus, the town below them owned a more commercial bend than it might otherwise have done without such royal interest.

"Which merchant plays host to him?" she asked.

"Robert Atte Cross, my lady, the goldsmith. Some folk say that the merchant is related to de Martigny's father in a business way." Walter shrugged to indicate that he didn't know if this was true or not.

Well now, that was interesting. The possibility of encountering Sir Michel on the town's lanes or, even better, in the smith's shop itself was just the sort of opportunity Ami craved. Only, Sir Michel was too clever by far. He would know that a poor ward like herself hadn't come to that specific shop just to gawk at the wares.

"That's all I know of him thus far," Walter said, his gaze fixed on Ami's purse.

"It's not enough." Ami shifted her leather purse from one hand to the other, then drew it open. Studying its none too cluttered interior, she continued, "I need to know who he keeps in his bed at night, with whom and where he dines. Most importantly, I need to know if he plans to leave Winchester." She paused to peer up at Walter. "It's protection for myself I seek. I won't have Sir Michel making free with my belongings now that he's in control of my estates."

Aye, yesterday she'd even written to her folk, telling them to hide what they could. That would work for the little items. It wasn't going to serve for a bed as massive as the one in her nearest manor house.

Walter grinned, expectancy written in the stretch of his lips. "Your concern is mine, my lady. I'll do what I can to help you."

Ami fished out a single pence and offered it to him. "My thanks, Walter."

The porter blinked, astonishment flattening his expression. Ami bit back a laugh. "I heard yesterday just how much those wagers of yours earned. Walter, if not for me and my firm grip on virtue in the face of royal threat, you'd still be a poor man. Dare I say I think you owe me this? It was a great liberty you took with my repute."

Chagrin twisted the man's lips. "Forgive me, my lady."

"Find all you can about this man and I will," Ami assured him and started down the steps. She was more than ready for that soak. Something about this sort of intelligence gathering always left her feeling soiled.

By the time Ami had reached the yard, Maud trotted out of the bathhouse and started toward the hall. When she saw her lady she waved. That motion was enough to convey that Ami's bath was ready, the water already warm, having been kept at a simmer overnight on yesterday's embers.

Once she was beyond the shade cast by the porch roof, the sun reached out to catch Ami in its embrace. Despite the chill air, the light felt deliciously warm against her back. Confidence soared. Walter knew his craft well. Better than anyone, the porter could sniggle out Sir Michel's secrets. Armed with intimate knowledge of the mercenary, she would soon have that baseborn soldier dancing in the palm of her hand.

Chapter 9

"**O**h, my lady, I'm so sorry your band is dented," Maud cried as she, Ami, and their soldier-escort picked their way down Winchester's mucky High Street. "I don't know how it happened. Truly, I'm always careful with it."

Guilt shot through Ami. She knew exactly how her gilded band had been dented; she'd done it herself. What she hadn't expected was for Maud to be so upset over this. "Sweetling, please, you mustn't worry so."

Maud's response was a sniffle, which only drove Ami's guilt a little deeper. This was what desperation did to a poor woman with no reason to visit a gold-smith's shop but to make a repair.

Maud's depression was Sir Michel's fault. Damn his stubborn refusal to give Ami the least bit of his attention. These past days, Ami had done everything she could conceive to invite him nearer to her, smiling, posturing, watching the mercenary through the flames, and even lurking around corners so he'd have to pass her when he traveled from place to place in the hall and castle. Nothing worked, not even her attire. The worst of it was that she'd spilled something on her scarlet gowns the first day he appeared for the castle's communal meal, only to spill something on the green and gold set at the next. So, today, for this very important confrontation, what did she have left to wear? Only her third best. Desperation rather than fashion sense demanded that she don her silken veil, although all she had to hold it in place was a leather band.

Frustration rose in Ami. She wouldn't have been desperate except for Sir Michel's wretched ability to keep a secret. Not even Walter could discover anything more about the mercenary than he'd already revealed to Ami.

Maud sniffled again. Ami glanced at her. "Truly, Maud, you cannot blame yourself. The band is soft. It has to be, else how would I wear it in any comfort? Besides, that dent gives us a perfect excuse to escape the hall for a time."

"That's true enough, my lady," Maud agreed at a murmur, her head bowed.

That her maid finally accepted some morsel of consolation made Ami eager to offer more. "I tell you, I've never been so glad to be out of reach of those women in all my days. What caterwauling! You'd think they'd been sentenced to death, rather than asked to endure a mercenary as their guardian for a week or two."

Maud offered Ami a soggy smile. "The worst was

that first day. That newcomer, Lady Roheise. She was the loudest of them all."

Ami nodded. Aye, Roheise had been loud, but Ami thought the noise more of a zealot's calculation than outrage. The only passion that noblewoman owned she spent on fomenting rebellion. At Roheise's urging, the highest of the noblewomen, women with the funds or influence to do so, had left the disparagement of Sir Michel's guardianship, trailing out the gate after their king. Some went to their families' traditional residences in Winchester, while others joined the queen presently at Kensington. Those who had nowhere to go complained daily, as Mistress Milicent did, that the world must be ending now that a commoner was the guardian of his betters.

Against so much prejudice, Ami could hardly blame Sir Michel for keeping to himself. His meals must be agony. As the highest ranking of the remaining ladies, Lady Sybilla and Lady Adelberta were required to sit at either side of him at the head of the room. However, both refused to share the meal with him; they claimed they'd rather die than touch their mouths to the commoner's cup, a golden vessel set with two jewels, each the size of a walnut, no doubt looted from a better man. Thus, each afternoon they turned their shoulders to him, Sybilla sharing her meal and wine with the castle's priest, while Adelberta entertained the castellan.

Unwelcome and unwanted, pity for the mercenary stirred in Ami. She knew all too well that sort of disdain. It was the same sort of snubbing she'd suffered when she first came to court and discovered she was the lowest ranked and poorest of the wards. Well, if their high-handed scorn had infuriated her, Sir Michel seemed to accept their contempt with ease.

Holding the hems of her third-best garments high, Ami ducked beneath the overhanging second storey of a tailor's establishment to avoid a housewife and her maid. The two women didn't notice Ami or her party as they sought to avoid an oxcart trundling its way up the street. The maidservant bore her mistress's shopping basket. A chicken, its gaudy feathers stirring, but its neck limp in death, sprawled atop a loaf of bread.

Ami gave a *humph*. If she'd been wearing her scarlet, they wouldn't have been so quick to shove her aside. She clung to the house wall as the oxcart groaned past. Darting around its other side came an apple seller, his handcart's wooden wheel spewing mud as he called out to all and sundry of the superior quality of his fruit. Huffing, a cheesemonger's apprentice squeezed between the cart and the wall, passing Ami whilst carrying a great wheel of his master's product on his back. From open shop windows up and down the lane, merchants shouted to passersby to inspect what they had to sell. Across the way, two workmen sang as they applied a new coat of plaster to a cook shop's front, while the scent of stewing lamb wafted out of the shop's open door.

Catching Maud by the arm, Ami thrust back into the traffic on the lane. It wasn't far before they came to Robert Atte Cross's goldsmith's shop where High Street intersected the lane leading to the cathedral. Like any other merchant, the master's shop occupied the lower level of his home, but that was where all similarity to the other dwellings on this street ceased.

The goldsmith's house was a monument to his success. At three storeys tall, his house towered over its neighbors. No mold or cracks marred the gleaming plaster covering his walls, and, although his roofing was only reeds, the thatch was new and its crest trimmed into fanciful shapes. Between his house and each of his neighbors' dwellings was an alley, wide enough to admit a horse and rider.

Ami peered down the nearest alley as they passed it. Just as she expected, a courtyard opened up behind the house, the cobbled expanse caught between the house and a high garden wall over which she could see the crowns of yellowing apple trees. In the yard stood a dozen horses, their tails switching as they waited. Their riders slouched or sat, dicing, near the stable wall. All of them wore the red of the de Martignys.

Sir Michel was presently in residence. Excitement soared in Ami, only to snag and droop back toward the earth. As the possibility that she would actually encounter Sir Michel woke, common sense whispered that what she did was too bold for a woman. Ami shut the door on sense. She couldn't afford to listen, not when her need to control Sir Michel was so desperate and her chances of accomplishing it narrowing with each day. It couldn't be much longer before he left Winchester to go to her properties. Once he was there, he'd make free with those possessions she cherished.

As with every other shop in the world, a long window ran the front length of the goldsmith's house. How else, save by watching, would potential buyers be able to judge the workmanship of the smith's wares? Ami stopped before the window. Fine coils of gleaming gold wire streamed from a brass bound chest in one corner of the workshop. A fire, complete with undersized bellows, burned upon a hearth at the back of the work chamber. Men, perched on tall stools, used tiny hammers and even smaller pincers as they created their pieces.

Her gaze wasn't on the workroom, but the stairway that crawled up the far side of the shop into the house above it. If Sir Michel truly was inside the house, then he'd use the kitchen stairs to descend to the rear courtyard and he'd need to cross the smith's hall to reach the kitchen, which was always at the back of the house. Ami needed to be in that hall to meet him. That was the trick, getting herself invited into the goldsmith's hall.

"Master smith," she called, not knowing which of the men bent over their work was the one she needed to address. "I pray you, do you do repairs?"

A tall reed-thin man turned at her call. Robert Atte Cross's nose ended in a bulbous knob, his eyes watered and his chin receded. Dressed in functional brown, a thick leather cap upon his head and an equally protective apron covering his torso, he stepped to the window. He blinked when he saw Ami's escort and recognized the dress of the king's soldiers. His gaze shifted to Ami in new consideration.

To compensate for her modest dress, Ami had worn every piece of jewelry she owned on the assumption that the richer a goldsmith thought a person, the better that person would be treated. A thick gold bangle decorated each wrist, while every shift of her mantle allowed a glimpse of her father's heavy golden chain where it draped across her breast. Rings decorated three of her fingers. Ami thumbed the one with the large red stone, her wedding ring.

"Aye, we do repairs, my lady," the smith said. If Ami's French told him she was from England's ruling class, his own words held only hints of the English that was his native tongue. "How is it I can aid you this day?"

Maud laid Ami's dented band upon the counter, then stepped back behind her mistress. Ami pushed it closer to the smith. "I fear it needs straightening."

He nodded, then nearsightedly lifted the band to inspect it. "So it does. It wouldn't hurt to do a little regilding as well. The foil's worn."

Ami stifled her flinch. To refuse would cost her the invitation she so wanted, but the thought of how much this would lighten her purse made her quail. It was the reminder of Sir Michel unchecked to make himself free with her properties that drove her. The only positive was that she didn't have to pay the smith today. Those who served England's gently born were good about extending credit, even if it meant waiting until their customer's death to collect their payment from his will. Ami certainly hoped her fortunes improved between now and her death.

"Then regild it," she commanded.

The smith smiled. "Happily so, my lady. It won't

take long, being such a small job. Would you care to wait in my hall whilst I work?"

Ami managed not to hoot in triumph. Aye, the cost was worth what it bought her. "How very kind of you, master smith. I would, indeed."

The man moved to the outer door at the far end of his long window, opened it from the inside, then beckoned for Ami to enter. "If it pleases you, while you wait you may look upon my samples, to see if anything catches your eye. I hope you don't mind that I have another guest in residence just now. He should be no bother as I believe he intends to depart shortly."

It would have been very bad form to grin like a madwoman, even if that was what Ami felt like doing. "Nay, of course I don't mind," she replied. "Come, Maud."

Leaving the soldier to wait for them outside the shop, Ami and Maud followed the smith up the steps to the first landing. Leaving the stairway to turn back on itself and continue up toward the third storey, Roger Atte Cross opened the door off the landing and stepped inside. "Welcome to my hall, my lady. I'll fetch my wife."

As the smith strode across the room toward a door at the chamber's opposite side, Maud gasped. Ami would have done the same, save she'd already lost her breath. If the exterior of the goldsmith's house announced his wealth, the interior screamed of it.

Sunlight streamed in through three arched windows in the east wall. The window openings had been filled with expensive glass that kept out the chill even as it admitted light enough to make the rushes strewn upon the hall's dark wooden floor gleam like the gold stored in the shop below them. Stenciled in red upon walls the color of butter was a crosshatch pattern. At the center of each diamond sat a bright blue flower.

Unlike the raised hearth stones at the center of the king's halls, this man's hearth was built into the back wall as was the newest fashion. Although Ami thought this wall hearth clever for the way it drew the choking smoke out of the house through a stone channel before it could stain ceilings and walls, she wondered how a fire this close to one wall could heat the hall's opposite end, even if the door could now be closed. Adjacent to the hearth stood a tall cupboard painted bright green with red trim, the household's dishware displayed upon its shelves. A silver tray and two golden drinking cups stood among the soup bowls and spoons.

As in every hall Ami had visited, the tables used for eating stood in pieces against one wall, waiting for the midday meal when they would be reassembled. Holding the tabletops against the wall were the benches used by the diners. That left only two chairs in the room for the time being and they stood before the hearth, their tall, curved backs toward Ami.

"Look," whispered Maud, pointing to the chairs, "they're just like the one in our house."

"So they are," Ami said, then sighed. "I love that chair."

The chair in her own hall, the larger of her two manor houses, looked like these, something akin to a barrel sawed in half lengthwise. The tall, curved back was meant to catch the heat from the fire. Even on the coldest winter nights it kept its occupant warm. Or occupants.

A wave of sadness took Ami by surprise. Despite the difference in their ages, Richard de la Beres had been a doting husband, lover enough to leave her gasping in spent passion when they were finished, and an easy man on whom to bestow her affections. For the six years of their marriage he'd indulged her every whim, all the while claiming he only did so because her whims were so sensible. He had liked nothing better than the evenings they spent in that chair of theirs, Ami seated in his lap. More than once, they'd fallen asleep together there.

"Here is my wife, Mistress Hughette," the smith called out as he reappeared through the doorway. The plump woman was dressed in heavy gowns of golden yellow, almost the same color as her thin blond braids. A pattern had been woven into the fabric of her overgown, then enhanced by hand-sewn outlining done in golden threads, no doubt spun by her husband. Her veil was as thin as Ami's, the silk tissue clinging to her round cheeks. Her bulging eyes were a bright blue.

That her hands glistened from a recent rinsing recommended her to Ami at once, for it meant she was truly a housewife. London had merchant wives as haughty as Roheise who lifted no finger in the daily management of their homes.

"I'll leave you to her and be on to your repair, then," the smith said and departed, leaving the door to the hall open behind him as he went.

The smith's wife smiled widely at her guest. The change was stunning, the dumpling of a woman giving way to a consummate hawkster. Ami caught back a laugh. No wonder the smith had so swiftly offered to bring her up here. It was his wife who sold what he made.

"Welcome to my hall, my lady," Mistress Hughette said, then nodded to Maud. "Would your servant care for a slice of cheese and bit of barley water while you wait? The barley water's fresh, just this morn."

Maud shot Ami a hopeful look. Ami nodded, just as eager for Maud to go as Maud was to take advantage of a treat. In case Sir Michel did appear, it would be far better all around if Maud didn't witness that meeting. As for a chaperone, Ami would have Mistress Hughette.

"Then, make yourself at home, lass," the smith's wife said, pointing to the door she'd just used. "The kitchen is just through there and Cook will see to you."

Offering Ami a quick bob, Maud hurried for the door, eager to claim what was promised to her. At the same moment the creaking of floorboards over Ami's head gave way to footsteps, that of at least two people, heavy enough to suggest men. The drumming of heels moved to the stairs.

Ami's heart jerked. More than life itself, she wanted to face the hall's door so she might see if it truly was Sir Michel. Unfortunately, the door was behind her and to turn her back on Mistress Hughette would be unbearably rude. In a world bereft of privacy, custom dictated that folk never allow their curiosity to stray past their own hemlines.

The footsteps ceased as they reached the landing, as if the owner of those feet had paused. At the same instant the smith's wife offered her better a quick bob. "Will you sit and perhaps take a cup of wine? But, before you do, might I know your name, my lady?"

The occupant of the landing freed a scornful snort. Triumph soared in Ami. She didn't question why a mere breath was all it took for her to know who stood behind her.

"Her name is Lady de la Beres," Sir Michel called, his words loud enough to reach them across the hall.

Chapter 10

The richness of Sir Michel's voice and the clipped
precision of his accented French sent a shiver
down Ami's back. If she'd noticed that about him a
week ago, she didn't recall. No matter what she had or
hadn't missed about him, his call freed her to turn.

She pivoted, crying out, "Why, Sir Michel, is that
you?" in her best portrayal of surprise, only to have
honest startlement pierce her.

He somehow looked bigger here. His form filled the
doorway, his shoulders nearly brushing the jamb at either
side of him. Rather than his black armor he wore a knee-
length tunic beneath his dark cloak, this one the red of his
family's house, a hue that suited his coloring. His boots
reached to his knees, dark garters holding their soft uppers to the line of his calves. His long sword was belted
over his tunic, his hat and gloves tucked into the belt.

With no hat to disturb its fall, his dark hair curled

lightly against the sharp lift of his cheekbones. Sunlight caught against his clean-shaven cheeks, then gleamed on the narrow line of his beard as it followed his jaw. Ami almost frowned. He looked different and it wasn't just his attire. It took her an instant to realize there was no tension in his shoulders and his jawline.

"Ah, so you know the lady, sir?" Mistress Hughette didn't sound particularly pleased over this turn of events. She glanced between her paying guest and her husband's paying customer.

"We are acquainted," Sir Michel replied, starting into the room.

"Aye, mistress, we know each other," Ami agreed as she watched the man who followed Sir Michel into the chamber.

Against his handsome master, this man was stunning in his ugliness. If he was Sir Michel's servant, there was nothing servile about him, not with that proud set to his shoulders. He was nearly as tall as his master, his build as powerful. It was a brown tunic and chausses he wore. Rather than a mantle, he'd opted for a leather ca-puchin, but left its hood dangling down his back. His hair was cropped close to his head, far shorter than was the fashion. A scar crossed his face from his left brow to his right cheek, while two fingers were missing from his left hand. His eyes were a flat mud-brown.

The two men stopped arm's length from Ami. Sir Michel watched her. For this moment, the frigid gray color of his eyes had given way to almost blue. Ami's triumph soured. Damn him, but he wasn't surprised to see her here.

The left corner of his mouth lifted. That simple motion was all it took. Despite all her admonitions not to let it happen, the remembered sensation of his lips pressed against her hidden ear tumbled through her. It was time to look someplace else.

She shifted to smile at her hostess, but Mistress Hughette's attention was fixed on her guest. Although Sir Michel moved in no way Ami could interpret as a sign, the goldsmith's wife gave a single nod of her head as if agreeing to something. She looked at Ami. Was it disapproval Ami saw in the woman's bulging eyes?

"My lady, if you will excuse me for a moment, I'd like to see that your maid is settled."

"But, of course, mistress," Ami replied, only because polite convention trapped her into agreeing. What was this? No woman left her female guest unattended in the presence of men who weren't related to her.

Ami watched the kitchen door swing shut after Mistress Hughette, grateful that Sir Michel's servant was still here. She wasn't ready for privacy with the mercenary, not after that dangerous encounter in the alcove.

As if he heard her thought, Sir Michel looked at the man beside him. "See that my horse is saddled and ready. I'll be down in a moment."

"Sir," the man said with a nod, then, offering Ami nothing but a brief sidelong glance, he followed Mistress Hughette to the kitchen door. Ami's heart went with him.

Reminding herself that all of society prohibited Sir Michel from touching her, especially with Mistress Hughette only a shout away, Ami girded herself for their confrontation. Perhaps she could draw him into conversation and protect herself with a wall of words. If she was clever enough she might even be able to lead him into sharing a bit of himself with her, then use that intimate knowledge to insinuate herself into his thoughts.

A torrent of inanity formed itself on Ami's tongue. She looked at Sir Michel. All her carefully contrived words dried into dust and blew away.

Gone was any trace of that warm blue from the mercenary's eyes, leaving only frigid gray. His mouth was a taut line while a muscle in his jaw worked.

"You trespass greatly, my lady, in coming here," he said, his voice low and harsh.

If he meant to provoke her it worked. "Trespass against you? How have I done that?" Ami crossed her arms. "Below stairs the goldsmith is repairing my veil band for me. I was invited into this hall by the householder himself."

Sir Michel closed the gap between them until he stood almost as close as he'd been in the alcove. Ami refused to shift even an inch. She wouldn't have him thinking she was afraid of him, when she wasn't, not of him at any rate. It was her own reaction to him that terrified her. She steeled herself, taking a firm hold of her already well-chained lusts.

"What?" the mercenary challenged, his voice so low that his word was barely more than a whisper. "No protest that you didn't know I resided here?"

Ami's jaw tightened. She hadn't expected him to be so blunt about it. Although Ami didn't mind twisting the truth back on itself to suit her purposes, she had never been able to spew a bold-faced lie. And since that meant the only answer she could give incriminated her, she said nothing. From the kitchen came the sound of voices, Maud's, then a man's.

Sir Michel gave a quiet nod. Something in the movement of his head suggested he accepted, even approved of this aspect of her character. "Heed my warning, my lady. Retreat to the castle, departing this very moment never to return," he said, his voice still held low.

Without moving her feet, Ami shifted back just far enough that she could look him in the face. "What is it about all you men?" she demanded at a whisper for no other reason than he had whispered to her. "What makes you think you have the right to command any woman you see?"

The coldness in his gaze wavered for an instant. Ami blinked. Although his mouth hadn't moved, amusement almost wafted from him.

"Because you are women and we are men," he replied quietly, then lifted his hand until his bare fingers were poised a hairsbreadth above her cheek.

Ami inhaled sharply. Scrambling to shore up her defenses against the coming onslaught, she reminded herself that this was the man who would impoverish her by stripping her estates bare, taking all she cherished. This was also the man who had declared her worth less than her true value. She absolutely refused to let her desires be stirred by him.

He stretched his fingers toward the wing of hair that lay against Ami's cheek as if he meant to smooth the strands. From deep in her woman's core, heat flickered to life. God help her, but it was happening again. She wanted, nay, she needed to feel his flesh against hers.

Aye, but no matter how deeply her body desired it, the mercenary didn't touch a single hair. Neither did he take back his hand. Instead, he cupped his palm above her cheek. A taunting warmth flowed across the gap between his flesh and hers.

The urge to feel his skin on hers demanded that Ami lean her head into his palm. With all her might, she fought to hold her neck stiff. His hand fell back to his side. Disappointment was strong enough that she had to stifle her cry, the one that would have begged him to bring back his hand. The only cry she ought to be making was to Mistress Hughette.

Ami's mouth refused to open. If the lady of the house returned, then Sir Michel would step back. More than anything, she didn't want him to do that.

"What are you doing?" she whispered instead.

His brows lifted. His eyes were that almost blue again. "This is the second time you've posed me that question," he replied, his voice as low as hers, "when you know very well what it is that I do."

Ami caught back a shiver. He was right. She knew exactly what he was doing; he was waking her passions in a way that no man had ever before done, not even her husband.

Before she knew what he was about, Sir Michel lowered his head until his lips once again hovered over her ear. A tissue-thin veil did nothing to stop sensation. Just as had happened in the alcove, his breath against her flesh sent a desperate need to feel his lips on hers careening through her body. Longing exploded past Ami's ability to control it. It kept her frozen where she was when what she needed to do was retreat across the room.

"You stray too far from the boundaries of your game by coming here. Enter my world again and you'll pay my forfeit for your error," he breathed into her ear, then began to shift back from her.

Startled by his strange message, Ami turned her head to look at him, her movement so swift that her lips met his retreating cheek. Although the meeting was nothing but a glancing brush of flesh to flesh, sizzling sensation shot through her, so intense that her knees weakened. It was contact enough for Ami to know that he'd shaved this morn. His skin was smooth and warm against her mouth.

With a gasp, she looked up into his face. The same desire that plagued her now filled his gaze. That he might want her as badly as she did him tangled Ami in languorous tendrils of sensation. The heat in her woman's core seeped through her until every inch of her felt on fire. The lines of his face softened in response.

Ami's gaze dropped to his lips. Never in all her life had she wanted to taste a man the way she wanted to taste him. All sense dissolved. She leaned toward him, lifting her head in invitation. He drew a long, slow breath, then stepped back from her.

His refusal was like the dash of cold water. Embarrassment scourged her, awakening anger, both at him and at herself. How could she have so brazenly offered him a kiss?

Even as she castigated herself, Ami kept her gaze locked on his. She wouldn't give way to shame in his presence, not when he might think he'd triumphed over her in some way. His eyes hardened back into that frigid gray.

Ami's shame melted into surprise as she recognized what he was doing. That coldness of his was nothing but a shield, a wall behind which he hid his emotions from the world. Aye, and just now, he was hiding how deeply she affected him.

Triumph stirred. Every smile, all those times she'd *accidentally* confronted him in the castle, they had all worked. Even though her victory had come at great cost to herself, she was well and truly planted in his mind.

As if he heard her thought, the mercenary took another startled step back from her, then another, until they were more than an arm's length apart. Ami's triumph crashed back into exasperation. God take him, why did he have to make this so difficult? He needed to stay close a little longer, so she could solidify her hold over him.

Seeking something that might bridge the chasm that had just opened between them, Ami posed the question she'd meant to offer a moment ago, when her intention had been only to engage him in conversation.

"So, now that you serve as guardian of the wards, why haven't you moved into the castle?" Her voice, raised to the level of normal speech, shattered the quiet enveloping them. Worse, the question sounded just as inane and pretentious aloud as it had when she'd first formed it in her mind.

The mercenary shot her a steely glance. Now, why should he be so irate over her question? It was a legitimate inquiry. The guardian of the wards had the right to use the second largest of the castle's bedchambers; Winchester's castellan used the royal bedchamber when the king wasn't in residence. The talk among the wards had been vicious regarding Sir Michel's reasons for not claiming the chamber. Some of the women even interpreted his absence as a slight against them. That stunned Ami, especially after they claimed they couldn't bear his presence in their midst.

"That is my concern, not yours," he said, his voice hard and cold, as he snatched his gloves from his belt and shoved his hands into them. Something about his tone said that Ami would see no more of him, not until he'd destroyed every iota of the good work she'd done here.

Ami's already shaken victory dissolved until all she held in her hands were ashes. No matter how hard she tried, she would fail. He would never give her a chance to leash him.

Offering her a brusque nod, Sir Michel turned, moving toward the hall's door rather than the kitchen. When he reached the landing outside the hall door the knight paused to look at her from over his shoulder. His face owned no more expression than a stone. His eyes were as hard as the glass in the windows and just as cloudy.

"Those gowns suit you. In them, you look like what

you are, a fresh-faced country lass." With that, he turned and started down the forward stairs, his footsteps ringing in the quiet.

Shock tore through Ami with such force that it left her gaping. How many times during her first year at court had someone said that to her? Why, that condescending bitch's son! He'd already stripped her of her pride by declaring her worthless. Then he'd stolen her dignity by stirring her desires and leaving her in a quivering puddle at his feet. That pompous commoner wasn't going to also strip her of the sophistication she'd worked so hard to cultivate.

Behind Ami, the kitchen door creaked as it opened. The smith's wife came to stand beside Ami, her hands folded. "My lady, whatever it is you plan for him, know that you can but fail."

Startled, Ami pivoted toward her hostess. "What say you? Plan? I only came here to have my veil band repaired."

Mistress Hughette's brows jerked upward in dismissal of Ami's protest. "Don't forget that I read your face as you looked at him. It wasn't any of my goods you came looking to buy this morn."

Ami's heart dropped to her toes. The woman thought she'd come here to offer herself to Sir Michel. And, hadn't she done just that, offered herself to the man both before and after his taunting? In her need to protect herself from being called lewd and forward, hasty words flew from Ami's lips.

"Nay, you mistake me, this I vow. While I admit coming because I knew Sir Michel dwelt here, my reason for confronting him is wholly decent. I seek only to protect my own properties. The king has named Sir Michel administrator of my estates. I know nothing of him and wished to judge the sort of man he is. Call that brazen if you may, but I'll name it desperate. I'm no rich woman. I cannot afford a guardian who might make free with what is my only support."

The goldsmith's wife shook her head at this. "Even if that is your purpose you couldn't have erred worse by coming here. Try to match wits with him, or to control him in any way, and he'll eat you up, then spit out your bones after without a shred of remorse over how he treats you. He has no patience with your kind."

"My kind?" Ami asked in startled question. "What do you mean?"

"You are gently born. He is not," the woman replied, using the same patronizing tone that the noblewomen adopted when they reminded Ami she was but a knight's daughter and unworthy of their notice.

Anger soared. By God, but she wasn't going to let the whole world trample her esteem into dust beneath its heels. "I cannot care what patience he has with me. I won't let him destroy what little I own in this world," Ami retorted, her shoulders squared.

Mistress Hughette shook her head, rejecting the idea. "Destroy? I doubt he'd do that."

Ami crossed her arms. "Thus, do you reveal how little you know of those above you. In a world where men are born to battle rather than to trade, looting another's property is a means of income. Why, I know knights who take another's sheep for no other reason than to

provoke a battle and exercise their warrior's skills.
Barons happily besiege the homes of their inferiors trying to win dowries for their younger daughters. Trust
me. Your boarder will take what he wants of mine,
without care or concern that he leaves me destitute."

Mistress Hughette shrugged. "Enough. You convince me that your reason for coming was honest. Here
now, why not join me in my kitchen? We'll share a bit
of something wet between us while you wait on Master
Robert to finish your band. While you linger, perhaps
you'll explain more about your world to me so I can understand it better."

Satan's own imp perched like a hawk on Michel's
shoulder as he started down the stairs. That wee devil
shouted that Michel should return to the hall. Once
there, he should accept the lady's invitation and kiss her
into yielding all to him. There wasn't an inch of
Michel's body that didn't agree with the imp's suggestion.

Somewhere, no doubt about the time Michel caught
the scent of roses on her skin, everything he intended
went awry. That brush of her mouth against his cheek
had been deadly. However brief the touch, it had been
enough to make the floor beckon, offering itself up as a
temporary bed. Indeed, it was this that had Michel leaving the hall through its front door, rather than making
the shorter trip to the courtyard through the kitchen. As
long as the hall floor seemed a perfectly logical place
for coupling, Michel couldn't afford to be within arm's
reach of Lady de la Beres.

Jesu, but she craved lovemaking the way a starving man longed for bread. Michel hadn't anticipated the enormity of her wanting. Her hunger was so great that he found it difficult to understand why she hadn't already given way and satisfied what ate at her. Yet, all the gossips agreed that the lady held tight to her virtue, although many a man had tried his best to breach her defenses.

Perhaps that was why Michel felt only amusement as Lady de la Beres stood at the center of Mistress Hughette's hall and pretended surprise upon seeing him. The lady wasn't the first gentlewoman to try and pierce his privacy. Even a noblewoman had once invaded his rented quarters while at Kensington, in an attempt to seduce him. All her boldness had won her was a tongue-lashing that had blistered her skin and driven her from his presence, never to return.

Then again, fornication wasn't this newest vixen's game. An almost-kiss, an apology, then days of chase with Lady de la Beres appearing wherever he was. How the lady had known where and when to appear had concerned him at first, but worry had soon given way to sheer enjoyment.

Nor had she come to him dressed as the lady he'd met in John's apartment, the one who tossed commands at him as if he were a servant. If she had, he might have reacted toward her as he had the noblewoman. This morn, Lady de la Beres's garments were as simple and honest as her unwilling desire for him, her manner lacking all disdain.

A careless man might be led astray by her appearance. He might think her the sort of woman who cared more for a man's character than his name or status. Michel shook off that thought as ludicrous. No matter her portrayal, the lady was still gently born. She would never tolerate marriage to a commoner.

No matter what reason brought her here, she couldn't repeat this visit. John would pounce upon her bold actions and decry Lady de la Beres's lack of virtue and refuse to allow a wedding. No doubt, John would use her perceived wrongdoing to justify taking Lady de la Beres into the royal bed the next day.

Anger exploded in Michel, catching him by surprise. No man, not even a king, futtered his wife!

He froze on the stairway about halfway to the ground floor. Wife? Damn his sense of connection to her. It was even worse now than it had been that first night. If only he knew what was feeding it, he could crush it.

The answer welled in him, leaving him stunned. Lady de la Beres prized her virtue highly, despite her enormous needs. Indeed, she prized it so highly that she starved herself to remain chaste. Yet Michel knew without question that she would give all to him if he but kissed her.

What she refused all other men, she would give to him and him alone. The thought was so seductive that Michel nearly turned on the stairs and climbed back to the hall. Almost.

Want him she might, but she was still gently born and he, a commoner. Her birth demanded that pride and the need to maintain her rank rule her. Hadn't she proved that when she asked about taking the apartment in the castle? Rank, and the privileges that went with it, were all that mattered to folk like her.

By the same token, his refusal had revealed more to her than he cared to consider. He'd hoped that his back-handed compliment about her dress would drive her into a fury so great that she'd forget everything that had happened here. Instead, she'd whitened in hurt, although he couldn't imagine why.

With that thought nipping at his heels, Michel paused at the base of the stairs. Here, the entrance stair to the house opened up on Master Robert's workshop. Michel eyed the smith, his journeyman, and apprentices, all at their work. Save for Lord Amier and his squiring, Michel might have been one of them, tapping away at some bit of frippery.

Nay, it had never been his fate to be a workman, even if he hadn't been squired. Although Michel's father and brother had begun their careers as goldsmiths, neither one worked at their forges. They still owned their shop, but now other masters and journeymen turned out gew-gaws for the well-to-do, much to the profit of his kin. That freed Michel's brother and father to operate a far more lucrative trade in currency. So profitable was the exchange of one country's coin into another that they now owned a number of estates and manor houses, neither man needing to lift a finger to earn his keep.

All this Michel had learned only after Lord Amier's death. It had been a condition of Michel's squiring that his father agree to give up all contact with his second son. Just as Amier had sold his daughter to the goldsmith to restore his treasury, Michel's father had traded his younger son into the gentry to advance his common bloodline.

After Amier's death, Michel had received a letter from his sire, inviting the prodigal son back into the fold. Michel had visited twice more since then. Although he wasn't yet comfortable with kinsmen he barely remembered and had been taught to despise, he wasn't Amier, so full of pride that he despised the wealth that arose from the merchant class. For the past years Michel had entrusted every extra coin he earned to his kin. They were better with coins than farmers with seed, reaping crop after crop of profit, something that had already greatly improved Michel's style of life even after this short a time.

Now, as Michel watched Master Robert smooth Lady de la Beres's narrow veil band, he regretted that he hadn't sought out his family the moment he'd reached his adulthood. Had he done so, then he might not have needed a king's uncertain promise to get him a wife. Instead, Michel could have simply bought himself a knight's daughter, free of all political ramifications.

With that thought came Michel's next move in Lady de la Beres's game, the way to wake the anger he needed to rekindle in her. Not only would the lady forget everything she might have learned of him, she'd come for him with murder in her eye.

"Master Robert," Michel called out, giving himself no opportunity to consider that what he did stretched past the needs of his goal into something a little more personal.

The smith turned to look at his guest, his brows raised and a smile upon his face. "Good morrow, Sir Michel. How may I assist you?"

"By allowing me to pay the cost of repairing that band," Michel replied. "It's a regal thing, certain to do justice to the head it adorns. Do be certain to tell its owner that I made it my gift to her."

"I'm certain the lady will be greatly appreciative, sir," Master Robert replied, smiling. As he should. Robert knew if Michel paid him he'd get his coin this week instead of years later. "It will be a pretty thing again, once I'm done with it," the smith said, admiring his own handiwork.

Giving the man a nod, Michel turned away, disgusted with himself. It was rude to turn his host into a messenger, especially with the sort of message Michel wound around the band. He'd just turned that bit of frippery into a symbol of Lady de la Beres's unwilling passion for him. Every time she looked upon her veil band she'd remember the day she offered her body to a commoner, begging a man beneath her to sate her physical needs.

Which meant she would never again wear it, when a good part of him wanted her to think of him, and only him. This had to stop. He was already more vulnerable to her than was comfortable. If he were fortunate, the hurt would destroy her passion for him.

He freed a harsh breath. Now, here was irony, indeed. Only days ago, her scorn had so set his teeth on edge that he'd sought to humiliate her by waking her passions. Today, believing he'd caught a glimpse of an honest woman beneath that scorn, he strove to reawaken her spite.

Michel strode around the corner of the goldsmith's house. Each step took him farther from the unwelcome sensations that Amicia de la Beres woke in him, so that by the time he reached the courtyard at the back of the house, he felt blessedly empty.

Chapter 11

Michel's troop waited in the courtyard for him, eleven of the twelve men already mounted. Yet afoot, Roger Twofingers, so called for the number of digits hewn from his left hand in some long ago battle, held Michel's horse. Although most of these men were English, they all wore the de Martigny colors. These were battle-hardened soldiers all. None of them cared that the man they followed was foreign born. For them, a man's worth was measured by his ability to swing a sword and bring those who followed him, hale and hearty, out of a battle. These were skills Michel owned in abundance.

Not one of them was any better looking than their captain. Michel had chosen them for their disagreeable appearance. The harder their look, the less likely a brave band of boys would lose their lives trying to prove themselves better than a knighted commoner and his troop. There were other reasons Michel kept these men, not the least of which was their ability to hold their tongues and their loyalty to the one who paid their wages, both attributes he appreciated.

Roger smiled as he saw his master, the movement of his mouth doing nothing to soften his disfigured face. "The lady departs?" he asked. His use of Michel's native tongue was accented by nearly two hundred years of separation from Normandy's French-speaking lands. No emotion colored his words.

The corner of Michel's mouth lifted as he gave thanks again that he'd sent Roger from the room. It wouldn't have served to have his captain see him panting in his need to satisfy the lady's hunger. "She does, with both her skin and repute intact," he replied, his tone flat.

"You are more merciful than she deserves," Roger said with a snort, trading on their friendship to speak frankly. "While I cannot fault her choice in servants, her brazen manner warrants punishment. Then again, I can't think of a single well-born vixen who doesn't deserve a good strapping."

Sharp anger again erupted in Michel, catching him unaware. No man spoke so about his wife! He reined in his reaction. Before this day was done, he'd find some way to sever his sense of connection to Lady de la Beres.

"Mount up," Michel commanded his captain, taking his own reins from the man and rising into his saddle. "It's time for our daily audience with the castellan. Each day is a new surprise as he struggles to hide his disdain for me while striving to follow our king's command to the letter," he said, making light of the contempt he endured.

In all truth Winchester's castellan, one Sir Hubert, was more tolerant than most Englishers. Perhaps this was because the man was the fourth son of a baron, a birth that guaranteed him no more inheritance than pride in his name. That didn't mean their meetings, naught but formality as they listened to each other's report on the state of the wards and castle, were easier. If the castellan never turned his shoulder, neither did his gaze meet Michel's. If not for that Michel might have offered Sir Hubert congratulations. Any knight capable of working his way from penniless extra son to guardian of a royal fortress was worthy of Michel's respect.

Once Roger was mounted, Michel led his troop out through the alleyway and onto the lane running in front of the smith's shop, then turned his horse's head toward the castle above the town. He moved no faster than a walk, being in no hurry. Once his meeting with the castellan was finished all he had to look forward to was that godforsaken midday meal.

Michel's shoulders tensed against the ordeal that dinner represented, once more cursing John and his game. It wasn't the derision that bothered Michel. It was how John counted on this exposure to thwart his mercenary's wedding plans. That, more than anything else, kept Michel at a distance from the lady. Well, there was no more distance now, not after this morning's meeting. He and Lady de la Beres were at last and all too clearly beginning to define the rules of this personal game of theirs.

All the breath left his lungs. "God take me for the idiot I am," he snarled as the magnitude of the error he'd just made reared up before him.

A woman as bold as Lady de la Beres wouldn't absorb a blow like the one he offered with that band. Nay, she'd plan retaliation at the earliest opportunity, and that opportunity arrived with today's meal. Jesus God, what had he been thinking? That was just the problem. He hadn't had a truly clear thought about anything except Lady de la Beres since the sensations that had sparked between them in the alcove, when all that should have been on his mind was the state of her properties.

"Sir?" Roger shot a sideways glance at his employer as they guided their horses through Winchester's main gateway, avoiding a departing oxcart.

"I've made a tactical misstep," Michel muttered in reluctant explanation.

Roger gave a snort. "Not an uncommon event when men spar with women," he said in gentle reproof. "Care to elaborate?"

Michel didn't question how Roger knew that his error had to do with Lady de la Beres. For all his brutish appearance, the man was surprisingly perceptive.

"I was perhaps a little too heavy-handed in my effort to see that the lady didn't repeat her mistake. She'll want to strike back, but I've made it clear that she's never again to approach me in private, which leaves only the hall and the meal. A confrontation with her before so many doesn't serve my purposes just now."

That was an understatement. Drawing more than

forty witnesses of all ranks to note an interaction between him and Lady de la Beres was exactly what John
had hoped would occur. Once again, the possibility of
leaving England without the prize he'd been promised
rose up before Michel. Damn, but he didn't want to turn
his back on what he'd accomplished here to begin again
somewhere else, under some other capricious prince.

"Then, perhaps you should dine elsewhere?" Roger
suggested. "It's not as if the king's wards much appre-
ciate you usurping your supposed place to sit at their
high table."

"If I could dine elsewhere, I would," Michel replied.
"As much as they despise me at their table, they would
resent my absence more, claiming the empty chair evidence of my disdain for them. Of those knights who remain here, some would use this to justify their hatred of
me and their swords will loosen in their sheaths. Others
will look upon that empty seat and see a coward. Again,
swords will loosen. Nay, the only acceptable reason I
have for not sitting at that table is to depart."

It was his only option, even though Michel had
planned to delay his trip to Lady de la Beres's properties until John no longer lingered at nearby Windsor.
"It's time we take that journey I mentioned, leaving this
very day."

"Then, you've devised some way to befuddle the
king's spies, so that they don't notice your absence?"
Roger asked.

Michel made an irritable sound and offered his captain another shrug. If he left now, he'd return to an irate
John, ready to offer a royal chastisement to his errant

mercenary. There was sure to be at least one nasty trap as punishment for Michel's disobedience. Still, one of John's traps was preferable to the damage the lady's open assault would do.

Roger's laugh was a deep rumble. "You do realize your plan will only make matters worse, giving the lady time to devise a more effective retort. Instead, seize the moment. Deliver her some crushing blow this day, something that will make her reconsider any future attack, then leave. That way she can use your absence to reclaim her dignity and convince herself there's no further use in trying to punish you."

"Good advice, but how can I use it when what you suggest means a public confrontation, the very thing I seek to avoid?" Michel sent his man an amused look. "Roger, you astound me. I never knew you were such a swain, so attuned to the thinking of the weaker sex."

Roger grinned. "What choice have I with this face of mine?" The lift of his hand indicated his scarred features. "No woman is going to tap at my door, hoping I'll open my arms and take her into my bed. I must woo by sly insight."

Still smiling, Michel turned his attention to the castle's yard as they rode into the gate. That Roger assumed the lady had come this morn to offer herself to him only reanimated that imp on Michel's shoulder. It whispered of the sort of kiss the lady might offer him, and where that kiss might lead.

As Michel's desires stirred anew, so did the need to indulge himself in a new round of that physical taunting. That alone was reason enough for him to ride from

Winchester without a backward look. He pulled his horse to a halt before the hall. Only as he dismounted did he realize that the lady could no more confront him in full view of the diners than he could her.

"He did what?" Ami's shocked cry rang in the goldsmith's hall.

The smile on Robert Atte Cross's face dimmed a little. He glanced to his wife who stood beside him. A frown pinched Mistress Hughette's brow. She pursed her lips.

Offering Ami a bend of his head, as if doing so might make what he said more palatable, the smith repeated himself. "Sir Michel instructed me to tell you that he wished to make you a gift of the band's repair, my lady."

Horror raced through Ami. She looked at Maud. Until this moment, Maud hadn't yet realized it was Sir Michel who dwelt here. While in Mistress Hughette's kitchen, they'd listened to the troop as the men left the courtyard below them. At Maud's question regarding the noise, the housewife had only mentioned that they presently hosted a knight as a guest.

Now, the maid's eyes were round as pence, her skin the color of almond paste.

Surprise drained from Maud's face. Ami watched helplessly as her maid added the identity of Mistress Hughette's guest to her mistress's dented band and this unexpected visit to a goldsmith's shop. There was no mistaking when Maud completed her calculation, or that she'd come to the wrong conclusion. Nay, not the wrong conclusion, but the conclusion that Sir Michel intended everyone to devise by way of his *gift*.

The maid pressed her hands to her lips. "Oh, my lady, what have you done?" she breathed through her fingers.

Ami looked at the band in her hands. It glowed with more brilliance than it had owned in years. Aye, but no longer was it a pretty and expensive bit of jewelry, something Ami cherished. Instead, it was a symbol of her destruction.

If somewhat shy, Maud was as clever as the next woman. If Maud thought Ami intended to lay with Sir Michel, so would any other of the king's wards who did the same figuring. Whispers would fly. That she had never been Sir Michel's lover wouldn't matter. The fact that he paid for the regilding of Ami's band was proof of intimacy; the gift was too expensive to be anything else.

Horror died beneath the onslaught of anger. God should have taken Sir Michel in the alcove when the mercenary had begged for it. Then again, God would have the man soon enough. Ami would fillet him for what he'd done. But first, she'd destroy his plot to debase her.

Ami raised her head to smile at the smith and his wife. At least, she hoped it was a smile and not a grimace.

"Master smith, although Sir Michel names this a gift, I fear the knight plays a jest on you, and me, one in very poor taste, I might add. I am a ward to King John, who has only just named Sir Michel as administrator of my estates. Thus, any coin the knight expends on my behalf is returned to him from my income."

"Ah, but of course. That only makes sense. I'm certain that's what the knight meant when he spoke to my husband," Mistress Hughette seconded.

The concern in the housewife's voice sent a wave of relief over Ami, even though Mistress Hughette's reason for aiding Ami was selfish. If rumors circulated that a gentlewoman had used the goldsmith's house for an assignation, then the smith's wife would be named a procuress, which destroyed her repute as well.

Satisfaction rose beneath Ami's angry panic. Such a fate would serve Mistress Hughette rightly, just punishment for a woman who dared leave her female visitor unchaperoned with her male renter, even if no one in the world might ever know of it.

"But, I'm quite certain he said this was to be a gift," the smith insisted, glancing between the two women.

His wife put her hand upon her mate's arm. Her fingers dug into his sleeve. "Nay, Master Robert, you misheard. It is as the lady says, a jest made at her expense. This is the knight's way of asserting his newly won control over her estates and purse. Assure yourself that the lady's coin, and no other, purchased this repair."

Frowning, the smith blinked as he realized there was a message for him in his wife's words. He puzzled over it a moment, then his eyes widened in shocked understanding. "Aye, I remember now. He did seem amused. I see how I misunderstood his prank for something else."

"My lady," Mistress Hughette offered Ami a deep

bend of her knees. "Thank you for your trade. You'll excuse me but it's time to begin setting up the tables for the midday meal. My husband will see you out."

No matter how nicely the merchant's wife smiled, Ami heard the message within the message. Ami was to please leave, doing so this very moment. It would also be kindly appreciated if she took her trade elsewhere, at least until Sir Michel gave up his use of this home.

Still reeling over how the mercenary had nearly managed to ruin her, Ami followed the smith down the stairs. At street level, her royal escort straightened from his slouch against the wall of a chandler's establishment across the lane, then stepped forward to join the woman he was supposed to protect. Ami barely noticed him as she strode out into the lane, her band clenched in her hand and Maud trotting to keep pace with her stalking mistress.

Anger grew with every step. It wasn't as if this blow was necessary. She'd heard Sir Michel's message, the promise that he'd extract his price if she ever again dared to visit him. Again. A second time, not the first.

But, of course, her debasement had always been his plan. Why else would he have sent away both the smith's wife and that man of his? Sir Michel had intended to stir her senses, awakening what she couldn't control no matter how hard she tried, then blame her for it. It was a common trick, one many a man had tried to use against Ami in the past, so common that Ami cursed herself for missing it and forgetting Sir Michel was a man like any other.

"That overbearing commoner! That arrogant foreigner! How does he dare abuse me so?" The words
streamed from Ami on a raging hiss.

Maud gave a panting squeak at this. "Oh, my lady, I
cannot bear it any longer. Tell me true. Why did Sir
Michel de Martigny pay for your band?"

That brought Ami to an abrupt halt. She turned on
her maid, her hand lifted in protest and her mouth open
to deny all. Before she could speak, tears formed in
Maud's eyes.

"I changed my mind," the maid cried. "Don't tell
me. I don't want to know."

That made matters even worse. Ami's eyes widened
in indignant disbelief. "How can you think that of me?"
she cried. "You know me better. Now you hear me and
you hear me well. That mercenary didn't pay for anything. It was my coin and no other that bought this
work. Moreover, you are to never again to repeat those
words, not before me and definitely not in front of anyone else. Better yet, forget that we ever left the hall this
morning. Now, holding your tongue tight in your head,
turn your feet in the direction of where we belong and
move."

Maud whitened at Ami's chide. Reaching out, she
caught her mistress by the arm. For Maud it was an act
more brazen than she had ever before attempted.

"God save us both, but as bad as this is, you aren't
finished with him," she cried, her voice shrill in fear.
"Tell me you know better than to try and soothe your
own outrage by shouting at him!"

Catching an arm around Maud's waist, Ami nigh on dragged the smaller woman to one side until they stood against the featureless wall of a beltmaker's house. The soldier started to join them. Ami sent him a pointed look, not so much begging privacy as commanding it.

The man, his brows already high on his forehead, caught the command in her look. He stepped a few paces away from the lady and her maid to stand in the beltmaker's shop window, pretending to examine the man's wares. When he was far enough away, Ami turned her back on him to address Maud.

"Have a care with what you say," Ami hissed, her voice low even though there was street noise enough to drown out what she said. "Do you want everyone around us to think I'm so forward that I'd shout at one of the king's mercenaries?"

"But, you are that forward," came Maud's all too truthful reply. Thankfully, her voice was no louder than a whisper. "My lady, I cannot let you do it. This is no ordinary knight, bound by honor and the constricts of his good name. This is a monster who paints his mail black. Confront him so boldly and he'll slaughter you." Maud's face began to crumple. "If you die I'll be alone here. Without you, how will I know what to do?"

"Maud, I promise you. No matter what anyone says of Sir Michel, he's not going to kill me." A harsh laugh tumbled from Ami's lips at the recall of how Sir Michel's gray eyes had softened into almost blue as she offered him her kiss. Nay, killing her was the last thing he wanted to do, not unless he could accomplish that slaying upon a bed and use pleasure as his weapon.

Unwelcome sensations stirred with that thought. Ami crushed them. This was the man who would soon be looting her properties.

Maud's eyes widened. "Nay, nay, nay," she whispered. "What I see in your eyes cannot be. Tell me that Sir Michel isn't the man upon whom you set your heart. Oh, please, it cannot be on his account that we've lingered time and again at the castle gateways, and near the hall's screen."

"He most certainly is not the one," Ami cried out loudly enough to make a passing housewife shoot her a surprised look.

What was it that Maud and the goldsmith's wife believed they saw in her face that had convinced them she had any interest in that mercenary?

Ami bent her head near Maud. "You may trust me on this," she snarled. "If Sir Michel was the only man remaining on the face of this world, I still wouldn't have anything to do with him. Now, come. I want to go back to the hall."

Ami dragged slight Maud back out into the street, not even looking to see if their escort followed. As she walked, her anger grew until a red haze wrapped itself around her heart. The truth was, if Sir Michel were the last man on earth and it meant the end of her own hopes for ever having a husband or a family, she'd still plan to murder him.

The need to twist his *gift* until it was ruined rode tandem with Ami's need to vent her rage on the mercenary. Nay, destroying the band wouldn't be good enough. What she needed to do was drive the expensive piece down that patronizing, overbearing, betraying knight's throat.

Chapter 12

Ami shifted from foot to foot in impatience. She'd picked the spot for her ambush with care, choosing the base of the stairs that led up to the queen's hall. Everyone who wanted their midday meal, and that was anyone remaining in the now emptied fortress, had to climb these steps.

And, so folk had. For over the last quarter hour, the soldiery, the stablelads, the laundresses, even the bathmaids had streamed up the steps. That stream was now a trickle. From the door a storey over Ami's head, the thrum of conversation abruptly stopped. The chaplain's voice rang out, bidding the diners to bow their heads in prayer.

Beside Ami, Maud sniffled, the noise meant as a complaint. Ami paid no heed, lost in concern. An hour ago Sir Michel had been within these walls for an audience with the castellan. A few minutes ago the castellan had made his way into the hall. So where was the mercenary? Hidden beneath the folds of her mantle, Ami's hand clenched around her band. That cad had best think twice about avoiding her. By God, but she'd never forgive him if he left her starving for both food and vengeance.

A movement across the yard caught her eye. Ami straightened in anticipation, only to relax in disappointment. It was only the serving men, each one bearing a tray of steaming food braced upon his shoulders. With their every step toward the hall, the day's meal chilled.

Trailing behind these men was Mistress Milicent. The old woman wore her working gowns, garments as grayed and marked with age as she was. The only splash of color was the bright embroidery that decorated the face of her cloth belt. It was a testimony to the old woman's rural roots, roots not so different from Ami's, that Milicent chose to participate in the creation of their meals, although she only did so when the female wards were separated from the full court. Trotting at the dowager's heels was a single maid, working to keep pace with her sprightly employer.

The old woman offered Ami a wide smile as she came to a halt before the stairs. "My lady, why do you linger? The meal begins."

"Mistress, how glad I am to see you," Ami said in greeting. The opportunity to shield what she intended to do to Sir Michel opened up before her, gleaming as brightly as the new gold foil on her band. "I've been hesitating here, torn in twain over right and wrong. Will you advise me on what is proper?"

Mistress Milicent snapped up Ami's sop, the depth

of her pleasure over being consulted on a matter of manners glowing in her creased face. "But, of course, my lady. What is your question?"

Ami caught the old woman's arm. The smell of boiled chicken clung to Milicent, suggesting the spots on her gown were broth. Ami led her a little way from their servants.

"Pardon, but it's nothing I care to share with others," she said, her voice low. It wasn't that she didn't want their maids to hear, only that she didn't want Maud protesting as she listened to her mistress bend the truth here and there.

"It's Sir Michel. A merchant in town tells me that the mercenary spoke to him, making a purchase supposedly on my behalf." There it was, her grain of truth soon to be buried beneath a layer of obfuscation. "That suggests to me that the mercenary already begins to spend what isn't his. Mistress, more than anything I feel I must approach the mercenary and ask after his intention, perhaps even correct him if he has overstepped. However, I don't wish to do this before witnesses, not when there's no man who likes to be chastised by a woman. In the case of a man like Sir Michel de Martigny, I fear my questions may encourage him to vindictiveness. Can you tell me if there's any way to confront him in a private place without compromising my repute?"

Approval softened the creases on Mistress Milicent's face. "You do well to think on this, planning your actions, my lady, but then I expect no less of you. You've always seemed more level-headed, less prone to unguarded flights of emotion than the others."

Ami caught back a derisive laugh at that. Milicent wouldn't be so approving if the old woman could see the sort of heat that boiled in her just now.

"As for approaching Sir Michel, the sooner you do, the better for your properties and your income," the old woman said. "If the knight refuses to heed you, as I'm certain he will, you must rush to pursue other avenues of complaint, even speaking with our royal master if need be." Milicent offered this as if Ami didn't already know how important it was to leash the mercenary.

Milicent leaned closer. "Now, as for where you can meet him, the hall would be appropriate, although you shouldn't approach him until after the meal. So too would the yard be acceptable." The sweep of Milicent's arm indicated the courtyard around them. "So long as you have a chaperone to watch over you as you meet with him."

"My thanks, mistress," Ami said, false humility hiding her sly triumph. Milicent had just given her what she wanted. "I truly feared misstepping and losing your good opinion, as well as that of my fellow wards."

Milicent drank in Ami's deference the way a cat lapped milk. "My lady, nothing you do can shake my opinion of you. Unlike many of those in our king's custody, your mother did a fine job raising you. She would be proud of the woman you have become."

That tore a hole in Ami's satisfaction. Pride would hardly have been her dam's reaction if she'd lived to see her daughter's misadventure of this morning. Nor would Ami's mother have approved of what her daughter now contemplated. Then again, her mother wouldn't have approved of much that happened at court.

"Now that we've settled the matter, come," the dowager said, again offering Ami her arm. "We'll dine, then I'll act as your chaperone as you confront the mercenary after the meal."

The last person Ami wanted as a witness was the dowager. "We can't confront him after the meal if he's not in the hall."

"He's not already above?" Milicent asked in surprise. "But he sits at the high table."

"What can I say?" Ami replied. "I've waited here, hoping to approach him as he entered, but he hasn't arrived. Now that you've assured me I do no wrong by using the empty yard for our meeting, I'd like to linger here a little longer, in case he's been delayed. That is, if my maid might serve as my chaperone?" Ami gave extra emphasis to the question in her voice, to make it seem that she was begging Milicent's approval rather than dismissing the woman.

"Your maid can serve, but why count on her? I'll happily bear you company," Milicent said, flickers of forbidden and lurid interest stirring in her aged blue eyes.

"Oh, mistress, I could never ask it of you. Please, you've worked so hard creating the meal, I couldn't bear to keep you from the just reward for all your labors," Ami protested, putting every ounce of sincerity she could concoct into her words. "Nay, there's no reason for you to stay, not when I suspect the mercenary truly doesn't intend to appear at all. It's only my own peace of mind that demands I wait another few moments before making my way into the hall."

Disappointment flashed in the old woman's eyes, only to disappear beneath a facade of propriety, proving that Milicent held herself to the same standards of behavior that she demanded of everyone else. She'd rather die than openly admit she owned a fleck of curiosity. "As you will, my lady. However, should the mercenary appear, remember to remain within sight of the hall door and keep your maid at your side the whole while," she said.

Here it was, everything Ami desired. With Milicent's approval came the old woman's tacit promise that no matter what someone inadvertently witnessed or overheard, Milicent would defend to the death Ami's right to meet the knight this way. The dowager never admitted to an error in judgment.

"My heart rests easier for your words, mistress," Ami said with a smile.

"As it should," Milicent replied with yet another nod, then beckoned to her maid. "Come, Alys."

The two women started up the stairs, weaving their way around the last of the serving men and their trays. Halfway up, Milicent paused to look over the railing at Ami. "My lady, I shall save you a spot next to me."

The invitation was nothing less than a demand for payment. Milicent expected to hear all the details of the coming meeting. Even as Ami nodded, her mouth tightened in refusal. Milicent would wait forever before she got the truth, that was if Sir Michel deigned to appear so Ami could vent her wrath on him.

Ami returned to stand next to Maud. Maud turned a teary look upon her mistress. "Please, my lady. He's not coming. Let's go up into the hall."

"Oh, he's coming," Ami snapped as she forgot the courtesy that Richard de la Beres had taught her to practice toward her servants. "He's slinking in late, hoping to avoid me. He'll not escape me as easily as that."

A quiet hiccough left Maud, then her spine straightened and her chin lifted. "Then, you can wait here by yourself, my lady," the maid said in a defiant whisper. "I'll not stay here when all you want to do is drive a brute into murdering you."

Ami's rage dissolved under the weight of her astonishment. "What? You can't leave me. You're my chaperone!"

Maud's shoulders squared. "A chaperone is more than a companion, my lady. If I'm to protect your repute, then you must heed my advice. Heed me now. What you intend to do here is wrong. Now, we are going up the stairs to eat our meal," she retorted, only to have her last word die into a gasp. She shrank back, her eyes wide, her gaze aimed over Ami's shoulder. "God save us both!"

Ami pivoted. Sir Michel and his ugly man were riding their horses into the yard. Both men had shucked their casual attire in favor of military dress. If Sir Michel's man looked all the more frightening in boiled leather armor sewn with metal rings, his employer's appearance was even more daunting.

Seated atop his massive warhorse, Sir Michel's mail

gleamed like ebony under a weak autumn sun. His head was bare, his helmet hanging from his saddle near his shield, his mail coif dangling down his back between his shoulder blades. He'd shucked the leather undercap he wore beneath his mail hood. The day's breeze made free with his hair, lifting the dark strands.

Smug satisfaction stirred. He came expecting rage, but she wasn't about to make a shrew of herself by shouting. Nay, that demeaned her. She'd keep a tight hold on her superiority and chasten him as if he were a misbehaving child, truly gouging his pride.

The mercenary drew his horse to a halt at the foot of the stairs not but two feet from them. Maud loosed a croaking sound, then whispered, "I told you he would come armed and ready to kill us."

"I'll tell you again that he has no intention of killing me," Ami spat out, boldly meeting Sir Michel's gaze, her voice loud enough that he could hear her. "The only thing his armor means is that he's afraid of me."

Chapter 13

Michel dismounted, his back to the women. Afraid of her? Amusement lifted the corners of his mouth, his pleasure rising until it finally vanquished that part of him resistant to the confrontation.

Roger was right. This was his perfect chance to prove to the lady that he was her rightful master. If nothing else he wanted to repay the damage she'd done to his repute by telling Master Robert that his payment for her band's regilding was stolen from her purse. In order to soothe his host and hostess, Michel had needed to offer them a part of the truth, that he'd asked in secret for Amicia de la Beres's hand.

Mistress Hughette had first been relieved near to tears, then she'd chided Michel for making the gentlewoman a gift before he'd declared his intentions, since doing so could only harm the lady's good opinion of him. As if Lady de la Beres had any good thoughts regarding him.

After that, the housewife's imagination had run wild. Mistress Hughette had suggested that Lady de la Beres suspected Michel's interest in her and had come this morn hoping to provoke a lover's declaration from him. Since relief and approval more than suited Michel's purpose, he didn't bother to correct the housewife.

Now, stripping off his steel-sewn gloves, Michel tucked them into his belt and turned to face the lady. Lord, but she was beautiful. Still dressed in her simple blue gowns, anger stained her cheeks a warm pink and reddened her lips. Her eyes flashed green fire. Gold glinted in one hand.

So, she meant to refuse his gift in public as part of her retribution, did she? From deep within Michel came the need to force her to accept the band and everything it meant. That would be tantamount to her admitting that he had the right to purchase intimate gifts for her, and more.

With that, all Michel's attempts at justifying the purpose of this meeting crumbled. There was but one reason that he stood in this yard. So many men had tried to breach Lady de la Beres's walls and failed. He needed to confirm her unwitting message of this morning. He wanted her to tell him that he was the one, the only one, she'd allow through her barriers. To do that he had to again provoke the lady's passion for him.

Roger joined him, then gave a jerk of his chin toward the waiting women. "It appears that the two of you have marshaled your pieces. All we wait on is the roll of the dice to see who makes the first move in this match. Go, sir," he said, holding his voice low enough that only

Michel heard him, "trusting me to divert all attention from you. It would greatly aid my cause if you drive the lady around the hall's corner. That would also protect you against accidental glances from above. What of the lady's maid?"

Michel watched the frail creature do her best to hide behind her mistress. As their gazes met, the maid reeled, colliding with the stair wall, then crumpled onto the hard-packed earth of the courtyard floor.

"Invite her to join you, then keep your backs to us," Michel said. He wanted no witness, not even Roger, if things went as awry as they had twice before done in his meetings with Amicia de la Beres.

Roger cocked his unscarred brow. "That I'll do willingly, the lass being a sweet thing. But what makes you think the lady will let her maid go so far from her?"

The corner of Michel's mouth lifted. "Trust me. A few words and yon lady will forget she ever had a maid at her side."

A slow smile stretched Roger's lips. "Why look there. I believe the dice roll in your favor, sir. You make the first move."

Michel gave a breath of a laugh, then turned toward his opponent in this glorious game. Four steps closed the distance between him and the woman he meant to wed. Amicia de la Beres watched him come, not a shred of fear in her gaze.

Pleasure again stirred in Michel. What reason had she to fear him? It was her own starvation for lovemaking that was her worst enemy.

The lady made a show of looking him up and down, then lifted scathing brows. "Most men eat their meals in more comfortable attire, Sir Michel," she began, only to make a startled noise as Roger stepped to the side of her fallen maid. The frail young woman freed a quiet cry as she looked up into Roger's face, the sound not shock over a ruined face but that of recognition.

Amicia de la Beres whirled on Roger. "You'll get away from her, you will," she commanded with all the imperiousness of her class.

Paying the gentlewoman no heed, Michel's captain offered his hand to the seated servant, speaking quietly in her native tongue. Perhaps it was what Roger said, or perhaps it was that recognition. Whatever it was, the maid accepted the soldier's hand, letting him pull her to her feet.

"Maud, what are you doing?" The lady reached out as if to grab her maid's arm.

Michel shifted to stand between the two. "Let her go, Amicia," he said, making the second move by using her given name when he had no right to it.

Amicia stepped back from him, her mouth ajar. "How dare you address me so," she demanded, doing just as Michel had promised; Roger led the unprotesting maid around the horses.

Michel shrugged off her complaint. "What can I say? It seems only right that we banish titles and formality. After all, we're no longer mere acquaintances, not after this morn."

Heat flamed in Amicia's cheeks. "You are despicable."

"I am," he agreed, fighting the urge to laugh out loud.

Michel glanced above him, toward the hall door and the noise of so many folk all at their meal. No one stood on the steps. Behind him, saddle leather creaked and horses chuffed to each other as Roger brought them around to stand like a wall between his employer and the world. Roger and the maid stayed on the opposite side of that equine wall, speaking. The rise and fall of their voices was hushed—Maud's sounded worried, Roger's soothing and something more.

It was privacy of a sort, but a strange one. Still, the sense of isolation wrapped itself around Michel. Here, with no one to witness save the sun and a few clouds in an autumn chilled sky, they might as well have been completely alone. The imp on Michel's shoulder squawked, Satan's cherub promising that once he had her around the building's corner there'd be even more privacy, and freedom.

Michel took a step toward the woman whom he couldn't seem to help claiming as his own. They now stood less than an arm's length apart. As she'd done this morn, Amicia held her ground. Her arms again crossed, she cocked her brows as if daring him to do his worst.

Sharp pleasure stirred in Michel at the thought of how wondrous *worst* might be. Lord, but he hadn't enjoyed a game this much in years. Then again, he'd never before matched wits with a woman while using her passion as his pawn.

He took the last step. They were close enough that he

could smell the scent of roses from her skin. Her eyes narrowed.

"You'll step back this instant, Sir Michel," she commanded, giving scornful emphasis to his title.

She wasn't the first person to twist the symbol of his achievement into an insult. However, her derision lacked impact when he knew she was using it to disguise just how vulnerable she was to him.

"Tsk, Amicia, such rudeness when all I want is to give you what you desire," he said, reminding her of this morn's events.

Her face flamed anew. She leaned toward him, her forefinger pointed toward the center of his chest. The corner of Michel's mouth lifted again. It was the kitten challenging the mastiff.

"Give me what I desire! You, sir, couldn't begin to know what I desire, much less be capable of providing it for me."

"On the contrary, Amicia. I know exactly what you desire. How could I not when you so clearly showed me what you need this morn?" he asked. "I know that I can awaken your hunger for me without even touching you. Imagine what would happen if I but rest my fingers on your cheek? Nay, I suspect I'm more than capable of satisfying any desires you may have."

"Cad," she gasped, staggering back from him, unwittingly moving in the direction of the corner.

"I thought we'd already determined that I'm a man lacking in the social graces," Michel replied, taking joy in following her. "Here is something I see as a great failing of your class, Amicia. All of you assume that everyone else in the world lives by the same strictures of polite convention that bind your lives and behavior."

Her green eyes flashed. "Arrogant buffoon! I've had enough of you playing me for the fool this day. I'm not about to stay here and dance for your enjoyment a second time. Here," she thrust out her hand. Her band glinted in the sun. "This is yours. You purchased it this morn but forgot to take it with you when you left the goldsmith's shop." She offered him a tight-lipped grin. "Oh, and by the by, your attempt to ruin me has failed. Neither the goldsmith nor his wife understood the intent of your gift. Despite your efforts to besmirch it, my name remains spotless and intact."

With an amused breath, Michel leaned toward her, craving the heat their bodies made when they were close. "You're wrong, Amicia. If your repute remains intact it's because of me. I saved you from yourself when I refused your kiss this morning."

Ami reeled in shock at Sir Michel's words. All desire to repay him for his insult died in the need to turn tail and run as far from him as possible. How could he be so horrid? No polite man gloated over how he stirred a woman, at least not to that woman's face.

Struggling to collect herself, Ami met his gaze. His eyes were again that warm blue-gray. The corner of his mouth began to lift in the motion that Ami now recognized as his smile.

"I forbid you to laugh at me," she snapped.

He blinked. The blue in his eyes immediately hardened back into gray. Ami drew a swift breath in triumph. It was good that he didn't care for how she could read his expression.

In her eagerness to prick him again, she let words fall from her lips without thought. "Commoner, think what you will about what happened this morning, but I'll tell you the truth. No woman would offer anything to one so bereft in honor as you, especially not me." She turned her body to the side as she spoke, aiming her shoulder at him in the ultimate dismissal.

He made a harsh sound low in his chest. Catching her by the upper arm, he wrenched her back around to face him. Ami yelped, stumbling. Her outraged protest died unspoken as she straightened.

Gone was the man of a moment ago, the one who had almost smiled at her, the same man who had nearly accepted her offer of a kiss this morn. This man's eyes were empty of all emotion, his jaw so tight Ami wondered that the bone didn't shatter.

"Hear me, madam," he said, his words edged in steel. "No matter what you think of my parentage, you will never again turn your shoulder to me."

Maud was right. He was a brute who could kill her without a thought. Ami wondered how she could have forgotten how dangerous he was. Dangerous or not, she'd rather die at his hands then let him know he could frighten her.

"Let me go," Ami demanded, lifting her chin.

She kept her voice low. Shouting might goad him into violence or, worse, bring the whole hall down on them. It wouldn't do to have everyone witness him holding her, not when this blunt-spoken cad might well spill the full tale of Ami's visit to his residence this morn. Not even Mistress Milicent could save her if that came out.

Rather than release her, he pulled her around the corner of the hall, his grip so tight that she flinched. Once out of sight of his man and Maud, he shoved her back against the wall, using his hands on her shoulders to pin her in place.

"You have no right to hold me," Ami cried quietly.

Bracing her hands against his mail-clad chest, she heaved with all her might. Her veil band, which she yet clutched in her fingers, shifted with her thrust until it lay flat against his chest. The gold looked all the brighter against his ebony mail. She shoved at him again. The effort popped the shank of her mantle pin from its hook. Still, the man in front of her didn't budge an inch.

Panting and trapped, she sagged against the wall and looked up at him. His face might have been carved from stone. All life was gone from his eyes. If this was his rage, then it was unlike any manifestation of anger that Ami knew. Every man of her acquaintance she'd had the misfortune to watch raging spewed his bile at the top of his lungs.

"You must release me," Ami told him, then did her best to soothe without actually taking any blame for having brought this moment down upon herself, which she had. "I am the king's ward. No man may touch those whom our liege guards in his household. Think on it. If someone sees what you do here, your life could well be the forfeit."

There wasn't a flicker of softening in his gaze. Ami sighed in defeat. He would have his apology.

"I beg your pardon," she said softly. "It was rude of me to turn my shoulder to you." And, so it was. Hadn't she despised Sybilla and Adelberta for doing the same to him when he was at the high table?

He went so far as to blink, but his hands didn't loosen on her arms. Worry stirred in Ami. What if he couldn't release her until he'd used his fists to relieve what boiled in him? All it would take was one of Lady Roheise's spies catching sight of a bruise and the lady would leap to the right conclusion from all the wrong reasons.

"Please, Michel," she tried using his Christian name, praying the feminine and familiar address might pierce his rage. "You must let me go."

His expression didn't soften, but his hands opened and he took a half step back from her. Ami let relief escape her on a heartfelt breath. With the lift of her breast her mantle slid off the pin's shaft and the garment spilled off her shoulders.

As Ami turned to catch it, Michel's hands again closed around her arms, this time at her elbows. Without the thickness of her mantle between them, she could feel the imprint of his fingers on her arms right through the fabric of her sleeves. His hands slid down the length of her arms until his thumbs moved at the crease of her elbows. The heat of his caress burned through her garments to sear her flesh, then pulsed through her body.

Rendered mute by the sensation, Ami looked up into his face. The tenderness of his touch wasn't reflected in his expression. His eyes were yet dull and lifeless. Still, as he gently, carefully, urged her to lean back against the wall, she did as he bid.

His hands slid down her arms until they rested atop her clenched fists. Neither of them wore gloves; Sir Michel's were tucked in his sword belt, while Ami had none on her person at all. Ami's heartbeat quickened. It had been years since a man had last touched her, skin to skin. Lord, but it was a wondrous sensation. Michel's palms were hard, made so by the demands of a warrior's work, his fingers startlingly supple as he traced the curl of her fingers and the landscape of her knuckles.

At the pressure of his touch, Ami's clenched hands opened. Her forgotten circlet clattered on the ground at her feet. Craving more of his caresses, she turned her palms toward his.

He traced her palms, then twined his fingers with hers. It was as their hands joined that Ami realized what she wanted from him. That was even more frightening than his anger. She jerked her hands away from his and pressed her palms against the wall behind her. Cold stones sapped the heat he'd left upon her skin.

"Do not," she commanded him at a whisper.

Michel only braced his hands on the wall at either side of her shoulders. New life flickered behind the flat

gray of his eyes. He leaned toward her, his mail jangling quietly.

Heat flowed from him, wrapping itself around Ami.
Her breath left her on a shaken sigh. Without thought,
she lifted her mouth in invitation. His lips brushed hers.
She gasped quietly, then her eyes closed.

The clean scent of his soap filled her nose; she tasted
Mistress Hughette's barley water on his lips. She shivered. How could she have forgotten that a man's beard
against her skin could be both rough and soft in one
glorious instant?

His kiss deepened. A wave of pleasure crashed over
Ami. With it came the image of tangled bedclothes, of
candlelight, bare skin and joy. Wanting this with all her
heart, Ami leaned into his body.

Where not so long ago she'd flinched at the thought
of touching his painted armor, now her hands slid up
his metal-clad chest to his nape, above the bulk of his
metal hood. She combed her fingers through his hair,
the silken sensation waking heat at her woman's core.

He made a noise low in his chest at her play, his
mouth again moving on hers. She pulled herself closer
to him, as she begged him to give her what she so
needed.

Even as his mouth clung to hers, he put his hands on
her hips and set her back from him, then began to
straighten. Wild refusal exploded in Ami. He couldn't
leave her unsatisfied, not now!

With her eyes still closed, she tightened her arms
around his neck. Remembering everything Richard de

la Beres had taught her of waking a man's pleasure, she raised herself to her toes and moved her mouth across his. Michel made a sound not unlike a growl. His arms closed around her, his hands slipping down her back until they cupped her hips and lifted her against him.

Ami didn't care that his armor tore at her gowns. Instead, she pulled herself closer still, craving the feeling of his body against her own. His mouth slashed across her, demanding that she yield to him. This she did without hesitation, her thighs opening. Joy's pressure grew within her with every move of his lips, promising that explosion of ecstasy she hadn't forgotten despite the years. Desperate for more, Ami tore her mouth from his and pressed a kiss against his cheek, then to his throat.

"Nay," he breathed.

Before she had time to resist, he reached behind him and caught her hands in his, then stepped out of her embrace. Space opened up between them, cold and empty. Crying out, Ami's eyes flew open. She strove to pull free of his grasp and reclaim what she so needed.

"Nay," he repeated, again twining his fingers between hers to trap her hands.

Warm blue now lurked behind the dull gray of his eyes. The hard lines of his face had softened. He looked younger, less careworn. Ami's heart responded. Maud was right. This was the man who had caught her eye, and more.

"I am the one," he said in a harsh whisper, echoing her thought. "You will give yourself to me."

The crudeness of his comment destroyed all Ami's pleasure. She yanked her hands from his to cross her arms. His kiss hadn't meant anything. Just like every other man who'd tried his hand at seducing her, Michel cared about one thing: getting her beneath him so he might brag to everyone that he'd done the impossible and futtered the unattainable Lady de la Beres. A hurt far greater than Ami wanted to acknowledge caught her in its grasp.

"In that you are wrong, mercenary," she said in her harshest voice, her chin lifted to its most imperious angle. "You are nothing to me, and I would rather die than give myself to you. Now, leave me."

The blue faded from Michel's eyes. Without a word, he pivoted and strode around the corner of the building. Once he was gone, Ami gave way to her weakening knees and slipped down the wall to sit on the ground in the pile of her mantle, feeling as crumpled as Maud had looked in the same position a few moments ago.

Her veil band lay within arm's reach, glinting in the afternoon sun, each spark a chide. How could she have forgotten Michel had made it a gift to debase her? What right had he, a commoner, a mercenary who refused to give his oath to any man, to insult her so!

She knew just how to repay him. Her eyes narrowed. She'd dispatch that note to Roheise. Who cared what became of her if Michel were torn limb from limb?

How could she will so horrible a death upon the man whose mouth tasted of barley water and whose touch could set her afire? Ami's anger collapsed, leaving a gaping hole inside of her. Tears rose to fill that space.

What was she doing, crying over a man she barely knew, one who insisted on mistreating her? Determined to keep those droplets from falling, she tilted her head back against the wall. She hadn't wept in years, not since Richard de la Beres passed and she'd come into the king's custody. To survive at court, she'd left behind any feminine softness as relics of her rustic upbringing, including tears.

Ami recoiled in surprise as the image of the woman she'd become rose before her. What had happened to the Ami whom Richard de la Beres had loved? That woman would never have toyed so casually with a man's life, no matter what that man might have done to her. Nor would that earlier Ami have used scorn to hurt anyone.

The effects of four years in this stinking, debased place blossomed in her, an ugly flower with a sickening stench. In her effort to protect herself and survive, she'd become one of the selfish, manipulative, uncaring women she despised.

This time Ami made no attempt to stop her tears.

Chapter 14

Saddle leather creaking, his mail jangling, Michel slowed his mount from a trot to a walk. The horse settled into the slower pace, his breath steaming above his nostrils. It was colder than usual for November, promising a deeper winter than the last. Not that the chill affected Michel. Between his cloak, the surcoat he wore atop his mail, and the thick undergarments that protected his skin from his armor, he was more than warm enough.

Although he and his troop had been on the road for only a few hours, the sun already hung near the horizon. Slanting rays of orange and mauve reached out across the earth's face to tint all they touched. The moon, showing only half its face, had risen hours earlier and now drifted almost directly above them in a sea of steadily darkening blue.

The men riding with Michel took advantage of this

rest period to trade comments and easy jests. Roger's whistle sang out, the tune that of a lewd ditty about a man pursuing a woman who left him with desires painfully unfulfilled. The captain hadn't needed to witness the events in Winchester's courtyard to know what happened between Michel and Amicia. As quickly as he could, Michel called for a return to their earlier pace; it put a blessed end to Roger's whistling.

This ground-eating pace was the most efficient way for them to reach Amicia's nearest property before sunset, but speed wasn't the only reason Michel chose it. He wanted as much distance as possible between him and Winchester and a game that had lost all its amusement.

It astonished him that Amicia turning her shoulder to him could make him so furious. Why? He'd known that her insults of the previous moment were but pretense. Moreover, unlike masculine contempt, which Michel always answered with his sword, the contempt of well-born bitches was unworthy of his reaction; they were, after all, only women.

But as Amicia turned her shoulder to him in rejection, something had exploded deep within him. It had taken all his will not to lift his fist to her. If she hadn't spoken to him, using his given name, dropping both his title and her contempt to embrace a new intimacy, he might still have been standing in the yard striving to control himself.

The sound of his name on her tongue had dissipated his rage, only to have unfettered desire take its place. Michel closed his eyes, once again savoring the sensation of their kiss. Even if events conspired to keep him from marrying her, Michel would never forget the way her mouth moved on his as she lost control of her own passion and strove to awaken his. It had been everything he expected, more even, than their encounter this morn promised.

In his lust for her, he'd forgotten the damage chain mail might do an unprotected body and snatched her close. A moment later, when she'd parted her thighs in invitation, he'd cursed his armor, for it kept him from what he needed.

Even now and as furious as he was with her, heat stirred. Lord, but with all his soul he wanted her beneath him. Better yet, she wanted him with equal hunger.

Or rather, her body wanted him. Michel opened his eyes and glared at his horse's mane. Damn that woman and her prejudice. All he'd asked was that she admit he was unique, different from the other men who pursued her. It was an admission that her breeding wouldn't allow her to give him, and he'd been a fool to expect it.

As he drew another angry breath, he caught the faint scent of woodsmoke. That scent brought with it the promise of walls, warmth, and food. Michel slowed his horse to a walk, looking for the bent birch that had been his landmark when he'd come this way to fetch Sir Enguerran to Winchester the previous week; then, he'd only ridden past the manor, having no legitimate reason to pry within its walls. It wasn't far now, only over the next hill.

The sun's orb now nestled upon its bed on the horizon. Golden rays stretched high above it, as if it strained to escape its nightly sinking into the earth's embrace. In the crisp air above him, starlings massed in their twilight ritual, a twittering and writhing black cloud against a painted sky. A raven's call rang out from a nearby copse, the caw a harsh, rasping question as it returned to its aerie. An answer came from a yipping fox, starting out on its nightly hunt.

Reaching the hilltop, Michel reined in his horse, studying the lay of the land with a new eye. The downward slope ended in a slight depression. So shallow a dip didn't warrant the name "valley." Not so long ago, Michel had visited England's north, in the king's company. There had been something awe-inspiring about the vast emptiness of those backward shires and the fractious men who inhabited them, but Michel far preferred this area of the world. Here, the hand of Man had been so long at the plow that there was nothing wild or uncertain left in the landscape. By God's will, forests of ash and oak had been harvested and a tangled wilderness tamed into placid, fertile fields.

The finest of Amicia's manor houses rose from the depression only a quarter mile from where he stopped, its enclosing wall embracing at least half a virgate of land. Set on a stone foundation as tall as a man, the hall reached two storeys before ending in a roof of thick thatch. The dying day stained its walls purple, while the night's newly awakened breath brought the smoke streaming from its roof vent in Michel's direction.

A village of a good two hundred dwellings, enough folk to support the manor and create a bit of profit for

its master, lay outside the manor's walls. There was
something about the way these houses squatted into the
earth, their reed roofs reaching almost to the ground,
that made them look snug, capable of enduring even
winter's gales.

All in all, what spread out before him was the ideal
reflection of the settled, fruitful future Michel had always imagined for himself. This was a place where he
could forge his legacy and bring forth sons, knowing
that they would carry his line forward long after he was
dust. Aye, but to have his piece of pastoral heaven he
had to marry Amicia de la Beres. Michel freed a harsh
breath, his hands tightening on the reins enough to
make his steed shift uneasily.

"All you do is sour your stomach and guarantee that
you won't sleep tonight," Roger said, urging his horse
to come abreast of Michel's. When Michel shot him a
narrow-eyed look, Roger only smiled, the lift of his
mouth decidedly cheerful. "What would you say to a
distraction, a chance to vent some of what boils in you?
Aye, that's what you need. A little venting and you'll
sleep like a babe this night instead of stewing until
dawn in your bitter thoughts."

"What are you babbling about?" Michel demanded.

"That," Roger said, pointing to the west. "The light
befuddles my eye. Tell me what you think. Are they
about half a mile from us, or farther?"

Startled, Michel shifted in the saddle to look where
Roger indicated. Silhouetted against the sunset on the
opposite ridge line was a troop of mounted men, the

gleam of metal on both horses and riders suggesting they had a military nature. They were making their way toward the manor house.

Irritation drained from Michel and he gave thanks to Roger. This is how men lost their lives. They let thoughts of females and pleasure divert them from more important matters.

Blinking against the sun's last bit of brilliance, Michel counted and came up with two dozen men, a force twice the size of his own. But were they a threat? At that instant, the one leading the riders called out, pointing toward Michel and his men. Whatever he said was lost in the distance, but Michel didn't need words to know the leader's intent. All the riders immediately turned their horses in this direction and set their mounts into a gallop.

Horse flesh was expensive. No man drove the wealth of his house across a night-darkening land, not when hidden burrows and jutting tree roots might ruin an animal—unless that man was desperate to hide something and believed he knew the landscape well enough to take the risk. Sir Enguerran was just such a man.

"To arms," Michel warned, with no particular urgency in his voice, to those who followed him.

"How many?" one of his own called back from the rear of his troop. They were below the hill's crest and couldn't see the threat they faced.

"Double our number," Michel replied. "Come forward all of you, shields at the ready and align yourselves along the hilltop. We'll make our stand right here on the lip. Our attacker must think he has cat's eyes, since he comes for us when we've got no more than a half hour of light left. I'm loath to lose any of you because we battle in the dark. Let's make this a swift victory."

And Sir Enguerran was doing what he could to aid Michel's victory. The attack Michel saw forming on the plain below him was the desperate ploy of a knight incompetent in matters of war. The first tactical lesson Michel had learned as a squire was that it was far easier to defend a height than to force an assault up a slope. Thus, were most castles raised upon mounds. If Sir Enguerran was representative of the sort of knights who inhabited England, then Michel knew why they'd refused to come to John's aid in the king's Continental war. They feared their own deaths.

"What, no suggestion that we run for the manor below us?" Roger asked with a laugh, his sword already in hand and his circular shield on his opposite arm. "We're as close to it as yon troop is. We could reach its walls with ease."

"I think not," Michel said, the tautness that always claimed his body prior to battle creeping over him. "If yon troop is led by the man I think, there may be no sanctuary for us within the walls. Besides, I believe I like this distraction of yours, well indeed."

Michel straightened his helmet on his head, then took his kite-shaped shield from its saddle rest. Trained to that sound, the big gelding's head lifted in anticipation. He danced against his rider's new tenseness. With his shield on his arm, Michel slid his sword from its sheath, his gloved hand fitting perfectly into its well-worn grip.

Their attackers were now within a hundred yards and closing quickly. Every man among them wore his cloak wrapped tightly around him, as if to hide any color or insignia that might identify their house. An anonymous assault.

Michel's lips tightened into a stiff smile. If Sir Enguerran wanted to hide his identity then he should have ridden a different horse. Twilight wasn't deep enough to disguise the creature's piebald markings.

With a rattle of armor and harness rings, the men of his troop leaned forward in their saddles, ready to deliver their first strokes. In response to the sound, Michel's mind emptied of all thought, even that of Amicia de la Beres. He lifted his sword, ready to use the skills his grandsire had taught him, skills that one of his class wasn't supposed to own.

Roger was right. This was the perfect diversion.

Chapter 15

So dreary was the pall cast by this dark, wet day that not even the cheery crackle of the fire could banish it. Save for Lady Adelberta's tuneless humming, something she did every time she spun, the women in Winchester's hall were swathed in a silence so deep that the rain on the shutters sounded like drumming to Ami's ears. She took another stitch in the framed cloth in front of her, resenting the project and giving thanks that it would soon be too dark to embroider.

It wasn't just that this length of linen was another in the endless yards of embroideries that she and the other wards produced to decorate the many churches that the king and queen patronized. It was that the chore demanded she sit. More than anything Ami wanted to pace furiously back and forth across the hall until she carved a rut into the floor.

Michel was gone, not just from the castle but from

Winchester and no one, not even Walter or his many eyes and ears, knew where the mercenary went and when he might return. Even Sir Hubert, Winchester Castle's castellan, knew no more than that Michel had begged leave due to personal business. Personal business. The only personal business Ami could contrive for Michel, a foreigner on England's soil, was the stripping of wealth from her properties.

Michel?

Ami's needle hovered over the taut surface of the linen in her frame. She stared unseeing at the pattern on the fabric. When had she started thinking of that horrid, thieving brute solely by his Christian name, the way a lover might?

Perhaps it had been because they'd almost been lovers. Shame heated her cheeks. Mary save her, she'd actually opened her legs to him.

Even as Ami tried to banish the memory of what she'd done in the courtyard, desire reawakened. Her wholly untoward need for that mercenary afflicted her like some dread disease, beyond her control. She only had to lick her lips to once again taste his mouth on hers, or remember the intensity of his need for her in the way he'd taken her mouth with his kiss. There was slight comfort in knowing that she hadn't been the only one lost in wanting in the courtyard.

Ami closed her eyes in a futile effort to escape what plagued her. There was no refuge for her, not even in her own inner darkness. Those remembered sensations had invaded her dreams. Each of the last two mornings she'd awakened her body was alive with longing. For him.

How could she want a man who stirred all her senses only to turn what had been a life-shattering moment for her into the simple conquest of a seducer over his victim? Aye, the moment had been life-shattering in more ways than one. Ami stabbed her needle into her embroidery, then yanked it back out as she completed her next stitch.

Fool, fool, fool. She'd been so intent on punishing him for behaving like every other man who'd tried to seduce her that she'd spoken without thinking. If she'd held her tongue for just a moment she would have noticed that the game had finished, that she'd succeeded in leashing Michel. True, she hadn't bound him to her with affection, but in that courtyard she had most certainly gained control of his lusts. Rather than reject him, as she had, she should have agreed to give herself to him, then kissed him again. After all, he could hardly have done anything untoward, not dressed in his mail. A few caresses and that private, stolen moment could have given her all the victory over him that she craved.

Instead, she'd sent him from her more furious than he'd been at the goldsmith's shop, or in the alcove. If her purpose had been to guarantee that Michel would steal from her, then she'd achieved it. He'd take her things for no other reason than to punish her.

And this was the man she now referred to by his Christian name? Ami breathed out a curse and jabbed her needle into the cloth again. The point stabbed into her guiding finger at the back of the frame.

Snarling, she leaned back on her stool, the injured

digit in her mouth as she sucked away the pain and blood. Sitting tailor-fashion on the floor beside Ami's stool, Maud lifted her head from her own sewing project, a new chemise for her mistress. The maid offered her employer a concerned and questioning look.

"I pricked myself," Ami muttered with her injured finger still in her mouth.

Compassion filled Maud's smile. "My poor lady. You're as nervous as a cat today, worse even than yesterday," she said, turning her gaze back to her own needle. "It's a shame Lady Eleanor took the minstrels with her. You could use an hour's dancing to settle yourself."

Ami caught back the desire to throw her embroidery across the room and bellow in frustration. Dancing? Her world was crashing down around her ears and Maud talked of dancing as if the movement of Ami's feet would solve every problem.

Her head bent, Ami crushed the linen in her lap between her hands. She hated being in the king's custody. And, she hated being a woman. Because of her gender she was trapped here, helpless and blind, unable to protect her house from Michel.

"Lady de la Beres?"

Ami sat up with a start to find one of Lady Roheise's servants standing before her. The maid was swathed in a thick cloak. The garment's hem was stained with mud and shimmered with moisture, just foul enough to suggest a day spent on the road.

"Aye?" Ami replied, gnashing her teeth in disbelief. Could this day really get any worse? She glanced around the hall to see if anyone watched. Every eye was aimed in her direction, when the last thing Ami needed was for any of the women in this room to believe she'd aligned herself with Roheise and her cause.

"My lady has just returned to Winchester from London this day, but fell ill on route," the maid said. "Not wishing to share her ailment with her fellow wards, she's taken temporary lodging within town for the night." Although the maid's voice wasn't raised, the hall was so quiet that her words rang around them.

The corner of Ami's mouth quirked at the implicit irony. Roheise didn't wish to share her ailment with others of her own rank, but thought nothing of infecting commoners.

"Remembering yours as a friendly face in this hall," the maid continued, "she wonders if you would consent to serve as her chatelaine for the night?"

It was a canny message, crafted to deflect curiosity over why a baron's widow might call a knight's daughter to her side. Nor was there a woman in the room who could or would refuse the summons. In their world, which honored service above all else, Roheise's request was a mark of distinction, so much so that Maud was already afoot and searching for Ami's outer garments in the chest.

Only Ami knew the message's true purpose. Roheise had learned that Michel was gone. The noblewoman no doubt raged over what she perceived as Ami's failure. Nay, Ami couldn't refuse, not without drawing more attention upon her than she could afford right now.

"But of course I'll come, doing so to repay your lady her favor," Ami replied, offering listening ears an explanation for why she should get this honor. "I cannot tell you how grateful I was for that posset your lady gave me last week. It did much to ease my distress after my audience with our king."

"My lady is nothing if not generous," the servant agreed with what seemed an honest enough smile.

Ami rose from her stool, the determination to find a way to be free of Roheise as soon as possible filling her. Wanting no delay in shedding this awful task, Ami didn't even consider changing into her better gowns. Roheise would have to receive her as she was dressed now, in her second-best, the green overgown atop a yellow undergown. However, she wasn't going to risk her fragile silk veil to the elements. Removing the fine headdress, Ami joined Maud, who yet bent over Ami's chest, her mistress's blue mantle and linen headdress in hand.

Ami took her mantle, but left the headdress. Donning it took two free hands. Maud was still bent over their clothing chest, searching for Ami's woolen winter scarf. For the sake of fashion, Ami's mantle had no hood. Thus, the scarf was needed to protect her head and headdress from the wet.

"While you're digging in there, find your own cloak as well, Maud. You'll come with me," Ami said, throwing her mantle over her shoulders.

That brought Maud upright with a start, her eyebrows lifted at this unexpected command. Lady Roheise's maid frowned a little. "There's no need to bring your own maid, my lady. Trust me, between my lady and the household where she stays, we've servants aplenty already."

Ami knew that, but she didn't want to be alone and friendless in the enemy's household. "My maid has certain skills when it comes to healing." Aye, and certain they were. Thank heavens no one in the hall knew that Maud's healing gifts were limited to wrapping linen around wounds and making an effective mustard plaster.

Maud blinked at hearing herself described this way. A tiny crease appeared between her delicate brows. A similar worried pleat appeared on the brow of Roheise's maid. That was the only protest either dared offer. Ami might not be a noblewoman, but no servant had the right to naysay a knight's daughter.

"My lady, if you'll bow your head a little," Maud said, holding out the linen headdress.

At the sight of that complex wimple with its chin strap, Roheise's servant shifted impatiently. "My lady, Lady Roheise hoped you might come immediately to her side."

So, Roheise was worse than furious. To delay would only worsen matters. "She's right, Maud," Ami said. "It takes forever to arrange the folds on that thing, and the lady needs me. The scarf will suffice for now."

Ami took her woolen scarf from a startled Maud and tied it over her hair. "Get your things and lock our chest," she said.

With their outerwear in place, Ami and Maud followed Roheise's maid from the hall to find a pair of de

Say household soldiers waiting at the base of the hall's stairs. All of them hunched their shoulders against a pelting rain and made their way in silence down Winchester's sodden streets.

Hidden behind the thick gray clouds that owned the sky, the sun was beginning to set, or so said the steadily darkening atmosphere. Night's coming was the signal for all merchants to cease their labors. Up and down the lanes, wood clapped against wood as shutters closed on shop fronts. Those workmen and journeymen who didn't live with their masters shouted their goodnights, anxious to be behind their own doors and at their rest. Apprentices sprinted home after the final chore of the day.

Wafting through that cookshop's open door came the scent of a hearty stew and the sound of male voices lifted in song. As Ami passed its entry, she glanced into its interior. Caught in the friendly flicker of firelight was a group of day laborers, indulging themselves in a bit of entertainment, along with a cup of ale and bite, before they retired to nests of straw in their shared and cheerless corners.

The soldiers stopped before a draper's house, its thick shutters closed and barred to protect the man's precious fabric from the skulking night. At three storeys tall, the building wasn't so different in form from the goldsmith's abode, which stood only one street over from this place, but it wasn't quite as fine. Perhaps Roheise had chosen Michel as her sacrificial victim because she couldn't bear an upstart knighted commoner renting what seemed Winchester's best residence.

Roheise's servant opened the house's street door, dismissing their escort with a wave of her hand. The soldiers retreated to the alley at one side of the house. From there, they'd seek the outbuildings in the rear courtyard where, Ami was sure, the others in Roheise's household guard were making their beds.

Just as in the goldsmith's house, stairs zigged and zagged up the house's end wall. At the first storey landing, Roheise's maid didn't pause to see if those she led followed. She opened the hall door—the sounds of a meal in progress cascaded down the stairs—then disappeared into the big room.

As she went, Maud reached up from the step below Ami to catch her mistress by the hand. "My lady, what are we doing here?" she whispered, the crease between her brows deepening. "Why would a noblewoman want you to be her chatelaine when she knows others among the wards far better than you?"

"I like this honor no better than you do, Maud," Ami replied, not willing to reveal that she'd foolishly involved herself with a scheming noblewoman. "We'll go in, but stay close to the door. As soon as I can, I'll find a way to excuse us."

Together, they entered the draper's hall, stopping just inside the door. Rich lengths of fabric decorated the merchant's hall, reflecting not just the quality of his goods but his wealth, since it seemed he didn't need to sell some of his most expensive goods. The draper's whole household was in the hall, seated at dining tables for a late meal. Behind them, the hall fire, set in a wall enclosure like that of the goldsmith's, threw its light, if not its heat, well into the center of the room. That rendered the branches of candles on the tables nothing but the affectation of the wealthy.

In the house's best chair at the middle of the high table, the one with its back to the fire, sat a hale and hearty Lady Roheise. Although this was but a casual meal in a commoner's household, the noblewoman's gowns were heavy blue sarsenet. A great sapphire glinted on one finger, while a necklet of pearls clung to her throat, the warm white of the gems the same color as the hair at the lady's temples, visible through her silken veil.

To Roheise's left was a thin elderly man with a mane of white hair. His rich attire alone named him the master draper. To her right sat a portly and equally as aged woman who wore a baron's ransom in jewels upon her pudgy fingers.

"Why, Lady de la Beres, how good of you to come," Roheise called out as her maid came to stand at her back.

Ami offered a smile and bob. "Lady Roheise, I give praise to our Lord. I came expecting to see you laid low, but you seem quite recovered."

"Aye, so I am, by God's good grace and Mistress Avelin's wondrous broth," Roheise replied, touching the bejeweled hand of the woman next to her. The look of affection that passed between the two women was so warm Ami knew Roheise would have chosen this house even if the goldsmith had offered his. Here was irony, indeed, an earl's daughter doting on a common woman while spurning all other commoners as unworthy of her notice.

"Well then, since it seems you have no need of me after all, my maid and I will return to the king's hall," Ami said, with no hope that she might so easily make her escape.

"Why such haste? You've only just arrived," the draper called out, the smugness in his booming voice saying he enjoyed hosting his betters no matter how much it cost him. "Please. My house is yours for the night. Stay and take your comfort with us. Lady Roheise has spoken of how you so charmed her last week. Come, come," he insisted, beckoning Ami nearer to the table. "My eyes are old, my lady, and no longer see with clarity. I'd like to judge for myself if you are as lovely as my noble guest claims."

The last place Ami wanted to be was deeper in this chamber. Yet, to refuse was rude and would expose to Roheise how nervous Ami was when Ami didn't need Roheise knowing another thing about her. Ami crossed the room and stopped before the draper. The old man looked up into her face. There was nothing weak about his eyes. Instead, they gleamed with enough masculine appreciation to suggest that he'd more than once strayed from his wife's bed, and wouldn't mind doing so again.

"See, Master Philip, she is all I said of her and more," Lady Roheise told her host with a little laugh, then looked at Ami. "And, my lady, I truly did speak to him of how you and your unusual ways charmed me. That's why I thought of you when I fell ill on the road," she said. "So, will you bear me company here this night?"

Ami blinked. Although Roheise smiled, the expression in her steely eyes said she no more wanted Ami to stay than Ami wanted to remain. That was fine with Ami.

"I really can't," she demurred, scrambling to concoct some reasonable excuse for refusing. "I didn't expect to be gone for more than an hour or so, thinking if you needed tending through the night that my maid might stay. I made no provision for my belongings and am loath to leave them unguarded in the hall when I cannot afford pilfery."

"What a pity," Roheise said, her voice heavy with disappointment. "However, I understand your hesitation. It's a sorry truth that our king and those base men who serve him are wholly untrustworthy. I only hope you can forgive me. I would never have called you to me at so late an hour if I'd realized I would recover so swiftly on my own." Roheise came to her feet, then rounded the table's corner to stand beside Ami. "Let me see you to the door while Master Philip calls my men to escort you back to the castle."

So confident was the noblewoman that her will would be honored she didn't even look behind her to see if her host did as she bid. Instead, Roheise linked her hand into Ami's arm and turned her erstwhile guest toward the exit from the hall. When they were far enough from the table not to be overheard, Roheise bent her head near Ami's ear.

"Why did you bring your maid? You should have known I expected a private moment."

"Your servant said you were ill and needed me to act as chatelaine in the merchant's house. What gentlewoman goes off to serve this way without her maid at her side?" Ami hissed in reply.

Roheise's eyes hardened at Ami's defiance. Her mouth twisted into a tight line. When they reached the landing outside the hall, the noblewoman waved Maud down the stairs and closed the door. Roheise's grip on Ami's arm insisted that Ami remain with her on the landing.

At the street door, Maud turned in surprise to look back up the stairs at Ami. "My lady?" she called, worry in her voice.

Ami smiled. "Wait for me outside. I'll be but a moment or two."

Once the street door closed behind Maud, Ami freed herself from Roheise's grip and stepped as far from the lady as possible on the landing's short space. "Let me guess," she said quietly. "You want to know what I've accomplished thus far. Well, there's not much to say. Sir Michel is gone. He left two days ago and no one knows where he went."

"And, let me tell you what I know of your efforts on my behalf," Roheise retorted, her harsh voice held to a whisper, her face a mask of anger. "You visited the goldsmith's house while the upstart commoner was in residence, then you met with him in the courtyard before he departed from Winchester. Why no message to me of your success?"

That shook Ami to her core, not that Roheise had been watching. If Ami could purchase Walter's eyes and ears to watch Michel, Roheise was capable of paying many more to watch over her own pawn. It was that Roheise knew about the meeting in the castle's yard. Only Milicent could have told Roheise that. Not that Milicent had more to tell than that. All Ami had related to her afterward was that she'd warned Michel she would complain if he spent her coin, and that he had listened.

That old gossip! Thank God, the dowager hadn't stayed that day. Otherwise Roheise would have known the truth. Then again, if Milicent had remained, there wouldn't have been a kiss, Michel would never have made his crude offer, and Ami might still have had a chance to save her estates from him.

"If you know that much, then you also know I've had no success," Ami snapped. "He's avoiding me, as he has for days. That's why I went to the goldsmith's and tried confronting him in the castle's yard, all to no avail. Tell me, my lady, how am I to drive a man into doing anything if he refuses to allow me near him?"

Roheise's eyes narrowed. "That, as you informed me over a week ago, was to be your problem. It is my problem to achieve rebellion against John, and that is all that concerns me. However, your continuing failure has now made your problem mine as well. It didn't take long for me to devise a new way to use you to awaken England's decent folk to the outrages of their king. Best you consider how much easier it is to destroy a woman's repute than to protect it, especially when that woman has gone to a man's place of residence."

There was no subtlety in the threat. Roheise didn't intend to wait any longer, nor did she need to wait. Ami's trip to the goldsmith's gave Roheise everything she needed to achieve her goal. Ami's heart sank as she understood.

Roheise's had never cared whether Ami succeeded. All Roheise needed was a woman known to be chaste throughout court, yet with a reputation for driving men to their edge as they pursued her. There was only one woman at court who was both. Ami.

"You may spread the tale as you like," Ami said, cursing herself for a blind fool, "but without me to stand beside you, claiming it's true, all you have is innuendo. There are witnesses, good and true, to testify that no wrong was done." And none of them would know that they lied when they swore to this.

Roheise dismissed Ami's defense with a wave of her hand. "It's amazing what people will say for coins. As for you, do what you will. I have what I need. Those who hear the tale will know it's true when John refuses to execute his mercenary for having had his way with you."

Mustering what remained of her dignity, Ami turned on the landing and descended to the foot of the stairs. It took all her will not to tear open that burly panel. She stepped outside, then gently closed the draper's door when she wanted to slam it with all her might.

When it was shut, she leaned her back against it. Maud stood a few feet from her, clinging to the house's side as she tried to find some relief from the rain under the short eaves. Ami turned her face to the darkening sky. The rain had lightened these past moments into a cold mist.

She was ruined. Her future would be as dry and barren as the draper's door, and it was all her own fault.

"My lady?" Maud asked, coming to stand beside her. "Are you ill? What did that noblewoman do to you?

Maud's words sparked a fire in Ami's belly. Her eyes narrowed. It was better to stand before the whole court and admit to being a whore than give Roheise her victory. Turning on Maud, she caught her maid by the arms.

"Not ill, Maud, but angry. That benighted noblewoman! I'll see to it she pays the highest price possible for what she does."

Maud's eyes widened to circles in her face. "What does she do to you, my lady?"

Ami wasn't listening. Instead, her mouth tightened into a smile. What she needed was a partner, someone motivated by self-interest to help her. Of the two potential partners who came to mind, Mistress Hughette and Milicent, Ami chose the goldsmith's wife. It wasn't so much that Mistress Hughette hadn't gossiped, but that her house was so close. With Michel gone and the workday at an end, Ami wouldn't be stealing time from the business of gold if she called upon the smith right now.

Thank God, Roheise's escort hadn't come for them yet. Holding a finger to her lips to signal silence, Ami pulled her startled maid a few yards down the street, then ducked into the alleyway leading to the next house's courtyard. Although Maud's eyes flew wide at her mistress's unusual behavior, she made no sound. Instead, the two of them clung close to the wall only a few feet inside the alley.

Ami's ears pricked. Maud's breath echoed harshly from behind her. Through the walls of the house beside Ami came the muted sounds of folk settling in for the evening. From the direction of the goldsmith's house a man's whistle sang out. Ami knew the tune, a lewd ditty, imminently better whistled than sung. A pair of lads made their way past the alley's opening, looking at nothing but the bucket of ale that they carried between them, each matching the other's step to prevent sloshing.

"What is this? With as long as it took to decide which of us had to tromp back through town, I thought they'd surely be down here, awaiting us." The man's irritable voice echoed to Ami from the front of the draper's house, his words spoken in the commoner's language. Although at court Ami used only the French tongue she'd inherited from her parents, she knew the English language well, indeed, having learned it at her nurse's breast.

"No doubt the lady changed her mind and decided to

stay," his companion replied. "Not that anyone would tell us that. Nay, they'll leave us standing here in the cold and wet."

"What now? Do we wait or call up the stairs to discover their intent?" the first man asked, sounding younger and more unsure than his companion.

"We're not doing either," the elder said in irritation. "We'll go back to the stables. When they're ready they'll call for us again, naming us dolts and churls because we didn't stand here and freeze our cocks off while we waited for them to make up their minds." Both men laughed, the sound receding as they retreated back behind the draper's house.

Ami straightened in surprise. The most she'd hoped for with this ploy was that the soldiers might believe she and Maud had started back to the castle without them and follow. That would have given Ami ten minutes or so to make her plea to the goldsmith's wife before she returned to the draper's house to ask when her escort meant to appear. If the soldiers had considered crying up the stairs about missing women, Ami could have stepped into the street and called to them, using escape from the rain as an excuse for being in the alley.

But this! This was a gift from God Himself, and a certain sign that she was meant to win this new turn in Roheise's game. Maud stepped closer to her mistress to take Ami's arm in a worried grip.

"What's happening? Why are we hiding here?" she cried, her voice low and not a little frightened.

"The lady wants something from me that I'm not at

all willing to give her," Ami replied, her voice grim. "Indeed, so little do I trust her that I won't even walk with her men."

Maud's face whitened. "But, my lady, night is falling. We cannot walk alone and unprotected."

Ami almost laughed. "Trust me, we'll be fine. We're going no farther than around the corner. Come," she caught Maud by the arm and stepped out into the street, turning toward the goldsmith's house.

Chapter 16

A mi drew Maud to a stop before the goldsmith's house, expecting her maid's protest after the debacle of their first visit. "Now, Maud, don't worry. Sir Michel isn't in residence at the moment."

Rather than shock or disapproval, Maud's expression flattened until she almost looked disappointed. "I know that. It's all you've talked about for the past two days," she murmured.

An apprentice, a lad of no more than twelve, answered Ami's tap. "Aye?"

Ami smiled, as if doing so might disguise the fact that she and Maud were two unguarded women, standing under a dripping, darkening sky. "I am Lady de la Beres. Might I have a word with your mistress?"

The lad's eyes widened as if he recognized her name. Ami could think of no reason that he should—that was, unless the tale of her veil band had made its way through the household. Hardly likely. Mistress Hughette had every reason to conceal that story.

"Wait here," the lad bid and rudely shut the door in Ami's face.

At any other time Ami would have stalked off, irate at such treatment by a commoner, vowing to never again frequent this place. She could no longer afford pretensions, not after Roheise's threat. Worse, if Mistress Hughette refused to see her, there was nowhere else for her to go save back to the draper's, and that meant the ultimate defeat.

A moment later the door reopened. Mistress Hughette stood in the portal, wearing her rich yellow gowns, only now they were covered with a stained apron, something a woman of her wealth and status should never need don. Her fine wimple had been replaced by a simple headcloth. All in all, she looked every inch the housewife.

Rather than frown as she looked upon Ami, Mistress Hughette's smile was brilliant. It was the last expression Ami expected to see on her face after their first encounter.

"Why, Lady de la Beres. Whatever brings you to our door so late in the evening?" There was an odd slyness to her words, as if she'd divined some intent for Ami's visit that Ami herself didn't know.

Clearing surprise from her throat, Ami offered the merchant's wife the clumsy tale she'd concocted. "I fear my maid and I find ourselves trapped in town, having been separated from our escort. I know you've no reason to offer me a boon, not after the mishap earlier this week, but might we bide with you for as long as it takes to send to the castle for a man to lead us home?"

Ami fell silent, certain of a blunt refusal. Mistress Hughette surely wouldn't invite in an ill-mannered gentlewoman whose actions had threatened her repute. The most Ami could hope for was the offer of an escort from the goldsmith's household, with she and Maud standing in the street while they waited for these men to appear.

Rather than irritation or rejection, cunning pleasure flashed in Mistress Hughette's bulging eyes. "But, of course, we can do that for you. Come in, come in." She opened the door wider, the sweep of her arm inviting the sodden women to enter.

"Thank you, mistress," Ami replied, her hope for recruiting an ally battling the sense that there was something intrinsically wrong with the invitation, given the woman's previous opinion of her.

As she and Maud entered, the smith's wife gave a tsk. "How your cloaks drip. It may be a while before you leave us. Why not remove them, so you'll be more comfortable as you wait?" The lift of Mistress Hughette's hand indicated a line of pegs on the wall where the household's everyday outer garments hung.

Ami unpinned her mantle and handed it to Maud, then tightened the woolen scarf around her head. She should have insisted on donning her linen headdress. Although the scarf covered her hair well enough to keep her decent, it felt uncomfortable to be dressed so casually while a guest in a strange household.

Smiling still, Mistress Hughette started up the stairs

to the hall. Ami followed her into the big chamber only to be stricken by how empty the room was, especially after the draper's crowded hall. The only sound was the cheery crackle of the fire in the hearth, the circle of golden light cast by the flames reaching almost to this doorway.

Perhaps the goldsmith liked a period of quiet and isolation during his evenings. Ami could see the man in one of the chairs before the hearth. Or rather, she saw one shirt-sleeve clad elbow, which was the only part of him that showed outside of the chair's enclosing back. Everyone else was in the kitchen, or so said the fragments of genial conversation that managed to waft past the closed door, accompanied by the scent of a hearty stew and warm bread.

Mistress Hughette strode toward the chair. Ami stopped at the room's center, waiting. Maud halted beside her.

Reaching the chair, Mistress Hughette glanced back at her visitor and smiled like a cat who'd gotten into the ducklings, then said to the man in the chair, "There's a visitor."

Startled, Ami glanced at Maud. Her maid was paying no heed to what went forward in the hall. Instead, Maud watched the kitchen door, her head cocked as if she listened. Her expression was intent.

The man in the chair shifted, its seat creaking with his movement. He came to his feet. It wasn't the goldsmith.

Ami stared as Michel set his golden cup down on the arm of the chair, the dancing firelight teasing colored glints from the jewels decorating it. He turned to face her. There wasn't time to manufacture barriers. Instead, subtle admiration filled her. Here, her betraying body proclaimed, was just the sort of man that any woman might cherish as a husband.

Firelight marked the aggressive jut of his nose and made his newly shorn cheeks gleam above the line of his beard. Made darker by dampness, his hair seemed as black as ebony. He wore his shirt, one sleeve rolled back to reveal a bandage around his wrist. The shirt hem hung to mid-thigh, while his legs were clad in a rough pair of stockings, which covered a man from his toes to his hips. Crisscrossing garters on his calves kept his chausses from sagging. All in all, they fit him well enough that Ami could see his were well-made legs.

The fire's flickering illumination pierced the fine linen of his shirt, silhouetting his lean form. Ami's heart skipped a beat. His shirt's neckline was slit nearly to the center of his torso. Its ties were loose and the garment fell open, revealing more than a glimpse of the powerful planes of his chest. His skin wore a dusting of dark hair.

The need to explore Michel's body with her hands caught Ami by surprise. She could still remember what it felt like to touch Richard de la Beres, but he had been an old man. Her body sighed, promising that touching this man would feel very different.

Shocked at herself, Ami curled her fingers into her palms and stepped back, her gaze meeting Michel's. "But, you're gone from Winchester." The unconsidered words leapt from her lips.

"I returned less than an hour ago," Michel replied. His eyes were as gray and hard as the stones that made up Winchester's town wall. Fury radiated from him.

Ami crossed her arms before her. If he was furious at her, it was because she'd refused his lewd proposal. "Well then, welcome back," she snapped.

Turning to Mistress Hughette, she said, "I fear my coming here was a mistake. Will you lend me and my maid an escort so we might make our way back to the castle?"

The pleasure in Mistress Hughette's face dissolved into confusion. "But I thought you came—" she began, only to be interrupted by Michel.

"Amicia stays. We have business to discuss," he said. It was no request, but a command.

All Ami heard was that he used her given name before the merchant's wife and Maud. That was it. Roheise didn't need to say a word. She was ruined.

"I fear *Sir* Michel"—Ami let her voice linger on his title so Mistress Hughette would know that she hadn't given him permission to use her given name— "mistakes himself for someone other than the mere administrator of my estates. Whatever business he believes he has with me can wait until the morrow and a more appropriate venue. I'll have that escort now, mistress," she demanded.

"I've just returned from your properties, Amicia," Michel said, speaking over her.

That brought Ami's full attention back to him. Outrage deflated with a bang. Panic loosened her tongue.

"So that's your reason for a meeting. You want to gloat over how you've made what was mine yours. If you think I'm going to let you loot my belongings without a fight, you're sadly mistaken. Come, Maud. We're leaving."

Ami pivoted toward the door and managed two steps before Michel closed his bandaged hand around her wrist. She yelped at the feeling of his warm fingers against her skin. Holy Mother, now he was touching her in public and before witnesses!

"Let me go," she demanded, jerking on her trapped hand as she strained away from him. His face might have been carved from marble. His fingers tightened around her wrist, then with a jerk, he pulled her back around to face him.

Ami's scarf slipped to the nape of her neck. With a wordless cry, she snatched for it, trying to rearrange it over her head with her free hand. Instead, it completely unwound. Bareheaded among strangers and mortified, Ami backed as far from Michel as her trapped arm would allow.

"Let me go." What Ami meant as a command came out sounding like a plea.

"A little privacy, Mistress Hughette," Michel said. There was no evidence of his fury in his voice. But, then, he was adept at hiding his emotions from those around him. From all save her, that was.

"But of course," the goldsmith's wife said with such alacrity that it knocked the breath out of Ami.

"Come, lovey," Mistress Hughette said to Maud.

"Join me. I could use your assistance in serving those who travel with our knight."

As the housewife extended a hand toward Maud, Ami's maid smiled so broadly that it seemed her cheeks might split. Ami gasped as she realized Maud intended to leave her without a backward glance.

"Where are you going, Maud? You have to stay. You're my chaperone." She strained away from Michel, reaching for her maid's arm, only to have him pull her backward before her fingers touched Maud's skirt.

Rather than rescue her mistress, Maud sidled a few steps nearer to the kitchen door. "Now, my lady, you cannot want me here, not when Sir Michel intends to discuss business with you. I've no desire to stand in the rain for a second time when the two of you decide your words are too private for me to overhear. Let me aid Mistress Hughette in her kitchen. Content yourself with the knowledge that I'm but a shout away, as is the whole household. After all, my lady, you yourself told me that the knight means you no harm."

Ami reeled at the betrayal. When had Maud become clever enough to rationalize abandonment by using her mistress's own words against her? Where was her shy and fearful Maud? The woman standing before her was some changeling, a confident stranger determined to flout all convention so she might get behind that kitchen door.

Only neither Maud nor Hughette had any idea how dangerous it was to leave her alone with Michel. Ami turned toward the goldsmith's wife. "Mistress, you cannot leave me unchaperoned with him."

"Listen to your maid," Mistress Hughette replied, once again smiling like that satisfied cat. "You may call out if you have need, but we both know that won't be necessary."

That left Ami nothing to do but watch in disbelief as the kitchen door closed behind the two women. She was ruined, ruined, ruined. If Michel used this private moment to once again rouse her senses, then make that lewd proposal, Ami wasn't certain she had the will to refuse him, not after two days of being tormented by the memory his kiss and two nights haunted by dreams of him in her bed.

Shivering, half in terror over what she couldn't control and half in anticipation of feeling Michel's flesh against her own, Ami backed as far from him as his grip on her arm allowed. Although his eyes yet reflected the icy depths of his anger, he studied her as if reacquainting himself with her face. His gaze touched her brow, the line of her cheek, then traced the curve of her lips.

It was only a look. Still, throbbing heat woke within her. God help her, but Maud and Mistress Hughette had only just departed the room and it was already too late to call for help.

"Let me go!" Ami yanked on her trapped arm with all her might.

Michel grunted. His fingers opened. He gave his hand a quick shake.

As he again reached for her, Ami stumbled back

from him, then wheeled into a turn. Her plait flying, her scarf caught in one hand, she sprinted for the hall door. It was safer to be bareheaded and unescorted on Winchester's streets than it was to be alone with Michel de Martigny.

She got as far as the landing before he caught her. Ami's cry ended mid-breath as Michel spun her around and shoved her back against the stair wall. His hands pinned her into place. Panting, she strained against his hold.

He loomed over her, his expression dark. "This time you go too far, madam." His voice was a raw whisper. "How dare you accuse me of thievery before others when you know very well that I have done no wrong."

Even if he'd shouted at the top of his lungs, Ami would still have sighed at his nearness. The warmth of his body reached out to envelop her. With that heat came his scent, all the more heady because she knew it.

Loosened, his shirt gaped far enough for her to see his torso almost to his waist. Need stirred sharply as Ami again eyed the powerful masculine planes of his chest. Oh, but he looked nothing at all like her former husband. Although Richard at two score and five, his age when they wed, had yet owned a sturdy frame, Michel's chest was broader, with heavy, hard muscles beneath his smooth skin. The hair covering his chest narrowed near his waist until it was but a thin pathway. Aye, and that path descended past his waist, leading down to sin—and her certain destruction.

That didn't stop Ami from wanting to use a finger to follow it. She swallowed and clenched her fists, crumpling her scarf, then forced her gaze upward. Yet damp, strands of his dark hair clung to his throat. The memory of the courtyard and of combing her fingers through his hair returned.

Ami tore her gaze from his throat to his face. His eyes were narrowed. There wasn't a hint of softness in his expression. Her gaze caught on his mouth.

All too well she remembered the way his lips had moved on hers, filling her with pleasure. A kiss was what she wanted. Nay, a kiss was what she needed.

Resistance dissolved. Lost in need, Ami's body relaxed. Her hands opened, her scarf drifting forgotten to the floor.

It didn't matter that he raged. The only thing that existed in Ami was her need to feel this man's mouth, his hands and his body upon hers. Lifting herself onto her toes, she touched her lips to his.

Chapter 17

Michel jerked in surprise as Ami rested her mouth against his. He arched back from her, still holding her against the landing's wall. Jesu, but he'd been ready to beat her for her false accusation, one no doubt meant to destroy him—and she wanted to kiss him?

Although night had crept up the stairs, cloaking the landing in dimness, the hall fire threw enough light into this small space that he could see her. Her head scarf was gone. Loosened by their struggle, tantalizing wisps of brown hair now escaped her plait. They clung to the curve of her cheeks and trailed in seductive promise along the slender length of her neck. Shadows marked the gentle slope of her cheeks and outlined her flushed lips. Her eyes glowed as green as emerald velvet. It was the promise in their depths that stirred him. The hunger he'd done all he could to awaken fair pulsed from her, enveloping him in a cloud of her desire. She'd lied in the courtyard, even if she wouldn't admit it. He was the one to whom she'd give herself.

But Michel couldn't afford to accept what she offered, not after what he'd seen of her properties. Amicia de la Beres was no longer the woman he would take as his wife. John and Sir Enguerran's greed had made certain of that. Without their potential marriage to protect Michel, accepting Amicia's offer tonight could mean forfeiting his life.

Amicia made a tiny, forlorn sound. With her shoulders yet trapped against the wall, she reached out, laying her hands against his waist. Even with the fabric of his shirt between her fingers and his skin, the heat of her hands seared him. Need thrust like a sword through his belly. If death was the price he paid, then so be it. Every man had to die and he wasn't going without having first tasted her passion for him.

Michel bent his head and touched his mouth to hers. She sighed. Her lips were warm and soft beneath his. The scents of rain and Winchester radiated from her skin, but beneath it all clung that faint scent of roses.

One of those wisps of hair trailed across his cheekbone. That woke Michel's desire to see her hair loosened about her. Releasing her mouth, he straightened and freed her arms.

"Nay," she pleaded as she clutched his waist. Although soft, her protest echoed in the silence of the landing. It was a worthy warning. One cry and they'd bring the whole house out here to see what they did.

"Ssh," Michel breathed, touching a finger to her lips

to silence her, then drew the back of it down the slope of her cheek. Her skin was wondrously soft against his.

Her eyes closed. She leaned her head into his caress. Michel's shaft stirred. Cupping his hand beneath her chin, he traced her lower lip with the ball of his thumb. She relaxed against the wall, her posture saying she was content to let him touch her as he would.

Michel drew a sharp breath at that promise, then stroked a hand down the length of her plait. At its end was a single leather thong. Slipping it off, he used his fingers to open her braid until her hair fell in smooth waves to past her waist. Gathering her tresses up in his hands, he savored the way the thick strands curled about his wrists and trailed down his arms, then again combed his fingers through her hair. If the gossips were to be believed, then he was only the second man to touch her this way.

She shivered at his play, her eyes opening. Her irises were dark with pleasure, but the tiny crease between her brows said she was coming to her senses. In another moment she'd recognize that what they did was wrong, especially for her. When she did, she would deny him, and herself.

This was one game Michel was no longer willing to lose. Leaning forward, he brushed his mouth against her, again and again, one light caress after another. It taunted them both, stirring his own needs as she gasped lightly and again relaxed against the wall. Her hands came to rest upon his arms, her fingers curling into his shirt-sleeves.

A moment later, and she tried to claim his mouth with hers. When he denied her, retreating just a little, she arched upward, trying to press her body to his. That made Michel smile against her lips. He'd won. She had forgotten all propriety in her need for him.

Stroking his fingers down the curve of her throat, something that teased another shiver from her, he trailed his hand downward until he cupped her breast. She cried out against his mouth. Through both her gowns he felt her nipple harden. Michel caught a sharp breath, then kissed her with all the need that now burned in him.

As Michel's mouth slashed atop hers, Ami lost herself in a storm of pleasure and held on to him for dear life. His clean-shaven cheek was cool against hers. His beard was both rough and soft in one glorious instant. The sweet taste of the wine he'd been drinking yet clung to his lips.

A moment later he tore his mouth from hers to press his lips to her ear, nipping, suckling, teasing. Arching against him in mindless parody of what she so wanted, Ami cried out only to be startled by the echo of her own voice. The mists of delight parted far enough that she could see the goldsmith's hall over Michel's shoulder.

Jesus God, but she was letting the king's mercenary futter her on the goldsmith's landing!

"Quietly, sweet," Michel murmured against her ear, then rubbed his palm over her breast as he again used his teeth to nip at her earlobe.

Even as Ami gasped, a joyous shudder dancing

down her spine, she released Michel to brace her hands upon his shoulders, meaning to push him back from her. This had gone too far already. He left off kissing her ear to press a line of kisses down the curve of her neck. The most marvelous sensation shot through Ami. The strength left her arms.

He moved his free hand from her waist to her hip, then drew her against him. Their thighs touched. All that lay between them were her gowns and his shirt. That wasn't thickness enough to prevent Ami from feeling his shaft against her belly.

Resistance evaporated. His lips had reached her shoulder. She tilted her head, begging him to kiss her nape. When he did, she melted.

She had to feel his skin against hers. Sliding her hands around him, she caught the back of his shirt in her hands and wrenched it up until she could lay her palms against his bare waist. His flesh was warm and smooth against hers. Yet shuddering and gasping at his play, she drew her fingertips up the column of his spine to his shoulders. Then, slowly, she used her palms to map every inch of his back as if claiming the territory as her own.

How could his muscles be so heavy yet his skin be so soft? Again she stroked his back, savoring the sensation against her palms. Both hands descended toward his waist.

Michel straightened to look down into her face. For the moment, his expression was unguarded. The gray of his eyes was warmer, made so by his passion for her.

At his waist she found the cord that held up his

chausses. With a sigh, Ami let her hands drop even farther, until she found the points of his stockings, the narrowed bits of fabric that fastened each leg to the waist cord. There she stopped her hands, letting them rest upon his bare hips.

His eyes closing, Michel leaned forward with a sigh and rested his brow on hers. "Your hands," he breathed in wonder, his voice so low that Ami almost didn't hear him, "there is such possession in your touch."

Then, before she had time to comprehend what he'd said, he reclaimed her mouth with his. This time, his lips moved across hers in deadly earnest as he demanded she yield all to him. All on their own accord, Ami's hips lifted until they pressed to his. When she found that fabric yet stood between her body and what she now needed more than breath itself, she cried out and brought her hands forward around his hips.

Michel gasped against her mouth, his senses afire. After his swift bath this evening, he'd donned only the minimal number of garments needed to be decent. There was nothing between Amicia's searching hands and his shaft.

She found what she sought. As she'd done with his back, she explored his shaft's engorged length with her fingers, tracing it, circling its head, making it hers, until Michel forgot about kissing her and drowned in a sea of sensation. It was intolerable that she could touch his body when he couldn't feel her flesh. He needed her now, stripped bare and sprawled upon his bed.

Amicia closed her fingers around his shaft and

stroked. Pleasure crashed over him, eating up common sense. His bed was too far away.

Bringing his hands to her hips, Michel gathered up the fabric of her gowns until her hems were lifted to her waist. Then, holding them out of the way, he again took her mouth with his as he stroked his free hand across her bare belly.

Her skin felt impossibly soft against his fingers. At his caress, she released his shaft and panted against his lips. He found the curls that covered her nether lips. Then, doing as she had done to him, he slipped a finger between them to explore her, only to groan at the warmth and wetness that he discovered. As his finger entered her, she arched against his caress, flooding his hand with her need.

"Michel—" she pleaded against his lips, only to free another breathless moan as he stroked her again.

Michel needed no more invitation than that. Cupping his hands beneath her hips, he lifted her until he could press himself between her legs, then braced her back against the wall behind her.

Amicia gave a startled squeak at this shift of position. "Nay," she gasped out, catching her hands about his waist as if to push back from him.

Michel's eyes narrowed. She wouldn't refuse him. He was the one she'd chosen. He shifted, his shaft finding the entry to her womb, then made her one with him.

Ami stiffened, overwhelmed by sensations. His body's heat, his smell, his mouth moving on hers, the feel of his legs against hers, the way his fingers dug into her hips, the inferno that was his shaft inside her, it all seemed too much to take at once. She tore her mouth from his and turned her head to one side.

She expected him to force her lips to once more meet his. Instead, he touched his lips to her brow, her cheek, her chin, then nuzzled her ear. At the same time he slid deeper into her. Ami's whole body wept with relief and pleasure. This was what she needed, and nothing had ever been more welcome. All that mattered was that he should move within her and drive them both into joy. Wrapping her arms about his neck, she tightened her legs around his hips. That brought him even more deeply within her.

He groaned softly against her ear, his pleasure feeding her own. When he again moved within her, she arched against him. Ecstasy welled, the promise of ultimate joy close enough that she cried out, straining to achieve what she so desired.

They were so close she could feel his amusement as it rumbled in his chest. The warmth of his quiet laugh filled the cup of her ear. "Hush, else we'll have company," he whispered, his voice strained and hoarse. "Now, kiss me," he commanded and once more thrust into her.

His movement drove her beyond thought. She did as he bid, turning her head to kiss him. Her lips and tongue danced with his as his shaft filled her again and again.

All at once, the pressure in her womb exploded. With a thrust of her own, she held her hips against his. As joy overtook her, her whole body shuddered in completion. Groaning against her mouth, Michel followed where she led, then sent her to a place where nothing but satiation existed.

Adrift on that sea of ecstasy, Ami relaxed against Michel, releasing his mouth to rest her head on his broad shoulder. Her body was alive with the feel of him. She touched her mouth to his neck in a gentle kiss and was rewarded by his swift tremor. Replete, she breathed in his scent and savored the beat of his heart against her own.

She never wanted to move again, nor did she want to exist without this man's arms around her. The fanciful thought of living forever in a man's embrace made her smile. Yet that was exactly what she wanted at this moment.

Nay, what she truly wanted was to make love yet again, this time in the warmth and security of a bed. A moment later he kissed her cheek, then released his hold on her hips. Her legs slid down the length of his, her feet once again returning to the floor. As her hands lowered to rest against his chest, he wrapped his arms around her and drew her into his embrace.

It should have been a soothing caress. Instead, Ami's skirts caught on the wall behind her. The draft from the door at the bottom of the goldsmith's stairs chilled her indecently bared legs almost to her thighs.

The embers of passion died as the reality of what she'd just done hit Ami with all the horror that such perversion deserved. She shrank back from him, only to remember that her hair was unbound. Mortification grew. Not only had she given herself to a man who meant only to debase and impoverish her, she'd done it in a way more unnatural than even her king might concoct. They hadn't even taken off their clothing!

Michel held Amicia close, savoring the way her body fit against his own as if she'd been made for him. Her head reached to just below his cheekbone, the perfect height if she wished to lay her head upon his shoulder. Her waist was at the exact spot for him to comfortably rest his hands.

Yet stunned by the power of their union, he sighed. No other woman, not even the inventive whore in his youth, had ever driven him so deeply into pleasure that he was past all caring. And past caring he had been. Even if the whole of the goldsmith's household had crowded around and demanded that he cease what he did, Michel doubted he would have noticed them.

Amicia stiffened in his embrace. Regret, deep and far too personal for Michel's tastes, shot through him. Her sanity had returned.

As Michel released her, he banished the memory of their shared pleasure to some distant sweet place within him. To cherish the emotions she stirred would render him vulnerable to her in a way that left his nerves on edge. He stepped back.

She watched him, her face pale, her eyes glimmering. Then she turned her head to the side. Her rejection was nothing less than Michel expected and everything he couldn't abide. Gentlewoman that she was, she couldn't bear to look upon the baseborn man to whom she'd given herself just as Eve had given herself to

Adam before the world had distinguished one man a king and another a commoner.

The sting of her rejection grew until brittle emptiness filled him. If his birth was all that mattered to her after what they'd just shared, then it was time he regained his own sanity. All he wanted from his wife was her estates and her gentle blood. Now that he knew Enguerran d'Oilly had stripped her estates of all wealth he could no longer want Lady Amicia de la Beres. On the morrow he'd ride to Windsor to tell the king that he'd thought better of marrying an English heiress. Turning on his heel, Michel climbed the stairs, leaving her behind him without a backward look.

Fifteen minutes of wild, debauched pleasure. That was all her years of well meant denial had been worth. Trembling, Ami kept her head turned until she could no longer hear Michel's footfalls on the stairs.

She couldn't watch him abandon her, even though she'd earned his rejection. The rules of seduction were very clear, and the peril of any woman who played the game of chaste love. The woman who let down her moral barriers and gave herself to the man who chased her rendered herself worthless in his eyes. Once a man's lust was sated, he discarded her and moved on to his next challenge.

Ami closed her eyes, trying to escape within herself. Instead, imprinted on her eyelids was the unwelcome image of Michel as he rested his brow to hers. Her heart twisted. He'd said that there was possession in her touch. There had been. She wanted to own him.

In that instant, the image shifted until it was one of Michel lying atop her, the homely curtains of her bed closed around them. Her eyes flew open and she cursed herself as a fool. He had rejected her without a word, and still she wanted him in her bed? Why, on the morrow he'd surely brag to every man he knew about taking the chaste Lady de la Beres.

God help her, but Roheise seemed to have eyes everywhere. If Michel spoke to even one man, the noblewoman would soon know it, then leap to cheat Michel of his life. Again, Ami's heart twisted.

Right or wrong, possible or impossible, she didn't want Michel dead. Nay, she wanted him in her bed, in her body, and at her side in life. Ami's head bowed as she understood herself.

The game was over. Michel had turned the table on her. Rather than bind him to her with his affections, Ami was the one leashed by her heartstrings.

Leaning down, she snatched up her forgotten scarf and gathered up her hair. Her fingers shook so badly that the resulting braid was misshapen and loose, and she couldn't find the thong. Tying on her scarf, she retreated down the stairs and donned her mantle, pinning it so her plait and gowns were completely hidden beneath it, then returned to the hall.

"Maud, it's time to leave."

At her call, the kitchen door flew wide. Mistress Hughette thrust her head out of the opening so swiftly that it suggested she'd been standing right next to the portal, as if waiting for Ami's call. She frowned when she saw the hall was empty and Ami was already wearing her mantle.

"Well then, you'll be needing a man to see you safely back," the woman said, sounding disappointed. She retreated into the kitchen, leaving the door open behind her.

A breath of stew-scented air flowed into the quiet hall, bringing with it the sounds of folk at their meat. This was spiced by snatches of gentle conversation and the occasional trill of warm laughter. Another time, the sounds would have been welcoming, comfortable sounds, but with Ami's life turned on her head, it seemed as alien as a foreign language.

"Maud?" Ami called out again, cringing as she heard the pleading edge to her voice.

"I come," Maud called, but still the maid didn't appear. Instead, Ami swore she heard Maud's giggle. A man's baritone laugh followed, the sound of his amusement low and intimate. A moment later Maud fair danced into the room, a brilliant smile on her face.

That Maud might have so enjoyed herself after deserting her mistress to debauchery should have awakened Ami's outrage. Instead, the energy it took to manufacture anger seemed miles beyond Ami's reach. Leaving her maid to follow, she retreated back toward the hall's door and stairs. As Ami crossed the landing, she averted her gaze, incapable of looking upon the place of her downfall.

Once in the street, with two of the goldsmith's journeymen as their escort, Ami hunched her shoulders against the cold and wet, and started up High Street for the castle. Beside her, Maud chattered happily, something about flavorings for stews. Ami heard not a word.

As they reached the walls of the castle, Maud's prattling ceased so abruptly that it jostled Ami out of her despair. They were where the land began its gentle upward slope into the castle's gateway. It was already full dark. Thus, the castle's massive main gate doors should have been shut and barred. Instead, one still stood wide. Torchlight streamed through that opening along with the sounds of shouting men and neighing horses when there should only have been the dark and the quiet of folk at their rest.

"What's happening?" Maud asked, more to herself than in expectation of any answer.

An instant later a man raced from the gateway and down the slope toward them. Ami recognized him as one of the castle's cooks. A purse dangled from his fist as he ran.

"What is it?" Maud cried out as he drew near them.

"The king," the cook panted out, his voice fading as he passed them. "He has returned without warning."

Ami's heart sank even deeper. Just when she'd thought life couldn't get any more horrible, it did. How long would it be before Michel told his patron and king about her? Once Michel did, it wouldn't be long before John made good on his threat to play another game with his ward.

Home. The image of her warm manor house awoke to call to Ami, promising welcome, isolation, and acceptance. That's where she needed to be. Once she was home, she would be safe, at least for a little while, from handsome and irresistible mercenaries, devious and betraying noblewomen, and a debauched monarch.

Chapter 18

Ami awoke the next morning, her head pounding and Michel's lingering scent still filling her lungs. Her need to go home hadn't receded any, but release from the king's custody meant another audience with John. Her monarch's promise to continue their game stood like an armed knight between Ami and that audience.

A few feet from her, Maud, already dressed for the day, leaned over her mistress's chest. Rubbing at her temples, Ami sat up and squinted into the darkness that yet held the hall in its grip. Outside the wind moaned around the corners of the hall and rapped imperiously at the closed shutters. It wasn't noise enough to drown out Maud's humming.

Ami's eyes widened. Maud was singing that lewd ditty they'd heard whistled on Winchester's streets last night. Shocked, she shifted on her pallet to look at her maid.

"Maud!" Ami kept her protest quiet as a goodly number of the women in this room yet slept.

Maud straightened with a start. "Pardon, my lady, I didn't know you were awake," she whispered, the hint of a smile clinging to her lips.

"I cannot believe what I hear you humming," Ami chided, managing to manufacture a little of the harshness that such behavior deserved. "That's hardly appropriate fare for your lips."

It wasn't dark in the hall enough to hide the way Maud's skin darkened at this. "Pardon. I didn't realize I was humming. As for the song, the tune's caught in my head. Someone in Mistress Hughette's kitchen sang it last night."

"What sort of housewife allows her folk to voice such filth among mixed company," Ami grumbled, not because she believed the song as bad as that, but to aim a belated and impotent blow at Mistress Hughette for her complicity in Ami's downfall.

"Oh, but Mistress Hughette didn't allow it. She demanded that he stop, then threatened to box his ears when he didn't." Maud giggled at this memory, her face softening.

It wasn't amusement over the incident that Ami saw in the maid's reaction, but affection for the singer of that song. That brought Ami the recall of Maud's intensity last night as she'd listened to those behind Mistress Hughette's kitchen door. As Ami recognized what it meant, disbelief shot through her.

"You deserted me last night to spend time with a man?" Ami cried, only to bite her tongue after the words were out. Roheise had ears everywhere, but especially in this room. The less said about last night, the better.

All the pleasure drained from Maud's face, leaving Ami staring at the hollow, frightened girl who'd come with her into the king's custody. The change was dramatic enough that Ami was almost sorry she'd spoken. Almost, that was, until the taunting memory returned of Michel making love to her while afoot and with her skirts above her hips.

"You shouldn't have left me," Ami complained softly, pressing her fists to her forehead. If Maud had stayed in the goldsmith's hall last night, then she would never have kissed Michel. Without that kiss Ami would still own her virtue and her pride.

And some modicum of Michel's respect. Ami crushed that thought. He had abandoned her. Why should she care whom such a man respected?

"My lady, I'm so sorry," Maud whispered, her head bowing. "You're right. I shouldn't have left you. Fie on me."

Ami sighed. For years, she'd encouraged her maid to find a little joy in life, only to complain when Maud finally did as she urged. If only Maud's timing hadn't been so awful. Awful or not, nothing changed the fact that Ami had enjoyed that perverse joining as much as the lyrics of Maud's song suggested it should be enjoyed. Worse, the longing woke for more of what she'd experienced last night, then refused to die. Between the king's game and meeting Michel again, encountering Michel was the more frightening.

Ami looked up at her maid. "Maud, I want a bath this morn, and you must lay out all of my very best. I'm going to request an audience with the king, now that he is returned. I want to return home for the holidays."

"Home?" The word exploded past Maud's lips. "Oh, my lady, you wouldn't be asking for release from court on my account, would you? If so, do not, since nothing I've done warrants it. You mustn't coddle me this way. Really, I'm content to stay, knowing how much you enjoy the festivities the king stages for the Christmas court. Think of the dancing." This last was almost a plea.

If Ami hadn't been so desperate to leave, Maud's turnaround, and her affection for the man who caused it, might have been amusing. Instead, she slanted a narrow-eyed look at her maid. "How good of you to sacrifice so on my behalf."

Maud wasn't looking at her, but the body of the hall. "My lady, the porter comes this way," she hissed.

Startled, Ami turned to look. Walter was picking his way in their direction through the yet sleeping women, something Ami couldn't remember him ever doing before this very morn. As a man Walter kept to his post, entering the hall only to dine. If he needed to contact any of the wards, he called for a maid to bring the message. Only there were scarce few maids up and about yet this morn.

Maud was right. He was coming to their corner. Ami frantically drew her bedclothes around her until she and her loosened hair were decently covered.

"Pardon the intrusion, my lady," the porter said, his

gaze aimed at the wall behind Ami rather than at her, "but the king commands you into his presence, wanting you to come to him this instant and alone, as you did the last time."

Ami froze in horror. Michel had already shared the tale of her perversity with his royal master! Now John wanted a taste of what she'd given Michel.

Walter's eyes flickered toward her, then back to the wall. He cleared his throat. "For the sake of your kindness to me, my lady, I feel I must warn you. Our king called for you upon his arrival last night. His chamberlain was none too pleased to learn that you'd gone into town to tend Lady Roheise. I offered to send a man to fetch you, but Master Chamberlain said it would take too long and the matter was better saved until this morning."

Relief washed over Ami like a flood. John didn't know what had happened with Michel, not if he'd called for her last night. He couldn't know. John had arrived about the same time that she and Michel were sharing that godforsaken landing.

Relief ebbed, leaving the specter of treason behind it. John knew she'd been to see Roheise. If the king had so much as an inkling of the noblewoman's plot to justify rebellion, and Ami's seeming participation in it, Ami could well lose her life. Once again, the game table shifted, only this time Ami faced a far more deadly opponent than Michel.

"It's just as well you didn't send for us," Maud said, with a nervous giggle. "We weren't at the draper's."

Ami's heart dropped. New curiosity stirred upon

Walter's broad face. Ami shot Maud a disbelieving glare. The maid's expression flattened as she realized her error.

"I mean, we weren't at the draper's for long," she corrected, wringing her hands.

Ami pasted on a smile and shifted to look up at Walter. "Maud's right. We didn't stay long at the draper's. You were away from the door when we returned, Walter. Would that I'd known about the king's call last night."

That was laughable. If Ami had known John was looking for her, she wouldn't have slept a wink. As it was, her torment over what she'd done with Michel had allowed her only two winks.

"Pardon, my lady, but our king arrived without a word of warning. That left the stablemaster short-handed and Sir Hubert asked me to assist with the horses." Curiosity lingered in Walter's face, something that didn't bode well for Ami's secrets.

"When does His Majesty expect me?" Ami demanded.

"I'd say the sooner the better for you, my lady. Take care and wear your heaviest mantle this morn. What was merely foul weather last night is a gale now." Then, with a blank nod in her direction, he retreated to his post.

Ami shifted on her pallet to again look at Maud. The maid's hands were folded and held against her heart as if she prayed. She looked sick.

"I'm sorry, my lady," Maud moaned quietly, then her face twisted. "Oh, my poor, poor lady," she cried, as if John had already ordered Ami's execution.

That restored the steel to Ami's spine. Never mind that she'd put herself in this position. She was sick of so many people all striving to use her as a pawn, even if it destroyed her. She'd find a way to defy them all.

"That's quite enough, Maud," she said and came to her feet. "Fetch warm water and be swift about it. No matter how badly our king wants to see me, he'll have to wait until I'm properly dressed and washed."

For the second time in a month Ami found herself in the antechamber that led to the king's bedchamber. Since there was no use trying to hide from John's lusts, Ami hadn't stinted in her attire, wearing instead every bit of wealth she owned, even that accursed band upon her sheer veil.

The band was a matter of practicality. With no hood upon her mantle, she'd needed it to hold her veil on her head this morn. Walter was right. Although it wasn't far between the king's and queen's hall, the wind had nearly blown her over as she made the passage. The day promised to work itself into a right fine gale.

"Master Chamberlain," Ami said, offering a curtsy to the cleric whose chore it was to arrange the schedule of England's monarch.

Dressed in a bright blue tunic trimmed with silver, the golden chain that signified his position crossing his narrow chest, the chamberlain's bald pate gleamed like alabaster in the antechamber's low light. As he saw her, his broad face wreathed in a smile, he bowed a little as if she were one of the king's more frequent and favored visitors—or would become one of the king's more frequent and favored visitors.

"Ah, here you are at last, Lady de la Beres. If you wouldn't mind?" He extended a hand toward the balcony Ami had just passed to enter the antechamber. "For your sake and his, his Highness wishes to keep your meeting with him private and he is presently attended. If you'll step into the alcove until the others have departed?"

That sent a bolt of worry through Ami, for she could think of but one reason for such privacy. "Can you tell me why our liege asks to see me?" The words were out before she could stop them. More than anything she wanted to go into the king's presence at least a little prepared for the fate that awaited her.

The man's bushy brows rose high upon his hairless forehead. The welcome died from his dark eyes. Although he surely knew most of the reasons behind John's meetings, retaining his position meant keeping a strict hold on his tongue when it came to the king's business and intent.

"Perhaps it is because Sir Enguerran d'Oilly has agreed to my bride price?" Ami prompted, holding on to the hope that this private meeting had the same purpose as the last, even though the thought that Sir Enguerran had managed to raise the fee John required made her stomach turn. Marrying her neighbor was no more attractive a fate than becoming the king's whore or being accused of treason with Roheise.

The chamberlain's face took on the blankness given

to those accustomed to keeping other men's secrets. "If you'll step into the alcove, my lady?" This wasn't a request, but a command.

Cursing herself for alienating a potential ally, Ami did as she was bid. She pulled the antechamber's outer door open until it stood across the front of the alcove, as it had when she and Michel had their tête-à-tête here. That wasn't shield enough. Ami shifted to the farthest corner of the tiny cubicle so the men leaving John's chamber couldn't see her, not even a glimpse through the little gap between the door and the balcony's wall.

Trapped in this dark little nook, she had nothing to do but stew in the possibilities. The image woke of herself standing before the church door with Sir Enguerran, only to mutate until it was Michel at her side. Ami blinked away the vision.

A moment later, the inner chamber's door opened. Men muttered, then the thud of bootheels rang on the balcony. There were at least three men, armed, judging by the jangle of mail and clank of empty scabbards against metal-clad legs. One man raised his voice enough that Ami heard him tell his companions that the day promised to be miserable, especially for such a long ride.

When they were well down the stairs, Ami exited the alcove, then swept through the antechamber, her head held high. The chamberlain opened the door to the king's bedchamber, then closed it after Ami entered.

Coals again glowed in the brazier's pan, but that didn't stop Ami's breath from clouding in the air before her. With the wind thrusting icy fingers through the cracks in the shutters, the draft was so bad that little heat stayed. Dozens of candles stood around the room. Although their flames fluttered and danced, the light was strong enough to force the shadows into soft piles in the corners. The dimness clung like cobwebs to the folds of the royal bedcurtains.

This time there was no servant and no game board, only John seated in his high-backed chair, the one from the hall. The king's legs were stretched out before him in a casual pose. His elbows were braced upon the arms of the chair, his beringed fingers steepled before his chin. There was nothing to read in his dark eyes as he watched her.

He looked far more regal today. Beneath a scarlet mantle, he wore one of his finest tunics, a garment made of blue and red velvet with the insignia of the Plantagenets embroidered with precious threads onto its breast. His belt was studded with pearls, the golden chain draped across his chest set with rubies. Resting upon his brow was his crown, the flickering light teasing colored fire from the massive jewels that decorated it.

At least such formal attire sent the possibility of bedplay to the bottom of Ami's list of horrible fates. Unfortunately, it advanced the potential of a charge of treason. Ami dropped into a deep curtsy before him, but refused to kneel. Such a pose felt too much like pleading, something she couldn't bring herself to do, not after her last audience, even if refusal cost her her life.

"Sire, I come as you have called."

"So you have, albeit many hours later than I would

have liked," John replied, his voice as neutral as his gaze.

"Sire?" Ami asked, pretending ignorance over last night's attempt to find her.

John's eyes narrowed just a little as he studied her. "I was amazed to learn that you attended Roheise de Say last night. I wouldn't have thought you the sort of woman to tolerate so arrogant a bitch."

His words felt like the opening move in a game of chess when Ami was heartily sick of game-playing. It was time for honesty, or at least the pretense of honesty.

"I didn't tolerate her, sire. She called for me, claiming illness, but when I reached the draper's house I found she wasn't as ill as had been suggested. At that point I refused to attend her."

A little of the blankness receded from John's eyes. The corners of his mouth quirked. He dropped his hands to his lap. "There's that fire of yours again," he said. "I cannot tell you how much I admire that in you. What say you that we put it to the test. I think it's time we play our next game, you and I."

Ami crossed her arms. It was the worst possibility, but at least she was prepared for it. "Once again, I must protest that I am no worthy opponent for you, sire. You would be better to choose a countess."

John's smile was slow and pleased, then darkened into something akin to a leer. "How you underestimate yourself, my lady. And me. Haven't I watched you strive these last weeks to repay my mercenary for the insults I goaded him into making? Dear Amicia, I was shocked at how you laid in wait for him, making certain that he saw only you at every turn. What I couldn't fathom was what you hoped to achieve by your efforts. Care to explain your goal to me?"

Ami stiffened as John used her given name, for it promised coming intimacy. That he watched her so closely suggested he used her in some greater game, one he was playing with Michel. Because she didn't know the purpose to this other game, she couldn't afford to dissemble.

"I wasn't trying to repay insults, but to fix his affections on me, sire," she replied, taking care with her words. John didn't like hearing that others thought of his mercenaries as unprincipled thieves. "I thought that if Sir Michel invested his heart in me, he might take better care of my properties."

John straightened in his chair at this, still smiling. "What diplomacy, my lady," he congratulated her. "Your efforts might have worked if you'd tried them on any man save Michel de Martigny. That Frenchman is damned cold-blooded, incapable of pleasing a woman. I doubt he'll ever satisfy you."

His words were a sword's thrust through Ami's chest. Michel had satisfied her all too well. As shame over last night faded, surprise welled. "What do you mean, satisfy me?" she demanded.

"In a moment, my lady," John replied, leaning over one arm of his chair. There, at its foot, stood several folds of parchment. He picked up the topmost skin, then straightened, turning the missive in his hands.

Candlelight caught on the thick red circle of wax that closed the parchment. He looked at her from over the top of the letter, his eyes now alive with enjoyment.

"Pardon me, my lady, but I've gotten ahead of myself with this other discussion of ours. We must needs return to the rules of this new game. I devised it just for you, believing you might play more aggressively in a competition a little more meaningful than backgammon. Before you begin, however, you'll have to prepare for a journey."

Ami only frowned at her king. "And where might I be going on so wet and windy a day as this one?"

Creases marked John's cheeks as he smiled at her, the turn of his lips apologetic. "Aye, it's a pity about the weather. Know that I hadn't expected it to be such a miserable day when I conceived this game of ours. If I could, I'd hold off, but all the players are gathered. It's too late to delay now. As for where you're going, it's Thame Abbey in Oxfordshire. Do you know the place?"

She nodded, confused. The king was the abbey's patron; she and the other wards had made a number of embroideries for its sanctuary. She'd actually visited the place during her first year of royal custody. On a mild summer day with the ground springy with rain, it could take at least a full day to reach the abbey from Winchester, moving at the pace that the king's court set, which was a walk. To reach it in a day in this sort of weather, she'd have to ride far faster.

"For your safety, you'll travel with a royal escort,"

John was saying. "You'll take this message," he held out the parchment toward her, "and give it to the abbot upon your arrival at the abbey."

Ami stayed where she stood, her arms crossed and her lips pursed. When he realized she wasn't coming to fetch the missive, John let his hand return to his lap.

Ami cocked her head to one side. "Dare I admit, sire, that I don't much like the sound of your game? Why not choose something warmer? Chess, perhaps?"

"How can you refuse when you don't yet know what participation in it might win you?" John protested, coming to his feet. "Don't worry, my lady. Unlike you, I'm not going to be miserly about confessing all my reasons for what I do and what I hope to accomplish."

Crossing the room, he stopped in front of her, closer than was appropriate between a man and woman who weren't relatives, or married. Ami was surprised to realize that the king was only a little taller than she and not nearly as powerfully built as Michel. Somehow, he'd always seemed larger and more menacing.

Nor did his nearness set her nerves on edge as it had in her last audience. But then two weeks ago she'd still owned something worthy of protecting from him. Now that she'd spent her pride on Michel and been rejected, nothing mattered. There was an odd sort of freedom in knowing that nothing John did could hurt her as deeply as Michel had, unless the king took her against her will. For reasons Ami couldn't name, she was certain that rape wasn't what John wanted between them. Raising a brow, she waited for his next move.

Again he smiled. "Fie on you, my lady. You really do abuse my majesty most heinously. It's fortunate for you that I am a forgiving man."

The corner of Ami's mouth lifted. "Sire, you may forgive, but I somehow doubt that you forget. I'll wager you hoard what others do, in case the opportunity to use it against them might arise."

England's king threw back his head and laughed at that, the sound of his laughter ringing against the beams that crossed the ceiling. Still grinning, he looked at her. "Sweet Jesu, but you are a wonder. I like you better and better. It's a shame that your boldness doesn't bode well for the other players in this game."

That caught Ami's attention. Still smiling, the king started to tuck the parchment between Ami's folded arms and her chest. The back of his hand almost brushed her breast. Ami snatched open her arms and stepped back to take the parchment from him.

"Pardon," John said, holding up his hand as if to claim innocence. "Have a care with that missive. If the seal is broken or even damaged, the abbot is commanded to disregard the message within it."

Ami studied the sheepskin in her hands. The abbot's name was penned across its front. Tension knotted in her neck as she recognized the handwriting as the same as that note she'd received after the feast, the one warning her of Michel's appointment as guardian of the wards. But why would John warn her of that?

"So, sire, what happens after I reach Thame Abbey?" she asked, keeping her other question to herself.

"That all depends on how you arrive at the abbey, my lady. If you are yet in the company of my escort, then you may present this message to the abbot. When he breaks the seal, he'll find my dowry contract for you, transferring your properties to him and permitting you to join the sisters attached to his abbey."

Ami gaped. "But, sire, I have no calling for the religious life."

"Then, it's fortunate for you that this is but one possible ending to my game," John said, that smile of his again flitting across his well-made mouth. "Right now, or at any point along your journey, you may decide to refuse holy orders. In which case your escort is commanded to return you to me where you will join me in my bed."

As he spoke, John raised his hand to touch a finger to the curve of Ami's cheek. Before she thought, she jerked her face away from his caress. John's eyes glinted, not in anger, but amusement.

"Think about it a little before you refuse, Amicia." His voice lowered into the realm of intimacy. "Between us there can only be pleasure. Nor is having a king in your bed such a hardship. Loving me can make your life easier. You can leave court. You can live in your home, managing your life as you see fit, save for those times when I have need of you."

As much as Ami wanted to return home, she wasn't ready to turn her back on all pride. John might be capable of wringing pleasure from her body, but it wouldn't be enough to drive her beyond caring that a whore was a whore, even if it was the king in her bed. Why was it so easy to reject a king and so impossible to refuse Michel, who wasn't even a gentleman? Ami sighed, feeling the knot Michel made in her heartstrings tighten.

"Sire, yours is a tempting offer, but my heart and conscience won't allow it of me," she said, forgoing all artifice to offer him the truth.

Disappointment flashed through John's gaze, but once it was gone, respect darkened his eyes. "I could command it of you," he whispered.

"You won't," Ami returned, her voice almost as low as his.

It was John's turn to sigh, this time in defeat. He stepped back from her until there was a decent distance between them. All hint of desire left his expression.

"Well, if you won't have God and you won't have me, there is another choice. You may marry."

Dismay shot through Ami. "Sir Enguerran?" she demanded.

The corner of John's mouth lifted as he returned to his game, both the one he'd plotted for Ami and the one he played in this room. "He's one candidate. Just to make the game interesting, I decided you needed a second choice. If Sir Enguerran doesn't please you, several weeks ago, before we arrived at Winchester I believe, Sir Michel de Martigny suggested to me that you might make him a respectable wife."

All the breath left Ami's lungs. In that instant the whole of the king's game became clear to her—from that first horrid interview, to her inflated bride price, to Michel being named as administrator of her estates, and finally to that note. John had always intended Michel to be her husband.

And Michel had known that. He'd known when he'd toyed with her senses in the alcove, and on her first visit to the goldsmith. He'd known when he'd dragged her around the hall's stairway to kiss her. And he'd known on that god-bedamned landing when he'd taken her.

A new image formed, that of Mistress Hughette, her smug smile and her eagerness to leave them alone last night. It was a matchmaker's look. Jesus God, but Michel must have told the smith's wife that they were to be wed after Ami's first visit! After he'd done all that, how could that bitch's son turn his back on her and leave her on that landing to torment herself with shame? He knew they were be to wed!

"No, I won't have him!" The words erupted from Ami's mouth.

John tsked, then grinned as if her refusal pleased him well, indeed. "If you intend to say that every time I mention a potential mate, my lady, you'll have to re-consider your first two options."

Ami took a backward step, her eyes narrowed. "I won't play this game, sire. It's wrong to toy so with my life."

"Your objection is noted, my lady," John replied with a shrug. "However, as I said earlier, it's already too late to retreat. If you wish to blame someone for that, blame Sir Michel. He set the game in motion three days ago when he departed Winchester without my leave. The sands are now slipping through the hourglass, as it were. You need to make haste in your preparations for travel, as your escort will come to fetch you from the queen's hall in but a quarter hour."

"It will take me longer than that to pack," Ami cried, protesting more to stall than because it would take any time to pack. She didn't have that much in the way of possessions. "I'll need to find a heavier cloak for my maid to wear."

John shook his head. "Not your maid, my lady. You go on this journey alone."

"But, sire, no decent woman rides without a companion among a troop of soliders," Ami protested, truly shocked.

"Thus, this privacy," the sweep of John's hand indicated his empty chamber. "No one will know, not even after you've completed your ride at the abbey, since whatever choice you make resolves any mark on your repute. Choose God and no one will care. Choose me and, well, folk will whisper, but you won't care. Choose one of your two potential husbands, and all you'll be is married." He offered her a quick smile and lift of his brows, then continued.

"Now, pay heed, my lady. In just an hour's time, your potential husbands will be sent from Winchester with instructions to capture you," John continued. "In order for one of them to make you his wife, he must arrive at Thame with you in his possession. Of course, if you prefer one man over the other, all you need do is re-main here at Winchester and offer yourself to him once he leaves my presence. Do you prefer one of them?" It was a sly question.

"Nay," Ami snapped.

This couldn't be happening to her. Home. She wanted to go home. She would go home. Once on the road, she'd turn her horse toward her end of Sussex and be done with her mad king. Crossing her arms, she lifted her chin. "I won't do this, sire."

John only smiled again. "Abdicate this game, and your royal escort is instructed to abandon you to the dangers of the road."

"Sire!" Ami cried in protest. "You wouldn't."

"Oh, but I would. Think on it, my lady. Can death, or your rape, truly be preferable to marriage, or to my bed? How can it be when I am your heir? Remember, your death makes all that was yours mine."

Once again, John raised a hand to trace a finger down the curve of Ami's cheek. This time, she allowed it without resisting. Consideration filled his face.

"Don't let me win unscathed, Amicia," his tone low-ering again until he spoke to her as a man speaks to a woman he desires. "Make me pay some price for what I do to you. Let revenge against me motivate you."

"I don't want revenge, sire, and I don't want to marry, not right now," Ami pleaded, with no hope that her king would show mercy.

John touched a silencing finger to her lips. "As you so wisely told me, Amicia, you are mine to do with as I please," he said, his hand dropping to his side. "Now, go, remembering that no matter what you and I have said here between us, I still hope you arrive at Thame, before your potential husbands, and that you choose me."

Chapter 19

"**S**ir Michel?"

Michel stirred upon the goldsmith's bed. The brittle emptiness of Amicia's rejection yet held court within him. It had kept him from his rest most of the night. Damn her. Was she so pompous that she could reject him when he was the only man she wanted? Damn him. He could no more afford to care what she thought of him or his birth than he could afford to marry her.

Rolling onto his side, he thrust open the bedcurtains. The thick gray of a stormy dawn held sway in this sleeping chamber. Outside the house, the wind howled.

One of the smith's apprentices stood at the bed's side. The child wore only his shirt, his legs but scrawny sticks beneath the oversized garment's voluminous hem. That the boy had only just now arisen from his pallet was proved by the way the birds still nested in his hair.

"What is it, boy?" Michel asked, speaking slowly. Some of the younger lads in the household hadn't yet mastered the French tongue.

"I hope you don't mind my coming to you, instead of the mistress, but she's not yet dressed. There's was a messenger, sir. His Majesty commands you into his presence upon the hour of Terce." Even in Winchester, which saw a great deal of England's monarch, a call to attend the king had the power to make the boy's eyes widen.

Michel bit back another curse. If John had returned to Winchester today, then the king must have received news of Michel's absence at Windsor on the very day Michel had departed for Amicia's properties. And now John wanted to extract his price for Michel's defiance.

The question was whether to tolerate the king's punishment, or leave for greener pastures now that his attempt to find himself an English wife was at an end. Only, he wasn't ready to leave England. Not wanting to examine too closely why he didn't want to leave, Michel swung his legs over the bed's side in preparation for rising.

"My thanks, lad. Will you tell your mistress that I and my troop must begin our morning sooner than usual?"

The child nodded, then picked his way through Michel's still sleeping men to retreat down the stairs. For a moment, Michel stared out into this, the upper chamber of the smith's house. It was here, in a chamber almost as large as the hall, that Master Robert, his wife, and their maids usually slept, while the house's journeymen and apprentices slept in the hall below. The smith and his mate used this bed, while the maids laid out pallets on the floor. For the time that Michel rented their chamber and this bed, the whole household slept in the hall.

Coming to his feet, he stepped over a yet snoring Roger to retrieve his shirt and chausses from where they hung on one of the bed's posts. When he'd dressed, save for the cross garters on his calves, he tapped his captain with a toe.

Roger snorted, his eyes flying open. "What?" he gasped out, then blinked and squinted up at Michel. "Sir?"

"The king has returned to Winchester and I'm to see him in an hour," Michel said, retreating to the bed to wind the garters onto his legs. He kept his voice low as he spoke; there was no need to share the news with all his men.

"Christus, he heard you left Winchester," Roger breathed, sitting up, then shaking his head. "I pray this won't be a costly meeting for you, sir."

The corner of Michel's mouth tightened, not in response to the question of whether John might wreak some sort of vengeance on him—that was a given—but in irritation. Kings and noblemen were by their very nature capricious creatures. It annoyed Michel to no end that he couldn't begin to guess what price John meant to extract from him, or how far Michel might have to travel to escape it, if it was excessively capricious.

"Rouse the men," he commanded Roger. "I want everyone up and armed before Terce, when I must leave. Pack everything, saving out my armor and underarmor. It's possible we may be leaving the king's service before day's end and I won't ride in my shirt-sleeves."

"Aye, sir," Roger said.

Directly upon the hour of Terce, Michel left Roger, his troop, and his water-stained cloak in the king's hall, and made his way up the stairs to the balcony that fronted the royal bedchamber. Unlike Michel's last audience, when John commanded there be no delay between Michel's arrival with Sir Enguerran and their appearance, this time Michel had dressed as befitted a knight granted a private audience with his king. It was his gray satin court tunic, the one trimmed in silver, that he wore. The garment wasn't as fine as he could afford, however it was suitable to his rank. At his waist was a supple leather belt, its tip encased in silver filigree. His only weapon was a small dagger in a silver scabbard. John was a cautious king and didn't tolerate armed men in his presence.

As Michel reached the top step, he glanced down the balcony's length. The antechamber's door was closed. That meant he could see into the alcove at the end of the balcony. Standing in that alcove was Sir Enguerran d'Oilly.

The man who had bankrupted Amicia's estates was smiling to himself as he waited to see the king, his stance relaxed as if he hadn't a care in the world. Like Michel, he had also donned finery, in his case a tunic of tawny velvet trimmed in golden embroidery; his chausses were a deep yellow, while his cap was scarlet.

The wealth on d'Oilly's back had been purchased with Amicia's stolen goods.

The portrait of an upstanding and well-to-do knight was marred. Sir Enguerran's tunic's right sleeve had been removed from the garment's body. Covered in only his loose shirt sleeve, Sir Enguerran's right arm was supported across his chest by a sling of undyed linen.

If Michel had ever had a doubt who his attacker of two nights ago had been, here was proof. He clenched the fingers of his right hand, again feeling the snap of his opponent's bone under his sword's blow. It was sheer luck on Sir Enguerran's part that he still had an arm; he'd already been twisting away from Michel as he took the blow. Except for that twist, Michel would have cleaved Enguerran's arm from his body instead of straining his own wrist.

The injury had ended their skirmish, for the meeting of their forces hadn't lasted long enough to be called a battle. Michel had let them escape unimpeded, and the troop had disappeared into the darkness just as swiftly as they'd come.

As Michel stepped onto the balcony, his footsteps ringing on the suspended wooden corridor, Sir Enguerran turned to see who came. The man's face, already pale against his injury, blanched further. He shifted deeper into the alcove, then as Michel drew near, turned to show the mercenary his shoulder. The insult had no sting, not when they both knew who the better man was. Paying d'Oilly no heed, Michel opened the antechamber door.

"Ah, Sir Michel," the chamberlain said, his gaze not quite meeting Michel's as he spoke. Bernard of London didn't approve of his king's mercenaries. "The king awaits you. You must come as well, Sir Enguerran," the cleric called out, motioning to the knight in the alcove. "His majesty intends to see you both at once."

Not waiting for the chamberlain to make the presentation—there was no point when John was already infuriated—Michel stepped into the king's bedchamber, leaving d'Oilly to follow. John stood before his tall chair, wearing formal courtly attire, even to his crown upon his head. That John might meet them dressed thusly could have given Michel pause, save for what lay in the bed at the back of the room. Or rather, who.

Ensconced in the bolsters was a plump lass. Having fetched her a time or two on John's behalf, Michel knew her as the daughter of one of Winchester's wool merchants. The man had been happy to trade his child's virginity for the modicum of royal favor that having his lass in the king's bed bought him. As far as Michel knew, the girl was no less delighted to be futtered by royalty. As for John, that he had a woman waiting for him in his bed said he didn't want to give way to rage. Instead, he'd temper his fury during this interview, and afterward spend what it cost him to do so in her body.

Thoughts of futtering dropped Michel right back onto the landing in the goldsmith's house. The memory of holding Amicia in that most interesting position and filling her with his seed returned with enough power that his shaft reacted. Before Michel could stop himself, the longing to once again meld his body with hers shot through him.

He resisted with every ounce of his will, for what he wanted wasn't a quick tumble but permanence. Amicia could never be his wife, and not just because she was impoverished. Marrying her meant giving up his mercenary life and the coins and wealth in spoils it earned him. Once he traded his oath of loyalty to John for her estates he was bound, body and soul to England. At the same time, rebuilding her estates would consume every coin he might earn through those financial ventures with his father and his brother for years to come, without offering an iota of revenue. Rather than advance himself and his potential children, Michel might find himself in the same position as his grandsire, needing to sell a daughter to a rich merchant in order to meet his obligations.

"Why, Sir Enguerran," John called out, offering Michel no greeting as he looked past his mercenary to his sworn liege man. "You're injured. Come forward, sir."

As Sir Enguerran made his way across the king's chamber, John turned toward the bed. "Bertha, love, pull the bedclothes over your head and go to sleep for a little."

"Aye, sire," the lass called, then burrowed under the blankets.

John shifted back toward his visitors in time to find Sir Enguerran struggling to kneel. The king waved his knight back to his feet. "Nay, we'll not ask that of an injured man. How came you by it? Pray tell us the tale," he commanded, playing the role of congenial, concerned monarch for the moment.

Michel thought it impossible for the man to pale any further, but Sir Enguerran's face grayed until he looked like death itself. The knight's gaze started to shift toward Michel, then he caught himself. Michel almost smiled. So, Enguerran d'Oilly shook in his boots, fearing that he was about to be named a thief before the prince he had defrauded.

Too bad for Sir Enguerran that he wasn't bright enough to realize a public accusation was impossible. No one at court would believe that Sir Enguerran had done the pilfering, not when Amicia's properties had been in the hands of one of the king's mercenaries, albeit for only two weeks. The rumors would claim that the king accused a good and true Englishman to disguise his mercenary's greed. Instead, Sir Enguerran came here desperate for some way to save himself.

D'Oilly's smile trembled on his lips. "My thanks for your kindness, sire. It's only a break. I was thrown from a colt."

"Ah, dangerous creatures, horses. Twice, we have almost been trampled, once while our brother Geoffrey was in the saddle," John replied, tugging thoughtfully at his bearded chin. "We're glad to hear you're not disabled. We've had news of armed men riding abroad at night in your area, attacking innocent travelers."

Sir Enguerran's expression flattened as he once more faced the potential of his crime's exposure.

Michel shot a swift look at John. Outside of Michel's own troop, the only other men who knew of that attack were those riding with Sir Enguerran and the bailiff at Amicia's nearest manor house. Since it wasn't likely that John had Sir Enguerran's men in his purse, that left only Amicia's bailiff.

Here was proof that John knew his ward was impoverished. If the bailiff was a royal spy, then John had to know the state of Amicia's properties. The iciness that had held Michel in captive since last night melted under new anger's heat. Just as he thought. John had been trying to cheat him from the first.

"Well then, given your injury, we must thank you for making the ride here on such short notice," John was saying to Sir Enguerran, his tone nought but pleasant.

Believing himself safe for the now, the fool knight ate up his monarch's bait like a hawk taking a lure. "How could I not come, sire, when your messenger arrived last night saying that you'd rescinded your bride price for Lady de la Beres. Sire, I cannot thank you enough for your generosity. The first amount was well beyond the limits of my purse."

So that's how D'Oilly thought to escape punishment for his wrongs. He meant to marry his victim. As his wife Amicia couldn't complain over what he did with her property.

The image of Amicia coupling with d'Oilly exploded within Michel. Every muscle in his body tensed in rejection. He was the one she had chosen. Only she had refused him. Michel forced the lewd image from his mind.

"Would that it were that simple, Sir Enguerran." As John spoke, his gaze shifted to Michel. A tiny crease marked his brows as if he were considering something, then he bent to retrieve two folds of parchment, each sealed with red wax and scribed with words across its face. John handed one of these to Sir Enguerran.

The knight took the skin in his left hand, holding it awkwardly as he stared at its surface, his brow furrowed. His was the expression of a man who had no acquaintance with the alphabet; reading was a skill Michel cherished, having hired a tutor for himself after leaving his grandsire's house. He hadn't needed his long-lost father to tell him that the more learning a man had the less likely he was to become another man's stooge.

"We want you to know that we tried, but we just couldn't convince the lady to choose you as her mate," John said, shaking his head as if he were truly powerless to affect Amicia's choice. "Given her reluctance, we were forced to contrive a bit of a competition."

D'Oilly looked up from the missive and blinked in surprise as John made the first move in his new game, one in which Michel and Sir Enguerran would both pay a price for their wrongs against him.

"An hour ago Lady de la Beres left Winchester, traveling for Thame Abbey. If you yet want her as your wife, Sir Enguerran, you will take this missive and ride out after her. When you meet her on the road, my escort will give her into your custody. You will then bear the lady the remainder of the way to the abbey." He paused for just a moment. "Now, listen carefully," England's king warned, holding a cautioning finger toward the knight. "If, and only if, you arrive with her at your side and with this parchment in hand, and no one challenges your right to marry her, will the abbot perform the wedding for you. Succeed in this, and we will rescind the lower bride price as well as the higher one. That means you'll have yourself a bride without paying us a pence for her."

John grinned like a merchant who had just closed a particularly fine sale. Sir Enguerran beamed.

John was giving Amicia to this tufthunting thief, the man responsible for ruining her! Michel caught back his anger and called himself a fool for overreacting. John never gave anything to anyone, especially not if he knew they'd wronged him.

"Oh, and just so you know," John continued. "You aren't the only man pursuing her. We felt a need to offer the lady a choice in mates. Sir Michel, here, shall also be seeking her along the road to Thame."

As he spoke, John shifted to look at Michel. His mouth smiled, but deep within his gaze anger crouched, ready to spring. John stretched out his hand, offering Michel the second skin he held.

Michel took it without hesitation, tucking it into his belt. This was no longer a game, not when Amicia was alone and friendless on the road. Anger stirred. Amicia was but a small and slender woman, delicate despite her bold behavior. What sort of king had such little respect that he threatened the life of a woman he was supposed to protect?

"All the same conditions apply to Sir Michel," John

said, once more speaking to Sir Enguerran. "If he arrives at Thame with her, she is his to do with as he pleases."

Michel blinked. John hadn't said *marry*. If not a wedding, then what?

Enguerran gaped as if his free bride, and the means to shield his theft, had already slipped from his one-handed grasp. "But, sire," he began to protest.

John threw up his hands as if to ward off the complaint. "Tut, Sir Enguerran. Haven't we done enough by agreeing to rescind her fee? Oh, there's one last thing you should know. If she reaches the abbey alone, even if only moments before you or Sir Michel, she has the right to choose a different fate for herself.

"Go now," John shooed Sir Enguerran toward the door with a wave of his hand. "What with your injury, it's only fair that we hold Sir Michel here for a half hour, to give you a bit of an advantage."

"Aye, sire," Enguerran said, then shot a look at Michel. Tangled in his expression was disdain for a common-born mercenary, surprise that Michel hadn't exposed his thievery and the idiotic certainty that he could still hide what he'd done by marrying Amicia.

Chapter 20

John waited until the door closed behind the man, then shifted to face his mercenary. All the amusement and warmth left his expression. Outside the wind still howled. A coal snapped in the brazier. Bertha snored gently, having done as her king commanded and fallen asleep.

"You left Winchester when I commanded you to stay." John's accusation was a quiet growl.

"I was right to go, sire," Michel retorted, barely preventing himself from accusing John of trying to swindle him. "The lady is impoverished, her every moveable item gone. Whether her belongings have been sold or were taken to d'Oilly's estates, I cannot say. Based upon their reactions to the news that I am now her administrator, two of her bailiffs colluded with the knight in this stripping of her wealth."

"Well, well, the worm has more spine than I thought,"

John said, pretending surprise. Then he smiled, the movement of his mouth tight. "It would serve you rightly if I forced you to marry her and left you to rot in penury. I am your king! You dared to defy me."

Michel only waited. He wouldn't excuse himself or apologize when all he'd done was see to his own affairs. Only a fool went blindly forward without watching where he put his feet.

When royal rage won him nothing, John sighed. Anger drained from him. "Damn you, de Martigny, but you're as bold as the lady. I don't know why I tolerate either of you. So, now that you know her estates aren't what you expected, have you decided you don't want her as a wife?" As John asked the question all expression left his face.

That gave Michel pause. How would admitting that he couldn't afford the lady serve John? He countered with a ploy of his own.

"Sire, you've already made me a part of this competition for the lady's hand." He touched the parchment in his belt. "Are you saying that I'm not to play the role you gave me and seek to make her my wife? Perhaps you intend that I should give her to d'Oilly if I find her first?"

Frustration danced through John's gaze, then was gone. "She seemed very upset when I mentioned that you'd asked for her hand some weeks ago. She then refused you most vehemently when I suggested that she surrender herself to you here so she might avoid the rigors of travel on a day such as this one," John added, as if that might explain or excuse the cruelty of this game of his.

That Amicia would reject Michel this morn was hardly surprising, not after her rejection last night. She was what she was born, a gentlewoman with all the arrogance and prejudice her blood demanded. Michel only waited. John gave a gentle shake of his head.

"Shame on you, de Martigny. All those times she sought you out. You avoided her. Why, she even went to the goldsmith's house to find you, only to leave cursing, or so I'm told. Not much of a swain, are you?"

Michel wished he hadn't played the part of swain at all. It was his own fault that Amicia's rejection yet stung. A wise man didn't make himself a woman's pawn. Instead, Michel had let himself desire her, even let himself imagine that she would accept him into her body without remembering the slight his lower rank did her own.

Taking the parchment from his belt, he offered it back to John. "Then, you'd rather that I left the game so d'Oilly might have her?"

The king stared at his missive as if it were a snake about to strike. Snatching his crown from his head, England's king loosed a blistering breath. "Damn you. All I want is the shred of triumph that is my due," he complained. "Tell me you desire her. Tell me that you care what opinion she has of you. You cannot be as impervious to her as you maintain."

Michel shrugged. He wasn't going to give John anything the king might use against him. "Sire, it doesn't matter what opinion I hold of the lady, or what I want from her. The fact remains that she is now impoverished."

John tossed the symbol of his regency into the seat of his chair. It fell with a ringing clatter. "Then, since you won't have her, will you take Lady Sybilla?" he demanded, naming the heiress he had wanted Michel to wed.

"I will not," Michel returned, all the more certain of his decision after those shared meals listening to Sybilla's conversations. The lady was no different than Amicia in how she despised him, but that was their only similarity. "Lady Sybilla is a reed in the wind, her opinions changing with her companions. As dull-witted as she is, she'd let anyone and everyone twist her into a tool and not have the sense to realize she's being used. Any marriage I make here in England is going to be unpopular. My wife needs to be bright enough to understand that if she betrays me she also betrays herself."

John's smile was slow and warm. "Amicia de la Beres would be such a woman, but you don't want her. So, if not Lady Sybilla, then what?"

That was John's final move. It was time to end this game.

"Sire, I never said I no longer wanted Lady de la Beres, only that she's impoverished. I'll take her, but only if her properties are restored to the state they held prior to her entering your wardenship. Do this for me and I'll participate in this competition of yours. Refuse, and for all I care Sir Enguerran may have her and be well rewarded for defrauding you. Meanwhile, I'll humbly request a release from your service so that I might seek a wife and estates in the employ of some other prince."

John's eyes widened. His mouth opened and closed as if he were a fish out of water, until he caught himself. "God take you," he snarled, his voice lowering into a whisper, then he threw up his hands in defeat. "Ach, you have my solemn and holy vow. The de la Beres properties will be restored to the same state they owned four years ago."

"And this restoration will be completed within six months' time," Michel added, in case John thought to drag his heels.

"In six months' time," the king agreed, then his eyes narrowed in affront. "Do you trust me so little? Perhaps you'd like me to scribe my words as a merchant pens his contracts?"

Michel would very much have liked that, but to ask it was to suggest that John's word was no good. Even if that were sometimes true, to speak such a thing aloud was an insult beyond any man's bearing. "Sire, I trust you to carry out your vow to its every syllable. All I'm saying is that her lands are so poor that without immediate restoration those who work her home farm could starve next year."

The indignance faded from John's eyes. "If it's as bad as that, then I hope Sir Enguerran hasn't spent too much of what he's stolen. It's he, not me, who'll restore her lands. He'll do better than restore, he'll pay an additional sum to soothe the injury he's done me and my ward, which you and I will split."

"He may protest that he's innocent of your charge and blame me in his stead," Michel countered, blocking the only remaining avenue of escape for John.

John dismissed this with a lift of his brows and a snort. "That worm won't say a word. He dare not, not when I can prove what he's done, then outlaw him, taking his properties for myself." The king caught himself and smiled. "Now, that's an attractive thought. Rather than force him to repay you, I'll exile him and make you warden of his confiscated lands. Use his profits to restore the lady's property. Then, when your income has returned to where it should be, you'll still have his profit until such a time as I see fit to forgive him."

"And if he has heirs, sire?" Michel warned. "I'd not have the world believe that I'm no different from Sir Enguerran, stealing from the properties I'm charged to protect."

"If he does have heirs, then I will make them your wards. You'll have the control and the use of their income until they reach their majority. Should they choose not to remain in your custody, they may pay you some fair amount to be released. Either way, the lady's lands will be restored and you'll have a tidy sum to keep you. Thus, whatever you do, don't kill the worm when you meet him on the road. I can't put heirs into the custody of the man who killed their father. You may, however, break his other arm if you like." John's sly, sidelong look said he knew very well it hadn't been a fall from a horse that had caused Sir Enguerran's injury.

It was more victory than Michel expected. Amicia and her restored lands would be his. To his surprise it was his body's longing to once again know hers that rushed through him. Not even the reminder of her prejudice and rejection could dampen it.

"Then, I'll be on my way to Thame, sire."

"Not yet," John stopped him. "There are a few details about this game that I saved just for you. First, although I warned the lady that her escort would withdraw if she left the game and the road to Thame, I fully expect her to turn her horse in some other direction."

John's gaze warmed as he savored the thought of Amicia's defiance. Dislike for the man who was England's king stirred in Michel. A ruler should have more concern for his subjects than to leave a fragile woman alone on the road in such weather for no reason save his own enjoyment.

"If she does separate from her escort," John continued, "I've commanded all but two men to turn back. Those two will follow her at a distance, leaving marks for their tracker. He and those marks will lead you to her. Once you have her, bear her directly to Thame and marry her."

Michel's brows rose at the amount of time and thought that John had invested in his game. "You never intended to force Lady Sybilla on me."

"I would have if you'd flinched even a little," John retorted, "but you wouldn't budge. Then I discovered what d'Oilly had done."

John stripped off his belt, tossing it into the chair with his crown. There was a gentle pattering as the pearls on the belt's surface struck the chair's back. "Here's another vow for you, Michel, as holy and true as my last one. I won't tolerate d'Oilly marrying the lady, for once those vows are spoken they cannot be undone. I don't want that woman wed to him. Fail me and I'll have your head, then make the lady a swift widow and take her for myself."

Michel's fists clenched at the thought of Amicia in John's bed. "Sire, for all we know Sir Enguerran has already captured the lady, given his head start. How am I to take her back from him when you've bound my hands by asking me not to kill him? He's not likely to give her up, believing as he does that marriage to her will shield his crime."

John removed his jewel-studded chain. Like his other princely accoutrements, it flew toward the chair with careless disregard for the wealth that decorated its face. Clattering as it hit the wooden back, it slid halfway off the seat, then caught, dangling just above the floor. His tunic followed.

Dressed in his shirt and chausses, he turned toward Michel. John's expression was closed and considering as he rubbed a finger against one temple. A muscle worked along his jaw. Creases appeared at the corners of his eyes as disgust mingled with respect filled his gaze. "You truly won't lift a finger to make her yours, will you? You want me to give her to you on a platter."

Michel rocked back on his heels a little. "That is what you promised me at Nantes, sire."

John's expression soured. "Here's the price I pay for giving way to a moment of heady triumph. I won that battle but lost the war. But promise I did. As you will. Here's your assurance that you'll have your bride—if things go awry and the lady arrives at the abbey in that thief's custody, or by herself—something I cannot fathom her doing—there is a phrase that the abbot and I share, a code of a sort. All you need do is speak it to the abbot, doing so where none might overhear. By this phrase he will know you come directly from me and that the commands you convey are mine and meant to supersede all other commands."

John fell silent, once again massaging his temple. A moment passed. His eyes closed as if giving Michel the bride he wanted pained him.

"And that phrase is?" Michel prompted, the need to be on the road after Amicia gouging at him. Only when she was in his arms could he be certain that she was his. She would be his, no matter how little she liked the disparagement their marriage did her. Whether she accepted him or not, she still desired him and that was more than Michel expected from his wife.

The king's eyes opened. The skin along the jut of his cheekbones darkened a little. "He and I were discussing the flight of birds. The abbot said something about an owl's knuckles, that being the name he gave the place where the bird's wing bends and from which feathers stretch like fingers. That is the phrase: owl's knuckles. Once you've used it, forget it. If you reveal it to anyone, your life will be the forfeit. Now go."

Still awash in triumph, Michel bowed and retreated, closing the antechamber door behind him.

Chapter 21

Without a glance at the chamberlain, Michel exited onto the balcony, then descended the stairs. Outside the hall, sleet spattered against the closed shutters. A gust of wind whistled into the big room's open door, blasting around the screen and across the hall with enough force to carry the smoke from hearth to ceiling vent with nary a curl or swirl. Amicia was out in this, no doubt already separated from her escort.

Driven inside by the weather, folk crowded in the room, laughing and talking, a few coughing against the damp. With the leaping flames upon the central hearthstone the hall's only source of light, they were gray hulks with but the occasional flash of color from a tunic or cap. Some people gamed, but most worked on personal projects, a bit of whittling or sewing, as was the wont for the winter months.

Michel located his troop near the door where it was

coldest. That was no hardship for men already dressed to travel in the foulest of weather, wearing two tunics beneath their cloaks and braies—the heavy leg covering that men in the northern reaches of England preferred for its warmth—rather than chausses on their legs, and boots. Roger, himself from the English hinterland, had introduced the garment to Michel.

Much to Michel's surprise, as he joined his men he found Amicia's maidservant nestled in the crook of Roger's arm. If the maid's face was as water-stained as her cloak, Roger's ugly visage owned a not so subtle pleasure. Michel sent his captain a vexed look; his men weren't supposed to seduce maids. Then again, who was he to chide? Roger hadn't been the one doing the futtering on the landing last night.

Roger only grinned. "Look, sweet Maud. Here is Sir Michel now," he said.

With a gasp, the maid thrust away from the ugly man who held her, not in fear, but to drop to her knees and catch Michel's gloved hand in her own. "Oh, sir," she cried, "you must help me."

Michel loosed an amused breath at this. Roger had worked miracles. What had happened to the woman who had nearly fainted upon seeing him in the castle's courtyard?

"Stand up, lass," he said, extracting his hand from her grip, motioning for Roger to aid her back to her feet. "Tell me what you expect me to do for you."

"It's my lady. You must save her," Amicia's maid cried, her face crumpling as her eyes watered anew. "The king's men came and took her. They wouldn't let me accompany her. Oh sir, she's going to die."

"But, Maud, how can she die when she's escorted by the king's own men?" Roger asked, his voice gentler than Michel had ever heard it.

"What? Do you think she's going to let the king force her to go where she doesn't wish to go? Not my lady," Maud cried, a touch of pride in her voice even as her chin trembled. She boldly wound an arm around Roger's waist and looked up at Michel. "Sir, I've never seen her so angry. Lord, but the things she said as she prepared to travel, about the king and game-playing." A hint of a frown flashed across her brow. "She said things about you, too, sir. Not very kind were they, but you should know she doesn't mean them, else she wouldn't look at you the way she does."

Michel barely had time to blink over this aside before Maud had rattled on. Then again, a blink was more reaction than he wanted to display before so many witnesses.

"I know her, sir," the maid continued. "She said the king has commanded his men to let her go if she chooses to leave them. It won't matter to her that she's a woman alone, not as angry as she is right now. Oh, sir, I begged her. I said that only pilgrims travel alone, that she's a gentlewoman with a repute to maintain. That only made her angrier. She said that you and the king had stolen all she had left to protect. Please"—Maud folded her hands as if truly praying—"if you have any care at all in your heart for her, help her. She'll die by herself."

If Amicia believed she had no repute left to protect it

could only be because of what they'd done on the landing last night. That made the way she'd turned her head in rejection of him look different, more like shame. For the first time, the possibility stirred that there was another explanation for what she'd done.

"Sir, are we free to offer aid to Lady de la Beres?" Roger asked, seconding the maid's plea.

"We are better than free," Michel replied. "It is already our mission. The king has commanded me to find Lady de la Beres and escort her to Thame Abbey."

"Oh, thank God," Maud breathed, sagging against Roger in relief. Scrubbing the tears from her face with backs of her hands, she added, "I can help."

"You? What could a wee thing like you do?" Roger asked with a kind laugh.

The maid shifted in his arms to look up into his scarred face. "I know where she's going and can lead you there."

"Where does she go?" Michel demanded. Knowing Amicia's destination meant he didn't have to trust John's tracker, who could have secret orders from his royal master that conflicted with Michel's purpose. Since John's phrase would only work if Michel arrived at the abbey in time to prevent vows from being said, a wasted moment could mean the end of his future.

"Why, home, of course," Maud said as if he'd asked a nonsensical question.

Michel almost smiled as tension drained from him. It *was* a nonsensical question. Of course she was going home. Where else would an unaccompanied gentlewoman go than into the protection of her home guard?

That Amicia believed her bailiff would offer that protection suggested she had no idea what had happened to her properties. When Amicia had appeared at the goldsmith's door last night, and only an hour after Michel's return, she brought with her the suspicion that she'd colluded with Sir Enguerran, especially after her accusation of thievery, spewed in front of Mistress Hughette. Michel had meant to grill Amicia over her unexpected appearance until she either confessed her part in the plot or convinced him of her innocence, but she'd kissed him and he'd forgotten about accusations.

He looked at Roger. "Strip off your hauberk and give it to me. You'll be wearing my mail and riding my horse while you journey to Thame on my behalf."

"Sir?" his captain asked in surprise.

"The king has turned the finding of Lady de la Beres into a competition of sorts. I need something to convince my rival that the lady still travels on the Oxford road and is already in my custody. To keep him distracted while I find the lady may mean that he tries you as he did us the other night. Can you resist him without killing him or any of his men as you did before, knowing that the woman he seeks to take from you is your Maud?" This last was a subdued tweak, meant to repay Roger's earlier taunts.

If Maud frowned in confusion, Roger laughed, needing no more explanation to understand his master's intent. "Sir, I can play my role as you with ease, what with your helmet covering my face. But, what of you as you try to play me? You may have my steel cap to wear in place of your helmet, but that will hardly disguise your pretty face. What pretense will you use to convince others that you are me?"

Had Roger tried this insolent jest earlier this morn, he might have earned himself a harsh chide. But now that Michel had John's vow and secret phrase, as well as the whereabouts of his wife-to-be, one corner of his mouth lifted. "What more disguise do I need save that whistle of yours? One stanza and everyone will know it can only be you. Either that, or they'll turn their heads away in shock. Mistress Hughette complained this morn that you sang it in front of the maids last night."

"What right had she to complain about him when she laughed right along with the others?" Maud protested, coming to her love's defense before Roger had a chance to reply. "He didn't even sing all the words."

As the rest of Michel's troop brayed in raucous amusement over this, a breath of a laugh left Michel. "How now, Roger? It seems she likes you well, indeed."

"So she does," Roger replied, his eyes glowing with pleasure.

"I accept your offer of aid," Michel told the blushing maid. If Maud lacked her lady's curves, she was roughly the same size. "Did your lady leave behind any garment that is distinctively hers?"

Maud nipped her lower lip in consideration. "Well, there is her mantle. I told her to wear it, it being fur-lined and far warmer than her hunting cloak, but she refused, not wanting it ruined by the weather, even though she could have worn it under her cloak." She gave a disapproving shake of her head at the foolishness of her better.

"Perfect," Michel said, confidence growing. "Will you wear her mantle and ride with Roger to Thame, pretending to be your mistress?"

"Oh, sir," Maud said, folding her hands, her expression creasing in reluctance, "I couldn't. That mantle is a very expensive garment."

"If it's ruined I'll replace it for her," Michel countered. It was an offer he could afford to make now that he had the king's vow to restore Amicia's properties, and control of Sir Enguerran's properties as well.

Maud's eyes flashed. Her chin lifted in unconscious mimicry of her mistress. "You once made trouble for Lady de la Beres by purchasing her band's regilding. Now, here you are offering to pay for an even more expensive mantle. I think I must know your intentions toward my lady, sir."

She was a mouse challenging a lion. "What is this? Will you play the chaperone today when you refused last night? Then you told your mistress I meant her no harm. Have you changed your mind?" Michel teased.

The maid clung to righteous reproach. "Is there a reason I should have?" she asked. "My lady did leave the smith's house nigh on in tears."

However bold her chide, Michel was grateful for it. So, it had cost Amicia dearly to reject him. Hope stirred, then persisted. He'd weakened her defense against him.

"Be at ease on your lady's account, little chaperone," Michel said. "I have the king's permission to wed your mistress."

Maud's face split in a broad grin. "I knew it!" she crowed. "I knew it after she was so upset with Lady Roheise, and the only place she could think to go was to the goldsmith's door." Still smiling, Maud dropped into a curtsy. "Oh, sir," she breathed. "Aye, I'll wear her mantle and pretend to be my lady to aid you, sir. Only give me a few moments to prepare for travel."

She didn't wait for him to dismiss her, only turned and sprinted around the corner of the screen. Michel watched her go, wondering what connection Amicia had with that haughty, lewd bitch, Roheise de Say. For the first time since Amicia appeared in the smith's hall last night, it occurred to him that she'd come truly unaware that he had returned.

Well, if he wanted answers he would find them on the road to Thame, or on the way to Amicia's nearest manor, if she had indeed turned for home. Taking the pack that contained his traveling attire from Roger, Michel retreated a little way from the door. As he dressed, the memory of the way his body had melded with Amicia's again rolled over him.

Hope grew. No matter how much the gentlewoman in Amicia despised his common bloodline, the woman she was desired him for the man he was. Her passion for him could be an effective tool. Once their vows were said, he could hold her hostage in his bed until sensation destroyed her pride, and she accepted him.

The thought of making love to Amicia until she admitted that he was her rightful master no matter his heritage was tantalizing, indeed. Aye, the longer it took to break down her barriers, the more pleasure there would be. In which case, it was well past time to catch himself a bride.

Another gust of wind screamed down the slope of the rolling hills in front of Ami. It tore across the plain toward her, through copses of white-barked birches along the way. Already stripped of their leaves by the season, the trees rattled, woody skeletons.

In a pattern made familiar over the past hours, Ami turned in her saddle to put her back to the wave of stinging rain that pelted her. The moment she shifted, her mount stopped. The mare's head hung, her mane and tail streaming.

Ami hunched her shoulders and waited. The frigid air penetrated her woolen cloak, then passed through her hunting attire—sensible and sturdy woolen gowns of forest green—as if the garments didn't exist. The hem of her cloak escaped from where she'd tucked it around her legs for warmth's sake. Her hood fluttered around her cheeks, straining against the scarf tightly wound around her face to keep the hood over her ears.

If only she hadn't been so angry this morn she might have listened to Maud and worn her mantle beneath her cloak. Aye, the garment would have acquired a few mud stains, but she would have had a layer of fur between her and the wind. That she might actually freeze to death out here, doing so because she'd been vain about her attire only made her angrier.

How dare John and that common good-for-nothing mercenary misuse her this way! Ami drubbed her heels into her horse as the wind died back to a mere howl.

The mare stumbled back into a sluggish walk, the fastest speed this horse could manage.

John's men had refused Ami her own horse, putting her instead on the oldest, most spavined mount in the royal stables. Ami was sure they'd done it to limit the distance she could put between herself and her pursuers. After all, the longer she was on the road, the better her chance of capture.

It was to make herself more difficult to find that Ami had taken the least direct and longest path to her nearest manor. However, an hour after turning off the main track she regretted her decision. Above her, boiling black clouds so thick that they seemed one seethed in the sky above her. It was the promise of more rain, or possibly an early and unusual snow, that filled the biting air. This, when her diversion left her still more than twenty miles from home.

With no sun, Ami's growling stomach told the hour, claiming that she'd now missed the day's main meal. She pressed her fingers to her purse, which hung from her belt beneath her cloak, right where John's men had left it, thank God. There'd been an alewife in the last village who'd called out the offer of a cup of stew for two pence.

Ami had almost accepted, as much for the stew as the prospect of being within walls for a time. Only, she couldn't afford to pause, not even to consume a cup of stew. It was dangerous enough that she traveled alone these few miles to her house. At the rate she was moving, it would be deep night before she reached her manor house, what with the days so short this time of year. A lone woman traveling at night was insanity, and Ami had a much more distant goal that Sussex in mind. Which was why she needed to go home.

Once she had her own escort at her back, men whose loyalty was to Richard de la Beres and *not* the king, Ami meant to depart for England's northern reaches. It wasn't any of Roheise's discontented and rebellious nobles, men like Eustace de Vesci who ruled the northern stronghold of Alnwick, that Ami intended to seek out, but a young woman she'd met at the wedding she'd attended last summer. No one at court knew Katherine Godsel, or that Ami was acquainted with Kate. That meant no one would think to look for Ami at Glevering, Kate's house, especially when Ami knew Kate's husband, Sir Rafe Godsel, was presently in London on business.

Once she reached Glevering, what then? Ami grimaced, again damning John and his mercenary, and this horrid game of theirs. Running to the north might put her beyond Sir Enguerran's reach, but not Michel's and surely not John's.

Again the mare slowed and, again, Ami drubbed the poor old creature's sides until it returned to plodding. If she couldn't escape her pursuers, she could make it as difficult as possible for them to find her.

It was especially Michel de Martigny she wanted to elude. After that experience on the landing, the thought of ever again facing him made Ami's stomach clench— as it had too often on this day.

Michel's rejection replayed itself in her mind, only now that she'd had time to absorb the news that he'd asked for her hand, it took on a new meaning. Men didn't marry lewd women who carried out trysts in full view of some stranger's hall while fully dressed.

In which case, she didn't need to worry about Michel pursuing her into the north, or even to Thame Abbey as the king suggested.

Something too close to hurt stirred in Ami. Damn him. If Michel intended to marry her, why had he taunted her, stirring her senses until she'd given way to sin and ruined herself in his eyes?

The answer lay in the echo of Mistress Hughette's warning. Michel had no patience with *her* kind, the goldsmith's wife had said, as if being born a gentlewoman were akin to having leprosy.

Ami gritted her chattering teeth. Just as Sir Enguerran would surely beat her to ease his degraded pride, commoner that Michel was he'd needed to prove himself superior to her. This he'd done by waking her desire for him, until her body betrayed her morals.

Once again the wind rose to a scream. Ami shifted in the saddle to put her back to it. The mare stopped. This time, when Ami applied her heels, the poor old thing only grunted in exhausted refusal and stayed where it stood.

Ami would have screamed if doing so would have accomplished anything. Instead, she dismounted. No matter how desperate, she didn't have the heart to drive a horse to its death.

Forcing her frozen gloves to bend, she curled her fingers around the reins, then walked, leading the horse into the wind. It was like pushing through brick walls, but push Ami did, even after her legs tired and her vision began to swim with exhaustion. She wouldn't give in to defeat, just as she wouldn't marry Sir Enguerran, she wouldn't bed John, or become a nun. That left her only options marriage to Michel de Martigny or death. Death was surely the better choice.

Chapter 22

What was wrong with that woman? Even chickens had better sense than to stay out of doors for any length of time on a day such as this one. Another blast of frigid air buffeted Michel, as if it were trying to drive him and Roger's horse off the road. He drew deeper into his fur-lined cloak. Sleet stung his face where his scarf didn't cover it. The air had grown colder since the advent of afternoon.

Beside him, John's tracker also bent to escape God's breath, drawing so far into his body that for a moment he seemed headless. As strange as this Ott was, the impression didn't improve much as he straightened. With his shoulders hunched, his cloak hood pulled low over his brow and a scarf wrapped around his lower face, his eyes were the only thing visible. Ott's gaze met Michel's, then slipped to the side, not with the disdain of Michel's betters but as if the man were uncomfortable with other humans.

Ott hadn't uttered more than three words since they left Winchester. Nor was he speedy at his task, moving no faster than a trot between marks. Michel hadn't minded the man's deliberate pace at first, for backtracking might cost time he couldn't afford to spend. Moreover, until this past hour and the last two marks, they'd kept to almost the same route Michel had used to reach the de la Beres manor only three days ago. They no longer did.

Although they still moved in the general direction of Amicia's nearest property, this change worried Michel. John's vow or not, he couldn't resist the thought that he was again being cheated. At the last mark he'd told himself he'd continue on in this direction for another hour, but if they found nothing or turned too far from where that manor house was, he'd bid Ott farewell and ride for Thame, hoping that Sir Enguerran would find his bride for him.

When the wind howled past Michel, this time the scent of woodsmoke and penned livestock filled its depths, the promise of civilization ahead on this track. A little farther on, grassy pastureland gave way to cultivated fields. The scars left upon the earth by plows ran at odd angles, plot by plot, as each family strove to take the best advantage of drainage and sun angles. Depending on the reek, Michel could tell which of these fields would rest beneath a layer of manure for the next season and which would soon put forth a crop of winter wheat.

The village that owned the plots was of good size, several hundred dwellings. Framed against the dark and raging sky, whitewashed cottage walls gleamed beneath thatched caps the color of tarnished gold. Rising from their midst, a holy island in a sea of the mundane, was the stone tower of their church, the village's heart and refuge in times of trouble.

A single rider came toward them. Beside Michel, Ott straightened in his saddle and gave a forward jerk of his chin as he recognized the traveler. Michel's concern fell away in a wave of relief. Urging his horse into a canter, he rode forward to meet the man.

"I am Sir Michel de Martigny," he called out over the whine of the wind. In case the soldier needed proof, Michel pulled his scarf down beneath his chin to reveal his face.

"Then you are the man I seek," the king's soldier replied. With his dark cloak hood drawn down over his brow and his receding chin covered by a sparse black beard, the man's great nose became a crow's beak. He was dressed much as Michel, in a leather hauberk, thick woolen tunic and a heavy cloak. Rather than braies, this man had cross-gartered a second layer of fabric over his calves and chausses for warmth's sake.

"Where is Lady de la Beres?" Michel demanded.

"She's still moves along the track, having exited the village a quarter hour or so ago," the soldier replied, giving a jerk of his thumb to indicate the cottages behind him. "The mare she rides has finally given out and refuses to carry her any longer."

"She's afoot?" Michel snapped in unwelcome surprise. If her horse was done in, they wouldn't be reaching Thame tonight.

"Aye, and Pip and I we're none too happy about letting her go on this way, not with no mount to carry her away from danger should something happen. His majesty commanded that she not see us as we followed. Now that her pace has slowed, we've had to drop even farther behind her. We wouldn't know until it was too late if she were attacked. Thus, did we decide it was time to see if you came after us as our king said you would, sir. As slow as we've moved, we calculated that Ott, there"—he raised a hand to the tracker who was yet plodding their way—"should have found us about now."

John's soldiers had more heart than their royal master. "Which way takes me to her?"

The soldier shifted in his saddle to indicate the village behind him. "You ride straight on through, sir, bearing on the leftward path as it rounds the green, then on past the church. When you're out the other side, stay leftward. You'll find Pip at the village's edge or thereabouts."

"My thanks," Michel replied. "Now, if you're so inclined, you can earn yourself a few coins by bearing a message for me."

The soldier grinned at that. "There was no one who said Pip and I needed to hurry back to Winchester, sir. Where does this message go?"

"To Reading." Before leaving Winchester, Michel had laid out his intended path to Thame with Roger. "At the priory there you'll find my man, Alan of Exeter. Tell him that I have the lady, but that she and I have only one good horse between us and won't make Thame this night."

Michel exhaled in frustration, his breath clouding before him. If Roger arrived at the abbey and there was no wedding to end the chase, Sir Enguerran would realize he'd been hoodwinked. It wasn't a pleasant thought, riding hell-bent for Thame on the morrow with Amicia at his side and no protection, knowing that the knight and his men were scouring the countryside seeking a missing bride.

"Tell him that Roger must leave Thame under cover of darkness to confound those who follow, and ride for Reading. If I'm not already at the priory to meet them when they arrive upon the morrow, then they should assume I'm working my way toward the city, moving from village to village as I come. If they do the same, we should meet each other at some point. If for some reason we miss each other, the lady and I will continue on to Thame, doing the same all the way." The only reason Michel wouldn't reach either Reading or Thame was that Sir Enguerran had killed him to claim the free bride John had promised him.

"Aye, sir," the soldier said, then hesitated. "Pardon, but is there great haste with this message? None of us believed the lady would dare to leave our custody this morn, even though our king warned us she would. Nor did we think we'd be out for more than an hour or two before you caught us. Pip and I have nothing to eat, unless we dine on our horses' oatcakes. There's an alewife in the village whose stew promises to be more appetizing," he said as Ott drew his mount alongside them.

It was a fitting end to a sour tale. John had sent Amicia from Winchester with a troop of unprovisioned men. If the soldiers hadn't eaten, neither had she. He'd have to feed her if he wanted to travel many more miles before they rested.

"Eat then, but don't linger overly long at it," Michel told the soldier, stripping off his gloves to dig out the promised payment. "Show me this alewife's shop. Perhaps she has something more portable than stew."

"That I'll do, sir," the soldier said smiling, "if you'll kindly send Pip back to join me when you find him."

In this village the alewife not only supplied the town's drink, but had turned her home into a decent cookshop as well. She provided Michel with sausages, a loaf of bread, and a wedge of cheese, then filled his spare flask with freshly brewed ale. Stashing their dinner in his saddle pack, Michel rode on to the village's edge only to find Pip no longer there. It was another quarter mile on the track and around a copse before Michel discovered the man.

Pip looked to be more fresh-faced lad than soldier, and a study in browns from his drab bundling and pale mustache to his horse's dull coat. The local who stood alongside his horse was the opposite; a bright spot in a winter faded world. The old man's tunic was a bright red, his capuchin a vibrant green. His curly beard and his hair were the same color as the creamy fleece draped over his shoulders. Instead of boots, he wore that same wooly covering on his legs. Between that and the shepherd's crook upon which he leaned, there was little doubting the man's profession.

The shepherd ranted at Pip in the English tongue, shaking a finger as if to chide. Already weathered by time into its own sort of leather, the old man's skin creased all the more in his irritation. As Michel drew his horse to a halt next to Pip's, the soldier said something. The shepherd fell into an immediate silence, then shot a narrow-eyed look at Michel.

Pip smiled. "You've come just in time for her sake, sir. She's afoot now that her horse has given out. But, where is your troop?" He peered back toward the village behind Michel as if expecting more men to appear.

"I'm alone for the now," Michel replied. The old man watched him, his brows drawn down over dark eyes as if he were trying to puzzle out what was being said.

"Ah," Pip said, then glanced at the sword belted to Michel's side. "I suppose that's no hardship for you, sir. You can protect her better than any other man."

"I suppose I can," Michel replied. Aye, he could protect Amicia as long as he didn't face Sir Enguerran and twenty men all by himself. "Now that I've found the lady, you can take yourself back to the village to meet your fellow at the alewife's shop. You and he will do an errand for me before returning to your royal master."

As he spoke, Michel began to turn his horse to follow Amicia. To his surprise, the shepherd reached up to catch the steed by the bridle. The old man said something in his guttural tongue. It had the sound of a question to it.

Pip frowned at the shepherd and snapped a command. The old man's face tightened in refusal, his retort given in a rude tone. Pip shrugged, then looked at the knight. "Sir, I told him to release your horse, but he insists on knowing if you're responsible for the lady. He passed her on the track and wasn't too happy about meeting her. What shall I say to him?"

"There is no harm in telling him that she is mine," Michel replied. A wave of satisfaction washed over him as he spoke the words. Aye, Amicia was his. She'd given her body to him, choosing him above all other men. If that's all the acceptance he ever got from her, it would be enough.

His answer sent the old man into another tirade, this time shaking his finger at Michel.

"He's upset about her traveling alone, sir," Pip said, translating as the man continued his rant. "That, and he's complaining about her rude reply after he told her this track was too dangerous a place for a gentlewoman traveling without an escort."

Laughter caught Michel by surprise, escaping from him as a harsh bark. "Tell him that the gentlewoman speaks rudely to all the commoners she meets, myself included. As for an escort, assure him that she shall have me at her side sooner than she wants and much to her displeasure."

Smiling, Pip translated. The old man's brows rose, then something akin to a strangled chortle left him. His grin revealed that he'd given up two of his lower fore-teeth to time's passage.

In that instant, wind again blasted past them, tearing at Michel's clothing as it stirred the fleece on the shepherd's back. It was colder now than it had been half an hour ago. The clouds had lowered to drag their ragged skirts across the land in the promise of a storm. Michel's hope of reaching Reading before nightfall disintegrated.

He glanced at the shepherd, then back to Pip. "Given the weather and the lady's mount, she and I may need a refuge for the night, before we complete our journey. This man knows this area. Tell him that it's toward the northwest and Reading that I intend to head. Ask him if he knows any place suitable for us to stop as we make our way in that direction."

Pip decoded the old man's answer. "Sir, he says that if you stay on this track it will turn eastward, taking you to the de la Beres manor about seven leagues on. However, there is a path about two leagues from here that breaks from it, heading northward once it enters the earl's properties. He warns that it has the look of an animal walk, but you'll know you've turned rightly for you'll cross a stream before the fork, then once on the track the water will cut back and forth before you. However, from that fork there's not much in the way of civilization, for the earl's chase stands between you and your route to Reading, and in that wild place no man may linger overly long."

Michel grimaced at the thought of sleeping out of doors on this night. The old man eyed him in consideration, tugging at his fleecy beard. He spoke to Pip, his tone earnest.

"Sir, he says just after the fork there's his summer hut," Pip translated. "He says it's not much, but it's snug enough to keep out the wind and rain. He's just returned from closing it up for the winter, so it's clean enough for the likes of you and the lady. There's straw in the lean-to, if you'd like to put it between you and the ground for a bed, and your horse can graze his fill in the area. He says that after you've gone a mile or so beyond the fork, you'll see the pens from the track."

A shepherd's hut might be nothing much, but it was in the right direction and far better than sleeping in the open. "Is there wood for a fire?"

When the old man was done spewing his thick, musical syllables, Pip said, "He says he doesn't leave wood at the hut, it being precious enough to attract thieves—"

Here the shepherd interrupted, this time his tone intense. Pip shook his head and replied, half-lifting his hand in Michel's direction. The old man's eyes widened. He released Michel's bridle, said something else, then tugged on his forelock, the nod of his head respectful.

Pip turned toward Michel with a smile. "He was warning you against the earl's parkers, who deal harshly with those who gather wood where they shouldn't. I told him that although you are as common as we, born of merchant parents, you are also the king's companion and a powerful knight. That changed his tune about firewood. He now says there's faggots enough for your stay hidden beneath the upturned trough in the nearest pen."

Which said that the old man had stolen his wood from the same earl against whom he'd warned Michel and knew the smell of woodsmoke might attract those same parkers. The corner of Michel's mouth lifted. It was a shame that Amicia wasn't as impressed as the old man by a merchant's son's achievements.

"Offer him my thanks," Michel said, giving the man a nod, "and say that I'll pay for anything I use."

The old man again tugged his forelock and bowed before Pip translated. It seemed he knew enough French to understand matters that concerned coins. Michel urged his horse into motion.

"Sir, are you certain you don't want Sim and me to ride with you?" Pip called after him.

"Nay, as I said, you've another task to do for me. Ride on back to the village and join your mate. The lady is mine now."

The phrase came even more easily from his mouth this second time. Michel savored the way it felt on his tongue, liking it all the more.

Amicia was his.

Chapter 23

Her horse was useless, she was exhausted, her gowns were sodden, her fingers and toes were so cold she couldn't feel them. Worse, the occasional spattering of sleet had become a steady icy rain. For the first time since separating from the king's soldiers, Ami let herself consider that her last move in John's game had been the worst of all the ill-considered and dangerous moves she'd made thus far. Even bedding her king wasn't as bad as dying out here, alone and unshriven.

Only it wasn't John's bed that Ami wanted. It was Michel's. Unbidden, the feeling of his mouth moving atop hers returned to haunt her. This was followed by the memory of their bodies melding as one. Unwanted lust stirred at her core.

She ignored it until it ebbed. If carnal warmth would have heated her cold toes, Ami might have let it linger.

Instead, all reawakened desire did was depress her when she was depressed enough already.

Another gust of wind hit her. The blast was so strong that Ami clutched the mare's bridle, huddled close to the horse, and waited. When the roaring air returned to its usual whine, she remained where she stood, her head against the horse's shoulder. It was time to admit defeat. What John did to her was unfair and wrong, but it wasn't worth her life. She needed to return to the village behind her and wait there in warmth and comfort for whatever her future held.

Releasing the mare's reins, not caring if the creature stayed or followed, Ami turned on the track. Framed against the dark sky was a single horse and rider, far behind her on the road. The image was so distant that it was nothing more than a blur of brown against the black of the sky.

Relief soared. Michel had come for her. Ami tromped on the thought. It wasn't Michel. He didn't want her; men didn't marry bold women who trysted on landings. Besides, it couldn't be him. Neither he nor Sir Enguerran would be riding alone as this man did.

If the rider wasn't one of her pursuers, then he was a threat. Ami closed her hand over the hilt of the dagger at her belt. If it was rape the man intended, she'd see he paid something for his outrage before she was taken.

The man increased his pace, the horse moving from a canter to a gallop. A moment later, Ami made out the billow of his cloak and the brown of the leather hauberk he wore. She didn't recognize the horse and could see nothing of the rider's face. Aye, but she knew the set of those shoulders and the way he sat in the saddle.

It was Michel de Martigny.

Relief, deep and complete, washed over her. Despite what had happened, or perhaps because of it, Michel still wanted her. As the last pretense of control over her own fate slipped from her fingers, anger and defiance faded. She'd not only live, but by the rules of John's game, she would marry the man who had taken her on the goldsmith's landing.

What of the way Michel had used her, turning her own sensuality against her until she betrayed herself and her morals? Ami sighed. The serenity and happiness of her marriage to Richard de la Beres had been unique; to expect the same from her second marriage was unrealistic. If the least problem she had in this union was that Michel needed to dominate her and her senses, then it was no problem at all.

If that was the only problem she faced in her marriage.

Stewing in uncertainty, Ami clung close to her horse and waited as Michel brought his mount to a halt before her. Wisps of steam floated up from his horse's hide and clouded in front of its nose as it huffed against exertion. Michel looked as warm as his horse, his legs covered in the braies of a Northerner. Ami envied him his fur-lined cloak.

He wore his sword belted at his side. His scabbard was black. A bit of silver tracery ran down its center to a solid silver tip. Modest embellishment, given his violent and skillful repute. More often, the greater the warrior's renown the gaudier the decoration on the tools he used to maintain his fame.

Such discreet decoration reminded Ami of Michel's gray tunic, the one he'd worn to the feast, and the circumspect embroidery that adorned that garment. This was not a man given to excess. That was certainly true in his emotions. Even in rage he kept himself under strict control. There were worse qualities in a husband.

As if he meant to speak, Michel pulled down the scarf that covered his face. Ami waited for him to gloat in triumph or upbraid her for running from him and the king's game. She marshaled defenses, ready to give back as good as he gave. Most of what rose to her tongue were accusations of lies and pained complaints of humiliation.

Michel's face might have been carved from stone. His eyes glinted, silver. The wind again rose, howling around them. The fur inside his cloak ruffled, the end of his scarf lifted. His horse's mane streamed across his gloved hands on its reins.

Still, he said nothing. Ami's defenses melted. There was nothing left but the only question that mattered. "Why didn't you tell me from the first that you'd asked for my hand?"

There wasn't so much as a flicker of emotion in his face at her question. "What would you have said to me if I had?"

It was a devastating strike. Ami's eyes closed. She knew exactly what she would have said. Before Michel had kissed her in the courtyard she'd been the king's ward, a courtier in every sense, full of overweening pride and self-importance. That woman would have railed over the outrage of a commoner daring to reach beyond his place, advancing himself through her disparagement. She might even have plotted with a noblewoman to achieve his death.

Opening her eyes, Ami again looked up at Michel. Sleet stung like an icy scourge. If he spent the rest of their marriage humiliating her, it would be just punishment for her previous arrogance.

"I would have refused you with every ounce of my being," she replied.

He nodded as if he appreciated her honesty, then stretched down his hand in invitation. "Ride with me. We need shelter more swiftly than you can walk there."

Ami stepped to his horse's side. Her face raised into the icy rain, she let her gaze mark the elegant lift of his cheekbones and the imperious jut of his nose. There was no warmth in his eyes for her, but that meant nothing. She knew very well what sort of heat she could awaken in his gaze, and in his body.

The woman she'd been before she met Michel was dead and gone. The woman she was now knew she could do far worse than to marry this uncommon knight. She caught her hand around his wrist, put her foot on his stirrup and helped him lift her sideways into his saddle in front of him.

Michel bent his head into the wind's teeth, a mix of icy rain and frigid air. Sitting in front of him, Amicia curled as close as she could to his body. Her back was braced against his arm, her head was tucked beneath his chin, her cheek resting on his leather-clad shoulder. Although he'd pulled his cloak forward to tuck as much as he could around her, cold yet radiated from her. Until a mile ago, she'd shivered so violently that he worried she ailed. As cold as she was it was no wonder that she'd given up so easily.

Roger's horse splashed through the stream. It was as the shepherd said. The track looked like one that sheep walked, the waterway meandering back and forth across it. At Michel's tug on her reins, Amicia's spavined mare entered the icy water with a reluctant grunt. The mare wasn't as exhausted as she portrayed herself, only clever enough to manipulate an unwitting rider.

The shepherd's pens appeared on Michel's right, nestled at the place where a hill rose from the base of the plain. It was more distant from the path than he expected, which was a boon, indeed. As they neared the pens, he saw that the chest-high fences were made of willow branches woven into a wall. They were efficient enclosures for a shepherd, being both flexible and portable, so the pens could be moved, rearranged or rewoven as needs demanded.

Beyond these willow walls was the hut, impossible to see from the track. It looked for all the world like an oversized mushroom thrusting up out of the earth, as round as the moon and topped with thatch grayed with age. Not much of its sole circular wall showed between the roof's low-hanging eave and the ground, but what little he could see revealed the remains of a long ago whitewashing.

Before he'd seen this hut, Michel had hoped they might bring the horses inside with them for the night. This wasn't just to keep them from being seen by Sir Enguerran, should the knight travel past this place, but to protect the animals from the weather and take advantage of the precious heat their bodies emitted. It would be far easier to escape detection if there was no need to light a fire, since the smoke and smell marked them.

That wasn't possible in this hut. The dwelling was barely any wider than Michel was tall, the door so low that he'd have to almost bend in half to enter it. From the look of the roof, he'd likely have to crouch the whole while he was inside.

As Michel halted his horse before the doorway, Amicia straightened in his arms, then caught the edge of the saddle and helped herself off his horse. Oddly disappointed that she hadn't waited for his aid, he dismounted after her, watching as she went to the hut's door. It didn't swing open as he expected, but slid to the side. She ducked beneath the lintel and disappeared into the construct's dark interior.

With her warmth his greatest concern, Michel went first to the shepherd's downturned trough. The wood was there, as promised. Returning to the hut, he left the bundle beside the doorway, then removed his pack from Roger's saddle. In reality, his pack was nothing more than a piece of fabric coated with goose grease to resist the wet, but the items he kept within it meant survival: the food he'd purchased from the alewife along with his own stash of dried meats, a blanket, and the means with which to make a fire.

With their continued life in his hands, Michel crouched low and entered the hut. The wind's shriek dropped to a distant whistle, muffled by the walls. The abrupt quiet was almost loud in its stillness.

Inside, it smelled of woodsmoke and fleece, and was warmer than Michel expected without a fire. The only source of light was the doorway as it allowed the gray day to pour into the hut. Framed in that watery light, Amicia huddled across the chamber from the doorway. Her cloak was pulled tightly around her, her head was bowed as she shivered again. The wall she leaned on lacked the whitewash and mud plaster applied to its exterior, thus looked like what it was, the same woven willow hurdling that made up the pens.

Standing at the room's center between him and Amicia was a thick central post, reaching up to the slightly pitched roof's midpoint. From it, saplings radiated to the encircling wall, support for the thatching. The blackened spot on the reeds at one side of the pole revealed the position of the ceiling vent, which meant the old man kept his hearth somewhere below that mark.

His feet cloaked in dimness and his shoulders hunched, Michel started toward the hearthstone, only to discover that the floor sloped downward to the hut's center, which was recessed into the earth to a depth around his knees. He straightened carefully and didn't collide with the ceiling. At his feet was a small stony platform raised about a foot off the hard-packed earthen floor, the old man's hearth.

Amicia looked up at him. "You have wood," she managed around the clattering of her teeth.

"Better than that," he told her, "I have flint and tinder."

Crouching before the hearthstone, Michel unrolled his pack and found the scrip that contained what he promised, then performed the miracle of bringing forth life-giving warmth from dead wood. Moments later, knife-edged shadows danced against the hut's walls. Smoke curled its way up to the blackened spot in the thatch. Newborn heat reached out to envelop him.

With a rustle of fabric, Amicia came forward to kneel before the hearth, her hands outstretched as if to embrace the flames. "Oh, thank you, thank you," she breathed. "I think it's already warmer in here."

The corner of Michel's mouth lifted. "You're easy to please."

Although she shot him a narrow-eyed sidelong look, her mouth twisted in wry amusement. The expression was strangely intimate, turning his halfhearted jest into something more private and personal. Every inch of Michel's body reacted. The thought of holding her hostage in his bed until she acknowledged that he was her rightful husband returned. His body's need for her caught him by surprise, the sensation so immediate and intense that it drove him back to his feet.

"I must care for the horses. There's food here"—he touched his foot to the half-unrolled pack—"and drink in the flask."

"You thought of everything," she murmured, then

threw back her hood and leaned nearer to the flames to bathe her face in the heat.

Michel froze where he stood. The fire's golden light gleamed against her damp skin. Her hair was again covered with that matronly linen head covering, the one she'd worn at their first meeting. It didn't detract from her beauty.

He studied the gentle slope of her brow, the perfect line of her nose and the alluring roundness of her lips. Another wave of need crashed over him. This time, it wasn't the desire to spill his seed within her. What he wanted was to hold her against his heart and feel her arms around him as she held him in return.

It was past time to regain his control. Turning, he left the hut. By the time he'd seen to the horses' needs, stowing their saddles just inside the hut's door, then rubbing them down before leaving them in the pen most protected from the weather to sip stream water from the shepherd's bucket and dine on oatcakes and grass, at least an hour had passed.

Stopping to gather straw for his and Amicia's bedding, Michel made his way to the hut, now drawn as much by the heat it offered as the woman waiting inside. More warmth than he expected flowed past him as he slid open the hut's door. Pushing the straw through the opening before him, he crept in, then left the door slightly ajar behind him. Life and health demanded it. Just as the fire needed a draft to breathe, those inside craved the draft to carry the smoke from the interior so that they didn't choke.

The fire's snap and pop welcomed him. The hovel's

dimness had been driven up and out along the roof's radiating saplings until it huddled at the line where the thatch and wall met. Blocking his view of the hut's interior was Amicia's cloak. It hung by its ties, stretched between two saplings as it dried. Her head covering dangled near the wall, draped over a knob on one of the radiating treelets.

Stripping off his own dripping cloak, he hung it from another knob on the saplings, then ducked around her outer garment. A damp, forest green gown hung behind it. On the next sapling over hung another. In the gap between that gown's hem and the floor he could see Amicia's naked feet braced against the hearthstone. Laid out on the pack's greased cloth was her dinner, their meal, untouched.

He stepped around the last gown. Swaddled from nape to shins in his blanket, Amicia sat close to the hearth, her chin resting on her upraised knees. As she looked up at him, her lips lifted into a small smile. Both his previous needs returned with all their intensity.

"Pardon the mess, but almost everything I had was soaked through," she said.

"You didn't eat." Michel's voice sounded gruff and overly harsh to his own ears.

The upward lift of her lips faltered. "I wanted to wait for you."

It was an unexpected offer of respect, one he wasn't accustomed to receiving from her kind. Something stirred uneasily in his chest. He turned away from her to remove Roger's hauberk, wiping it dry as best he could before setting it beside the saddles; although it might not be as precious as Michel's own mail, Roger's life depended on this garment. Then, unwinding the garters from the soft uppers of his boots, he removed his footwear. His braies followed, laid out upon the floor to dry. Even after the first of his tunics was dangling from a sapling near the door, sweat still beaded on his brow.

The other tunic went, this one dry enough to be folded and laid upon his saddle's seat, ready to wear on the morrow. That left him dressed in his finest shirt and his better chausses; he hadn't bothered to remove them in Winchester's hall, knowing they would be protected from the elements by all else he wore.

The only cold he felt was the hut's hard-packed earthen floor beneath his toes. Leaning down, he gathered up the straw, then made his way through the maze of damp clothing to spread it on the floor behind Amicia. While hardly an enticing mattress, with the blanket she was using laid atop it and his fur-lined cloak to serve as their blanket, they would weather the night in a modicum of comfort.

Amicia watched him work in silence. When he was done, he straightened and brushed what remained of the straw off his shirt.

"Michel?"

Jesu, but hearing her voice wrap itself around the syllables of his name did the oddest thing to him. "Aye?"

Her eyes were an emerald green. Her brows lifted in gentle question. The firelight turned her complexion to gold and cream. She bit at her lower lip, hesitancy flowing from her.

"Will you eat with me?"

Her request was barely louder than a breath, but the gesture screamed through Michel. It wasn't just respect she was offering him. She was treating him as her husband.

Emotions tangled with sensations until it was nothing less than wild need. He lowered himself to sit beside her. She watched him, her expression wary and unexpectedly shy. Outside, the howling wind droned on. The fire danced, wrapping them in its warmth.

His wife. Lifting a hand, he traced his fingers down the curve of cheek. The fire had burned its warmth into her skin.

She sighed at his touch, then leaned her head into his caress. He ran the ball of his thumb over the fullness of her lower lip. She shivered, only not in cold this time. Desire's heat rose to stain her cheeks. The passion he knew he could stir in her darkened her eyes.

"Amicia," he said, stroking his knuckles along the slope of her jaw.

"Ami," she murmured.

It was an even more intimate offer than her first one, admitting him more deeply than he'd ever expected to plunge into her life. Michel leaned forward. As he'd done on her first visit to the goldsmith's house, he put his mouth near hers, but didn't kiss her. She sighed, her breath warm against his cheek, then relaxed toward him in an even more blatant invitation. The thought of holding her hostage with his body returned, only now in his imagination she was a very willing captive.

"Ami," he whispered, savoring the way taunting her teased himself, "what say you that we dine a little later?"

Chapter 24

As Michel breathed his question against her skin, Ami forgot her stomach's needs and her exhaustion. That glorious warmth he made in her stirred anew, promising more of the pleasure she'd known last night. Only this time they wouldn't be hurried or exposed. The thought of leisurely lovemaking had her quaking.

Michel's fingers moved from her jaw down past her ear to her neck, setting fire to her skin where he touched her. The caress stopped where the blanket blocked his path. Will she, nill she, on the morrow she would be his wife. That left no reason to deny him, or herself.

She released her hold on his blanket. The woolen sheet slid from her shoulders to puddle about her hips on the hut's floor. All she wore beneath it was her chemise, the best one she owned. The king hadn't given her time enough to trade it for her everyday garment. Made of linen, it was so fine that it was nearly transparent. With a slow breath, Michel drew his hand down to her breast to trace the outline of her nipple beneath the fabric. Ami shivered, only it had nothing to do with the cold.

At her tremble, Michel looked up at her. Ami sighed in a tangle of admiration and surprise. His eyes were impossibly soft, their gray depths filled with the heat of his desire. The lines of his face were relaxed. Stripped of his expressionless mask, he was even more handsome.

From that moment in the alcove, when he'd put his mouth so close to hers, Ami had known what she wanted from him. It was his body, his flesh—all of his flesh—against her own. Now, when there was no longer a reason to deny herself, she'd not wait another minute before getting what she wanted.

Coming to her knees, Ami pulled off her chemise, tossing it aside without care for its expense. Michel caught a startled breath at what she did. Before she had a chance to tell him she wanted him to remove his shirt, he put his hands upon her waist. His touch rendered her mute. His fingers were warm and strong against her skin, his palms hard.

Holding her where she knelt before him, he studied her body. His look was enough to make Ami tremble in longing for their union. His gaze traced the outline of her breasts, then descended to her nether lips. He lowered a hand and traced his fingertips across the curve of her belly from hip to hip, then stroked the hair that concealed her womanhood. It was wondrous torment.

Rather than use his finger to awaken her lusts as he had the previous night, Michel brought his hand upward again to cup her breast in his palm. His thumb stroked its crest. Ami gasped as her insides took fire. He brought his other hand up to capture her other breast.

"Nay," she panted, catching his wrists and pulling his hands from her body. "You'll not do me so."

He looked up at her, a frown touching his brow.

"Not yet," Ami amended.

Then, keeping his hands captive, she lowered her mouth until it almost touched his. Slowly, taking care not to touch his skin with her lips, she shifted her mouth until it hovered over his ear. "I want to see all of you. I want to feel all of you against me," she whispered.

Her reward for turning his game back upon him was his swift intake of breath. He yanked his hands from her grasp. Rather than remove his shirt, he sat where he was and watched her. His face was blank, the look in his eyes almost distant.

Ami eased back to sit on her heels in disappointment. More fool her for thinking that he hadn't judged her lewd for what had happened on the landing last night, or that hc might desire her as deeply as she did him. Now, even before their vows were said, she'd stepped awry with him.

Slowly, the corners of his mouth lifted. Creases cut into his cheeks, then his gaze took fire, his eyes warming to that almost blue. To her astonishment, he smiled at her, not that secret quirk of his mouth, but a true smile. A noise rumbled from his chest. Ami gaped. The sound of his laughter was warm and deep.

"For shame, Ami. You are hopelessly brazen," he

said, then reached for the hem of his shirt. An instant later and it joined her chemise, forgotten. He came to his feet and untied the cord to his chausses, swiftly stripping the stockings from his legs.

Admiration held Ami hostage. Nay, Richard de la Beres had looked nothing like Michel. There wasn't an ounce of excess flesh to mark Michel's powerful frame. His legs were long, his belly flat. Firelight gleamed against the dark hair that covered his flesh and lay shadows upon the masculine planes and angles of his chest. A single scar marked his chest, white with age.

She let her gaze follow it as the line descended from his left shoulder almost reaching his nipple. From there, her gaze followed the narrow pathway of hair farther down his belly to his shaft, only to find proof of how much he wanted her.

Stooping, he caught the blanket that she'd discarded and flipped it over the straw he'd laid behind her, then offered her a hand to aid her to her feet. It wasn't the fire's heat that darkened the skin across his cheekbones.

"Come and feel all of me against you," he offered, his voice hoarse and low.

Desire grew until Ami felt drunk with it. She accepted his hand, then came to her feet and into his embrace, her arms sliding around his waist. Pressed against his chest, her breasts tingled as they brushed the hair that covered his flesh. It was every bit as glorious as she'd hoped.

Her hips met his. Trapped between them, his shaft seared her with its heat. He lowered a hand to her hip and pressed her even more tightly to him. With his other hand, he caught the tail of her plait. As he'd done the previous evening, he slipped the thong from its end and freed her hair from its confinement.

Ami shivered as he combed his fingers through those strands until her hair hung free about her, then leaned back from him. The expression on his face was intense as he watched her in return. The need to familiarize herself with his body grew beyond any care of what he might think of her. She set her hands at the base of his neck, then stroked her palms along the broad span of his shoulders.

His skin was warm against hers, the muscles beneath it seeming impossibly hard. At his left shoulder, she let her fingers find that scar. Flat and smooth, she traced it down until her palm rested atop his nipple.

He gave a quiet groan at her play, then caught her face between his hands. Touching his lips to hers, he let his kiss tell her just how much her caresses pleased him. Then, breathing deeply, he released her lips and braced his forehead against hers.

"Again, you touch me as if I belong to you," he whispered.

Startled, Ami eased back from him to look up into his face. Only now did she remember that he'd said a similar thing last night. She gave a tiny shake of her head.

"But you do belong to me, just as I belong to you. We will marry on the morrow," she replied, her voice low in her confusion.

The expression in his eyes softened, darkening in some emotion Ami didn't recognize. He drew a long, slow breath, then the corners of his mouth lifted again. "So we will."

Rising on her toes, Ami brushed her lips across his. As she did so she felt his shaft move between them. Heat spiked through her. She moved her hips against his, trying to elicit the same reaction.

"Jesu," he groaned.

His arms tightened around her, then, before Ami knew what happened, she found herself laid upon the blanket. Straw crackled beneath her as Michel lay atop her. His mouth took hers, slashing against her lips as he demanded the response he knew she would give him.

Ami lost herself to need. Her legs parted to let him rest between them. She closed her arms around him, stroking her hands over the smooth skin of his back, then arched beneath him to again tease her breasts against his chest. Gasping against her mouth, he slipped a hand between them. Ami cried out as he found the entrance to her womb.

He toyed with her, sending wave after wave of pleasure over her. Wanting all of him and so much more, Ami brought a foot across his thighs to hold the mound of her womanhood against his shaft. He groaned against her mouth, his kiss deepening until she lost her breath.

Then his shaft pressed at her nether lips. With a quiet moan, she shifted and took him into her, locking her other foot over his legs. When he moved, thrusting into her, she lifted with him. Her hands came to press his hips against hers, forcing him more deeply into her.

He arched against her hold. Pleasure greater than any she'd known unfolded within Ami, her womb weeping with it. He panted against her mouth and moved again, the stroke of his shaft slow within her. This time, her joy was so sharp and wondrous that she cried out with it. Again and again, he tormented her with this slow, steady pace, his mouth owning hers.

Just when Ami thought she might well die from pleasure, ecstasy exploded within her. She released his hips to dig her fingers into his shoulders, then tore her mouth from his, pressing away from him into their makeshift mattress, lifting her hips, wild to feel his seed enter her. With a ragged cry, he drove himself into her, his breathing short and harsh as he gave her what she so needed to feel.

There, trapped in ecstasy's hold, she remained, adrift in a warm, hazy place, where there was only pleasure and Michel. With no strength left to hold back exhaustion, she slipped into sleep.

Cold nipped at Ami's nose. Hunger gnawed at her belly. One side of her body was covered by glorious softness, while something small and sharp poked into her lower hip. Something heavy lay across her upper shoulder, pinning her in place. She opened her eyes.

Night had crept into the hut like a slinking cat to curl around their fire. It had eaten up the warmth and light until it was nothing but hissing, ruddy embers. Outside, the wind no longer howled, but only moaned.

It was a wayward bit of straw that stabbed at her hip,

having breached the blanket barrier. Michel's cloak lay atop them, the fur lining warm and soft against her bare skin. It was Michel's arm that lay across her shoulder. Her back was to his chest, his knees behind hers, his skin warm against hers. The steady roll of his breath said that he slept.

She could feel the beat of his heart against her. The sensation made Ami smile. She eased closer to him, wanting to feel more of her flesh against his.

The rhythm of his breath broke. His arm atop her tightened. He drew her closer still, fitting his body into the contour of hers. Ami sighed. It was as if they were made for each other.

At the sensation of his skin against hers, a ripple of remembered joy rose from the embers of their previous lovemaking. The recall of pleasure was both a taunt and a promise. Ami shifted her hips against his. His hand stroked down from her waist, then he spread his fingers across her belly. Wondrous need stabbed through her.

"You're awake," he whispered, touching his lips to her nape.

Those inner embers hissed back into flaming life. "I am," she whispered in return, feeling his shaft stir against her back.

"Are you hungry?"

Ami smiled, torn between the needs of her empty stomach and the needs of her empty womb. Her womb won. "Very," she breathed, pressing back against him and his shaft with just enough pressure to suggest that there was more than one sort of hunger gnawing at her. His hand slipped upward to close about her breast. It was Ami's turn to shiver.

He touched another kiss to her nape. "Before we were distracted, you asked me to eat with you. Do you still want my presence at your table?"

"We haven't got a table," she murmured, reaching behind her to rest her hand upon his shoulder, the arch of her body against him offering him more of her breast to touch.

His amusement was warm and soft against the back of her neck. "True enough," he replied. "But if we had a table, would your invitation stand?"

There was something about his tone that sobered her, taming her newly roused lust. Ami shifted away from him, turning to lay upon her side and face him. The embers shed just enough light to show her the outline of his face and mark the line of his nose. His eyes were a quiet glimmer in the dimness.

The stillness of Michel's expression brought the recall of how Adelberta and Sybilla, indeed the whole of the world, turned their shoulders to him. Ami sighed. Michel wanted confirmation from her, he wanted to know the exact intent of her invitation.

Bending an elbow, Ami rested her head upon it. Then, lifting her free hand, she traced the line of his beard as it followed his jaw. Finding his lips in the dark, she outlined them with her fingertip. "I would."

His eyes shimmered as he caught her hand in his, and pressed a kiss to her palm. Releasing her hand, he reached out to once again comb his fingers through her hair. Ami's shiver had nothing to do with cold.

"Amicia de la Beres, will you be my wife?" Michel asked, his voice low and intimate.

The instant his words were out, he rolled onto his back. Both his movement and his question startled Ami. Wanting his nearness and hoping to read its meaning in his expression, she followed him, coming to rest half atop him, her forearms braced upon his chest. Her hair fell forward to enclose them in its curtain.

"But, of course we will marry. By the rules of our king's horrid game, you found me. On the morrow you will take me to Thame, where the abbot will perform the ceremony."

"Nay, there is no game," he insisted, his voice strained as he reached up to again comb his fingers in her hair. His touch was gentle, the sensation making a lie of his fearsome repute. "There is only you and I here in this place. Tell me your answer. Will you give me your vow, cleaving to me as woman to man, wife to husband?" His voice was strained and quiet.

As Ami understood what he asked, the success she'd expected when she set out to conquer him dropped into her hands. Whatever had drawn Michel to request her hand in marriage, it was no longer enough for him. It was her heart and her loyalty that he wanted now.

If Ami's victory came too late to use to control him, it was also too late to save her from what she'd done. "Are you certain I am the woman you want to ask?"

Her heart aching, she eased down to rest her head upon his chest, her cheek upon the curve of his shoulder, her gaze aimed at the center of his chest. She could see the steady lift of his ribs as he breathed and feel the thud of his heartbeat beneath her cheek.

"I fear I'm not worthy of your affection," she whispered.

He stroked her hair. "Why is that?"

Ami's eyes closed. "For years I was careful not to involve myself in any of the schemes that forever fly about this court. But after our king made you administrator of my properties, I was angry. I was certain you'd be another Gerard d'Athlee, looting my properties unless I found a way to control you. Roheise de Say approached me. She offered me your death."

"Did she?" There was a new hint of amusement in his voice.

That startled Ami enough that she shifted, now bracing her forearms on his chest to look down into his face. All she could see of him was the gleam of his eyes.

"And how was I to be killed?" he asked, sounding completely unconcerned by what she told him.

"Drawn and quartered for raping me." Ami whispered this, still thoroughly appalled at herself for ever participating, even in her small way, in such a plot. "Roheise meant to announce your outrage against me to all of England in the hopes of raising rebellion against John, not just within her own noble rank but among the gentlefolk as well."

"And you agreed to let me rape you for her cause?" That amusement was definitely there. He twined a tress of her hair around his fingers. His play made her shiver.

"I only agreed because I was certain you would never rape me and that her plot was doomed to failure," she replied, glad she could say that and know in her heart it was true.

"Now, how could you be so certain of me?" He was definitely laughing at her. Michel reached up to catch her face in his hands, then pull her mouth down to his. His kiss was gentle, his lips soft on hers.

"Because you didn't kiss me in the alcove," she whispered against his lips.

His amusement was a quiet rumble in the darkness of the hut. "Lord, but I wanted to," he said, touching yet another kiss to her lips, then releasing her to relax back into their makeshift mattress.

"Not as much as I wanted you to," Ami replied, just as quietly.

His teeth showed white against the night as he again smiled at her. "As for rape, that we almost had in the courtyard a few days ago. If not for my armor, you'd have forced me down onto the ground and taken me right there, even if I'd cried you nay."

Ami stiffened in shock. She shoved back from him, her arms straight, her hands braced upon his shoulders. "That wasn't all my doing," she cried out in protest.

Michel's chuckle filled the tiny room, as warm as the coals on the hearthstone. "I cede the point. It was a joint effort, both there and on the landing."

Ami stared down at him, beyond understanding. "Don't you care that I schemed against you? Not that I meant to destroy you. All I wanted was to repay all of you for trying to use me, John for his game, Roheise for thinking she could use my pride to twist me into destroying myself, and you for leering at me, then using my own body against me. All of you treated me as if I were nothing but a pawn to be moved here and there as it suited your plans."

Michel wrapped his arms around her and pulled her back down to lay atop him. Their faces were but inches apart. The gleam of his teeth said that his mouth was again lifted into that rare smile of his.

"You were never a pawn to me. You were the woman I meant to marry."

"But I didn't know that," Ami protested.

"Now you do," Michel replied. "And here you are confessing your wrongs because you think yourself unworthy of me and my heart," he said, "when I am the commoner who will disparage you and your rank when we are joined in wedlock."

Ami frowned at him. "I might have thought that once, but that was before I knew you. Now, all that matters is that I'm a knight's daughter and you are a knight. No one will care for more than that when it comes time to find mates for our children."

For a moment Michel lay so still beneath her that she worried about him. Then his arms tightened around her until his embrace was almost painful. "Ami, tell me I am the only man you desire, the man you will marry, the man who will be your husband, not the winner of John's game. Tell me it is me you want."

In that instant Ami understood why none of what she'd schemed with Roheise mattered to Michel. She leaned forward to touch her mouth to his. "You are the man I desire, the man I will marry, and I want you because you are Sir Michel de Martigny, the man who has captured my heart."

Michel laughed, the sound of his amusement filling this tiny hut. Ami's smiled in response. So it would be in their marriage. She would be one of the few in whose presence he allowed himself to relax. When he knew her better perhaps he would share with her his deepest secrets, raising her to beyond precious in his eyes and heart.

Michel took her mouth, his lips slashing over hers as he demanded the reaction he knew she would give him. Longing once again for the joy he could make in her, Ami gave way to his plea. A moment later, she panted and eased to lay full atop him, her legs straddling his as she settled her hips on his. She didn't notice and didn't care that his cloak slid to the side as she moved, leaving them both exposed to the chill air.

Michel tore his mouth from hers. "What is this? Do you intend to ride me this time?"

Ami's cheeks took fire as she realized she was again playing the aggressor in their game of love. Lust's heat ebbed. "What a shameless hussy you must think me," she murmured.

She leaned forward and would have buried her head against his shoulder, but he stopped her, once again catching her face in his hands. His thumbs smoothed the heated flesh along her cheekbones.

"If a shameless hussy is what you are, then don't you ever change," he commanded, his voice husky. His hands on her face urged her to lean lower as he guided her mouth to his. "Now, ride me," he demanded against her lips.

Chapter 25

The next day dawned as dark and miserable as the previous one. Ami didn't care. Nothing mattered, not after last night, save that she reach Thame Abbey today with Michel and marry him.

They had finally eaten their dinner an hour or so before the sun's rising. That meager meal had turned into a battle, Michel pressing her to eat more, Ami striving to see that he had the larger portion. This became a laughing argument over who could do with the least amount of food. Somehow that resulted in them feeding each other, bite by bite, which had led to yet another round of lovemaking, much to both of their enjoyment.

When Ami had again awakened an hour or so later, she found Michel already up and dressed. He sat across the hearth from their makeshift bed, watching her, his eyes alive with pleasure, his expression so open and unguarded that it had taken away Ami's breath.

She'd washed as best she could—the water from the stream was frigid—then once again donned her clothing, cursing to herself as she struggled to wrap her wimple around her head without Maud's assistance. If not for the fact that she needed its warmth, she'd have gone without it. Michel offered her the use of his cloak, claiming that with his many layers of clothing his blanket would serve him well enough for an outer garment.

Before yesterday, Ami would have had no choice but an abrupt and swift refusal. The conventions of moral behavior were very clear. Borrowing a garment from a man to whom a woman wasn't related suggested that they'd shared more than clothing. But then, all Ami once held true no longer applied. Michel was right. Such polite notions were nothing but pretensions, the vain constructs of one set of humankind as it used mindless ritual to lift itself above the rest of the world.

Ami snatched that wonderful, fur-lined garment from him and snuggled into its warm depths. That his bride-to-be would so easily turn her back upon the dictates of rank teased another laugh from Michel. The sound of his amusement had sent a new shiver of longing climbing Ami's spine. Oh, she'd done well, indeed, accepting this man as her mate.

With Ami once more seated atop her spavined mare, the horse resisting with every step, they left the shepherd's hut to make their way northward toward Reading then, from there, to Thame. To save time they trespassed into the earl's chase, using pathways carved out by decades of hunting. Maintained for a nobleman's private pleasure, the chase had long been spared the hand of man so the boar and deer might prosper. All around Ami, trees swayed in the wind, their naked branches rattling. Fallen leaves, their autumn brightness giving way to the mottling of cold and damp, danced around her, skittering across frostbitten grass.

Bowing her head to escape today's far less frequent spattering of icy rain, Ami almost smiled. She was warmer today and it wasn't just Michel's cloak that made her feel this way. She looked up at him. A day's worth of beard growth left a dark shadow against his cheeks, giving him a rakish air. Her smile widened at the thought of careful and considered Michel ever giving way to the destructive impetuosity of a rake.

He caught her look. "What, do I amuse you?" A lover's warmth and confidence filled his voice.

"Deeply," Ami said, only to watch guarded surprise flicker through his gaze.

She bit back a laugh. Just as she thought. He'd expected a lover's denial, perhaps even that she would protest that he was perfect in all ways.

From that first day in the alcove, Michel had been able to read her, just as Ami had been able to decipher his careful expressions. Now that they knew each other even better, it took him less than an instant to realize she teased. One corner of his mouth lifted in the expression Ami was coming to cherish.

"As deeply as I please you?" he asked, his passion for her coloring his question.

"Never." Ami replied so swiftly that her word nearly overran his.

Michel's laugh rang out. Again the hearty sound of

his amusement stunned Ami, mostly because it was so unexpected in this taciturn man.

"You, Amicia de la Beres, are an insatiable woman," he told her.

"I am," Ami agreed, very content with herself and her appetites, "but only when it comes to you."

He shot her a smug sidelong look, his gray eyes warm. "I know. I am the one, the only man, who could breach your chastity."

Ami made a face at him. "Ach, but don't you dare let that go to your head, do you hear me, Michel de Martigny? I cannot help that you stir my senses beyond all control."

"A fact for which I am amazingly appreciative." Michel made a show of leering at her, only to break off, his head lifting. He tugged his horse into a turn so he could look back the way they'd come.

Ami watched in confusion until the next gust of wind brought her the distant sound of a neighing horse. Like him, she turned her mount to stare in that direction. She didn't know what Michel saw. All she could see were the trees and grassy meadows they'd left behind them.

"Who is it?" she asked, not certain why she thought he should know this.

"It could be the earl's huntsmen, tracking us, thinking we're a pair of poachers." Michel didn't say what they both thought, that the riders might be Sir Enguerran and his men, on the trail of a runaway bride.

"The only certainty is that they aren't my own men," Michel continued. All the warmth was gone from his voice and his face. It was the warrior, that knight with a fearsome repute, who took the place of her gentle lover.

Before they'd left the shepherd's hut, Michel had told Ami how he came to be chasing her alone, without his troop at his back, and how he'd sent word to his men that he and his bride would make their way northward toward Thame. Concern stirred in Ami.

Michel was right. The mummery he'd staged yesterday to distract Sir Enguerran couldn't have lasted past sunset. Even as thick-witted as Enguerran d'Oilly could be, he surely had thought to ask Thame's abbot if Lady de la Beres had ever arrived.

Ami berated herself for the same pretensions she'd thrown off this morn. Because gentlewomen never rode alone she'd turned toward Sussex and home. She should have ridden due north from Winchester, toward the safety she'd hoped to find with Kate Godsel at Glevering. Sir Enguerran wasn't clever enough to conceive that she'd go anywhere but her own properties. If she'd gone north, then she and Michel would now be making their way to Thame without worrying they would encounter Sir Enguerran. But yesterday, she hadn't known John's men were marking her route for Michel, and that he would have found her no matter which way she'd gone.

Leaning over, Michel caught Ami's mare by her reins. She gave a quiet cry as she lost control of her mount. "What are you doing?"

"What you cannot, forcing some speed from this ancient beast. From here on, we must needs ride as fast as we can. If they are the earl's huntsmen, I don't want them catching us within the boundaries of the chase. Explaining what we're doing here will cost us precious time," he said. "If those who follow us exit past the edge of this place, then we'll know they aren't the earl's men, but someone pursuing us."

"Perhaps it's only someone traveling in the same direction as we do," Ami offered in forlorn hope.

Michel shook his head at that, then kicked his horse into motion. Even at his faster pace it still took a goodly while to put the chase's northern boundary behind them. From the mare's coughs of complaint, she didn't think much of being asked to expend such effort. Michel didn't slow after they'd reached the road to Reading.

The mare's sides began to heave, this time in no pretense. They were but a half mile from the city, its church tower visible over the top of the shallow rise in front of them, gray stones against a gray sky, when the mare at last gave out. Once again, the horse simply stopped, refusing to take another step.

Ami dismounted next to her spent mount while Michel rode to the top of that rise. From there, he scanned the landscape behind them. Ami knew the moment he recognized who followed them from the way his shoulders tensed.

"What did you see?" Ami asked as Michel returned and dismounted beside her, needing to know but really not wanting to hear what he had to say.

"There's a good-sized troop on the road, led by a man who rides a piebald horse," Michel replied, his voice harsh.

"Sir Enguerran," Ami breathed as he confirmed what they feared. Her neighbor was the only knight she knew who rode a spotted horse; he was also the only man in this shire or any other likely to be following her. If there were more than twenty with him, then he'd borrowed men from someone else to help hunt her. "How far behind us is he?"

"Less than half an hour," Michel replied, his jaw tight and his mouth but a slash across his face. "They're moving faster than I would have expected for Sir Enguerran, given his injury. His arm is broken," he added.

"Ah," Ami replied, not caring if Sir Enguerran were stabbed through the heart, but only that the man chased her.

And Michel. No matter how skilled a knight Michel was, he couldn't face Sir Enguerran and his troop, not when he was alone and without the protection of his mail. He didn't even have a shield at his side. The mere thought of him injured or dead made Ami's heart twist in the worst way.

"Can we share your horse?" she asked, even though she already knew the answer to that question.

Michel shook his head. "Not for long, and exhausting Roger's gelding would buy us only failure. We aren't even far enough ahead of d'Oilly to give us time to find and buy you a new mount before he and his men will be upon us. Even if we did manage to purchase you another horse we'll still leave the city only a hairsbreadth ahead of them. I'm not enamored of us riding all the way to Thame playing the mouse to that knight's cat."

Ami tried another tack, trying to avoid the obvious. "Perhaps your troop has already reached Reading?"

Michel's expression softened just a little. "Even if my men waited for us, we'll be no more protected than if we were alone. The king has tied my hands, forbidding me to harm Sir Enguerran, making my sword, and theirs, useless to me. If yon knight"—the sweep of his hand indicated the approaching Sir Enguerran—"dies in a confrontation with me, whether by design or by accident, His Majesty may choose to renege on all he promised me to placate those in his court who despise mercenaries. That I will not tolerate, for it means losing you. Sir Enguerran has been given no such stricture. Thus, he can harass us all the way to Thame, doing who knows what harm to me and mine as he seeks to take you from me."

Stripping off his gloves, Michel tucked them into his belt, then touched a hand to Ami's cheek. His fingers were warm against her chilled skin. The corner of his mouth lifted as he freed a quiet breath. "In all my days I never thought to hear myself say this to any woman, but especially to a gentlewoman. I cannot bear the thought of losing you, or of leaving you widowed and once again available to some man other than me." His voice was gentle as his fingers moved against her cheek in a sweet caress.

His words of love startled Ami, for they were more than she ever thought to hear from a man as hard as Michel. She sighed and leaned her head into his caress. "Nor do I wish to lose you," she told him at a whisper. "So, what are we to do?"

Michel leaned forward to touch his lips to hers in a

brief kiss, then retreated a bare few inches. "The only thing we can," he said quietly. "I must let Sir Enguerran have you."

"What!" Ami thrust back from him in disbelief, all her joy destroyed. "Are you mad? Have you forgotten that Sir Enguerran has the same right to marry me if he arrives at Thame Abbey with me in his custody that you do?"

"What sort of confidence is this?" Michel demanded. "Just because I intend to allow Sir Enguerran to carry you safely to the abbey doesn't mean I intend to let him keep you. Trust me. The only man you'll wed when you reach those abbey walls is me."

"That's supposed to reassure me?" Ami retorted with a snort, her hands dropping from Michel's chest. She took another backward step and crossed her arms. "If you want to encourage me then offer me a better plan for rescue than that."

Michel made an impatient sound. "Enough arguing, Ami. Accept that I can not only do what I say, but I give you my word that I will do it. You will have to be content with that."

As he spoke, his expression shuttered, his features flattening into those stony lines Ami knew all too well. Ami stared at him as she understood what that new blankness meant. He was hiding something from her. No doubt because he knew she was adept at piercing his facade to read what lay beneath it, Michel was making certain he left her no opening to exploit as she sought to divine whatever it was that he concealed.

"How can I accept when your plan is so obviously

flawed?" she snapped, doubt sharpening her tongue just as it ate away at all his loving promises. "You just told me that our king has bound you and your sword. If that is so, then pray tell me how you intend to reclaim me from Sir Enguerran if you dare not lift your hand or your sword to him. You cannot mean me to believe that he will simply give me to you."

She ladled a little sarcasm onto this last comment, meaning to prick his masculine pride. Her question implied that he didn't mean to honor his vow to her. She expected that he would rage or be so shocked that she would dare question him that he'd be startled into offering the explanation she craved.

There wasn't so much as a flicker of anger or surprise in his gaze. "But that is exactly what I expect you to believe," Michel replied, his voice flat.

Shock tore through Ami, followed by hurt. He couldn't be serious, nor could he possibly believe her so simple. Doubt woke. Or, perhaps he believed her so blinded by want for him that she would trust with equal blindness. She'd played games with men like him for too many years to trust that way; in those games, men offered women promises all the time that they never intended to keep.

Ami desperately battled her sudden fear that Michel might prove himself to be the most adept of these faithless seducers. "That can't be all you'll say to me when you plan to leave me, and I could be forced to marry against my will should I arrive at the abbey in his presence."

"Have you not heard me say that you are precious to me beyond all else and that I will allow no other man to have you?" he repeated, still no trace of emotion in his voice. "How I accomplish what I promise can be none of your concern. Now, say no more, only return my cloak and free me to reach Thame ahead of you."

His cloak! The recall of their shared laughter as she'd taken it from him flashed through Ami. That only drove her hurt higher, until she had never felt so alone and bereft. She clutched his garment's collar close to her. Its fur was soft against her cheeks. Michel's scent clung to both the fabric and the fur.

"I won't," she said, despising herself for needing his scent and his garment when everything Michel now did suggested that he intended to betray her.

Not so much as a flicker of irritation appeared in his flat gaze. Instead, he only reached out to open the garment's pin. Ami shifted back from him. Michel let his hand drop to his side. They stared at one another in silence.

Ami's hurt grew by great bounds. Rather than retreat from him, all she wanted was to soothe her pain by wrapping her arms around him. She wanted to grab him by the front of his tunic and demand that he become again the man who'd won her heart. Fear of betrayal stopped her. As he'd done yesterday when he'd found her on the road to her own properties, he but watched her, saying nothing. At last, the need to speak overwhelmed Ami.

"Wearing it will make it seem as if you still rode with me," she said, her voice low, her tone defeated.

Some of the blankness softened from Michel's face, while a little warmth returned to his gaze. He reached out to take her face in his hands. So great was her need to feel his touch that Ami didn't care whether he might intend to betray her. She sighed as he lowered his head to touch his mouth to hers. He filled his kiss with all the passion he owned for her.

Lord, but he was a dangerous man. It didn't matter that he offered her nothing but a lover's suspect promise, or that the something he wasn't telling her might be his intention to betray her—the heat of her desire for him returned with all its intensity. She couldn't stop herself from relaxing against him.

Michel slipped his arms around her, pulling her close to him. The need to once again hold him against her body flared. Ami's mouth opened under his kiss, then the lines of her body melded to his in primal invitation.

As that happened, Michel released her to look down into her face. "This is why you must give me my cloak," he said, his voice gentle when his expression wasn't. "Ami, what sort of gentlewoman so brazenly offers her body and her lusts to a commoner?"

Ami blinked to hide the hurt his question did her. Here at last was one reason for why he might be leaving her behind with nothing more than some harebrained scheme for rescue as his explanation. Brazen she had been, both last night and on the landing the previous day. The only sort of gentlewoman who did these sorts of things was one foolish enough to reveal to a man who wasn't yet her husband just how much she needed and desired him.

As for the details of Michel's birth, what did that matter? She'd dismissed them as unimportant the instant she decided he was the man she would marry, and so she had told him last night. What remained to be seen was if she would be the woman he meant to wed.

Commoner or gentleman, a man was still a man. Priests taught that females lacked the ability to control themselves and their baser natures, something that Ami felt they had backward until she met Michel. However, having heard such things all his life and despite what he had said to her, deep in his heart did Michel think her incapable of controlling herself, not just with him but with any man?

"More to the point, cheri," Michel continued, the word falling so stiffly from his tongue that it lost any sense of endearment, "tell me what wellborn men think of gentlewomen who offer themselves to commoners. If you wear my cloak and Sir Enguerran recognizes it, he'll rightly assume we spent the night together. Ami, how would a man who prizes his lineage react if he learned the woman he must marry spent the night with a baseborn brute, one who most assuredly made free with that same woman?"

That knocked all thoughts of betrayal from Ami's mind. She knew just the sort of violence this could elicit from most knights. But Sir Enguerran wasn't just a knight. He was a toady who'd long since traded a man's natural esteem in hope of advancement, only to fail, destroying both his career and his pride.

"He'll kill me," she said. It was a statement of fact, nothing less.

"That he might," Michel agreed, so little emotion in his voice that it made Ami ache, "but only after the two of you have shared your vows, of that I am absolutely and utterly certain. Sir Enguerran wants you, and not just because John removed your bride price. The knight believes that marrying you will protect him from the wrong he's done."

Ami looked up at him, once again bereft. This was the man Michel expected to carry her safely from here to Thame? How could he believe a man so desperate would simply hand her over to his opponent once they arrived? He was mad. Or determined to be rid of her.

"So, not only must you return my cloak," Michel was saying, "but you must lie if he asks with whom you traveled this day. Tell him that I was one of the king's men, commanded to protect you until you came into the custody of one of your pursuers. You can convince him of this by offering a few of your choice and unladylike words regarding our king and his game."

He paused to smile at her. It wasn't that wide, easy grin she'd seen in the shepherd's hut, or even that amused quirk she enjoyed. Instead, the corners of his mouth twisted with into what was a grim upward-moving line. Ami couldn't bear it. He was retreating from her, word by word, turning his back on her, becoming again that fearsome and distant knight.

"Having found myself on the wrong end of your clever and blunt-spoken manner, I hereby testify that you can be very convincing," he said, no softening in his voice to indicate that he meant this as a compliment.

Ami gave a pained laugh, for his words pierced like

a spear's thrust. "It's a facet of myself that I will always cherish," she said, so he would know that she valued that about herself and still valued it, even if her manner cost her him. "And, you're right to say that Sir Enguerran isn't likely to question me too deeply, not if John gives me to him without asking for a single pence in return for my hand."

These were bitter words, indeed. More than Michel's betrayal or the chill wind buffeting her, the thought that John had stripped away her bridal value ate up Ami's remaining warmth. No wonder Michel risked riding out alone and unarmed save for his sword to find her. Then again, if all he wanted was a free wife, her forward behavior shouldn't prevent their marriage—that was unless, after last night, he had decided not even a debt-free marriage was worth a wife whose morals he mistrusted.

Michel opened the pin that held his cloak around Ami. At his tug, the thick garment slipped from her shoulders. Yet standing frozen where she was, she watched him toss the garment over his arm. It was only as he started to turn away from her that Ami's pain grew past the point that she couldn't bear it.

Reaching out, she caught him by the arm. Michel looked back at her, his brows raised in question. All she read in his gaze was his need to be on his horse and riding from here. From her.

A thousand questions crowded onto her tongue. She wanted him to repeat his promises of marriage. She wanted to know which was true, all the lover's words he'd spilled to her last night or what he'd said that first day in John's chamber, that she was worth less than the forty-five pounds John named as her original bride price. She wanted to tell him that she couldn't believe Sir Enguerran would simply hand her to him at the abbey. Most of all she wanted to plead with him to say that he still respected her, even though she'd given him no reason to do so.

Instead, all she could whisper was, "Don't leave me. I cannot bear the thought of marrying Sir Enguerran."

Not so much as a flicker of warmth filled his gaze. "Trust me," was all he said, then turned to mount his horse.

Chapter 26

Ami watched Michel disappear along the road toward Reading. He took with him all the confidence he'd striven to instill in her. For a long moment she stared at the empty roadbed. The wind blasted past her, bearing in its depths the low of distant oxen from some nearby farmhouse. On the verge, browned grasses flattened, then rippled back to standing as the gust died.

Trust him? How, when the only thing she really knew about him was that his kisses could drive her past the point of sense, and that the feeling of his body atop hers was wondrous? She drew a pained breath.

Wasn't this just the appropriate comeuppance for a woman who had spent four years playing the game of love? The goal in that game was to use loving words and the promise of passion to destroy better judgment.

And if Michel proved false, then he would have done what no man before him had achieved by besting her at her own game. Last night, she'd given him her heart, her body, even her soul. All she got in return was his unwitnessed oath to marry her. Without family and friends, or even strangers, to note such a promise, it was nothing more than meaningless words. She knew a dozen songs all of which told the tale of some foolish woman accepting her seducer's private vow of future marriage, only to have him deny her claims of betrothal after they'd lain together. The men in those songs then went on to cry to the world that she was no wife, only a woman of loose morals.

That scenario struck too closely to what had happened last night. The worst of it was that knowing Michel might betray her before the sun set today, Ami still wanted him. Michel had ruined her—not her repute, for that she'd given to him by her own free will—but her senses. She was so besotted with him that all she wanted was his arms around her again.

Going to her mare, Ami retrieved her own outer garment from where she'd tied it to the back of the saddle. As her cloak unrolled, the sealed fold of parchment the king had given her fell from it. She picked up the missive, holding it between her hands as she studied the imprint of the king's seal.

Here it was, her only remaining hope of escape from Sir Enguerran should Michel prove false. Becoming a nun was a better fate than marrying her neighbor, especially if the only reason Enguerran wanted her was to protect himself from something. Should that wrongdoing of his be revealed, then Ami would become useless to him and that could be dangerous, indeed.

However, if she wanted to use this missive, she had to find a way to reach the abbot ahead of Sir Enguerran. Escaping him once they were near the abbey would take an act of God. Nonetheless, if a miracle did happen, she wanted the option to act.

Ami shoved the parchment up inside the tight-fitting sleeve of her dark green undergown. As the vellum absorbed the warmth of her skin, it softened, molding itself to the shape of her arm. When she was certain it would stay where it was, she donned her cloak, pulling it tightly around her and waited for her neighbor's arrival.

She didn't wait long. Far sooner than Michel had predicted Sir Enguerran's troop crested the hill in front of her. Ami gave a surprised hiss. About this, Michel was right: her neighbor rode with almost twice the number of men she knew he kept on his estates. The woman riding next to him was the reason why.

Even swathed in a thick cloak lined with dark fur, with her hair hidden beneath a thick wimple, Ami recognized Roheise de Say. It was the noblewoman's household guard who had expanded the number of Sir Enguerran's men.

So great was Roheise's determination to spark rebellion against England's king that she willingly rode alongside a toady that she otherwise wouldn't have deigned to notice.

Ami's besotted and betraying heart gave thanks that Michel had chosen not to stay at her side, and that he'd taken his cloak with him. One hint that Michel had been in her presence would have given Roheise all she wanted. Ami hadn't absolved herself of the part she played in Roheise's scheme; even if the future proved Michel false, she wouldn't have his death on her soul.

Ami let her gaze shift to Enguerran d'Oilly. Atop his spotted horse, the knight slumped in his saddle. Rather than his chain mail, her neighbor wore only a sleeveless leather hauberk beneath his thick cloak, not unlike the one Michel wore. As Michel had said, one of Sir Enguerran's arms was splinted and bound across his chest in a sling. Her neighbor looked hollow-eyed, his face gray and drawn in pain, or exhaustion. Or both.

What sort of idiot rode around the countryside with a broken arm? Ami answered her own question. Only an idiot desperate to protect himself from something that he knew could hurt him worse than the pain of a moving horse. But if Sir Enguerran were that desperate, then how could Michel believe the knight would simply give his only defense to him without a fight?

As the knight and noblewoman brought their mounts to a halt in front of her, Ami drew herself to her tallest. Roheise looked far younger with a thick woolen wimple concealing her graying hair, but then she'd been known as a beauty in her younger years. The noblewoman smiled as if this meeting were only an encounter in the bailey of Winchester's castle.

Ah, but behind that smile Ami caught a flicker of desperation. By now the noblewoman must surely know about the king's game. That was, Roheise knew John had promised his ward's hand in marriage to whomever caught Ami first, be that Sir Enguerran or Michel.

That must have terrified Roheise. If Michel won, the noblewoman's plot shattered, for at that point the only thing her false charge would accomplish was to speed the abbot's wedding ceremony. The most common legal redress for rape was to force the victim to marry her attacker.

"Why, Lady de la Beres, at last we've caught up to you, after following you half of yesterday and all of this morning," Roheise said, her smooth voice revealing no hint of worry. "I cannot tell you how appalled I was when Sir Enguerran deduced that you must have left the custody of the king's escort. When night fell yestereven, I despaired on your behalf. What horrors I imagined, you traveling alone upon this road."

Ami bit back a scornful breath at this. The only horror Roheise dwelt upon was the possibility that her sacrificial lamb might have escaped her.

"Horrors?" Sir Enguerran said to Roheise before Ami had a chance to reply. His voice was rusty and thick as if he ailed. No doubt he did. Between two days on the road in this weather and his injury, he was fortunate he wasn't already raving with a fever. "You may have suffered such thoughts, my lady, but I never did," he said. "And wasn't I right not to worry? See, here she is just as I said she'd be, whole and hearty. Lady de la Beres was never in any danger, not on the roads at this end of England. Indeed, the only horror the lady could have suffered in this neighborhood was that baseborn Frenchman finding her before me."

Enguerran offered a laugh that sounded more like a cough. "I've done it, I've bested the lauded Sir Michel de Martigny and brought my wife, safe and secure, into my hands," he crowed, right well pleased with himself.

"On the contrary, Sir Enguerran," Roheise told him, the impatience in her voice reflected in her steely eyes. "Who do you think kept Lady de la Beres from reaching her own manor house yesterday, then forced her to turn toward the north? Who do you think also forced himself into your bride's bed last night?"

Sir Enguerran frowned, a single crease forming between his brows marking his befuddlement. "Who?" he asked.

"Why, that very same Michel de Martigny," the noblewoman said, her voice sharp in exasperation. "The commoner has already had his way with her. No doubt he took her by force." Roheise made this pronouncement with as much drama as she would have given the accusation, had she offered it before John's full court as she originally intended.

Sir Enguerran straightened in his saddle with a jerk. For that instant the dullness of pain and oncoming illness ebbed from his gaze. He gaped at Ami.

She waited for him to curse her or Michel. Instead, the surprise in his face returned to befuddlement. With his good hand, he reached beneath his cloak's hood to scratch at his head, then shifted again to face the noblewoman.

"But that's not possible," he said. "A man cannot be in two places at one time and we saw Michel de Martigny on the Oxford road yesterday. He and his men spent the night in Thame. Don't you remember that we located the house that de Martigny leased in Thame proper? That was before the abbot told us the lady hadn't been presented to him and we realized that de Martigny, honorless and base commoner that he is, had tried to drive me from the competition by convincing me he already had my bride." Sir Enguerran made a scornful noise. "I must say that I wasn't surprised by such behavior from one like him, who lacks any of the refinement of his betters. Nor do common brutes like him have the wit to puzzle things out the way men of purer birth do. I daresay he's now scouring the way from Thame to Winchester, perhaps just now beginning to understand that Lady de la Beres left the road yesterday."

Disappointment, surprise, and exasperation played across Roheise's face. Ami pressed her gloved fingers to her lips to hide her smile. This was what happened when someone tried to make a tool from a fool. Too bad for Roheise that she hadn't learned more about Sir Enguerran before she tried to make use of him. Had she done so, she'd have realized just how effective Michel's ruse would be.

Sir Enguerran's reaction also proved that Roheise hadn't shared the details of her plot with him. Ami supposed that shouldn't startle her. Nobles didn't trust unaligned tufthunters like him. The only toadies they tolerated were those spineless creatures permanently bound, tongue, soul, and fortunes, to their own houses.

"How clever of you Sir Enguerran, to divine that I left the Oxford road to go home," Ami said. If she played her next move just right she might well be able to stop Roheise and her plot, thus freeing herself of the burden of Michel's life. And perhaps if she did that, she might someday be able to extract her heart from his hand.

"You are also right to say it wasn't Sir Michel riding with me." Ami folded her hands as if to plead. "I pray you will forgive me, sir, for not doing as His Majesty commanded and making my way to Thame. Know that it was never my intention to escape you, only this foul competition. I was angry that the king had made me into a prize, like the purse offered at a joust. I was so angry that it didn't matter a whit to me that I'd lose my escort if I turned my horse in any direction save Thame."

Here, she offered a helpless shrug as she threw herself into a tale as fabulous as any shared to pass the hours on long winter nights. "Had I taken the time to think, I would have realized that His Majesty couldn't afford to abandon me for fear of courtly reaction to his deed. While the troop at my back did leave me, a soldier was sent to track me. When he found me, he took control of my horse as Lady Roheise suggests, forcing me northward again toward Thame where he thought you and Sir Michel would be waiting."

Lady Roheise gave a sharp laugh at this concoction. "If that were true, and the man was commanded to protect you, then why would that soldier abandon you along the roadside?" she demanded, her jaw tight as she poked at the weakest point of Ami's story.

"That's what I asked him as well, not but a few moments ago when he left me," Ami replied. "He said he recognized Sir Enguerran's spotted horse and there was no point in lingering with me when Sir Enguerran's approaching troop was the only movement he could see for miles. He complained that he was cold and tired, that all he wanted was the nearest cookshop in Reading, where he could get a decent meal."

As Ami spoke these words it was as if the sun rose within her head. She knew exactly what she needed to do to destroy Roheise's plot. Not only would it free her from responsibility for Michel's death, but it might even make Sir Enguerran reconsider marrying her.

The very distant possibility that she might reach Thame Abbey without either Sir Enguerran or Michel rose. If that happened, she could use the king's unconditional right to choose her fate to demand that she be married to Michel. Ami blinked in shock. Could she really be so besotted with him that she'd consider forcing marriage on a man who might not want her? Startled with herself, she bowed her head, for fear that Roheise might read her thoughts upon her face.

"However," Ami continued, "Lady Roheise rightly feared for me. Because of John Plantagenet and this despicable game of his, I am ruined, my good name destroyed. His Majesty commanded that his man remain at my side once he found me, to see that I didn't again leave the road. No matter how I argued, that soldier couldn't be persuaded that our king didn't intend for him to sleep in the same chamber with me. Either that, or he was loathe to sleep out of doors on a nasty night. I had to share a shepherd's hut with him last night."

When she was done speaking, Ami peered up from her pretense of shame. Patent disbelief filled Roheise's face. Rightly so. That Ami had traveled unescorted and unchaperoned was ruination enough. No woman would ever blurt out the tale Ami had just told. Instead, she would have buried it beyond the ears of any man, woman, or child.

As for Sir Enguerran, new concerns creased his pasty face. He eyed Ami as if she were soiled. Disgust curled the corner of his mouth. "You spent the night in the same hut with a common soldier?"

"I had no choice," Ami protested. "However, if you now deem me a less than suitable bride because of this, I suppose I cannot blame you."

"You lie!" Roheise snapped with enough vehemence to startle Ami into staring at her. Bright color flared in the noblewoman's cheeks as her eyes narrowed. "That was no soldier I saw riding with you a few moments ago. No matter the distance, I know it was de Martigny, just as I knew it wasn't either de Martigny or you we saw on the road yesterday."

"It was Sir Michel on the road," Enguerran growled, his face tense. "Didn't the man we saw yesterday ride the mercenary's horse? No stranger could do that, not when a knight's warhorse is trained to his owner's seat and touch. Did that man not also wear de Martigny's painted mail? A man's armor is fitted to him and him alone, and doesn't move easily to another, not without giving an armorer time to tailor it. Nay, my lady, if there's only one thing in this world that I know as God's truth, it's that the man we saw at Lady de la Beres's side a few moments ago wasn't Michel de Martigny."

Ami caught a breath. Enguerran wasn't just deter-

mined to reject Michel's presence, he was desperate to
see that everyone else rejected it as well. For good reason. Word that he'd been duped by a common mercenary's ruse would spread like a fire in London if
Roheise were proved right. Before the week was out,
folk would no longer only chuckle up their sleeves
about him, they'd laugh openly.

"By God, but you are impossible!" Roheise snarled
at the knight, her hands tightening on her reins until her
mount danced. "I am tired of arguing with you over
every obvious detail. Think! If de Martigny was clever
enough to hire a woman to play the part of Lady de la
Beres, then he is also clever enough to hire a man to
play the part of himself."

Excitement shot through Ami as Roheise offered her
yet another chance to save Michel's life, as well escape
Enguerran. Better yet, she had an audience eager to do
what needed doing once they heard her words. Every
man in the troop behind Roheise and Enguerran
gawked at their betters, some leaning far to the side in
their saddles so they could take in this unexpected bit of
entertainment.

"I pray you, my lady, say no more of Michel de Martigny in my presence, else I may be ruined beyond all
redemption." Ami cried out, knowing her words would
carry to the farthest soldier. "You know how easily rumors fly, and how folk care nothing for whether the
tales they spread are truth or not. It's bad enough that
the king's soldier will return to his barracks eager to
talk about His Majesty's strange competition and how
he spent the night in a gentlewoman's presence. The

tale will swiftly take on a life of its own until folk believe something untoward happened in that hut when it didn't."

With the clouds hanging so low overhead and the wind moving past Ami in the direction of the listening soldiers, no man missed what she said. Some shook their heads over her claim that some of their own might exaggerate or gossip, while others muttered in agreement.

Now determined to destroy Roheise's plot no matter what it cost her, Ami raced onward before she gave way to cowardice and thought the better of what she meant to do. "Are there not more soldiers here today, listening to every word we say?" she asked, raising a hand to her audience. "Won't they want to repeat your assertion that it was Sir Michel with me? Before long, there will be two rumors flying about me. Even though neither are true, everyone will soon believe that I trysted with both the mercenary and the king's soldier. Poor Sir Enguerran." Ami shifted to look at the man she decidedly didn't want to marry. "He already does me a great kindness, yet wanting to marry me even though he knows folk will talk about how I am a brazen vixen who dared leave the king's game and my escort. What sort of reward does this do him, turning his new wife into a woman the world names a whore unfit for either marriage or convent?"

There it was, in all its destructive glory. With those few words, Ami lost all she'd worked so hard to protect these last four years. Ah, but as she ruined herself, Roheise's plot crumbled. There would be no charge of rape, and no rebellion at least not from the noble-woman's spur. No whore could be raped.

A note of warning sounded within Ami. There was no turning back from here. If Michel did prove false, then her next home wouldn't be a whore's brothel but a king's bed. Then again, better John than Sir Enguerran. And it was far better to be a royal whore than to live in barren, religious isolation while Roheise and her family profited from her lie.

Ami waited for Enguerran's rejection. He couldn't still want her, not after that. True, the Church taught that a fallen woman's respectability could be restored through marriage and that the man who wed a whore went straight to heaven for his good deed. Most men weren't willing to dirty their children's names just to buy their way out of hell.

The repulsion curling Sir Enguerran's lips proved him a man like most others. A moment later, disgust drained from his face. He swallowed, his chin lifting in reluctant decision.

"She's right, my lady," the knight said, shifting in his saddle to look at Roheise. "You must have a care with what you say here. I don't want my new wife's name besmirched any more than her participation in the king's competition has already done. No one," he shouted, so all the men behind him could hear, "will ever again discuss anything you heard here or the events of these last two days."

Triumph and disappointment warred within Ami. Michel was right. Sir Enguerran was desperate to marry her. She wondered what wrong he'd done and why he thought their marriage could possibly shield him from it.

Roheise freed a furious sound. "Fool! Can't you see that she makes a dupe of you? Best you ask her why before you go dancing to her tune." In her anger and her native arrogance, Roheise forgot herself and went too far. "Or perhaps you don't care that she plays you for a poppet. Is that the sort of man you are, a woman's toy?"

"Enough!" Sir Enguerran bellowed, his shout breaking off into a chest-aching cough. When he could breathe again, he glared at the noblewoman. Painted on his face was the outrage all men suffered when named a dolt one too many times by some female. "Hear me again, Lady Roheise," he said, the rasp in his voice worse now. "I won't have you falsely disparaging the woman I intend to take as a wife, especially when we here all saw the same thing. Distance or not, the man who left Lady de la Beres was dressed like one of the king's soldiers, not a knight. Therefore, it wasn't Sir Michel."

Sir Enguerran's tone was final. Whether or not he believed what he said, he'd cling to it as truth from this moment until eternity. He had to, to shield his own self-image. Half of what Ami hoped to accomplish fell into her hands. Roheise would have to find some other way to spark her rebellion.

The knight yet glared at Roheise. "When I met you on the Oxford road yestermorn, you said you wished to aid me in finding Lady de la Beres. That you have done. Don't make me regret that I invited you to also attend the exchange of our vows."

Roheise wore an expression of steaming, hopeless frustration. Over time, Ami had seen that look at least once on the face of every woman she knew. Its cause was always a man who blindly rejected the truth solely because some female dared to point it out to him.

In the next instant, the noblewoman's jaw tightened in refusal. Rage took fire in her gray eyes. She shifted in her saddle to look back at her household guard.

"Go," she commanded them with a wave of her arm. "Sir Richard, you saw the man who parted from Lady de la Beres and the direction in which he went. Find him. When you have him, return to me with him as I continue onward to Thame with Sir Enguerran's company."

In response to his lady's command, the knight pulled his horse out of the ranks and signaled to his lady's men. More than a dozen soldiers separated from Sir Enguerran's party. With Sir Richard in the lead, their horses thundered past Ami and toward Reading at a near gallop.

Triumph drained from Ami. If Roheise hadn't watched her like a hawk, she might have moaned in fear. Damn her and this awful game. She'd just made yet another mistake by not thinking through her last move. Instead of protecting Michel, she'd just sent more than a dozen men to hunt him down when he rode alone and unsuspecting toward Thame. Even if he did manage to meet his own men before Sir Richard found him, all was lost. Roheise's guard outnumbered his troop.

"Have you lost your mind, my lady?" Sir Enguerran demanded, astonishment, pique, and the fear of being proved a dupe once and for all dancing across his expression. "Call them back this instant."

The noblewoman's eyes flashed at being so rudely addressed by an inferior, then her expression shifted as she donned the mask that every clever woman adopted when dealing with the pride-blinded men God had seen fit to put in command of their lives.

"Forgive me if I have erred or insulted you, Sir Enguerran," Roheise said sweetly, "but I think only of your honor and your new wife. Please let me do this for you, and for Lady de la Beres. As she says, with a few thoughtless words on the part of any of us, she could be ruined. Isn't it better that we find the king's soldier? That way we can hear from his own lips that he did no wrong whilst he guarded Lady de la Beres. That will go far to restore her name and your trust in her, and make you easier about marrying her. By the same token"— Roheise shot Ami a wicked little smile—"if my men find this soldier and it is revealed that this man has done wrong by Lady de la Beres, you'll know before you marry her what sort of woman your future wife is. In that case you'll have the satisfaction of avoiding marriage to a woman who will bring no honor to your name, and see that common soldier dead for misusing his better."

Panic twisted Sir Enguerran's face, trapped as surely by Roheise's words as were Ami and Michel. Since Enguerran's own wrongdoing demanded he marry Ami, he'd have no choice but to speak those vows even if every man in the world derided him for marrying a light skirt.

"No wrong has been done," he insisted, his voice breaking, then looked at Ami. "Why couldn't you have stayed on the Oxford road as you should have?" Despite all the years he'd spent trying to cultivate it, there was no subtlety left in Sir Enguerran. Desperation and disgust filled his face. It was an easy message to read. Enguerran d'Oilly didn't want her or their marriage any more than she did.

Michel was right. She'd survive the exchange of their vows. She might even survive as long as it took for her body to produce Enguerran's heir. After that, Ami's life would be worthless. Ami's hand went to where the king's missive was hidden in her opposite sleeve. There had to be a way to escape him.

"Go, mount your horse, so we can be on our way," he commanded.

"I cannot," Ami replied. "The mare is done for. That's why the soldier left me. She won't go another foot."

"She may ride with me," Lady Roheise offered a little too eagerly. "My horse is strong enough to carry both of us."

Ami's shoulders tensed in refusal. The last thing she wanted was to be subject to Roheise's control. Judging from the set of Sir Enguerran's jaw, he thought even less of this idea than Ami did.

"Gerard," he called.

At the sound of his name, a man drew his horse out of the pack, riding forward to halt next to his master. The soldier was young, slight and small, mounted upon a horse big enough to carry twice his weight. Gerard shifted in the saddle to grin almost lewdly at Ami, pulling his head deeper into his cloak's hood so Sir Enguerran couldn't see what he did. What with his fair hair and well-modeled features, he apparently took himself for a swain.

"You'll ride with my man," Enguerran told Ami, his voice cold and hard. "Now, mount up."

Ami didn't look the soldier in the face as she put her foot in his stirrup and hoisted herself up behind him in the saddle. Once she was in place, she yanked her skirt hems down as far as she could. She wouldn't bare any more leg than necessary to any of these men, even though all they could see were her calves modestly covered by thick woolen stockings.

"Forward," Sir Enguerran called, only to have the word break into another cough. "We proceed at a walk."

"A walk?" Roheise offered, an impatient edge to her voice.

Enguerran shot the woman a raging sidelong look. "I'm not jostling my arm just to please your sense of urgency. Now that I've found my missing bride, there's no longer any need for haste, not when the king set no limiting date on his offer. At a walk, we'll reach Thame by nightfall and that's good enough for me. If you don't like it, you may do as Lady de la Beres did yesterday, and separate from your escort to ride wherever you will."

With that, Sir Enguerran kicked his mount into motion. As Gerard urged his horse forward, the horse's first step made Ami slip in the saddle until she was pressed against the soldier's back. She pushed herself as far from him as she could, only to have him press back in the saddle, seeking contact between their bodies.

Ami braced a hand at the middle of his back, trying to keep him away from her. It didn't work. Their thighs still touched.

"Now, that's not very comfortable, my lady," Gerard said, his tone unacceptably familiar and his voice low enough so his master wouldn't overhear. "Why not put your arms about me and rest your head against my back?"

Ami didn't deign to respond. When it came to dealing with an inferior, the silence of disdain was far more effective than any angry word could be. As for what Gerard thought of her, or any of the others, she didn't care. No matter what happened, she wasn't going to become their new mistress.

With nothing else to occupy her except the fate she faced at the end of this ride, Ami set herself to devising ways to escape Enguerran. It was a good thing that they were yet miles from the abbey. She was going to need every inch of that distance to come up with something.

Chapter 27

Michel again slowed his horse from a canter to a walk so the gelding could catch its breath. While they walked, he glanced behind him. From near the top of this latest hill, the cottages in the distant village behind him looked like children's toys. There were but a few dozen homes, every one of them shuttered against the weather, their front and back gardens sleeping for the season beneath a blanket of straw. Cattle and sheep stood like dark dots against the empty sweep of sere pastureland, while the long expanse of fields that fed them and their stock flowed like rich black velvet over the sweep of the landscape.

But it was the road to the south of the village that Michel wanted to see, that and the men upon it. It wasn't the first time in the last hour he'd noticed them. With the earth rolling ever higher in this part of England, each hill's crest offered him the opportunity to see the men traveling the road behind him.

Even though he had no reason to think these men followed him, concern continued to grow as they steadily closed the gap between him and them. That might mean nothing but that they had some serious purpose that didn't include him. Still, a cautious man tended to live longer than an impetuous fool, and Michel knew he presented a tempting target to an opportunistic band of thieves. Not only was he traveling alone, without even a shield or a helmet, but his horse and sword screamed of wealth. Roger's gelding owned a fine lineage, his parentage displayed in the powerful lines of his body; Michel's blade was the best that he could afford, which was substantial for a bachelor knight. He could easily find himself overwhelmed and dead, his body left to return to the earth from which God had made it.

Michel touched the purse at his belt. It was in it that he had stored the fold of parchment John had given him in the presence of Sir Enguerran, before the king had offered that secret word. On the wax that closed it, the royal seal had imprinted clearly enough to be identified for what it was; the man who killed the king's messenger paid with his life. Ah, but to make use of that seal, Michel needed the chance to display it to his attackers before he was overwhelmed.

What Michel needed was Roger and his own men, or at least a shield. He sent the gelding over the top of the hill in front of him. There, the land flattened into a long plain, stretching for as far as his eye could see. He turned the horse off the road, mucky track that it was, toward a nearby stream. The gelding needed his rest, as well as food and drink if they were going to remain ahead of the distant men.

As the horse ate an oatcake and drank, Michel peered to the north, as deeply into the rain-shadowed distance as he could. Michel was sure he must be at least halfway to Thame by now. Not so much as a rabbit moved southward on the road ahead of him. There certainly wasn't a troop of soldiers missing their master.

There could be only two reasons that he hadn't already met his own men. The first and most logical was that he had gone astray. Foreigner that he was, he could well have misheard directions at some point. The folk in some of the previous villages spoke little French, and had the most atrocious accents he'd ever heard. He'd strained to decipher their meaning.

The second was that Sir Enguerran might have incapacitated Roger and the rest of Michel's men yesterday. While certainly a possibility, it seemed hardly probable, not when a few days ago Sir Enguerran's men hadn't been well drilled enough in arms to do more than annoy his own battle-hardened men.

When the gelding was rested, Michel again mounted, then backtracked for a last look at the approaching men. There were at least a dozen of them, maybe a few more. That meant it wasn't Sir Enguerran racing for Thame with the woman he thought he was going to marry. The knight's injured arm wouldn't tolerate this group's bruising pace.

Again he squinted at the distant troop. What if Ami hadn't convinced Sir Enguerran that the man he must have seen, just as Michel had seen him, was one of John's soldiers? A vicious curse aimed at both John and Enguerran dropped from Michel's lips at that. In that case, this could be a portion of Sir Enguerran's troop sent to chase down his opponent.

Michel turned Roger's horse and sent the gelding into his fastest canter. As he rode, he vowed to himself that if he and Amicia both survived to reach Thame Abbey, he would forgive her her doubts, her questioning his honor and his word. Then, he'd marry her.

The thought teased a laughing breath from him. John was right. Marriage to Amicia de la Beres would be like riding an unbroken horse, but sometimes the colts hardest to break tamed into the finest horses.

Lord, but she was far too perceptive for his good, realizing almost immediately that his refusal to explain meant more than a man's rightful demand that his woman trust him. Michel regretted that he'd left her wondering if he meant to betray her. Still, better to leave that impression than to give her even a hint of John's secret phrase. It startled him that rather than rage over her questions, he'd felt the glimmerings of pride and respect. Then again, he hadn't expected her to demand the same explanation Roger would have wanted had Michel tried to palm so lame a plan off on his captain. Michel promised himself that if he yet lived once this day was done, he'd honor her forever more with the honesty she deserved.

It was thoughts of England's king, secret phrases, and the knuckles of owls that suggested yet another identity for the men following Michel as well as their haste. John might have again reconsidered his offer of Ami's hand. Michel gave vent to another curse. The king would have no trouble finding his mercenary, not when John's own tracker had led Michel to Ami.

If those were the king's men, then they weren't likely to spare their horses. Michel's shoulders tensed. If this competition came down to a race, then he was doomed. While the gelding had a stout heart and decent stamina, he wasn't fast. That meant Michel had already let those behind him get too close. Nor did he dare leave the road, to elude them, since that made it impossible for Roger to find him. That left him only one thing to do: ride on.

Foam began to fleck the gelding's mouth. His breath huffed from him in rhythmic snorts. With the landscape now so flat, Michel could watch those behind him continue to close the gap with each mile, while the road ahead of him remained empty. They were close enough now that Michel could count fifteen men. Chain mail glinted from the nearest man, naming him a knight.

The leader took Michel's glance as a prod and shouted encouragement to his men, exhorting them to more speed. If any doubts lingered about who they chased, that settled it. Michel turned his gaze back to the road, seeking something, anything, he could use to his advantage.

The track dipped out of sight ahead of him, falling into a shallow valley. Praying there was some sort of cover or even a stand of rocks from which he could guard his back as well as time enough to position himself to use it, Michel whispered his apologies to Roger and his horse, then sent the gelding toward that lip of earth at a full gallop.

His pursuers howled out a battle cry at this change of pace. Rage tore through Michel as he recognized whose it was. He threw another look over his shoulder, seeking confirmation. The knight's cloak streamed behind him as he rode, the de Say insignia on the breast of his surcoat revealing his allegiance.

Michel leaned low over the gelding's neck, drove Roger's horse down into the valley, all the while begging God to take that arrogant, devious bitch, Roheise de Say. Ami had been every bit the noblewoman's pawn, only not because Roheise wanted to spark any rebellion, although if the bitch could use his death that way, she would. Nay, Roheise craved his blood, because Michel had not only refused her when she boldly propositioned him, he'd done so with words that conveyed his hatred for the women of his mother's class—all the women save Ami, that was.

At the bottom of this gentle dell lay a small hamlet, its defensive walls nothing more than the same woven willow fencing that had made up the shepherd's pens. Ah, but coming around the curve of those delicate walls was a man dressed in mail that had been painted black, followed by nine more soldiers. Michel tore off one glove and put his fingers to his lips to loose three short, piercing whistles. Having no family motto to trumpet as the men behind him did, this was Michel's code, a way to communicate on the battlefield when they were separated.

Roger's hand lifted in acknowledgment. His mount, Michel's horse, exploded into a gallop. The rest followed, warned by their master's whistle to come to him at their fastest speed and with swords drawn.

That was all the assurance Michel needed. Turning Roger's gelding, he galloped back up the road, stopping far enough below the valley's lip so those chasing him wouldn't see him until they were upon him. With Roger's horse trembling beneath him, his sides heaving, Michel shoved his hand back into his glove. He flexed his fingers once, to gauge how much more damage he could do to his already strained wrist—then he drew his sword.

Just as he hoped, the de Say knight came racing over the lip of earth ahead of his own men. Not expecting his prey to be waiting for him, the armed man's shield yet hung from the side of his saddle. The knight gave a startled shout as he caught sight of Michel, sawing on the reins as he tried to turn his horse and keep himself out of reach of Michel's sword. It was too little, too late.

Ami smelled the town of Thame before she saw it. The chill wind brought her the ever-present scent of woodsmoke, only here, as with every other pocket of humanity, the stench of city life, the reek of offal both human and animal, twined with that homely scent. The distant, frightened bellow of some dying bovine rang out, no doubt from the town's shambles as the butcher made his last slaughter of the day. The growing dimness said that, hidden behind the sky's cloudy cloak, the sun had reached the western horizon and prepared for its nightly rest.

As if to confirm the hour, the bells of Thame's sole church began to ring. Following on its heels came the more distant and deeper clanging of the abbey bells, as both called the faithful to the Vesper service.

Ami had long since ceased struggling to keep herself separate from Gerard. For both of them, this was the end of the second day in the saddle; they were too exhausted to care about propriety or the lack thereof. Indeed, Ami's back ached and she could barely feel her legs. If escaping Sir Enguerran meant running at top speed once they reached the abbey, she'd be hard pressed to manage it.

D'Oilly's men trailed behind Gerard's horse with no order or discipline in the way they arranged themselves on the track. Roheise and Sir Enguerran rode in front of them. Or, more precisely, Sir Enguerran rode in front of Roheise who rode in front of Gerard and Ami.

Bitter amusement teased a new tenseness to Ami's lips at this. Roheise had tried to ride in front of Sir Enguerran as her rank allowed, but Sir Enguerran's horse would have none of it. The piebald was no respecter of protocol. Every time Roheise advanced he nipped at her mare's flanks, driving Roheise back into the lower position. As for Enguerran, Ami doubted he knew or cared where Roheise rode. He swayed in his saddle, his head hanging, whether in illness or exhaustion Ami couldn't tell.

The town's main gateway appeared to their right. Like its walls, Thame's gate towers were constructed of wood, a far less impenetrable substance than stone. But then, this wasn't much of a city, what with less than six hundred inhabitants, all of whom profited in some way from the bishop of Lincoln's service, for he was the protector of the place.

Shivering as a frigid day chilled into an even colder twilight, Ami shifted in her shared saddle to peer ahead of Sir Enguerran. Thame's abbey lay outside the city to the north, and Ami craved the sight of its walls with the same intensity that her stomach begged for something more to eat than a single strip of dried meat. There was nothing for her to see but dimming fields and darkening orchards.

As Ami straightened in disappointment, Roheise shifted in her saddle to look behind her. Despite her warm furs, Roheise's face was pinched with anxiety. The noblewoman's guard had never returned, a fact that had both of them frantic, Ami for Michel's well-being and Roheise over what her missing guard might mean.

Their panic had its roots in a site some leagues past. They'd passed a place where it appeared a battle had taken place. Torn by iron-shod hooves, great gouts of sod had been strewn across the grassy clearing, those earthy chunks testifying to some sort of violence. Patches of flattened and darkened grass suggested men had laid upon them and bled. Ami's only comfort, and it was cold comfort, indeed, was that she'd seen no ravens or crows circling anywhere near the site. Those carrion eaters were the scourge of the battlefield. Drawn by the sound of clashing weapons, the fearless creatures didn't even wait for the fighting to end or death to claim the victims before feasting on the fallen.

If no birds meant no dead bodies, that didn't mean Michel was safe, for someone might have thought to carry off the dead. Even though Ami yet struggled to trust that Michel meant to honor his promise to her, everything in her revolted at the thought of him cold and still. If just thinking of it could make her ache so, what if imagination became reality? Ami drew a ragged breath. She was truly beyond hope. Michel's death would be as devastating to her as Richard de la Beres's passing had been.

Richard's death had been a peaceful passing, long expected, even before he began to ail. Her first husband had been a man far past his prime. Knowing that, Richard had spoken often to her about the time when he would be no more, preparing her for his permanent leave-taking. Moreover Ami had had years to love and cherish him before God had taken him. She'd only had a few brief hours with Michel.

Ami closed her eyes. Oh Lord, she wasn't just besotted. Rightly or wrongly, she loved Michel de Martigny.

At last, a tall stone wall rose up out of the damp earth ahead of them, the abbey's perimeter. There was enough light left to reveal the pale yellow and flinty black of the wall's surface; the Cistercians had done so well with this house that they could afford a stone defense.

Outlined against the now pewter sky was the abbey

church's tower, its square outline solid against the ragged clouds above it. Someone must have left the church door open, for caught in the rush of the setting sun's wind was the haunting sound of men chanting out the Vesper service.

Around the wall's corner Sir Enguerran's horse went, everyone else following, then on toward the arch of stone that marked the abbey's main gateway. Ami's heart rose into her throat. Here it was, the last chance for Michel appear and do as he vowed, demand that Sir Enguerran release Ami to him.

"What's this?" Sir Enguerran croaked, straightening with a start as he drew his horse to an abrupt halt.

Michel! Ami leaned around Gerard, needing to see him to prove to herself that he still lived. There was no one standing in front of the doorway, not even a porter, although one side of the gate's twin doors yet stood wide in defiance of the deepening night.

Shock closed its hand around Ami, sapping the strength from her muscles and the life from her heart until she was numb from head to toe. She'd gambled on one man and lost all, her name, her repute, her future, and any hope for happiness. There was no one to stop her marriage to Enguerran, who wanted her only as long as she could serve as his shield.

"Why is the gate open?" Enguerran asked, his voice thick with exhaustion and illness.

"Perhaps they know that we come, sir," Gerard suggested, concern filling his voice. Twice, he'd needed to ride forward to catch his master when Enguerran seemed a little too unsteady in his seat. The knight had gruffly rebuffed him each time, insisting that he was well enough and to leave him alone, when even Ami could see that he was fevered.

"Of course they do," Roheise snapped. "I sent a man first thing this morning to warn the abbot that I would be arriving late in the day and that I expected them to prepare me a chamber in their guesthouse." She urged her horse ahead of Sir Enguerran and into the compound, although it was no place for a woman; the guesthouse lay outside the abbey's walls. Her mare's shoes rang against the entrance's cobbled apron.

Yet locked in shock's deadening grip, Ami heard the clip-clop as if it were a distant echo. Her vision blurred until Enguerran seemed but a shadow in the deepening night as he followed the noblewoman inside the monastery's walls. Darkness had laid to rest upon the world, her inky hair streaming over the abbey's church and all its outbuildings, save one, where a pair of torches burned in brackets at either side of its door.

It was toward this fine house that Roheise rode. Set atop a tall foundation, the house rose nearly three storeys tall. Wide steps allowed access to its doorway, which stood about a man's height above the courtyard floor. A large window marked what would be its second-storey hall. For the now, shutters blocked the opening, closed against the chill. However shutters were no bar to candlelight. The expensive golden light slipped through the shutters' cracks and slats to lay a bold yellow pattern onto the muddy courtyard floor.

Roheise drew her horse to a halt near the house's bottom stair. Enguerran and Gerard stopped together a little bit to one side. So accustomed was Roheise to someone leaping forward to aid her in dismounting that she didn't think to call out for assistance, only waited as the rest of Sir Enguerran's men trailed into the court-yard, doing so at their own lackadaisical pace.

Sir Enguerran tried to lift his leg to swing down from his horse, only to moan quietly and fall back into the saddle, clutching his arm close. Gerard made a worried sound. "Dismount, my lady, so I may help my master." He threw the command over his shoulder at Ami, having long since forgotten that he meant to se-duce her.

Yet too devastated by her abandonment, Ami did not move. What point was there to race for the abbot's door to arrive first when nothing in her life had mean-ing? Marriage to Michel was the only one of John's four fates she could tolerate, and Michel had aban-doned her. She was betrayed, whether by his death or by his will.

"My lady?" Gerard said, more insistently.

With a quiet groan, Ami did as he demanded. Gerard dismounted after her, then hurried to assist Enguerran. By the time Enguerran was out of his saddle; he was panting. Gerard caught him just before he fell. Before the knight had waved away his soldier. Now he could no longer afford the pretense. He leaned heavily on Gerard's arm.

"To the porch," Enguerran managed to say, his voice now just a quiet rasp.

As the two men turned, Ami came face-to-face with

the husband who would be the cause of her death. In the jaundiced light of the torches, his face glowed yellow. Gray and brown stubble covered his unshaven cheeks. Night turned his eyes into black holes on his face. His teeth glinted as his lip lifted in a sneer.

"I should have known when the king waved his bride price for you that it meant I'd end up with something of equal value, nothing," he spat out, coughing around his words, his voice a growling whisper. "No matter what I told that noble bitch over there"—the jerk of his head indicated a now impatient Roheise—"I know the truth. You laid with the mercenary, you whore. Don't think that I won't make you pay for it. Now, up the stairs with you. I want this farce finished."

His words did what Ami couldn't do for herself and shattered shock's hold on her. Rage exploded in her. Her fists clenched. She leaned forward until she was nose to nose with her neighbor. Both Gerard and his master leaned back, startled by her aggressive movement.

"By God, but I've had enough of men using me," Ami snarled, keeping her voice low, "whether that man be you as you try to protect yourself from whatever wrong you've done, or John entertaining himself by tormenting me, or Michel making me care for him, only to abandon me when I need him. Well, no more, do you hear. I won't have you. Run, Enguerran d'Oilly, run your fastest and I'll still be the first to climb those stairs. By John's word, if I reach that doorway before you, I can choose my own fate." She pivoted and started toward the steps.

"I knew it! De Martigny took you!" Roheise yelled in triumph, excited enough by this to begin dismounting without assistance.

Ami whirled on the noblewoman, torn between rage and grief. "Nay, I took him," she shouted in reply, no longer caring who heard what.

"Stop her! Don't let her say anything else," Enguerran croaked in panic from behind Ami, but even frantic his voice was hardly more than a whisper.

Gerard grabbed Ami by the arms, and hauled her back toward him. Ami turned and, with all her might, kicked him. The soldier yelped and stumbled back from her, hopping a little. He collided with Enguerran, striking the knight's injured arm. Enguerran shrieked and crumpled to the courtyard floor.

Pivoting, Ami strode toward the steps, her hems flying. Who could have guessed that ruination brought such freedom? With her name and repute gone, she could do exactly what she pleased. And at this very moment it pleased her to become a royal whore. Her mouth lifted in a tight little smile. John wanted her as badly as any man wanted a woman and that made him vulnerable when she had her vengeance to wreak. She'd make England's king pay any and every way she could for how his game had cheated her of all she'd ever wanted in life.

"Where are you going?" Roheise demanded, grabbing Ami as her intended sacrifice reached the steps.

Her heart on fire, Ami did just as Richard de la Beres had taught her to do when accosted. She closed one hand into a fist and drove it into the noblewoman's mid-section. Gagging, Roheise released her, then dropped to sit on the courtyard floor. Ami continued up the stairs.

Above her, no doubt warned by the shouting, the door opened. A tall man stepped out, haloed in the torchlight, then closed that door behind him. The abbot. Ami remembered him from her first visit here. His was a narrow, Norman face, clean-shaven as monks were wont to be. His cowl was thrown back to bare hair the same silver as the metal threads that decorated his habit. A big cross rested against his breast, held in place by a golden chain, while a massive jewel gleamed upon his finger.

"My lord abbot, I am Amicia de la Beres," Ami said as she stopped in front of him. "I pray you witness that I have arrived in your presence ahead of Sir Enguerran d'Oilly. According to the rules of His Majesty's game, if I was the first to arrive I was to be allowed to choose my own fate. I demand that right."

As she spoke, she took the king's parchment from her sleeve. The wax, softened by her body's heat, had lost the imprint of the king's seal to wear the pattern of her skin instead. Did that make it any less official? She handed it to the abbot. He nodded as he took it.

"I've been expecting you," he said, his voice smooth and musical.

"My lord abbot," Roheise panted, staggering onto the porch, her arm clutched about her midsection. "Michel de Martigny used this woman against all that is right and proper. I believe he has also assaulted the men of my household guard. I demand that you find that base and foreign mercenary and see that he suffers his rightful punishment for these outrages."

The abbot held up a hand to stop her. "I can only deal with one woman at a time, Lady Roheise," he said. "You must wait until I've dealt with Lady de la Beres's difficulties before I can pay any heed to your needs."

A hiss of surprise escaped Roheise. "What is this, cousin? Ignore me at your peril, for what I demand is nothing less than the will of Lord Geoffrey," she said, referring to her powerful brother by marriage.

The churchman's expression tightened at this not so subtle threat. "Be that as it may, Roheise, Lady de la Beres presently holds my attention. Brother Martin?"

The door behind the abbot opened just far enough to allow a monk to exit. As he stepped onto the porch, the brother carefully pulled the door closed behind him until it was barely ajar, then stepped to his abbot's side. Slender and middle-aged, the circle of shaved skin at the top of his head gleaming in the torchlight, he studiously avoided looking at either woman on the porch as he tucked his hands into his wide sleeves. It was his manner more than anything else that named him his abbot's chamberlain. "Aye, my lord abbot?"

"Go into the courtyard and see if Sir Enguerran ails," the abbot said. "If he is in need of Brother Infirmerer's services, have his men bear him to our infirmary. They may follow you there as you lead Lady Roheise to the chamber she requested in the guesthouse."

Roheise's eyes widened, her mouth tightened as her

cousin put an injured knight and knight's daughter ahead of the child of an earl. "One hour, Maurice. Put me off for any longer than that and you'll regret it." She turned and strode down the stairs ahead of the brother directed to lead her to the guesthouse.

Maurice of Thame watched his kinswoman go, a faint air of dislike clinging to his features. Only when he could see her no longer did he turn his attention to the parchment in his hand. With the wax softened it opened easily. He unfolded it, stared at its surface for a moment, then looked at Ami from over its top.

"So, what fate was it you expected to claim with this when you arrived?" he asked in gentle question.

"I want to—" Ami started, intended to shout out that she would become the king's whore, only to stop and eye him in confusion. Expected to claim? Tears welled at what fate she'd expected to claim upon this morning's rising.

When she said nothing, the abbot turned the parchment in his hands, holding it up so she could see its surface. Ami stared at an empty piece of vellum. Not so much as a greeting was scratched upon that skin.

"That royal bitch's son," she snarled, hating John with all her heart. The king had played with them the way a lass made people of her poppets. For his own amusement, he'd turned them into the hunted and the hunters, and let them scurry about, thinking they had something to gain at the end of his game. In that instant Ami was ready to call Roheise back and offer to do whatever the woman needed to see her king destroyed.

The abbot smiled at her. "Having known our king's

mother, I must disagree. She would have torn out her son's liver if she'd lived to see this game of his. But tell me, what were the choices you believed you'd have in this game of His Majesty's?"

"If I arrived first, I was to choose between entering a convent, becoming our king's lover"—that sent the abbot's eyebrows flying toward his hairline—"or marrying either Sir Enguerran d'Oilly or Sir Michel de Martigny."

"I see," the churchman said quietly. "And of these four, which would you have chosen."

"Does it matter any longer, my lord?" Ami asked tiredly. "There were never any choices for me to make. Our king isn't willing to free even a ward as inconsequential as me from his custody."

All she wanted was a warm, private corner where she could rage, weep, and sleep for days without interruption. There was little chance of that. Instead, on the morrow she would return to Winchester where she would rejoin the other wards. Only she would no longer have her name or her pride to protect her from the scorn of others.

"Humor me," the abbot persisted. "Which fate would have been yours?"

The memory of waking in that hut with Michel's arm heavy on her shoulder made tears again sting at her eyes. She swallowed them. "I would have chosen to marry Sir Michel de Martigny."

The abbot released a relieved breath. The sound was loud enough to be heard above the hiss and pop of the burning torches and the agitated discussion going on between the abbot's chamberlain and Sir Enguerran's men. The churchman turned to face the door to his residence.

"So it is as you say. She does choose you," he said to the panel. "You may come out now."

Ami's heart stopped. The door groaned open. Michel stepped through the portal and onto the porch. He wasn't alone. In the vestibule behind him was Michel's ugly soldier and Roheise's knight, his head bandaged and his cheek stained with crusted blood.

Michel's hauberk was gone, his hair was a tangle. Dark spots stained the sleeves of his tunic and the right one had been rolled back to reveal his heavily bandaged wrist. He had never looked more handsome or more alive. Ami's knees weakened. She would have fallen if the abbot hadn't caught her by the arms.

Then Michel had his arms around her as he pulled her close to him. Ami pillowed her head against his shoulder. She could feel the beat of his heart against her cheek. This time she made no attempt to stop her tears.

"I thought you were dead," she wept against the warm, living skin of his neck, not willing to admit that she'd also feared he lived still and had betrayed her.

He bent his head over hers. "But, I am not dead, so why do you weep for me?" His voice was gentle and rich, as if he liked it that she might mourn for him.

Ami leaned back to look up into his face. "Because I love you," she replied, her voice quivering, "and I didn't want to lose you."

The corner of his mouth quirked up at this. His eyes

warmed to nearly blue. "Even though you believed I might play you false?" he asked.

Shame for doubting him tore through Ami. "How did you know?" she cried, new tears trickling down her cheeks.

He reached up to wipe them away with his finger. "Did you forget that I read you as well as you read me, cheri?" This time when he used the endearment it sounded more natural, as if he'd tried it a time or two since first uttering it and found it more comfortable now. When he smiled, it wasn't that hidden lift of his lips, but a full, wide grin.

"What a greedy thing you are, my lady, craving proof of my affection. Can you believe me now when I tell you that you are a treasure beyond any price to me?"

Rather than answer him, she rose onto her toes and touched her mouth to his, needing his kiss to know that this moment and he were both real. His lips were soft beneath hers for only an instant before their kiss shifted and it was his mouth moving atop hers as he demanded again she prove to him that he was the man she wanted.

Ami forgot that a monk watched them. All that mattered was that he was alive and she was in his embrace. Her arms encircled his waist as she drew herself against him, lost in the sensations he could wake. One of his hands stroked up her back to cup her head in his palm.

"That will be quite enough of that," the abbot said, sounding as if he held back laughter.

Ami gasped against Michel's lips, then pushed back

from him. Pleasure, joy, relief and so much more filled Michel's gaze. He looked at the abbot, turning so he could wrap an arm around Ami and pull her against his side.

"So, are you content that she was and still is my willing bride? She will testify that we did exchange promises to marry last night, if you like."

"I think," the abbot said slowly, "that the sooner we put the blessing on this union, the better for both your souls." He shifted to look at the men in the doorway. "You have witnessed this, Sir Richard," he said to Roheise's knight. "By the lady's words and actions here does she prove the truth of Sir Michel's tale. If they exchanged vows, even without witnesses, then there can have been no rape for they were well and truly married from that moment."

"But Lady de la Beres's missive from the king was blank, as was Sir Michel's," Sir Richard protested. "No doubt, the parchment Sir Enguerran carries is blank as well. The lady and the knight had no right to exchange vows if they didn't have the king's permission to wed."

"Neither Sir Enguerran or Lady de la Beres had the king's permission, but Sir Michel did," the abbot said. "He carried a second private message to me from His Majesty, one whose veracity cannot be doubted. I prefer to believe these other missives are blank because our king didn't wish to risk giving the lady to anyone save Sir Michel."

Sir Richard nodded slowly as if he'd like to deny what was said, but couldn't. "Then, as you say, there can have been no misuse on the mercenary's part. If I may, my lord, Lady Roheise is no doubt concerned over my whereabouts and condition. Will you release me to join her?"

Roheise's kinsman nodded. "Go to her, telling her that she should give thanks to Sir Michel that you still live and that it will cost her nothing to keep you at her side. I think if I had been Sir Michel and found you chasing me, I wouldn't have been as generous. I would have demanded a steep ransom from your noble mistress. You, after all, were the aggressor in this instance."

Sir Richard stepped out of the door and started toward the steps, only to stop. Turning, he eyed his fellow knight for a long moment. "The churchman is right. If you yet choose to demand that ransom, know that I will honor the debt." He hesitated, then bowed. "It was an honor to yield to you, Sir Michel. There aren't many men who can knock me from my saddle with a single blow," he said, then whirled and strode down the steps to disappear into the darkened courtyard.

Ami looked up at Michel in astonishment. He had been without any defense, yet knocked that knight off his horse? Michel didn't notice her surprise. He was watching the departing knight, making no attempt to hide his surprise.

"Sir Michel, might I borrow your captain to direct Sir Enguerran's men?" the abbot asked.

"Of course, my lord," Michel replied, even as Roger stepped out of the door to make himself available.

"Captain, if you will first send them into the kitchen

for their meal," the abbot told Roger, "then go to the barn and fetch the rest of Lady Roheise's guards to come watch them as they eat. They should be no trouble for you, since they don't yet know that their master is to be exiled for the theft of Lady de la Beres's moveables, should he be unable to repay the cost of what he's taken."

"He what?" Ami cried, stiffening in Michel's arms. Her bed! Enguerran had stolen her precious bed.

Michel shot her a glance, warning her to hold her comments. The urge to argue lifted in her. On its heels came the urge to demand explanations. Aye, but she'd mistrusted him once and been wrong.

She let both urges drain from her, then relaxed against his side, content to let Michel take care of what was hers, just as he cared for her. Surprise flashed in Michel's gaze, only to be followed by deep pleasure. His arm tightened around her.

Roger looked at his master. "When I have done the abbot's will, sir, I'll be returning to town and the house we rented. It's the miller's house, near the edge of town. Will you be coming soon?"

"There's the matter of their vows to tend to first," the abbot replied before Michel had a chance to speak. "They will be free to leave after that. I assume you will find your private accommodations more appropriate than sharing the guesthouse with Lady Roheise."

Roger nodded, then looked at Ami. "Shall I warn Maud to have a meal and a bath ready for you, my lady?"

Ami stared at the man. It was a mundane question, commonsensical even. The answers were easy enough. Either she wanted to eat and bathe, or she didn't.

Yet, after a day during which she'd found love and ecstasy in Michel's arms, only to crash into utter despair believing she'd lost him not once but twice, then once more know joy as she found him again and won all she'd thought never to have, she couldn't answer.

A sob caught her unawares, then another broke past her lips. Tears began again to flow. She turned in Michel's arms and, secure in his embrace, she wept in earnest.